WHAT'S
LEFT
UNSAID

ALSO BY EMILY BLEEKER

Wreckage

When I'm Gone

Working Fire

The Waiting Room

What It Seems

WHAT'S
LEFT
UNSAID

A Novel

EMILY BLEEKER

LAKE UNION
PUBLISHING

Text copyright © 2021 by Emily Bleeker
All rights reserved.

Published by Lake Union Publishing, Seattle

www.apub.com

Amazon, the Amazon logo, and Lake Union Publishing are trademarks of Amazon.com, Inc., or its affiliates.

ISBN-13: 9781542027205
ISBN-10: 1542027209

Cover design by Rex Bonomelli

Printed in the United States of America

For the real Evelyn—
thank you for letting me tell your story.

CHAPTER 1

Hannah hit "Send" and closed out of her email inbox, checking her dingy mug for one last stale mouthful of coffee. The empty cup clanked when she plopped it back on her desk. She sighed and then cringed, her breath sour even to herself.

Another article about nearly nothing for a weekly paper in small-town Mississippi. Just what she'd always dreamed about as a journalism student at Northwestern University. She chuckled somberly at her private joke. But if she let herself think about her life too long, it did sound like a joke, even if it was a gloomy one.

One year ago, she was writing for the *Chicago Tribune*'s community section, delving into things she was passionate about, like the outbreak of heroin usage at affluent suburban high schools and the negotiation tactics used in the hotly debated CPS teacher strike. It wasn't just the story, but also chasing the story that had been addictive, fulfilling. Hannah sighed again. And now, she was sweating through her T-shirt at the beginning of November, working in a small newsroom in Senatobia, Mississippi, where the two most exciting parts of her day were when Dolores would put on a new pot of coffee in the afternoon and when Hannah got to go home.

But Dolores left for a doctor's appointment after lunch, and there was still an hour until Monty would even think about locking up, which meant killing time as the sun was finally setting.

The pinks and oranges of the sunset made the dusty, ancient newsroom look nothing like her formerly brilliant real world of assignments and deadlines, of her boyfriend and parties and potential futures and life. She now lived in all the moments in between, in a suffocating monotony that briefly lifted when she could stalk social media for a peek of the fall colors in Millennium Park or the snow flurries crowding the headlights during rush hour on Michigan Avenue. She missed home. And she missed . . . him.

Alex. Hannah clicked on his Facebook profile for the tenth time that day. Thank God no one had cracked the code that would unveil all the amateur stalkers the internet had fostered over the years because she'd certainly be on a watch list by now. But Hannah had woken up next to that face for six years, nine months, and fourteen days. She'd kissed his shoulder when he was still asleep after a late shift and whispered "I love you" before she left for work. She'd held him in her arms when a toddler bled out in his ER after being hit by a stray bullet. And, damn it, she'd taken that photo he was still using as his profile pic nearly a year after he'd moved out of her house and into the arms of a young, perky resident who "gets me like you never did."

But she couldn't stop looking, even if every picture reminded her of how Alex smirked when they'd locked eyes in a speech class at Northwestern eight years ago. And the little scar above his lip made her remember what it felt like to kiss him. Even when it hurt to see the engagement ring she'd always longed for sparkling on someone else's hand. Sure, her work and personal life had fallen apart around her while she obsessed over Alex, but that was the punch line to her not-so-funny-after-all existence, wasn't it?

"Ms. Williamson." Mr. Montgomery Martin, round-bellied, silver-haired editor and owner of the *Tate County Record*, stood in front of Hannah's desk, glaring at a single page of printer paper.

"Yes, Mr. Martin?" Hannah minimized her browser tab without glancing at her screen like a pro. *A pro stalker?* Damn it. The joke got less funny every minute.

"Please be sure to call on sources in the future. Ms. Lou Ann Delany is spelled with a space between the *Lou* and the *Ann*." He wiped at the white crust that always seemed to be at the corner of his mouth like he'd just had his way with a glazed donut. But Hannah never saw a donut. Not once. He continued in his thick but dignified southern drawl. "And no *e* at the end of *Ann*. She'd have a full-on hissy fit if it went to print this way."

He dropped the overly reddened page on the keyboard in front of Hannah. It didn't take that much ink to make a straightforward name correction, but Monty had made it his personal mission to keep his newest and totally overqualified employee humble. She could point out that he'd been the one to take down the initial incident report with the no-space name and the superfluous *e*, and she could pull out the email and prove it, but what was the use? She wasn't trying to impress Monty Martin—she was trying to survive him until Mamaw Mable recovered from her fall and Hannah figured out what to do with the rest of her suddenly sidetracked life.

Then again, Mamaw hardly needed her help now with all the supports she had in place even prior to Hannah's arrival in Senatobia. As soon as her full-time housekeeper, Carla, introduced the night nurse and the day nurse and reviewed the daily schedule of activities that already seemed to be keeping Mamaw's world afloat, Hannah knew that "helping" her grandmother was really her mother's attempt to get her off the couch and out of her lingering depression. The first step in her mom's multistep plan to get old Hannah back after losing her boyfriend, job, father, and sanity all in a matter of a few months.

"Sounds good," Hannah muttered, glancing mournfully at her empty coffee mug. Caffeine was required to deal with a micromanaging Monty, who was still standing in front of her desk. She rearranged her keyboard and the edited page of writing, but he didn't seem to get the message.

He was still there—staring.

"Uh—do you . . . do you want to watch me fix it?" she guessed, stuttering, lost on how to relate to the sixty-something walking stereotype.

"No. I think you can apply those corrections on your own time," Monty said, slinging his thumbs through the belt loops. "I have a more pressing assignment for you."

So help me, if he says anything about cats—

Mrs. Mulvaney had been in today to tell the story of her miraculous cat being hit by a car eight separate times and still surviving. What was this, the *National Enquirer*?

Monty pointed to a green door to the right of her desk. The water cooler sat half in front of the opening and half against the wall by the back window.

"Down there is the basement," he said, like everything suddenly made sense. "Once it's cleaned out, I'm gonna rent out the space to Tonya Sellers for her weddin' dress shop. Now, I don't know if you've noticed, but I'm not much of a computer fella." Hannah had to hold back a smirk at what Monty's idea of a "computer fella" must be. "But somebody needs to get all those archives backed up on the internet so I can get that place cleaned out."

Shit. Hannah's smugness dropped. That was her new assignment—grunt work. She rushed to interject.

"Monty, don't you think Dolores could—"

Monty cut her off. "Dolores is sixty-six years old and has two bad knees. She's not making it up and down those stairs. I can barely get down there, and I'm—"

"How about Terry or Carl or—"

"Miss Williamson." Monty slammed his massive fist on the corner of the desk, rattling her mug, waking up her computer screen, and startling Hannah into silence. "This is not a debate. You are the most junior member of this staff, and I've given you an assignment. You will continue to write the traffic column and start digitizing the archives in the basement. I trust you can manage both responsibilities?"

He said it like he wasn't sure she could handle any assignments, much less the two completely inane tasks now on her plate.

I should quit, she thought. *I should stand up right now, grab my mug, tear up Ms. Lou Ann (with a space and no e) Delany's fender-bender article, and storm out the door.*

She could go home to Chicago and reclaim her spot on her mother's couch, where she'd been hiding for the past six months since her dad was sent home with hospice care to die in his own bed, her mom echoing that his premature decline was likely "for the best" so he wouldn't be in pain any longer, and Hannah wanting to scream every time she said it. After he passed away, four months ago, she tried texting Alex for support, but he didn't reply. That night she ended up telling her mom the tears were because she missed her dad, when they were also for "that asshole Alex," as her mom liked to call him.

The minimized profile at the bottom of her screen caught her eye. She couldn't go back to Chicago and live in the same city where she fell in love, continually touring the landmarks of her heartbreak. And there was Mamaw Mable, with two broken ankles and a heart that had suffered the harsh pain of standing at the edge of the deep holes she had to put her husband and two sons inside. So she didn't need Hannah to wash her hair or change her bedpan or make meals, but Hannah and her brother, Brody, and his two kids were the only living relatives left in Mamaw's life and the only tie to her children, who had both preceded her in death. Hannah just existing helped her sweet, lonely grandmother make it through each day. She swallowed and wrestled her mouth into a smile.

"Yes, sir," she muttered, out of options. Just like Chicago reminded Hannah of Alex, Senatobia reminded Mamaw of everyone she'd lost— but unlike Hannah, Mamaw craved the blanket of memories from her life, and kept them gathered around her in this town. And the small

Mississippi town provided Hannah with a hideaway from the garbage heap she'd created over the past year. So she wasn't leaving—not yet. Mamaw could heal, and Hannah could keep herself hidden and her mother semi-satisfied with Hannah's job at the *Record*.

"That's a good girl," Monty said, like he was praising his golden retriever. She'd seen people written up for less at the *Trib*, but the *Record* didn't exactly have an HR department. "I had Terry bring the PC down there and hook it up to the scanner. I'll send you an email with all the details." He looked at his watch and wiped at the corners of his mouth again. "You know what? It's too late to get started tonight, so why don't you get on home."

"Really?" she blurted, straightening her back and clenching her knees together. Monty rarely let anyone go home early without a doctor's note or docking sick days.

"Yes, ma'am. I mean after you fix those errors, of course, and"—he glanced around the office and slipped his other meaty thumb out of his belt loop, pointing to a stack of boxes by the door to the basement— "carry those boxes over there downstairs, and then you can go. They'll need to be sorted and scanned along with everything else. Might as well keep it all in one place."

"Okay," Hannah squeaked, hoping that was the end of the list, or "going home early" would undoubtedly become "working late."

"I'll be on a call with Momma, so you can just slide your revision under the door when you go." Momma was what Monty called his wife. It creeped Hannah out, but no one else was bothered by the undertones of that nickname.

"I could, uh, email it." She offered the most apparent solution while fiddling with her mouse to make the screen saver of bouncing lines disappear.

"That's fine." He sighed and then asked the question he always brought up whenever there was an awkward moment of silence. "So . . . how's your grammy?"

"Better each day," Hannah answered succinctly, practicing some of the shallow pleasantries that veiled most southern interactions. She opened the traffic report as Monty chatted.

"You know your grandmother used to write for the *Record* back when it was still the *Tate County Democrat*. She was also teaching at the community college . . ."

"Yes, I think I heard that somewhere," Hannah said, somehow withholding any touch of sarcasm as she highlighted the errors in Lou Ann's name. She didn't mean to be rude, but Monty had told this story three times in the past four weeks, and Hannah still hadn't figured out how to stop him once he got rolling. Saving the document, she glanced up briefly at the line of analog clocks above the front door, labeled by country as though the *Tate County Record* dealt in international affairs. Precious seconds ticked away in unison.

"That was back when it was still a girls' college. My daddy taught there too. Said half the teachers on staff were in love with Miss Mable Patton. Before she married your papaw, of course, and had your daddy . . ."

Hannah's throat tightened. She dreaded this part of the story, when Monty tried to talk about her dad. Like just because they went to high school together, he could make jokes about his "odd" laugh or how half the school thought he was a "homosexual." The phone rang in Monty's office.

"Oh, that'll be Momma," he said, waving Hannah off apologetically, as though she'd been an anxious participant in his story time.

Thank God for Momma.

Hannah hit "Send" on her email, tossed the edited page into the recycling bin under her desk, and logged out, seeing her escape window. She clicked off the monitor and looped her worn gray messenger bag over her head, letting it hang listlessly at her side.

Nowadays it was a glorified lunch bag that held little more than snacks, an occasional library book, and a tauntingly empty notebook, but she couldn't seem to break the habit of taking it wherever she went.

"Oh, Miss Williamson!" Hannah froze midstep.

"Yes, Mr. Martin?" she asked in a sugary way without turning around, using her "southern belle" filter. If Mamaw wouldn't say it, she shouldn't say it. She glanced back at Monty, who was pointing with one hand and clenching the receiver to his ear with the other, phone cord stretched to its limit. "Don't forget those boxes."

"Why I'd never," Hannah whispered in an exaggerated Scarlett O'Hara southern accent and pushed in her desk chair, eyeing the stack of dusty brown-and-white file boxes.

"Speak louder, dear," Monty called.

Hannah flinched at the inappropriate endearment and shouted back, "I've got it, Mr. Martin! Thank you!"

She grabbed the first two boxes off the tower, which must've been enough to convince him of her cooperation because he muttered something into the receiver and closed the door to his office without any further instructions.

So this is my life, she thought, balancing the boxes on her hip while twisting the cold metal knob to the basement door. It took an extra yank, but when it opened, the ancient, glossy topcoat crackled, hinges screeching in protest. When she turned on the bare light bulb nestled in the ceiling, a set of gray painted wooden stairs with a worn brown trail down the center pointed her in the direction of the archives. The stairs creaked loudly with each step like they were about to crumble beneath her, the musty scent of old books and mildewed plaster growing stronger the farther she descended.

On the other side of the room, there was an additional set of stairs that led to the street, blocked by a row of filing cabinets. As Hannah rounded the shadowy corner of the staircase, she could sense the clutter of tall towers of boxes like the ones in her arms, even in the dimness. When she clicked the light switch with her elbow, a series of hanging bulbs flicked on, swinging ever so slightly on long cords like the electricity had set them in motion.

"Damn it," Hannah cursed, nearly dropping her cargo as the room came into focus. Virtually the whole fourteen-by-eighteen-foot space was filled with files. The walls were lined with shoulder-high filing cabinets, each with four legal-size drawers. The middle of the room consisted of three rows of the same cabinets, back to back, all with dusty filing boxes stacked on top till they nearly touched the light fixtures. The aisles between them were similarly stuffed, scarcely leaving a footpath of bare cement down each row. Only a small desk in the back corner looked freshly tidied, a computer and printer set neatly on its surface.

This is going to take forever.

Her arms ached, but there were no clear spots in any of the aisles. The desk. Hannah wiggled her way toward the only open spot in the room on her tiptoes, twisting her hips from one side to another. Halfway down the aisle, focused solely on finding a place to step where there were no papers to trample—bam. Her hip caught the corner of a half-closed drawer, and stars flashed in front of her eyes.

"Ouch!" Hannah barely held back a whole string of curses, her side throbbing. She propped the load on her knee, foot up on a drawer handle, and rubbed at the painful spot.

"Owwww," she moaned, tugging at the waistband of her jeans to get a better look. All she could see was the top of a deep red triangle imprint that undoubtedly extended toward her thigh and was sure to leave an ugly bruise. She pulled the heavy jean fabric back over her injury and tried to chuckle. *At least I'm the only one who will see it.*

Her mental joke was about as funny as all the other jokes she'd been telling herself. She shoved at the guilty drawer, suddenly furious but not sure why. It didn't budge. A wave of rolling anger warmed her midsection. She clenched her fist and hit the drawer again. It creaked, and the sting of metal felt almost good. With both hands clutching the boxes this time, she rammed her elbow and bicep into the drawer in one last massive effort. The drawer slipped shut.

Finally, she thought, continuing on her way when a thunderous rush, like rain in a thunderstorm, made her turn around again to a deluge of yellowed pages and newspaper clippings pouring into a paper puddle on the floor from the top of the cabinet she'd just shoved.

"Shit!" she cursed, unable to hold it back this time and not caring who heard. "Shit, shit, shit!"

Stumbling the rest of the way to the computer desk, Hannah dropped the file boxes and lunged toward the waterfall of papers, trying to dam the flood, but the damage was already done. One empty filing box sat upside down on top of the pool of spilled papers. Another was on its side, still on top of the filing cabinet.

"That's just great," Hannah said, absentmindedly wiping her tingling hands on her jeans, not sure where to even start.

"Miss Williamson, everything okay down there? I heard a noise." Monty's voice echoed down the staircase. Hannah sighed. Monty was the last thing that needed to be added to this shitstorm.

"Uh, yeah, it's fine!" she shouted, straining her voice to sound reasonable.

"I'll be locking up in a few minutes. Why don't you leave these last few boxes for Terry and head on home? He can bring them down in the mornin'."

In the morning. Ugh. Terry would surely notice the addition of a paper moat in the archives. Hannah dropped to her knees and started shuffling pages into a pile.

"Uh, okay! I'll be up in a second!" She flipped over the upside-down box and placed the first pile of documents inside, then started on another batch, dreading her bike ride home with her throbbing hip.

"All right, then," Monty replied, sounding uncertain but also not curious enough to subject himself to the rickety stairs. Hannah stuffed another two stacks of papers into the box until she could barely get the lid on top and then pulled down the second box from the cabinet and made quick work of most of the pages on the floor.

They were letters to the editor and clippings made of newsprint and a few other random items she didn't take the time to examine. But as that box filled, Hannah had to gather pages more carefully; many of the items were thin typewriter paper that had to be at least sixty years old.

They were articles. Old, very old. From the typed dates on the pages, it seemed all were sent in the early thirties. In the corner of each item was a red *R* for rejected, scribbled in grease pencil. And as she looked closer—women had written most of them.

Of course, Hannah thought. Being a woman in this industry was still not exactly easy even now, but back then? She flipped through three more pages with female names in the byline. Most of the stories related to social occasions or religious conversations, but one caught her eye. The writing was less polished, more like someone was talking and less like she was trying to mimic the short, detail-oriented narrative of a "newspaperman."

My name is Evelyn. Next week, I'll be all of twenty, living in an institution for cripples, with a sixth-grade education. When one is asked what Evelyn is like, you might say fairly good-looking, a blonde with blue eyes, fair skin, and a turned-up nose.

Evelyn? It seems as though you've heard that name before? Well, maybe back in 1929, you did happen to pick up a paper and read where a fourteen-year-old girl was shot in her bedroom, not expected to live. Not one chance in a thousand . . .

Three knocks from the top of the stairs startled Hannah and brought her back to the present. She inhaled, and the dust that floated in the basement air clung to the back of her throat, nearly making her gag.

"Miss Williamson? You still down there, dear?"

She coughed and cleared her throat, but nothing came out.

Frozen, she glanced down at the tattered pages, the red *R* in the corner, and that name written at the top: *Evelyn*.

"I'm coming!" Hannah called, in her sweetest singsong voice, and on a whim slipped Evelyn's article into her messenger bag instead of back in the box with the rest of the stack. She tossed the last few pages from the floor in the box and shoved the lid on before restacking the wobbly tower. Hannah stood and dusted herself off, readjusting her no-longer-empty bag.

CHAPTER 2

"Mamaw, I'm home!" Hannah called out as she entered the house through the garage after stowing her bike on the rear wall. The same two steps Hannah bounded up without any effort, Mamaw had tumbled down six weeks earlier.

Up until that moment, Mable Williamson had been an independent ninety-one-year-old senior citizen, with a packed schedule that included a quilting group at the Presbyterian church she'd attended every Sunday since she was girl and a nearly-as-religious beauty regimen that included weekly manicures and a blowout every Thursday. And though she hadn't written anything of her own since losing Uncle Samuel, she also frequented a writing group at the local library, where she put her skills as a former teacher to use helping the burgeoning writers of Tate County find their voices, even if she'd misplaced her own.

Hannah closed the door into the house, leaving a large, tan 1974 Buick sitting parked in the garage behind her. It was the only car she could remember ever being outside Mamaw and Papaw Williamson's ranch home.

The house smelled of fried chicken and biscuits even all the way out in the laundry room, which meant that Carla, Mamaw's housekeeper, had already started on dinner. It was a different world from the one Hannah was used to, a world where a particular group of people paid a different group of people to make their lives easier. A housekeeper, a handyman on call, and a full-time nurse seemed like more than enough people to keep the household of one ninety-one-year-old woman running. Hannah was just used to paying the delivery boy a nice tip to bring her Chinese food.

Carla peeked her head around the corner of the kitchen wall, hands wrapped up in her apron, wiping at the flour that clung in a light film over her palms.

"Hey, girlie. I thought that was you," Carla called, her eyes crinkling heavily at the corners. "How was work?"

"Oh, you know, Monty was there so . . ."

Carla chuckled, and her laugh was as warm and fluffy as one of her biscuits straight out of the oven. Carla had worked in the house alongside her own mother long before her first wrinkle carved itself into her deep-brown skin.

Now, at sixty-six, the housekeeper was growing older herself, still taking on all the same duties but at a much slower pace. The food was perfection. The furniture polish was always spot-on, but the amount of time it took her to complete any task was as overwhelming as the archaic methods she invested in stubbornly. But she was an integral part of the Williamsons' home. Just like her momma before her, and granny before her. Much to Mamaw's disappointment, Carla's daughter hadn't taken up the mantle and was a third-grade teacher in Strayhorn; Hannah couldn't help but cheer inside that she had gotten out of this suffocating little town.

"Your spunk will be good for old Monty," Carla said, a loving smile adding more lines to the road map of her face.

"Oh, I'm not sure he'd agree with you."

"Well, sometimes a man doesn't know what is good for him even when it's lookin' him in the eye."

Hannah smiled half-heartedly. *Alex.* Damn it. How did everything make her think of him? Even here in Senatobia. Running away was supposed to save her from his specter, but most days he was there.

And where Alex wasn't, her father's specter *was*. He'd grown up in Senatobia, had ridden the same streets on his own bicycle and lived in this very house. There was a chip on the linoleum counter where a rogue baseball had crashed through the back window and into the kitchen, and the large oak tree out back still had nails and lingering chunks of lumber from his and Samuel's treehouse.

But the boy who grew up here was much different from the man Hannah loved, respected, and lost. And though Patrick Williamson had brought his family back to his hometown for holidays now and again, and had been the backbone of the entire family when Papaw died suddenly of liver failure when Hannah was eight and when they lost Uncle Samuel only a few years later, he never considered returning to his southern roots. "My branches grow over a different yard now, Momma," she'd heard her father say as he was trying to convince his mother to move into their spare bedroom in Oak Park, Illinois, after she'd asked him to consider transferring closer to home, offering him his childhood house as collateral. Despite their similar people-pleasing tendencies, Mamaw would never leave Mississippi for good and her son would never return to it.

"Carla, are those biscuits I smell?"

Carla's biscuits were her father's favorite and, even with the proper recipe, one item Hannah's mother could never successfully replicate.

"Maaaaybe," Carla teased, crossing her arms, circles of flour on the lap of her faded pink-and-green apron.

"I'm starving."

"Well, dinner will be ready at half past six. You can eat then."

Hannah bit her lower lip and stepped toward the kitchen. "I mean, I'm starving now-ish. And you know what would help a lot?"

Carla's face turned playfully stern. "Not a chance. You'll spoil your dinner."

"Carla, I'm a grown woman. I should be allowed to spoil my dinner if I want to."

"As far as I can remember, you are barely old enough to wear a brassiere."

"I'm thirty-one, Carla. And a brassiere?" Hannah roared this time. "No one even says that anymore."

"Yes, a brassiere. Hannah!" Carla scolded as Hannah dashed into the kitchen and across the squeaky-clean linoleum floor, where she snagged a hot biscuit off a cooling rack. It burned her fingertips, but she bounced it up and down in her palm, letting the heat escape.

"Sorry, I'm a better listener when I'm not starving."

"Who are you kidding? You are never a good listener."

"Who, me? I don't know what you are talking about . . ." The still-too-hot-to-eat biscuit muffled Hannah's words.

Carla poked at the chicken in the pan and shook her head. "If I weren't so happy to hear you laughing again, I'd spank your behind, Hannah Williamson."

The buttery bite turned to dry crumbs in her mouth, and she swallowed hard, forcing the dry lump down. Carla was right. She'd been smiling. No wonder something had felt so strange.

"Hannah? Is that you? We're in here, darling!" Mamaw called sweetly from the master bedroom in the back corner of the house. It was her "we have company" proper southern accent this time, which meant Nancy, Mamaw's in-home care provider, was finishing up her duties. Carla didn't count as company because she'd washed underwear, cried at funerals, and helped Mamaw clean the bloodstain off the wall of Papaw's study when Uncle Samuel . . .

Hannah cleared her throat, her tongue dry and sticky. "I'll be right there," she called out before finishing off the biscuit in two big bites. She cradled a few crumbs in her palm.

"I'm sorry," Hannah muttered an apology as Carla silently held out the wastebasket she kept under the sink and stared wide-eyed with pursed lips like she was waiting for something. Hannah quickly corrected herself. "Oh, I mean, I'm sorry—ma'am."

"You better get moving," Carla said, with an exaggerated sigh, "or I'm gonna burn your dinner."

"You? Never!" Hannah bantered as she ducked out of the stifling kitchen, just in case Carla's mood was actual irritation and not just a playful game. She could hear Mamaw chatting with Nancy in her bedroom. With Mamaw temporarily distracted, Hannah made a detour to her room—Papaw's study. During the day, the door was always opened a crack, just like when Hannah would visit as a girl. Even when Papaw was working from home, he kept it unlatched. Mamaw said it was because he got lonely; Hannah's dad said it was so he could hear when Mamaw was coming and hide the Jim Beam.

The room still smelled of his pipe tobacco and peppermints. Hannah could sometimes make out this strange, masculine mix of scents on her clothes during work. She didn't get to know her Papaw, but staying in his office made her feel like they were getting to know each other by osmosis.

After unlooping the strap over her head, Hannah dropped her bag by Papaw's massive oak desk. Inside were the pages she'd snuck out of the *Record*'s basement. She was about to retrieve them when an email notification vibrated on Hannah's cell phone. She jumped. There was another itch she hadn't scratched in over an hour. She took out her phone, but instead of checking her email, which undoubtedly contained some annoying message from Monty, Hannah touched one of three social media icons on her screen. As Facebook opened, she filled with a familiar cocktail of anticipation and hesitation.

"Hey, Hannah. I'm heading home." Nancy, the perky, perfect day nurse, stood in the doorway. Hannah froze in a half squat by the couch that was also her bed every night, reluctantly pushing the off button on the side of her phone.

"Okay, Nancy. Thank you." Hannah stood up. She placed her phone on the cushion and put on her well-practiced smile.

Nancy gave a glossy-lipped, electric smile that was either genuine or a compelling fake that had probably been perfected during her time in the pageant world. Her bobbed blonde hair was still in the same shape and style as when she'd arrived that morning as Hannah was leaving for work. Maybe she slept like that.

"Uh, she's still asking for you."

"Oh, I'm sorry. I got a little sidetracked with"—she glanced back at the phone on the couch—"work. I'll go say hi."

"I should warn you, she's gettin' pretty good at the wheelchair. I don't think she'll be stayin' in her room in the evenings for much longer," Nancy said with a playful wink. "Tomorrow I can teach you her bedtime routine. Or . . . I know Mrs. Williamson didn't like Tara, but if you need a night nurse, I have a few other references."

"I'd love to learn," Hannah blurted. She'd agreed to come down to live at Mamaw's house to help her, but she'd never been allowed to contribute.

"Okay! Can you get here a little early tomorrow? Like, by five thirty?" She adjusted the large floral bag at her shoulder.

"I might have to make Mamaw call me in an excused absence with Monty, but I'm pretty sure I can worm my way out early."

Nancy laughed. Sometimes Hannah wondered if she and Nancy could be friends if they spent time together away from Mamaw's motorized bed and Nancy's purple scrubs.

"Dang, girl. You're so funny. You should come out with my friends and me sometime." She swatted at Hannah's shoulder, her giant diamond engagement ring flashing in the light.

"Yeah, maybe," Hannah said, losing her humorous edge. "But I'd better get to Mamaw."

"Oh yes! Definitely." Nancy waved that glittery left hand again and stepped toward the front door. "See you tomorrow?"

"Yup! Tomorrow!" Hannah said, waving.

As soon as Nancy turned her back, Hannah's smile washed away. No. They couldn't be friends. Not really. Nancy had a perfect doctor fiancé. Hannah knew—she'd looked them up on Facebook weeks ago when Nancy sent her a friend request. She could unfollow Nancy online. But in real life, she'd have a front-row seat.

She almost felt like she was wrapped up in figurative barbed wire. As long as she stood perfectly still and didn't allow anything to disturb her, the jagged edges of the fence wouldn't hurt as badly. Intellectually she knew the only way to stop hurting altogether was to get out of the trap—by blocking Alex, discarding any lingering hope of reconciliation, and moving on. But she'd nearly died the last time she faced that amount of pain, so Hannah had convinced herself that she'd let go when she was stronger—when it wouldn't hurt as badly. She'd move on when she was sure she could handle it. Until then, she'd stay here in her safe bubble of faraway and stand as still as possible.

Anyway, what would Nancy and her friends find interesting about a northerner with a lousy attitude, dirty hair, and zero desire to wear ChapStick, much less a full face of makeup? She'd be the oddity, the charity case, the friend they all talked about with a hand on their chest crooning, "Bless her heart."

Bless my heart, she thought, rolling her eyes. She placed a hand over her heart, where it was pounding beneath her shirt like it didn't know it was broken. *I forgot to check my messages. Maybe he . . .*

"Hannah!" Mamaw called again, her voice getting scratchy from overuse.

"Coming!" she shouted back, shutting the office door with a click and slipping the folded pages from the *Record*'s basement into her back pocket where her phone usually sat.

"There you are, darlin'," Mamaw sighed in her smooth southern drawl that sounded the way butter looked when melting. In her mechanical hospital bed, Mamaw sat upright on top of her comforter, changed into the quilted dressing gown she wore each evening before settling in for the night. Her hair was a lighter brown than when she was younger, but both shades were straight from the corner hair salon, where she had her hair done on Thursday afternoons.

"Sorry, Mamaw. Nancy was just telling me the good news about your wheelchair. I'm going to learn how to help you with your night-time routine so you don't have to go to bed so early."

"I told Nancy and I'll tell you the same thing: I do not want to be a burden. I don't mind goin' to bed early if need be."

Mamaw's attempt at a stern voice cracked Hannah up. When she was a little girl, both Hannah and Brody knew that if they wanted a cookie, they should ask Mamaw. In fact, if they wanted anything, they knew to ask Mamaw, who was loving and overly generous with her only grandchildren. It was easy to see where Patrick Williamson had gotten his soft edge, and Hannah liked this reminder. It made her feel like the empty space he'd left behind was being filled in a way.

"You are not a burden. I moved here to help you. Let me help," Hannah said, her stern voice much more convincing. She couldn't help but be a bit annoyed. Not by Mamaw, but because there was no doubt in Hannah's mind that her mother, Pam Williamson, had blabbed to just about everyone in town of her daughter's recent "emotional decline and hospitalization," as she liked to call it. And now everyone who knew about her experience was treating her like a glass doll.

"Well, as long as you are sure it's not too much."

"That's not even possible," Hannah said, leaning in to kiss Mamaw's cheek. She took in the smell of her delicately applied perfume. As a little girl, she'd once tried to find out what scent it was by searching through the glass bottles on Mamaw's vanity, but all she found were label-less containers with mystery liquids, which just made everything seem that much fancier. Everything about Mamaw was beautiful, and Hannah didn't need Monty's stories to see that. But Mable Williamson's ultimate beauty wasn't her always-flawless skin, which made her wrinkles look like decorations rather than detractions, or her nails, painted a glossy version of some hue of pink or red. No, it was how she made everyone around her feel about themselves.

That was the most selfish reason Hannah hadn't left Senatobia yet. Mamaw didn't need Hannah, not with Carla and Nancy and the ladies from the women's group down at the Presbyterian church and even Charlie Davenport, her eighty-six-year-old gentleman caller who came to flirt over coffee and cake a few mornings a week. But Mamaw made her feel loved unwaveringly, and Hannah needed some of that in her life.

"I'm sure the last thing you want to be doing when you get home from a long day at work is to jostle these old bones around."

"I mean, I know Mr. Davenport would offer to jostle your bones . . ."

"Oh, now, Hannah! That's terrible." Mamaw laughed, not scandalized but conditioned to think she should be. She patted Hannah's arm, her vibrant brown eyes sparkling behind her oversize glasses.

"If by *terrible* you mean hilarious, then yes, it's terrible." Hannah grabbed a lotion bottle and a small container of nail polish from the nightstand and walked to the end of the bed. Both legs were in large plastic boots. The only way to know that human appendages were enclosed were ten petite toes sticking out at the bottom. Hannah applied a thin line of lotion to each toe like she did most nights before dinner.

"Sometimes you remind me of my brother, Jerry. When he was in fourth grade, a little girl gave him a dime and asked him to be her boyfriend. All the other boys circled to tease him, but he wasn't embarrassed. Instead, he shouted, 'Hell yeah!' and kissed the girl right on the lips. Got sent home from school for it. It was smart, though. The boys left him alone after that."

"Ohhhhhh, Great-Uncle Jerry was a player!" Hannah joked, gently massaging each toe individually. Nancy said it helped with circulation, but Mamaw said it reminded her of a mani-pedi.

"Well, he *was* all-state in football but not till high school . . ."

"No, Mamaw." Hannah swapped the lotion for the nail polish bottle and unscrewed the top. "Not a football player. A *player*. Like, he was popular with the ladies."

"Oh my." She giggled again, blushing like a teacher might come in and send her to the principal's office for talking dirty. But then her face became still. "It's not far from the truth, I guess. There was a rumor he got a college girl pregnant, climbed into her dorm window. She said she lost the baby in a car accident, but nobody saw her for nine months after, so Momma always thought she had the baby and adopted it out."

"Wait." Hannah applied a quick refresher coat, screwed the top back on the nail polish, and then took out the lotion bottle. "You're saying you don't know? Like, no one tried to find out?"

As Hannah massaged her feet, Mamaw shook her head subtly like she was shy about her response. "No, it was just a rumor. People love a little scandal."

"But what if it was true? Don't you wonder?" Completing her nightly routine, Hannah put the container away and rubbed the rest of the lotion into her palms. She couldn't *stop* wondering about things. That was part of the problem.

"No, people try to mind their own business for the most part. And besides that, I guess Daddy didn't want the gossip of it all. 'Cause of his business."

Hannah's great-grandfather was one of the few businessmen to benefit financially from the Depression. Cotton became the only fabric most families could afford, and the Williamson family was the biggest cotton distributor in northern Mississippi and southern Tennessee. And with a warehouse just off the train tracks, Williamson and Son brought in enough money to buy a lovely house on the main square, a new organ for the Presbyterian church down the street, and care for at least two elderly spinster aunts.

I'll be a fantastic spinster aunt one day, Hannah thought ruefully. Then again, she was a terrible spinster aunt right now. Her older brother, Brody, had two adorable little boys she hadn't seen since her father's funeral. But that wasn't only Hannah's fault. After becoming close to Hannah's now-ex, Brody took Alex's departure almost as hard as she had, but his reaction was less about crying and more about "making him pay." Hannah had too many of her own emotions to manage; she didn't have the wherewithal to manage Brody's too—so they hadn't talked in four months. Truthfully, everyone was tired of Hannah's depression and hyperfocus on Alex; even Hannah was, but that didn't mean she could snap her fingers and make it stop.

"But *we* don't have to worry about his business. They have all that genetic testing now. There could be more Williamsons out there some-where. We could—"

"Now, Hannah." She patted her granddaughter's hand gently, her baby-soft skin contrasting her swollen, knobby joints and brown age spots. "That's enough of that. My momma always said that you need to let people have whatever fiction makes their life tolerable. And I agree. There's no use in churning up the past."

Fiction. As a reporter, Hannah had become accustomed to fighting the easy fictions people tried to act out and digging deeper into the elusive truth. It was that craving for truth that made her call Alex through the nurses' station rather than his cell phone when he was working late, only to find out he wasn't on the schedule. And it was what made her ask about a contact named Max, who always seemed to call at the oddest hours of the night. And in the end, it was what made her take the El home on her lunch break and find "Max" and Alex enjoying some afternoon delight. Janie and Alex had been sleeping together behind Hannah's back for months, in her own home and bed.

Before the rejection and devastation hit, there was a brief wave of relief that she hadn't been as crazy as Alex had made her seem.

What would her life look like right now if she'd let Alex have his "tolerable fiction"? Perhaps being with him and pretending she didn't notice the inconsistencies in his stories or significant gaps in his timelines would've been worth keeping him in her life. But probably not.

A tinkling bell rang in the kitchen, signaling that dinner was ready.

"There's dinner," Hannah said, learning how to avoid awkward topics of conversation like she'd been born south of the Mason-Dixon Line. "See, once Nancy teaches me a thing or two about bone jostling, we can go back to having dinner at the table."

"That sounds lovely, dear." Mamaw smiled sweetly as Hannah slipped her hand off the bed, sending a puff of gardenia scent into the air.

"And maybe I'll call Mr. Davenport for some tips . . . ," Hannah snuck in as she hurried out of the room, Mamaw's scandalized rebuke echoing down the hall.

Passing Papaw's study, Hannah thought of the folded cluster of papers still in her back pocket. She'd read them later when she was alone. Mamaw might not want to know about the secrets hidden in the world around her, and Mr. Martin might agree with her, but Hannah couldn't help her urge to know someone else's ugly truth—especially when it distracted her from her own.

CHAPTER 3

"Yes, Ma, I know. I'll get it done," Hannah muttered as she entered the *Record*'s offices and headed toward her desk. The low rumble of traffic on the 290 came through Hannah's headphones.

For twenty-five years Hannah's parents made the commute into the city together, her dad dropping his wife off at her law firm before heading into his office at Columbia College on Michigan Avenue. Now that Pam Williamson had to make the trip alone, she'd fallen into a predictable pattern of calling every weekday morning at 7:30 a.m. or on her ride home at 5:30 p.m., seeking out a virtual companion for her drive. Hannah only picked up maybe 20 percent of the time, which likely meant she was a terrible daughter.

She felt for her mother and the loneliness of widowhood, but Pam didn't act lonely or sad when she talked to Hannah. No—most conversations were thirty-minute treatises on all the things Hannah needed to change in her life, with follow-up emails and the occasional spreadsheets that had been the norm since Hannah was two and enduring potty training.

"Larry Norris said he'd put a good word in for you. I know it's not the same as the *Trib*, but it's all online, so you could work from home. Once Mable is up and moving again, you could come back to your room here. Or Brody said you could use their guest bedroom until the baby comes. Try out California for a bit, maybe?"

"I said I'd fill out the application, but I have a job here with a newspaper—"

"You have a job at the *Tate County Record*, Hannah. They don't even have a website, and the Facebook page hasn't been updated since you got your first period."

"Ma!" Hannah clicked down the volume in case Dolores could hear from across the room. "I'm here now. I gotta go."

"Fine. Just make sure to turn in that application *today*. I don't want to offend Larry. Plus, he has a son who is around your age. Just went through a divorce and is having a hard time, like you did with Alex. Maybe you'd like to talk—"

"Bye, Ma."

"You gotta get on with your life sometime, Hannah—"

"GOODBYE, MA," Hannah said with an extra punch and then hung up the phone.

Hannah plopped down in her office chair and dropped her messenger bag on the floor. For the first time in nine and a half months, she'd shot out of bed in the morning, anxious to get to work and find more distraction like she had the day before. She wasn't going to let Pam Williamson, powerhouse attorney and helicopter mom of the century, ruin all that.

Waiting for the screen to wake up, she noticed the pile of file boxes that'd been left by the top of the basement stairs last night was missing. Terry had likely put them in the basement as promised. Hopefully, he hadn't touched anything else. The filing system was chaotic and random, but if Hannah could find the rejection box she'd spilled, hopefully she'd find more of Evelyn's story.

Last night, after Carla had gone home, Mamaw slept soundly in her room with the hum of cable news on to help her sleep, and Hannah finished drying the last dishes from dinner. Carefully, she stowed them on top of their tower in the cupboard, pulled the plug in the sink, and wiped her hands on a dish towel with a sense of satisfaction.

Before Senatobia, she'd never taken much to the domestic side of life. Meal planning and laundry folding weren't just boring necessities like they were for most people. For Hannah, the tentacles of her lingering depression made them feel like soul-crushing wastes of time. But here, when the night was quiet and the last suds of Lemon Sparkle were gurgling in the drain, Hannah almost understood how a homemaker's life could bring moments of fulfillment.

But the odd calm of domestic bliss was fleeting. She flicked off all the lights in the front room except for the one over the sink, then tiptoed down to check on a safely snoring Mamaw before finally returning to Papaw's study. She'd been away from her phone for a three-hour eternity. Whenever she hadn't looked at that screen for a chunk of time, she'd pick up the device expectantly, knowing anything could be waiting for her. A call from her mother, an email from her former boss saying they made a mistake, or even a "like" on Instagram from Alex.

Her lock screen was empty except for one Facebook notification. When Hannah touched the prompt, a picture popped up that made her heart thump. It was one of those Timehop memories showing images that were posted on that date some years earlier. This one was from three years ago when she and Alex had gone on a cruise to the Bahamas. Hannah was slender and glowing white in a modest bikini, and Alex was finely toned and bronze in his trunks. He was holding her up in the waves, both frozen in laughter. They'd played in the water like children that day, collected seashells, and dove headfirst into waves. They'd made love that night in their bungalow, and Alex said her skin tasted of the salt from the ocean that coated their bodies in a fine crystalline film.

Hannah dropped her phone.

That was the past. Laura, her therapist of the past several months, said Hannah had to stop reliving every good minute of her relationship, or she'd never move on. "Relationships are made from the hard moments, not the good ones," she'd remind Hannah, trying to guide her back to the reality of the broken trust and fidelity that characterized her relationship with Alex. But so far she didn't want to move on, she just wanted to go back in time.

Back in time.

This article was exactly what she needed to help her stop thinking about Alex. Hannah retrieved the folded typewriter paper from her back pocket. It was flimsy, with little tears forming down the crease lines as she unfolded the pages and settled onto the floor. The typewritten words were difficult to read, and Hannah had to turn on the light on Papaw's desk to make out all the words. She started again—from the beginning—realizing that the letter was addressed to her boss's father.

```
Editor in Chief Montgomery Martin
The Tate County Democrat
3556 Bedford Ln
Senatobia, MS 38668


May 19, 1935


Dear Mr. Martin,
Thank you for taking the time to read my
letter. When I told my friend Marion my
story, she said that it was a real good
story and, being from Senatobia her-
self, said I should tell it to you, and
```

maybe it could be in the newspaper like
the stories I read there sometimes.

My name is Evelyn . . .

Hannah rushed through the familiar first paragraphs, where Evelyn introduced herself, and picked up where the unread section began, flashing back to when the writer of the article had woken up in the hospital with her father and sister by her side. Hannah felt the same flip in her midsection that she'd felt when she picked up the article accidentally. The promise of a tell-all was always exciting to a journalist, and the first few lines of this article read like the opening to a true-crime podcast she would have binged on during her commute to and from the *Tribune* building. She kept reading, intrigued.

Myrtle wailed in the background,
"Who did this, Evey? Who did this?"
but I couldn't remember what had happened, and I wasn't sure what to make
of the bright lights, scratchy sheets,
and the heavy sensation in my lower
body. Daddy patted my arm.

"Don't worry, baby, you'll be all
right," he said. I wasn't used to seeing tears on my daddy's face. But lying
in that bed, I hated that I was the
reason for his tears.

"Daddy, do you forgive me? Do you
love me?" I whispered in response to
his chant, wanting to make it better,
to remember what happened.

"Sure, we love you," he said. "Close
your eyes now, and try to sleep."

Hannah's breath hitched at the tender recollection of Evelyn's father sitting by his little girl's bedside, the roles reversed in her own family only a few months ago. Hannah holding her father's hand each night as he fell asleep, trying to memorize the feeling of his fingers in hers. To think that he felt and heard her, even in the last few days of his life when he could barely open his eyes, touched Hannah.

I listened, but in the darkness, I slipped too far back in time—into childhood days when my momma was alive. Momma wasn't just beautiful. She also knew things no one else did. I remember when she was carrying Daddy's fourth child and hiding her newly swollen figure under aprons and tented dresses. I sat by her side in the living room with Daddy staring like he always did and with me sitting with a sewing needle in my hand for the first time.

"Daddy, these quilts will keep my babies warm when I am gone," Momma said, dreamy like a fortune-teller.

"You'll keep your babies warm, Ava," Daddy mumbled back, half paying attention to her.

A few months later, Momma stood in the kitchen, showing me how to peel and preserve peaches while Daddy read the newspaper at the table. Momma kept cutting but started talking to Daddy without looking at him.

"This fruit I'm canning will keep my babies from hunger when I am gone," she said.

Daddy dropped the newspaper, staring at Momma like she was speaking the Cherokee she'd learned from her momma's side.

"You'll keep your babies from hunger, Ava," he said, maybe angry, maybe sad.

And in November, my baby brother was born. Momma didn't leave her bed after that, and one night, Daddy called us all in to say good night. I was the oldest at eight. Myrtle was next to me at six, a brunette, very much like Momma with the sweetest disposition on earth. Vivian, also of the brunette type, was four years old and the prettiest of us three girls.

Momma kissed each of our heads and said she loved us and then weakly passed my brother to my daddy. When he took William, Momma traced Daddy's thick, calloused fingers.

"See these hands?" she said, sad like she held a thousand sorrows instead of a tiny newborn. "They will keep my babies safe when I am gone."

Daddy didn't correct her that time. He stared, kissed her fingertips, took my brother, and rushed us out of the

room so Momma could sleep. She never
woke up.

Never woke up. The image of her father taking his last breath, Hannah on one side, Pam on the other clutching his hand, flashed through her mind. When he didn't take another inhale, Pam kissed his cheek and said, "Goodbye, my love, I'm glad you have found rest."

But Hannah wasn't glad. She didn't have the room inside her to be "glad" in any way that her father was gone. He'd promised that he'd be okay. A professor of mathematics at Columbia College, he comforted his children and his wife with statistics when he was first diagnosed, stating the odds of survival like they were an equation that was beyond basic. It was the only time his numbers didn't add up the way they were supposed to. And even though she knew he didn't choose to die, and even though she knew it was crazy, she felt abandoned in a way, and she wasn't even a young child like Evelyn. She returned to reading, curious how the death of a parent affected young Evelyn and her siblings.

Left with four small children, Daddy
did the best he could. An aunt who lived
in a small Mississippi town took William
and has had him ever since. Daddy's
daughter by a former marriage then kept
house for us for a while. She was rather
fond of me, and I was crazy about her.
She came down with pneumonia the following year and died. Daddy then sent in an
advertisement to a city in Tennessee for
a housekeeper, and Mrs. Brown arrived
at 11:00 p.m. one January night to keep
house for us.

That took away our last chance for complete happiness. Every day I think this thought: if it weren't for Mrs. Brown, I wouldn't be crippled in this chair.

There is more to tell, so much more, but my hands are tired, and I have to wait till next week to get more paper from Mrs. Stallion. Please don't try to send a response here. I left the address and my last name off on purpose. Mrs. Stallion wouldn't look kindly on my meddling and digging up old dirt. But someone should know what happened to me, and if Marion says I can trust you, then I will listen to her.

Sincerely,
Evelyn

Hannah put the letter down, tears swimming in her eyes. She could see why the "article" had been rejected. It was long, had too many details, and was written like a letter home rather than a polished feature or the serial fiction of the time. But it also sounded human and real, and Evelyn came across on the page like a friend. This woman knew what it was like to suffer the sneak attacks of life and end up wounded. She knew the domino effect that could be initiated by one traumatic loss that would lead to a mess of tiles on the floor.

In Hannah's life it had started with Alex's infidelity, which tumbled her into a deep and paralyzing depression and addiction, which toppled into losing her job, which crashed into wondering why she needed to

Emily Bleeker

be alive at all, which dropped into an attempt on her own life, which collapsed into moving in with her parents and watching helplessly as her father faded and then disappeared in front of her eyes. Hannah didn't end up in a wheelchair at the end of her spiral, but she did end up paralyzed and living in a place where she was numbing herself with monotony and memories.

Right now she knew Evelyn's first domino, the loss of her mother, and her last, paralyzed by a bullet that was meant to take her life. But what about the in-between?

CHAPTER 4

Hannah rummaged through the loose boxes close to where she found the first letter. The day was a blur of frustration and chaos, emptying boxes and leafing through pages aimlessly. She developed a plan: She couldn't just dig through the documents recklessly. She needed a systematic process to get through the piles in a productive and organized manner. She scanned the documents in the next four filing cabinets and dug through countless random boxes, hoping to find another article with Evelyn's story.

For nearly a week she'd go home smelling of the browning, crinkling paper she'd spent scanning. Lately, there was a mysterious itch that started at her scalp and crawled down to her wrists as she handled some of the older pages. But it didn't make her give up. She popped an allergy pill and kept on digging.

She had copied the letter, so she didn't have to carry the frail original document around, giving her the ability to read and reread it anytime she had a spare moment. And her notebook pages were full of names, leads, phone numbers, websites, and plenty of dead ends. But it was a much-needed mental escape from the usual twister ripping through her thoughts.

And although she did submit the application her mom had been nagging her about, she hadn't lost her drive and curiosity in the time she spent shuffling through the files. Every day as she walked down the stairs to the basement, she'd think, *If I don't find anything today, I'll ask for a new assignment.* But then every night when she walked up the stairs, she knew—there was no giving up. And by day five she'd decided that even if she never read one more word written by Evelyn, just the act of searching was a valuable exercise.

On the sixth day, she started in on a filing cabinet with browning manila folders and labels that had peeled away from a stiff, crackled mystery adhesive. The dates on the files were in general proximity to the 1935 date on the first article. She went through those pages slower than she had through the cabinet with more modern files. And when a red *R* started showing up in the corner of the items in the middle drawer, she read the first sentences of each page, hoping to find Evelyn's voice again.

That's when she found it.

Yes! Hannah cleared her sticky throat and sat in the dusty green vinyl rolling chair by the corner desk. As she scanned the article, it didn't seem to be the next one in Evelyn's story, but it wasn't too far off from the story of a little motherless eight-year-old folded up in the original pages. She devoured the letter, almost too fast, like gulping water after a long run.

It started the same as the first article with the address of the newspaper and Monty Sr.'s name on top. There were a few sentences of greeting, but then the narrative picked up where another article must've left off, and immediately Hannah was there, back in 1925 with a nearly ten-year-old Evelyn.

> I'd kept house for Daddy then, all on my own. I sent Myrtle to school, Vivian to a neighbor's, and after the house was cleaned up, I went to school myself. It wasn't hard, at least not as hard as living with Mrs. Brown, who had a temper

and looked harshly on my every mood. But Daddy still didn't have a job, and we'd run out of Momma's preserves long ago, and her quilts couldn't keep us as warm as fuel in the fireplace or coal. So when Daddy got a job in Memphis, I let out a sigh of relief and wrapped my arms around his big ole shoulders as a thank-you. But that's really when the heartaches and unseen troubles began.

Hannah clutched the pages and forced herself to read slower.

On my tenth birthday, we again find Mrs. Brown, the ex-housekeeper, in our lives. Daddy never told us why she up and left that night, disappearing like that magician we saw in Coldwater. She'd been living with her daughter and son-in-law in Memphis, and Daddy said he'd run into her in the street one day, though I doubt it was an accident (Myrtle says I'm too conspiratorial in my thinking).

At first, we all got along pretty well till it was clear Daddy had taken a liking to the housekeeper. Mrs. Brown had always had a dull, sour face, and I could not figure out for the life of me what Daddy saw in her after being in love with such a beautiful woman as Momma. She was rightly labeled, though,

in the name Brown. She never brought
a lick of light into the world and did
her best to dampen any glimmer of hope
around us all with constant complaints
and criticisms. Daddy didn't seem to
notice, but us three girls saw.

On November 1, my daddy and
Mrs. Brown were married.

The information hit Hannah like a punch in the gut. How treacherous must it have felt for Evelyn's father to have replaced her beautiful
mother with a wretch. It must've been a slap in her face, a stab to her
mother's memory. Hannah knew what it was like to be replaced, and
it had made her question everything about herself. If Evelyn's momma,
who her father loved so dearly, could be replaced by an inferior version,
and if her brother could be given away to strangers, Evelyn must have
wondered what that meant about her value, her future.

With Mrs. Brown in the house (Daddy
made us call her Mother), we kept
boarders, and Daddy kept working. There
was a lot of work to be done in the
house, with Mother there now and the
two boarders, who needed feeding and
caring for.

I liked having the strangers in
the house, one a teacher at the high
school, and the other a Yankee book-
keeper saving up to bring his girl
to Mississippi, where his business had
transferred him. The men were genteel and treated me like I was nearly

a lady. They also kept Mother from
screaming at me when they were home
because she couldn't stand the embarrassment. I tried to stay away as much
as possible when both of the misters
(as my sisters and I called them) were
not home.

I started learning housekeeping at
Daddy's request and found I was better at that than I was at school, but
my disposition seemed to grow worse
instead of better.

Hannah almost related too much. Her father had been caring,
understanding of Hannah's deep dive into depression, checking on her
daily with phone calls and occasional swings by the apartment. But
Hannah's mother, Pam, couldn't see why Hannah wouldn't just get out
of bed and get on with her life. And though her friends were sym-
pathetic and unified in a tide of anger and outrage at Alex at first, as
weeks turned to months, and anger turned to sadness, which turned to
despair, her friends dropped out of the picture one by one, which just
made Hannah feel less worthy, less wanted. It wasn't until after Hannah
met her therapist, Laura, in the hospital that she understood that the
symptoms of depression don't always look like basic sadness and that
her ill temperament was one of them. Evelyn must've felt the same coil
of anxiety and despair that had spring-loaded Hannah's easy temper. It
was impossible to blame her.

Mother and I didn't get along together
at all. I was always doing something I
shouldn't do or wasn't doing something
I should do. Like when I put too much

starch in the misters' shirts and had to wash them and dry them again before Mother found out. But she did find out and slapped my hands for being wasteful. Or when the stew boiled over and doused the fire in the stove because I was doing my homework while trying to tend dinner. I worked very hard to do the things that I thought she would like, but for some reason, I just couldn't.

She would whip me. Never when Daddy was home, but soon she took the horse-whip to me every day for the littlest error. I'll admit, I got stubborn after some time of it. If she was going to whip me anyway, she might as well know what I thought of her and her plain frock and her ugly, crooked nose and her face that looked like it had never held a smile. But it only made her whip me more.

Even now, stuck in this chair, I can remember the pain of the twine and leather hitting my legs and back. I wish I could remember what other things felt like, like running or dewy grass or even pinchy heeled shoes, but I can't. Yet I can still feel the whip and can remember how it burned each time the fabric of my dress grazed my raw skin. When Daddy came home, it was always the same way. She would have a "heart spell" and I would have to ask her forgiveness. My only redeeming feature was that I was always sorry and could ask her to forgive me.

Daddy had forbidden her to whip us with that thing, but after some time, the tink of the shiny silver handle against the plaster on the wall where it hung was enough to make me straighten up. Besides, Mother didn't listen to Daddy anyway. She made his food and wore his ring, but I don't think she loved him or even cared about him. And when he started getting sick, she'd water down his stew and cut his bread helping in half, saying he didn't need as much because he wasn't out working much of the day "like all the other husbands."

I remember one day when Daddy had started to become increasingly weak. I tried to switch his stew with one of the misters'. Mother caught me. Her daughter, Louisa, and son-in-law were visiting for the night, and they were sitting in the front room entertaining the boarders, so she whispered, "You sneaky little thing. I saw what you did."

She smacked my face. I was so displaced that the tray dropped from my hands, spilling stew all over the clean floor and chipping one of the bowls. I knew I was in for it then, so I tried to run, but she caught me. I fought her back, but then her daughter came in to check on the commotion, and she hit me too and then held me down so Mother could whip my back till blood soaked into the gingham.

I'll never forget Mother's face, and whenever the preacher screams of demons possessing bodies, I think about Mother on that night. When the spell passed and the whip went still, Louisa told Mother to tend to dinner and then dragged me up the back stairs to my bed, handling me roughly as she changed me into my nightgown. She told me I'd never be forgiven if I didn't beg Mother on my hands and knees. She said that I was making Daddy ill with my behavior, and I had better change or he'd die.

The thought of Daddy dying hurt worse than the welts on my back and legs. Back then, I thought that if Daddy died, I'd want to die too. But foolish girl that I was, I didn't know what death was other than something that happened to everyone I truly loved.

The pages trembled in Hannah's hands as she imagined the pain of the whip tearing her skin, and how impossible it must've seemed to escape. No wonder Evelyn had considered death preferable to life without her protector. Evelyn was a child. This was her home and her supposed family. If she left—where would she go? And worse—no one was helping her. It stirred a disquietude in Hannah that said, "Do something." But this was in the 1920s—barring time travel, there was nothing she could do other than read.

Even with that, for the first time ever, I did not beg for Mother's forgiveness, and she never offered one apology. I grew rather mean to Myrtle and Vivian. They loved me dearly, and I did love them, yet they were afraid of me. They would never tell Mother anything I did or said. And as Daddy got sicker, his son by a former marriage (a brother of the sister who died) took my little sister that Christmas, and it nearly broke my heart, for I did love her so very much, though I hadn't been as kind to her as I might have been. And the frailer Daddy got, the more I wondered about Mrs. Brown. She was endlessly cruel and as hard as iron and hated all of us, even Daddy. I thought about the broken bowl of stew and the individual serving she always had me bring Daddy. I couldn't say it out loud, I barely dared to think it, but my thoughts lingered on the possibility that Daddy wasn't just getting old—he was being poisoned.

This poor girl, Hannah thought, sitting up in the squeaky old chair. Evelyn had endured the loss of nearly everyone she held dear in her formative years, and was forced into hard labor at a young age and beaten regularly. It was unnerving knowing that these were the least of her traumas. In a matter of four years, that child was headed toward an even more violent confrontation.

It felt like when Hannah and Alex had decided to follow the Cubs to Cincinnati for a game in the summer of 2016 when the World Series hopes were building. On I-74, a group of college-aged guys sped past them in the right lane. Hannah, in the passenger seat, sleepy from watching fields and small towns droning by in a comforting blur, lazily followed the speeding vehicle with her gaze when it swerved. The overcorrection was just enough to send the car off-balance and, as though it were happening in slow motion, the 1992 Chevy shifted just enough to make the tires on one side lift and start a barrel roll off the paved highway and onto the tall grassy knoll past the gravel shoulder. The car flipped four times, and Hannah watched as the young men in the back seat of the Beretta tumbled around like rocks being polished. She knew it was bad. She knew people didn't walk away from accidents like that without seat belts and miracles.

Reading Evelyn's story was similar—Hannah, the helpless stranger, was peering through a small window into a world of chaos that would inevitably lead to tragedy. And just like with that burgundy car, no efforts to change the outcome for those anonymous figures through the window, even with Hannah's call to 911 and Alex's attempt at first aid, could keep them from having funerals after that kind of disaster.

There was nothing left to do but watch and bear witness to the end of a life, and the only way to do that was to keep going. Hannah opened the empty lower drawer of the metal desk, the rollers screaming as she pulled on the handle. She placed the new article inside it, flat and minuscule in the spacious space. She shoved the drawer closed, noting the echo as it slammed into place, and reset her focus from the hollow drawer to the seemingly endless lines of cabinets. It wouldn't be empty long—it was the least she could do.

CHAPTER 5

The sun was setting as Hannah exited the basement, closed the green door behind her, and slid into her office chair. It had been a long but productive day. She'd found two additional articles and added them to the newly minted Evelyn drawer. On a roll with her scanning, Hannah hadn't had time to read the letters all the way through yet, but she'd taken pictures with her phone and was counting down the minutes until she could hole up in her room and devour them slowly, like she was eating a plate of tender BBQ ribs.

Waking up her computer, this time she bypassed any temptation to open social media and skipped to a search engine instead.

Hannah had been working on confirming that Evelyn's story was true. If so, it must've been a somewhat notable scandal in a small town like Senatobia, but it was nearly a hundred years in the past, and all Hannah had to go on was a first name and a general location.

It took a few searches for Hannah to find her groove. But over the past few days, she'd come to discover enough information about locations and a few small leads from the names mentioned in Evelyn's article that her empty notebook had started to fill with notes.

Hannah was working off a list of last names from that era that might match Evelyn's age and description. On another page, she listed the surnames that belonged to members of Evelyn's community like the leering plumber and the postman.

Oh! Postman! Hannah thought and flipped to another empty page. Perhaps there was a way of finding out Evelyn's name if she could locate her address. The postman seemed to be a great lead. She labeled the page, *Postman.*

She hadn't felt very much besides sadness for a long time, so to feel—pretty much anything else—was invigorating. Most days she wanted to get back in the basement to search the archives without Terry's prying eyes or Monty's commentary. And she'd found that when she escaped to the other side of the basement door and rushed carefully down the stairs, which no longer seemed as steep, that the creaks sounded less like warnings and more like invitations. She was even starting to enjoy the sound of a scanner bouncing off the cement walls. The dank, vaguely mildewy smell still scratched at Hannah's throat, but the mass of papers and confusion in the filing room no longer seemed like a daunting, massive waste of time.

Usually, Monty stayed later than all the regular newspaper employees, but recently Hannah was the one overstaying her welcome. Most nights for the past week and a half, he'd ended up standing at the top of the staircase, bellowing, "Miss Williamson!" from a safe and effortless distance.

And, like today, she left every single item in place so she could pick up in the same spot the next morning and then bounded up the stairs, which had somehow become less rickety. It'd become a game to see how fast she could collect all her belongings, avoiding Monty, who had a never-ending list of questions about her family, Chicago, and her job at the *Tribune.*

Thankfully, the one topic of conversation he hadn't forced his way into was what kept her so enthralled in that basement. Monty was such a control freak that Hannah was sure he'd hate the idea of anyone investigating a story without his express permission. But she reasoned that at least she was doing a bang-up job at organizing and archiving the files, as she'd been assigned. And the purpose of scanning the scraps of paper, letters to the editor, reference materials, old photos, and more was to one day put them online for public access, as so many other newspapers had done over the years. So she was setting aside a few items that needed to be filed together—nothing weird about that. Plus, without the hope of discovering more of Evelyn's story, Hannah would've bored of the activity within a day. Well, before that even.

Tonight she was at work even later than usual. Sweet little Nurse Nancy had taught Hannah how to help Mamaw in and out of bed and to perform the nightly routine of visits to the bathroom and distributing medicine. But Hannah kept losing track of time. If she biked home at full speed, she'd be able to spend a little time with Mamaw before she retired for the night.

Now that the days were getting colder, she'd started bringing her bike into the entry of the offices. It would be called a mudroom in Illinois, but Monty called it a vestibule. He sniffed when she'd deposited the ancient blue-and-white ten-speed there a few days ago.

Hannah wrestled the bike away from the wall, where it had gotten tangled with the dark walnut coatrack, like it always did. It was easy to drop it in the vestibule in the morning, but leaving was more complicated. The space was already tight with the rack, and there was also a pastor's bench and a small bookcase with an ancient arrangement of dusty silk flowers on top. Escaping gracefully was not an option.

Hannah kicked open the screen door with her foot and rolled the bike out backward onto the cement steps, trying to juggle the door, the metal frame, and her half-stuffed work bag. With one last shove, she forced the bike out into the fresh fall air. The door screeched and slammed shut, making Hannah jump forward and crash her shin into one of the metal pedals.

"Oh!" she gasped, leaning against the doorjamb to pull up the bottom of her pant leg. There was no blood, but she rubbed the deep red mark roughly to help make the pain dissipate.

"Are you Hannah?" a deep male voice asked from the bottom of the stairs.

Hannah glanced up from her leg. A tall man, young looking but old enough to have the beginnings of a neatly trimmed beard, stood on the cement path that led up to the newspaper offices. He wore worn blue jeans and a clean white T-shirt with a blue flannel unbuttoned over it that complemented his dark complexion. If it wasn't for the throbbing pain in her shin, she might have wondered how a stranger knew her name. Instead, she looked back down at her injury and mumbled a reply, distracted.

"Uh-huh, but I'm on my way out. Mr. Martin is inside if you need anything." She rolled down the fabric of her boot-cut jeans to cover the evidence of her clumsiness and started to force the bike down the stairs when the man rushed up the steps and grabbed the front wheel.

"Hey!" She jumped, surprised when the bike slipped out of her grip as he carried it down to street level effortlessly, like some kind of magic trick.

"I don't need Mr. Martin," he said, with the casual respect a good southern boy gives his elders. "I'm here to retrieve you."

Hannah pulled the strap of her bag up onto her shoulder, awkwardly aware that her dingy, beige bra strap was clearly visible at the edge of the deep V of her T-shirt, frumpy and unkempt. This man was objectively attractive, with dark brown eyes that looked like they were laughing at her and a firm chest that showed through the thin material of his shirt.

"Here, I got that," she said, rushing down the steps and reaching for her bike.

But the man didn't move or let go. Instead, he examined Hannah and squinted his dark eyes as he spoke. "You're Hannah? Not what I expected, but okay."

"What the hell is that supposed to mean?" Hannah blurted, yanking the handlebars out of his grip.

"Nothing, I just thought . . ." He let his words drift off into silence, likely trying to be polite, like every other damn person in this state. Ironically, the constant search for decorum left Hannah offended more often than she'd ever been in the more unfiltered North. Down here, instead of hearing what someone was thinking about her directly, she filled in the blanks with her most anxious thoughts and insecurities.

"Well, I need to get home," she said, gesturing to the darkening sky and taking a step away.

But the man didn't move out of the way. Living in Chicago had trained Hannah to always be on edge, and if she was still in the city, she'd have let go of the bicycle and called for help. But in small-town Senatobia, she planted her feet firmly on the sidewalk and glared up into the man's smooth and undisturbed face.

"That's why I'm here. I do some work for your grandma . . . Mrs. Williamson. She asked me to come by—"

Hannah stopped in her tracks. "Wait, Mamaw?" She felt like she couldn't breathe. "Is she okay?" At ninety-one, anything could be wrong. She didn't pause for a response, flipping open her messenger bag and riffling through to find where she'd tossed her phone. Mamaw didn't have a cell phone, but she did have a landline by the side of her bed. Maybe she'd called and Hannah had missed it.

She found the device and turned on the home screen. It was filled with notifications from a local number, but it wasn't Mamaw's. Someone had been trying to get in touch with Hannah, and it was urgent.

"Shit," she cursed under her breath. Touching one of the messages, she held the phone up to her ear.

"I can just tell you . . . ," the mystery man said, waving at Hannah like he wanted to take the phone out of her hand. But Hannah turned away and pressed it closer to her ear.

Mamaw's shaky voice came through the receiver. "Hannah, sweetie—I'm at Aria's Salon. My appointment ended a little early. Now, the girls and I are gossiping, but if you could head on down here as soon as you get home, that would be so nice of you. Love you."

Damn it—her hair appointment. Nancy had to go home early for a cake tasting with her fiancé, so Hannah had offered to leave at four, get Mamaw's Buick, and then pick her up at the salon by four thirty. It was now past six. She tapped on the next message, this one from four thirty on the dot.

"Hannah, darlin', maybe you're running behind today, or maybe you forgot about my appointment. The girls close up in half an hour, so I hope this gets to you soon. Carla is not picking up at home, and Nancy is already in Looxahoma, so if you could please give me a call here at Aria's Salon. The number is . . ." Mamaw read off a list of numbers and said her goodbye, hanging up.

There were three more messages, but Hannah couldn't bring herself to listen to them. She slipped the phone into her back pocket. It was an hour past closing time for the salon, but luckily it was only three miles across town, just a few blocks south of Mamaw's house. If she went fast enough and didn't get stuck at any intersections, she'd be there in fifteen minutes. After checking in on Mamaw, she could go home, get the car, head back, and pick her up.

Her cheeks burned, and the pain in her leg barely registered anymore. She tossed one of her legs over the bike and was finding her balance when the stranger cleared his throat.

"Thank you for your help, but I should go," she said, moving past the stranger, uncomfortable with the on-edge way he made her feel. As soon as she was balanced, Hannah started off down the sidewalk.

"Hey, would you just stop for a second?" He followed her, his long strides matching her hurried pace easily.

"Listen, I'm already late, mister . . ." She let the statement trail off, realizing she'd never even caught his name.

"Guy," he said, filling in her blank. "Just Guy. No mister." Even through his somewhat softened southern tone, he sounded annoyed.

"Okay, Guy," she said, putting one foot down momentarily so he could catch up. "I screwed up big-time and need to pick up my grandma."

"Your grandma is already at home," he said, not even a little out of breath. A fine line of perspiration at his hairline was the only evidence of his over-the-top effort. "Eileen dropped her off half an hour ago."

"Oh, thank goodness," she said, some of the tension in her joints releasing. Eileen was the owner of Aria's Salon.

"Well, good to see you've decided not to run away," he said, his grin charming. "I'm George Franklin's son. I'm helping build the addition out back of your grandmother's house."

"Oh, you're the handyman," she said, the pieces clicking into place. As soon as Mamaw got the news that Hannah would be moving in, she'd hired a crew to convert the screened-in back porch into a bedroom suite so Hannah wouldn't have to sleep long-term in Papaw's office. Hannah had rejected the idea, offering to take one of the upstairs bedrooms once she wasn't needed on the main floor anymore, but the crew had already started by the time Hannah arrived, and there was no stopping it now. The renovations were moving along, but with winter weather coming soon, even in mild Mississippi, they were rushing to get the insulation and walls up so that the work could move inside before it got too cold. But that meant that most of the time, the work was being done on the outside of the house. She hadn't met any of the men working with George, but Mamaw had mentioned that his son had done a few odd jobs around her place.

"I don't know about handy, but I *am* a carpenter. I help out my daddy when he needs it."

"Oh, sorry. I guess *handyman* is a bit of an outdated term," Hannah corrected herself, sure she was blushing.

"Yes, ma'am." He chuckled. "We prefer *handypersons* if you don't mind."

"Ah, noted." An awkward silence passed between them.

Guy did them both a favor and filled in the gap. "And you are the granddaughter I've heard so much about."

"Oh yes. Though my grandma likes to exaggerate," she said, grateful the sun was low enough in the sky that her embarrassed blushing could be explained away by the time of day.

"Nice to meet you, officially," he said. His smile was bright, teeth perfectly straight from fantastic orthodontics in his youth or really great genes.

Hannah took Guy's offered hand, likely a few moments later than would've been considered normal, but at least she didn't space out on it completely.

"You too, Guy. And thanks for passing on Mamaw's message. I should probably give her a call and head home." She let go after two short pumps, his hand large and mildly calloused in a way that matched his profession.

Guy didn't give her space to leave, putting his hand on her bike once again. "That is why I'm here. Your grandma wants me to take you home. I brought my daddy's truck for your bike. I know you thought I was tryin' to steal it." He smirked, joking but also serious enough to make Hannah's cheeks warm for the tenth time in their conversation.

"I never said that," she tried to counter, but decided midsentence it was better to be straightforward. She'd never been very good at BSing, and down here, it was a unique art of social grace. She was pretty sure you had to be born and raised into it to become proficient at it. "I've lived in Chicago for the past ten years, so when a stranger tries to take your bike on the street, you kick him in the—"

He interrupted just before she could say *balls*, for which she was immediately grateful.

"I'll count myself lucky, then. But for now, I should get you home," he said, sounding a little too much like a southern gentleman making sure a vulnerable lady wasn't out past dark to "protect her reputation."

She should let him take the bike and put it in the back of the truck. She should climb into the passenger seat and spend the next two minutes in polite conversation with a man who was, more than likely, a friendly, hardworking guy. Yet she found herself straightening her shoulders and pulling the bike closer to her body. She hated this part of herself that had become inflated since her life had started falling apart—defensive, anxious, especially when she felt insecure. She wanted to be strong and independent, and this man, through no fault of his own, was making her feel weak.

"I appreciate the offer, but if Mamaw is home safe, I think I'd rather bike," she said, tugging the handlebars out of Guy's loosened grip. He held up his hands like he was the one being robbed. She had tried to blow him off, had wasted his time, and had unintentionally insulted him. There was no way he wanted to do her a favor. She'd save both of them the awkwardness.

"Yes, ma'am, if you're sure . . . ," he said, backing away toward a boxy red-and-white Ford truck.

"Yeah, I'm sure. Thanks again, Guy," she said in her formal "I'm a professional" voice.

Guy put one hand in his pocket and rubbed at the stubble on his face with the other. "Have a nice ride, Miss Williamson." He retrieved his keys from his pocket and flipped them around his index finger, the hint of a smirk tugging up the corner of his mouth.

"You too," she called back, mounting her bike with one smooth kick of her leg, hoping that she looked like a skilled cyclist. She didn't dare look over her shoulder to see if he was watching. As she picked up speed, she lifted from her seat just a little. She was turning the first corner on her path home when a raindrop hit her wrist.

"What the . . . ?" She glanced up at the sky. She'd thought the rapid descent into darkness had been from the sun setting, but a rumble of thunder in the distance reminded Hannah that she'd forgotten to check the weather today. The raindrops continued to hit her skin in increasingly rapid succession, rolling down her arms and back and soaking into her hair.

Her foot slipped off the pedal and she wobbled, almost swerving into the street. A car sped by, the tires sending up a light mist from the rainwater already collecting on the ground. With one foot on the grass next to the road and the other on the sidewalk she'd veered off, Hannah squinted through the increasingly torrential downpour at the brake lights of the truck that had almost hit her, and her heart sank as she noticed it was Guy Franklin taking a right turn on Gilmore Street, heading toward Mamaw's house.

"Damn it," she muttered, dabbing her face with the inside of her T-shirt to clear the rainwater from her eyes, finally understanding the strange way he'd been looking at her when Hannah said she wanted to ride home on her own. The rain was cold, and her sweatshirt wasn't warm enough to keep out the chilly fall wind once it was saturated. But despite her hands feeling frozen around the handlebars and her face stinging with the impact of each angry raindrop, Hannah was warm all over. Not just from the speed at which she pedaled her bike but also from that cocky grin she wished she could wipe off Guy Franklin's face.

CHAPTER 6

Hannah hung her bike on the hook at the back of Mamaw's garage. Rainwater dripped off her sleeves into her face and onto the ground, creating a halo of droplets on the floor around her. In the fifteen or so minutes it took to ride from the office to Mamaw's house, every square inch of her body had been saturated. Shoes sloshing with each step, she hoped that the contents of her work bag were at least somewhat dry inside the supposedly "waterproof" lining.

Fighting off a deep shudder, Hannah stomped up the wooden steps that led to the house. Even the doorknob felt warm to her touch, and when she swung open the door, the smell of cornbread and chili welcomed her like someone had wrapped her in a heated blanket. Dropping her bag with a clunk, she stood still in the linoleum-floored laundry room for a second, letting the comforting air surround her. Carla rushed in wearing her apron and smelling of cooked onions.

"Oh my, you are a mess," she gasped, covering her mouth, without so much as a greeting. "You poor thing. Now, take off those wet things, and I'll get you a towel."

Hannah stripped off her jacket and drenched T-shirt, and wormed out of her heavy-soled boots. Carla could be straightforward and opinionated, but she always had a softness, even in her sharpest comments, that kept Hannah in the same state of respect and awe she'd learned as a small child when visiting at holidays. Papaw would smoke his pipe in the armchair in the front room, and when she and Brody got too loud, he'd escape to his office. Uncle Sammy was pure fun—piggyback rides and games in the local swimming pool—and her daddy would get a southern drawl from out of nowhere, pointing to every corner of the town with a new story. And Mamaw, even more polished and pristine. The only thing Hannah hated was that they had to change into fancy clothes for dinnertime and she'd have to be extra careful to not get a stain on her dress.

When Carla returned, she handed Hannah a fluffy towel that smelled of dryer sheets. On top of that was a neatly folded housecoat, a light-pink gingham material with an embroidered pattern around the collar and cuffs on the short sleeves.

"I'll give you your privacy. Just leave your things by the washer. I can toss them in for you later." Hannah always insisted on doing her own laundry, which usually led to procrastination and wearing the same pair of jeans longer than was probably socially acceptable. But today she didn't fight Carla's offer. She was already shivering, and any item of dry clothing was preferable to her pants' heavy denim material, which was clinging to her like alligator skin.

Once Carla left, it didn't take long to change out of her wet clothes, even with all the shivering. Leaving her damp bra and underwear on under the housecoat, she slipped on the warm pair of grippy hospital-style socks, wrapped her hair in the towel, and put her soggy bag on her shoulder.

Hannah tiptoed out of the laundry room and took a wide right turn, avoiding her usual path through the kitchen. Instead, she made her way through the formal dining room, avoiding the square pass-through that connected the two rooms, when she heard a familiar male voice resonating in the kitchen.

Sure enough, Guy Franklin was standing in the kitchen, shoveling spoonfuls of Carla's chili into his mouth. Hannah wanted to walk into that kitchen with her head held high, pretending she was confident in her calf-length housecoat and grippy socks, but instead she took a giant step back. It must've been enough movement to draw attention because Guy's eyes shot up from his bowl and connected with Hannah's. He raised one eyebrow, and that annoying smirk developed along the edge of his mouth as he slowly chewed a bite of cornbread.

She tried to think of something to say, but when he didn't look away and no clever words filled in the blanks in her mind, she broke off from his stare. Stumbling into the safety of the hallway, Hannah threw herself into Papaw's office.

Still chilled from the rain, she leaned against the closed door and wrapped her arms around her midsection. Under all the attractive young handyman's "yes, ma'ams" and "no, ma'ams" she knew he must be judging her.

The real person she was mad at in this house was herself. It was like she could only focus on one thing in her life at a time, whether it was mourning her father or longing for Alex or digging into the story of Evelyn or taking care of her grandmother. She had so few responsibilities in this Mississippi purgatory she'd found herself in, but she still couldn't function. And rather than be reminded of that frustrating fact, it was just easier to be mad at Guy.

There was a tap on the other side of the door. Hannah jumped. She reached for the throw blanket on the back of the office chair and draped it over her shoulders before responding.

"Yes?" she whispered through the crack.

"Hannah, your Mamaw is callin' for you. She wanted to wait for you to get home to have dinner, so I'll make up a tray and bring it to you in her room after you've changed."

Oh, thank God—it was Carla.

"Okay, I'll be out in just a minute," she said. Her cheerful singsong reply sounded false to Hannah's ears, but Carla didn't seem to notice.

So, this is why they do it, she thought as she threw on her sweatpants, a sports bra, and a long-sleeved Bears shirt that used to belong to her dad. There was a sense of relief in being in control of the parts of herself other people were allowed to see.

As had become a habit, Hannah picked up her phone to make a quick social media check. But as she tried to turn on the little rectangle, it didn't make so much as a beep.

"Damn it!" She tried a hard reset with multiple buttons, but still nothing. It was waterlogged from being in her back pocket during the downpour. "Shit!"

She dropped the temporarily useless device onto the desk, cringing at the loud thump. Yet another annoying result of her overly stubborn ride home. To think she might have to wait till morning to have access to the internet. Hannah ran a brush through her tangled, wet hair.

She'd apologize to Mamaw, smile, and do her best not to swear or mention how Monty's new shoes made fart noises or say mean things about almost-too-charming Guy Franklin.

"Thank you, darlin'," Mamaw said sweetly, as Hannah removed the portable tray from across her lap and pulled the quilt up to Mamaw's shoulders.

"Oh my gosh, it is the least I could do. I'm still so, so sorry," Hannah said, reaching for the horsehair brush on Mamaw's bedside table and running it through Mamaw's fine hair. After one stroke, Mamaw pushed Hannah's arm back gently.

"Oh no, dear. I just had my hair done today, so I won't need it brushed."

Hannah couldn't remember anything right today. "Damn it," she swore under her breath.

Mamaw must've heard because her mouth twisted in an odd, entertained way, her lips still a faded pink from the lipstick she'd been wearing on her trip to the salon.

"I'm sorry," Hannah apologized reflexively. Mamaw didn't find swearing ladylike.

"It's okay, darlin'. I'm getting used to it," Mamaw teased. It was nice, Hannah had to admit, to not have the conversation devolve into a big fight like it would've with her mother. Pam Williamson would toss around aggressive terms like *irresponsible* or *untrustworthy* or *ditzy*. It reminded Hannah of her father's gentle, serene temperament and how safe he always made her feel when he was around. No one calmed her anxieties like he used to.

She recalled when she was nine, and one week out from the fourth-grade bike rodeo she was the only one in her class who didn't know how to ride a two-wheeler. The rodeo was a rite of passage at Garden Grove Elementary in Oak Park, Illinois, and she'd been dreaming about it ever since Brody had won a red ribbon for Master Maneuvering when he was in Ms. Carter's class a few years earlier. But it wasn't just Brody. Everyone knew her father was an avid cyclist, and she'd done a whole research report about his last triathlon, so there was no way she'd show up to that rodeo with training wheels on her bike.

"It's okay, darlin'. You're doing a fantastic job," her dad told her as she sat on the curb after her eighth fall that night.

"Can I stay home from the rodeo? Please?" she begged, starting to feel desperate.

"No. You've got this," Patrick Williamson said, hefting the crashed bike back up on two wheels.

"But I keep falling. You and Brody are so good at it . . ."

Patrick Williamson put down the kickstand, sat next to his daughter on the curb, and examined the scratches on her knee.

"Hannah, you might not know this, but I didn't learn how to ride a bike until I was in high school. Your Papaw told me that I couldn't get my driver's license until I learned. I fell down a thousand times. Your uncle Samuel . . . he helped me in an abandoned lot so none of my friends could see how bad I was. But after lots of practice, my brain and my body figured it all out, and riding my bike became like walking. You know what I found out?"

"That you should never give up?" Hannah filled in a generic encouraging phrase she'd heard on one or two afterschool TV specials.

"Ha, well, not exactly. I found out that once you've learned to do something really well, nobody asks how many times you fell down while you were learning how to do it. You didn't walk the first time you tried, right? You didn't talk that way either. Same with reading and math and T-ball and soccer. So you'll fall down a few times. That's fine! Just try to fall into the grass, okay? No reason to get hurt every time if you can help it, right?"

Fall into the grass. That soft place to fall—that had always been her relationship with her dad. Her mom was the scratchy asphalt, and since her father's passing Hannah couldn't seem to find a safe place to land. But if Patrick Williamson was a neatly manicured lawn, Mamaw was a pile of freshly raked leaves.

Mamaw oozed grace with every genteel greeting and carefully controlled half smile. Her dark eyes were beautiful, but since Samuel had died, they also held a sadness in them that made you want to look a little longer than was polite. And those wells of sadness seemed deeper and darker since she'd stood by her eldest son's grave a few months earlier. Hannah was growing to understand the hidden sorrows gathered in her grandmother's eyes now that she was able to recognize the beginnings of her own pools every time she looked in the mirror.

"I'll keep working on it," Hannah said as she fluffed Mamaw's pillows. She liked to sleep a little upright after having her hair done so it didn't get all "flattened out." Just who Mamaw was keeping her hair fluffy for, Hannah didn't know. Maybe her beau, Mr. Davenport.

"No, dear. Times have changed, I know I'm old-fashioned. The ladies at the salon say"—she hesitated, then swallowed like she'd tasted something sour—"many colorful things. I'm startin' to wonder if maybe instead of you stopping, I should give it a try," Mamaw joked mischievously, tugging at the collar of her nightgown.

"Ha! Well, I think you'd raise a few eyebrows, but I say—go for it. I'd start out small if I were you. But you know how I feel about it—a few little *hells* and *damns* never hurt anyone." Hannah touched the metal on the lamp next to Mamaw's bed so it turned on and then dimmed with two more taps.

"I've been thinking," Mamaw continued, as though she'd put hours of thought into the topic, "if Reverend Moss can say it over the pulpit, why can't I say it in the privacy of my own house?"

"Amen!" Hannah added, like one of the church ladies from the Senatobia Presbyterian church, where Mamaw liked to go on Sundays when she was feeling up to an outing.

"And is one little curse word going to keep me from passing through the pearly gates?"

"Never!" Hannah urged emphatically, finding her grandmother's rebellion at the age of ninety-one beyond endearing. She flicked off the overhead light and retrieved the remote from on top of the sixteen-inch ancient tube TV on the dresser across from Mamaw's fully adjustable hospital bed.

She tried not to watch as Mamaw wrestled with her conscience, setting her lips in a firm line and mashing them together like a whole string of words she'd been dying to say was cued up right inside. She took a deep breath through her nose and held it. Hannah also held her breath without meaning to. She had given up being like her grandma long ago. It wasn't possible. It could be her mother's northern bloodline, or just being raised in a world that was colder in more ways than were reflected on a thermometer. She'd never be like Mamaw—but what if Mamaw became a little more like her?

Mamaw let out her breath but didn't say a word, losing her battle with her conscience and bred-in-the-bones belief system. More than a little disappointed, Hannah clicked on the humidifier, and the room filled with a relaxing hum as she took a deep lungful of the moistened air.

"Maybe tomorrow," Mamaw said, mostly to herself, wistfully, touching the bouffant of her hair.

"Maybe," Hannah added, reasonably sure she'd never hear a questionable phrase escape her grandmother's lips. Moving on to the next step in the routine, Hannah counted out Mamaw's nighttime pills. Most of them she didn't recognize, but there were a few that were familiar. Ambien, which looked like a small version of ibuprofen, had been prescribed to Hannah when she couldn't sleep after Alex moved out. The emptiness of that apartment was like a bell continually ringing. The doctor had warned the pills could be habit-forming, but she was desperate to sleep through the pain of his loss.

She didn't realize that the habit she'd form from taking Ambien would be time travel. When she took those pills, she slept so deeply that she would lose all track of time. She'd wake, take another, and another, until days had vanished. She kept thinking that when she'd wake up the pain would be gone—but it was always there waiting for her.

Hannah's flirtation with those pills and her subsequent firing and hospitalization dragged her through life only a few weeks before her dad took a turn for the worse. He was the sole reason there was only one funeral in the family this year instead of two. A few weeks before his sharp decline, he'd forced his way into Hannah's apartment because she didn't answer her phone for twenty-four hours and he had a "bad feeling about it." He'd called 911 and then had her involuntarily hospitalized after seeing the state of her trashed apartment and finding the empty bottle of pills on the floor beside her bed. Hannah cringed, still ashamed of how low she'd let herself get.

She recapped Mamaw's pill bottle and picked up the next one.

The Prozac was easy to identify, green-and-white capsules. It'd been the first antidepressant they gave her in the hospital, and the only pill she still took every morning. Apparently, in some ways, she was just like Mamaw.

"Hey, before I forget, I have a town history question for you," Hannah said, wanting to wash the memory of her father's rescue out of her mind. The sleeping pills worked in a matter of minutes, so she'd have to ask her questions fast.

"I'm not a historian, but I'll do my best," Mamaw said, putting each pill in her mouth one at a time, with a sip of water between. She always acted like she knew little more than how to host a Ladies of the Library luncheon or organize bingo night at the church, but Mamaw taught English at Gulf Park College for Women and years later at Senatobia High. She liked to play it down. She'd been raised in a time when it was unseemly to be a smart woman, but even after nine decades and with her body growing frail, her mind was sharp.

Hannah sat in the chair next to her bed and put her hands on her worn gray sweats. "When you were younger, did you ever hear a story about a teenager being shot in her home here in Senatobia? A girl, around fourteen years old?"

Mamaw handed the cup back to Hannah. "The only shootin' I can recall from when I was a girl was my cousin getting ahold of his daddy's pistol and killing the little Stanford boy. My momma made my daddy lock away all his guns after that. Now, there's always some kind of commotion at the trailer park . . ."

Mamaw, lovely as she was, still seemed to believe there was a right side and wrong side of town. Hannah corrected her more brusquely than she'd planned.

"No, it's not the trailer park, Mamaw. There was a shooting, a long time ago, before you were born. You wouldn't remember it happening. I'm wondering if you ever heard a story about a fourteen-year-old girl who was shot and paralyzed and then lived in a home for"—Hannah tried to find the right word, refusing to use the term that Evelyn called herself—"disabled individuals. I'm not sure what the institution would be called now. Um, like a nursing home. For younger people."

Mamaw smacked her tongue and blinked slowly like she always did as the sleeping pills were hitting her bloodstream. Her shoulders slumped and her head lolled to one side. Hannah kissed her dozing grandmother on the forehead, deciding not to push her for any further information; she'd waited too long to bring it up. Hannah carefully slid a hand behind her grandmother's back to adjust the pillows to support her head. She startled awake.

"Be careful of the hair, darlin'," she said, her voice as droopy as her body. Even half-awake, Mamaw was aware of the importance of beauty. Which was just another way Hannah was different; she didn't inherit much of Mamaw's beauty and had never been willing to put in the effort to assist where nature had left her lacking.

"You still look beautiful," Hannah said, plumping the pillows and carefully guiding Mamaw's head back to rest in a semi-reclined position. With the storm that had come through and the sunset hours earlier, the room was shadowy. Mamaw liked to fall asleep with the TV on the Hallmark Channel, so Hannah clicked it on, turned the volume down low, and then slid the controller under one of Mamaw's hands so she could reach it easily when she woke. Grabbing the dinner tray heavy with their empty chili bowls and scattered with cornbread crumbs, she backed away from the flash of the TV screen and Mamaw's steady breathing. With a bit of a balancing act, she used her foot to swing open the bedroom door wide enough to pass through with her loaded arms. Just as she was about to leave the room, Mamaw called out, making Hannah jump and the silverware gathered on the tray jingle.

"There *was* a home in Memphis for crippled children."

"In Memphis?" Hannah asked, a brief memory of a black-and-white image filling her mind. When scrolling through a list of historic hospitals, she'd seen a few potential institutions, but one ended up being a sanitorium for women with "female weaknesses" and the other had closed in 1912. Hannah had scrolled right past the children's hospital, recalling that Evelyn was twenty when she submitted her articles. But having Mamaw mention the children's hospital made Hannah pause. Evelyn was only fourteen when she was shot, so technically still a child.

"Yes," Mamaw said, as though she was dreaming. "Little Cory Mayfield went there after he nearly drowned in Coldwater River the summer I turned seven. He was Jerry's friend. Daddy visited him there a few times, I think."

"It was for children. Injured or disabled children?" Hannah asked, feeling like she'd finally homed in on a solid lead.

"Mm-hmm," Mamaw murmured her response, only minimally awake. Her breathing went back to the steady, throaty rhythm from earlier. She was asleep.

It didn't matter—the spark had lit the kindling Hannah didn't even know she had stored in her brain during one of her online research binges. She backed out of the room, leaving the door open a crack like Mamaw always liked it.

Hannah rushed to the kitchen to deposit Mamaw's tray, swearing to herself that she'd get the bowls cleaned before Carla returned the following day. Then she hurried to the study, nearly slipping on the floral carpet runner in the hall. There were two more articles on her phone from Evelyn, which held the potential of a wealth of information. Plus, there was a list of research items she could get started on even without reading the new articles.

But she knew almost as soon as she saw the black screen that her phone was still dead.

"Damn it," she cursed, picking it up and pressing the buttons, but nothing happened. *Stupid.* She chastised herself. Why had she let Guy get her so flustered? If it had been Mr. Franklin or Carla or Nancy, she'd have gladly put her bike in the back of the truck and taken the free ride home. But nooooooo, she had to get all strangely "I am woman, hear me roar" on the man.

Hannah rushed to the kitchen and searched the cabinets. Above the sink, next to a stack of brown-paged cookbooks, was a yellow Tupperware container labeled *Rice*. She scooped two cups of it into a gallon-size Ziploc bag, buried her phone in the white mass, and set the whole thing on the counter.

"That should do the trick," she said, placing the plug in the sink and turning on the hot water. Even if the rice method didn't work its magic, one night without a phone shouldn't cause too many issues. She could go to the *Record* in the morning and get caught up in a matter of hours. She'd have to call her mom when she got to the office and let her know about the phone issues and then email Laura to cancel their phone session for the third week in a row.

The only other person who might reach out would be Alex, and who was she kidding? She shook her head and shut off the faucet, damp with the condensing steam from the sink. Alex had had nine months to reach out since their breakup—he wasn't going to suddenly come to his senses now.

Hannah dunked the bowls in the soapy water. The sink was a bit too full for the volume of dishes she needed to scrub. If Alex happened to reach out, then—he could wait. Just like she had since the day he walked out. Sure, it was easy to say when she couldn't turn on her phone and while her hands were busy, submerged in the citrus-scented water.

In the future, if her phone buzzed and his name came up, she might not have the same philosophy, but tonight she was grateful for the break from that nagging need to check as her brain flooded with thoughts of Evelyn.

CHAPTER 7

Hannah headed to work early the next morning and ended up sitting outside the locked *Record* office, waiting for Monty. With her bike leaned against a tree, she sat on the front step, scribbling in her green notebook, jotting down a few ideas for a potential story based on Evelyn's letters. It was still embryonic, just a few bullet points, but she couldn't ditch the idea that there was something bigger here.

The morning air was chilly and smelled of fall, not altogether unlike how fall smelled up north. But the rising sun added just enough warmth to stunt the crispness she'd always found so invigorating when she'd walk her dog through the forest preserve with her dad when she was a kid, or when the first gust of lake-effect wind hit her face each September as she rushed down Stetson to the *Tribune* building.

God, she missed her dad. He'd sat in many of the homes and walked the halls of the Senatobia school she zoomed past each morning. This lukewarm autumn morning was his childhood understanding of fall. It was his nostalgia.

She rubbed her hands together, hoping this was one of the mornings Monty would bring in coffee so she wouldn't have to wait for Dolores to make it. She needed the warmth but also the caffeine. Plus, another addiction was dragging her down. It'd been over twelve hours since she'd last had access to her phone, and it was driving Hannah a little crazy. The freedom from the constant checking was making her think clearer, but the withdrawal was real. She dug around in her satchel and took out the Ziploc bag she'd brought with her, breaking the seal. The earthy, slightly mildewy scent of moisture and rice puffed out into her face, making her ill.

"That is a pretty lousy breakfast you have there," a familiar voice called out from the street. Stopped in front of the *Record* was Guy Franklin, driving the same red-and-white truck he'd offered her a ride in the night before, one elbow draped halfway out the driver's side window.

Great, she thought, internally mortified. Seeing him right in front of her place of work after a less than restful night of sleep, when she was wearing a slightly different baggy V-neck from the day before, under the same Army green flak jacket, her hair unwashed and unbrushed and pulled back in a messy ponytail, and running on zero coffee or access to social media, made her want to toss the bag at his tires.

"Not my breakfast." She smiled, opening no windows to the inner workings of her mind and emotions, wishing she'd done more than run a toothbrush across her teeth before rushing out the door. "Carla would be mortified if I let you think this came from her kitchen," she said.

Guy sent a matching smile back at Hannah, and she couldn't help but wonder if it was real or just as fake as hers.

"My momma taught me never to make assumptions . . ."

"Because they make an ass out of you and me?" Hannah completed the phrase.

"Uh, yes, ma'am. So I've heard." He didn't laugh, though something like amusement touched his lips, but not because she was fascinating or hilarious. It was the same way Mamaw looked when Hannah said something she considered unfeminine, or when her mother was disappointed in her fashion sense, or when Alex would roll his eyes when she left the light on in the car overnight and killed the battery. He was smiling because she'd made a mistake, said it wrong, or maybe it wasn't ladylike for a woman to swear—which ironically just made her want to swear more. This was precisely why she'd taken her bike home in the rain.

This man could make her feel like this—like a shook-up bottle of pop or the time she'd put regular dish soap in the dishwasher in her first apartment instead of dish detergent and the kitchen had flooded with suds.

"I'm headed to Broken Cup Café," Guy went on. "You want something?"

Do I want something? Hannah repeated in her head. *YES!* Yes, she wanted a large cappuccino with two shots of espresso, but she shook her head.

"Uh-uh." She smiled with closed lips this time. "Dolores makes a fine pot of Folgers Instant, but thank you." She didn't even forget to be polite. Damn. She was *owning* this.

"No problem. Hope you get inside soon."

"Thanks!" she said, chipper as all get-out. "You too!"

He smirked and drove away, the exhaust from his ancient transmission stinging her almost as much as the embarrassment.

"You too? You too, what?" she muttered under her breath, shoving the bag of rice with her waterlogged phone deep into her bag and replacing the flap, feeling like an idiot.

"Miss Williamson?" Monty stood in front of her, somehow ninja-like in his silent approach despite his size 12 loafers and the slight rasp in his labored breathing.

"Oh, hey! Good morning." Hannah was on her feet in an instant, twisting to switch places with Monty, who looked equal parts surprised and confused.

"I'm sorry, hun, am I late for a meeting?" Monty checked his wristwatch and dug around in his pocket for an overloaded, clanking key chain.

"No! No, I just thought I'd get in early today. Make some headway in the archives." She carried her bike up the steps behind Monty and slid it into its storage space in the foyer, hoping he wouldn't question her about it. He didn't seem to notice.

As Hannah hung her bag and jacket over the back of her office chair, then retrieved her notebook, Monty paused by his office door and called out, "Miss Williamson, a moment?"

Hannah froze. *Damn it.*

"Coming!" she called out across the room, glancing longingly at the basement door as she rushed into Monty's office.

She'd only been inside his cluttered work space a handful of times, including the day of her interview. It was filled with stacks of files and overflowing filing cabinets; should've been a clue as to what the whole organizational system of the *Record* was like under Monty's guiding hand. Back then, when she was newly arrived in Senatobia and still unsure if she even wanted to stay, the dusty electric typewriter in the corner and large oak desk that was covered in papers like a tablecloth had blurred into the background of this otherworldly place her father had once called home.

Since settling into life here, she'd found that everyone avoided Monty's office, especially at lunchtime, when he'd heat his leftovers from "Momma" in the crusty microwave he kept on the counter next to the broken typewriter. Hannah had never been called in first thing in the morning, and the office had a stale scent of old food smells and aging paper. Monty was crouched over, placing a microwavable container of something into the minifridge behind his desk. He stood with some effort and pulled up his slacks by his belt when Hannah walked in.

"Miss Williamson, why don't you take a seat," he said, pointing to the chair opposite his desk. It had a stack of neatly piled files with newspaper clippings pouring out the sides. She hesitated. "Oh, put those on the floor. I'll get to them later," he said, flapping his hand at the files like he was moving them himself.

Hannah cleared the chair and sat, the springs inside creaking and one poking up through the fabric at the back of her thigh.

So help me, if he wants me to clean this place . . .

Monty finally sat in his large, high-backed rolling leather chair. Bits of filling poked out of cracks on the armrests. He steepled his fingers in front of his face and pressed them against his lips, making Hannah wonder what the hell he was being so dramatic about.

"Miss Williamson, I do appreciate all of your hard work in the archives. I know it's a big job, and Terry says he's seen some good progress even in the little time you've been down there." He paused, as though Hannah was meant to respond.

"Thank you," she said, hoping the less she spoke, the sooner she could get back to work.

"No, thank *you*. I fear you may see this project as somewhat of a demotion after your time at the *Tribune*, but I assure you that was not my intention," he said, folding his arms.

Nothing like a good ole clearing of the conscience, Hannah thought.

"Seeing you sittin' on the front stoop this morning made me reconsider this assignment. Your eagerness to complete your tasks is apparent, and I can't help but think your talents are being wasted in that basement. I talked to Terry this morning, and he said that if you'd be willing to help him in the classifieds, he could trade time with you in the basement. What do you think about that?"

"No!" Hannah answered, faster than she'd intended. The only thing worse than acquiring display ads and inserts for the paper was listing weird shit for money like a common hustler. Selling puppies, soliciting love matches, exchanging half-broken junk for cash—wasn't there an app for all that? Her boss at the *Tribune* always said she had a strong sense of journalistic truth and something about gumption. Which was why it was so devastating when he called her up and explained she didn't need to come into work anymore because she was out of warnings and extensions and was being let go. She wanted to explain everything, but it was too hard back then and too embarrassing now. But this search made her feel like a journalist again.

"Pardon me?" he sputtered.

"I mean, no, thank you . . . uh, sir." Her attempted use of polite language seemed to calm Monty enough for her to continue. "I like my current assignment."

"You do?" he asked, incredulously.

"I do."

He scratched the top of his balding head and pulled at his belt again like his pants were falling down even while he was sitting.

"Well, that's fine, then. I may need to pull you back up here for some actual reportin' at some point."

"Of course," Hannah said, biting her tongue and standing to leave. Monty had already wasted a good chunk of the time she'd gained by coming in early. "I should get to work now."

She didn't wait for Monty to change his mind or say anything else that could make her temper flare. It was already smoldering just beneath the surface. He'd said it like she was shirking her responsibilities, when he was the one who'd relegated her to the dank, concrete story-cemetery.

Rushing past her desk and by Dolores, who was fiddling around with the coffee maker, Hannah speed-walked to the green door and swung it open. It took all her self-control to not stomp down the stairs. Sometimes she wondered if Monty just didn't like seeing her happy, so as soon as she got comfortable in one place, he wanted to shake her out of whatever tiny bit of enjoyment she'd settled into. Mamaw would say she was paranoid, and that Monty Martin was a sweet man trying to make everyone happy. But Hannah was pretty sure her frail Mamaw didn't have enough experience going up against men who wielded their power like a weapon and a shield. And if she ever had faced such a patriarchal figure, Hannah had no doubt her grandmother would've bent to his strong will with a smile and wink.

When she hit the bottom of the staircase, she bounded off the last step and onto the concrete floor. She considered letting Monty in on the story. He potentially had new information as well. There were original copies of every newspaper ever printed at the *Record*, way back to when it was the *Tate County Democrat*, filed away in Monty's office, and his father must've been on the job when the shooting occurred. But it was a risk. A huge risk. If she told Monty about the story and he rejected it, which he most likely would, the already nearly impossible task would become insurmountable.

Hannah flicked on the lights in the archive room, and the chaos of the disheveled filing cabinets and piles of half-sorted files in teetering stacks welcomed her. There was a buzz in the room, either from the electricity surging through the hanging bulbs above her head or from the tractor-beam-like draw Evelyn's story had on Hannah.

Evelyn's world was different, but there was no doubt she would understand what it was like to stand up to a Monty. And Hannah was confident that the girl with a sixth-grade education had a writer inside her, one that could've contributed so much to her world if people hadn't given up on her when she ended up in a wheelchair.

Finally seated at the basement desk, she forced open the rusty desk drawer, where the original letters were starting to pile up. The two she'd taken pictures of and intended to pick through at home before her phone became a paperweight were in folders on the top of the stack. She took them out, and the electric humming in the room ticked up a notch. She craved a lot of things that morning—coffee, a working phone, the ability to forget any and all exchanges she'd had with Guy Franklin in the past twenty-four hours, a text from Alex, a chance to hear her father's voice with his nearly imperceptible southern accent calling her "darlin'" one more time . . . but right now the one thing she wanted most of all was more of Evelyn's story. As she took out the original documents and started to read, Hannah understood two things: one, Evelyn's story deserved to be told, and two, this search was becoming personal.

CHAPTER 8

June 5, 1935

Dear Mr. Martin,

I hope you enjoyed my first efforts at storytelling. Though this is a dramatic tale, it is a true one from beginning to end. I've changed some names and places so that I am not stepping on any toes, if that was a worry. Which is also why I've kept my surname private as well. I will keep searching your paper with all the hope in my heart that one day I shall see my story printed there. If you do happen to publish it, I need no compensation. You may state the author's name as: "A crippled young girl."

In August 1928, I was operated on for appendicitis, or at least that's what the doctor thought it was. Mother always called it a "useless expense," but she never said if that was because she found me useless or because my appendix turned out to be just fine. All I know is that I'd been struck with terrible stomach pains one night after dinner. I thought for sure it was poison but didn't have the gall to tell the doctor that.

While I was in the hospital and laid up after surgery, Daddy got sicker and could hardly work. I'm sure Mother was hoping he would just get on with dying since she'd get his life insurance and the house and wouldn't have anyone stopping her from kicking out the rest of Daddy's kids.

To make up for Daddy's extended illness and my medical emergency, we took on more boarders. After the whipping and my surgery, I was a good, obedient girl for a while. In September, I returned to school and started back again into the routine of work.

I did all the housekeeping and most of the cooking. In the morning, I was the one who built the fire, mopped the stairs, fixed breakfast, called everybody to eat, and while Mother took Daddy to work, I'd clean the house up while Myrtle washed the dishes. Myrtle and I would go to school, always coming home to leftover lunch. Then, when we came back after school, the house was to be straightened and Myrtle and I had to get the coal in. Then I would go to the store, for Mother said I always did such things with numbers and budgeting better than Myrtle. Mother would fix supper, and then Myrtle and I would wash the dishes. Even if we got money to go to a show, Mother would make us take the two children who boarded with us, Mother's two boys, and her daughter Genevieve.

So, you see, I never had a moment to myself to think. By the time school was out for the summer, I was a nervous wreck. Daddy had surgery in the spring and was never the same after that. He never held a real job again. He cried easily and often called me Ava, forgetting my momma had died so many years ago.

I missed my momma in those days more than ever. Her canned peaches were long gone by then, and the blankets she'd knitted were being used by strangers sleeping in a bed I was only allowed to touch when I changed the bedding each week. And my daddy's hands were knobby and weak, and it was now my hands taking care of him. I can't blame Momma for not knowing what it would be like when she left us behind—she didn't know

there would be a Mrs. Brown or that
Daddy would get "sick" or that Myrtle
would die or that my baby brother and
sister would be raised by strangers.

Hannah's elevated feet dropped off the desk, sending up a cloud of dust. She blinked against the grit, rereading the last few lines again. Even though death stole Evelyn's mother, she was left feeling abandoned, like the woman should've been strong enough to outmatch mortality. Hannah hadn't ever admitted that out loud about her father, not to her mother or her therapist. But Evelyn knew.

She swapped one article for the next, placing the typewritten pages in a manila folder labeled on the tab with the date listed on the article. So far, she had five folders, including the new pages she'd found that day while archiving. The materials, sent more or less monthly in 1935, were coming together into a focused story line, which looked to be the beginnings of a potentially tragic love story between Evelyn and an older boy she'd met at the fairgrounds in the summer of 1929.

Hannah usually hated love stories, finding them too sugary and far-fetched. The way the boy fought through all odds to be with the girl, who was oftentimes artsy, flighty, and either a waitress at a coffee shop or the VP of a fashion magazine at the age of twenty-six. The pragmatic side of Hannah had always won out when faced with such implausible scenarios.

But Evelyn's naive little love story was different. It wasn't even about the boy she found herself in love with at the young age of fourteen—it's that she fell in love with him despite her stepmother's disapproval. It was a flash of rebellion that Hannah identified in Evelyn's "love" story. It showed an ownership for her own life that Mrs. Brown had tried to horsewhip out of her at a young age. Hannah was fascinated by that trait and was starting to wonder if this stubborn rebellion was one of the reasons Evelyn survived whatever assault led to the gunshot wound that took her mobility.

August 7, 1935

Mr. Martin,
It is me again. I have not heard from your offices on my previous submissions, but I will continue to write them in case you find them useful as a true story.

In May, the fair came to town. Myrtle and I were permitted to walk down to the fairgrounds with the youth group from Mother's church. But when we got there, Myrtle and I ditched them and went off to explore on our own. The smells of popcorn and cotton candy made my mouth water, and I was dying to remember what they tasted like.

Neither of us had much money, so when a teenage boy and his girl tossed their half-eaten bags of popcorn in the trash can right next to us, when no one was looking I took them for Myrtle and me without an ounce of shame, though Myrtle looked like she might die from embarrassment.

And when the cotton candy man wasn't looking, I snatched a stick of candy floss off a stand at the rear of his concession stand by slipping my hand through the flap at the back of the tent. I should be ashamed to admit these youthful follies, and I am a bit, but it has to be told.

No one saw us, but our guilty conscience made us run through the field behind the fairgrounds and into the dark woods to enjoy our sweet, stolen treasure. As the sugar melted on our tongues and our fingers grew pink and sticky, we lost track of how deep we had wandered into the woods. We heard the river and settled on some rocks there to enjoy the last bit of sweetness we'd have for a long time. Moments later, Lucy from school and her crew broke through the brush.

I'll never forget pinch-faced Lucy in her spotless handkerchief-hemmed dress, wearing her hair in pin curls from the salon like she was a grown woman, standing on that muddy bank, staring me down.

Behind her were three boys and two girls. Molly, a sweet, brainless little thing, was, as Mother liked to say, pretty enough to get a husband, though he'd have to be a dumb one. And then Gracie, a girl two grades older than me who still held on to some of her baby fat around her middle, even though Mother said that her momma made her drink ipecac syrup after dinner most nights.

I used to feel bad for Gracie, but then I got a peek at her lunch one day when she was working with Mr. Clayton in the library and I was waiting for Myrtle to find the library book she wanted to bring home. She had cold chicken, rolls, fried potatoes, and a bottle of soda pop.

I could smell it as I was standing at the checkout desk, and my stomach grumbled so loudly that the librarian gave me a slanted look as though I'd cursed. I'd gladly drink ipecac every night if I got to eat like Gracie. At that point in my life, standing by the swollen waters of the gap, seeing her dress pulling at her belly and the buttons straining to stay closed only made me feel envy, the stale, stolen garbage popcorn rumbling against the melted sugar in my mostly empty stomach.

"What are you doing here?" Lucy asked, like Myrtle and I had no right to be anywhere Lucy wanted to be.

"Cooling off," I said. It was a hot night, sticky for more reasons than the sugar clinging to the corners of my mouth.

"Well, cool off somewhere else," she said, shooing me away with the flick of her wrist. Her fingernails were painted a bright red, I remember that, and they caught a bit of the moonlight through the trees.

"Oh, Lucy, who cares? Let them stay," Gracie said, and I felt a little guilty for not caring that her momma made her throw up her dinner every night.

"Yeah, who cares?" said one of the boys.

Two boys from the high school stood behind Lucy, blurry-eyed from beer. They were both less than handsome. One with a spotted complexion and the other with such a robust body odor that I could smell him six feet away. But there was one other boy there, one I hadn't seen before. Unlike the local boys I'd seen grow into manlike figures from their days in knickers, this boy was new to town. He watched as we girls talked, and there was a bright-ness in his features that made me think he'd seen more in this world than I could ever imagine. I wanted that boy to notice me. I handed the last bit of the cotton candy to Myrtle and stood up from the rocks we'd been resting on together.

"We came here to swing the gap," I said, bluffing but wanting to sound adventurous to that handsome boy Lucy had roped into following her around in the woods. Myrtle let out a little gasp behind me.

When we were little, swinging the gap over the West Ditch River was a rite of passage every year before the summer break. Before Mrs. Brown lived with us, Myrtle and I could come and go as we pleased as long as Daddy never found out. Daddy was far too sad and busy after Momma died to care where we were much of the time as long as we were quiet.

One Sunday afternoon, when he was in Memphis still for a business trip, Myrtle and I met up at the gap with six or seven children from the primary school. Myrtle could never bring herself to swing over the water. She was always so timid and ladylike. But life without a mother had taught me to be strong, and even at nine years old, I was brave. It had long been known I was the youngest girl to swing the gap ever in the history of the school.

But later that summer, another boy from my class drowned in the river. No one knew if he fell off the rope or had tried to swim by himself one night, but after he disappeared while playing they found him in the river, neck broken and drowned too. Some people whispered that his drunk daddy did it 'cause he used to whup Bobby and his momma when he was cork high and bottle deep, but all the same, Daddy forbade me from going near the river. It was getting cold anyway, and Mrs. Brown joined our family soon after as my new mother, and my life stopped being my own. But that night by the gap I felt more in charge of my life than I had in a long time.

Hannah read the story hungrily. She hadn't felt that overly alive buzz Evelyn was referring to for far too long. Everything in the past several months seemed more like she was simply going through the motions. Even burying her father felt like she was watching herself through a window or a TV show in slow motion. She welcomed the numbness that distance gave her, but she missed the highs that were eliminated when she started running away from the lows. Recently she was starting to feel something—a subtle sizzle that ignited each time she read Evelyn's words and followed leads about her story.

"I dare you," Lucy said, her painted red lips just as pinchy as her face.

"I can do it with one hand," I said back to Lucy, willing to do anything to show her up. Boys followed her like mad.

I was prettier than Lucy; everyone knew it. I might not have been beautiful like Momma, but I saw the way boys

watched me like they used to watch
her, like sneaking a little peek of
my figure was a sin. It probably was,
but I didn't care. My body was the
one thing I owned that was mine and
not Mother's. She could beat it, and
she could starve it, but she couldn't
take it away from me. And one day, if
I stayed pretty enough and learned to
be charming enough, I thought I'd find
a boy who would take me away. I could
take Myrtle and adopt baby William and
bring back beautiful Vivian, and we
could be a family again.

"Ha, you skinny little thing? I
doubt it. You're bluffing. Now, stop
making a fool of yourself. Come on,
boys." Lucy turned on the ball of her
foot and started to walk as though
she were leaving the woods. Gracie and
Molly and the town boys followed her
like they were playing Simon Says. She
was probably going to kiss one of those
boys. Maybe my boy.

"I'm not bluffing," I shouted, leap-
ing over underbrush to the mossy rope
hanging limply over the rushing river.
I'd never swung the gap when it was
that full, no one ever did that I knew
of, but I wasn't going to back down.

"Evelyn, don't," Myrtle called out
timidly. She had learned how to make

herself small and forgettable over the years. Maybe to keep away from Mother's horsewhip, but I think it was so Daddy wouldn't send her away like he had everyone else.

"You'd better listen to your sister," Molly said sweetly. I didn't stop.

"You're not gonna make it," one of the boys, I think his name was Jimmy, slurred.

I carefully removed my shoes and tucked my socks inside so they didn't get muddy and then grasped the slimy rope with one hand and put one foot up on the knot tied at the bottom, beyond listening to any voice of reason.

"It's not safe, Evey!" Gracie used my childhood nickname and made me remember how we used to swing on the playground together when we were in primary school. She sounded like she was begging.

I reeled back, and with a big hop and using both of my arms at first, I held myself up while my feet found their footing and jumped into the gap with my eyes closed tight. The rope creaked but held my weight. It was wet against my face and smelled of twine and mildew, but the mist of the rapids felt fresh against my skin, and I knew

I was flying. Cheers echoed from the shore, and as I reached the highest point of my journey over the river, I opened my eyes and tossed up my hand in triumph.

Then I heard a crack, and my perfect curve over the water faltered, shaking my already insecure grasp of the rope. Crack. Again. Suddenly it was all gone—the wind, the weightlessness, the fluttering in my stomach, and the feeling of triumph as I plummeted into the river along with ten feet of rope and the broken branch it was tied to.

I'd like to say I remember struggling to the surface or swimming against the rushing rapids, but I don't. When I was under that water, tangled in the rope and helpless to find the surface, I didn't try to rescue myself. It was the closest to freedom I'd felt in a long time. No one would miss me, not really. Daddy would be sad, but he'd gotten over Momma and given away William and Vivy. Myrtle would be left alone, but maybe I was bad for her? Perhaps she could be the angel she was born to be without my negative influence. Besides, I didn't want to do it anymore, life. It was too hard. I was too alone. I was too hungry and frightened.

Stunned by Evelyn's dreams of death, Hannah's mouth was so dry, it hurt to try and swallow. She recognized those confused thoughts only too well. After Alex, but before her stay in the hospital, she would sometimes think, *If I let go of the wheel, it would look like an accident,* or *Just one more step off the platform and it could all be over.* Evelyn's life was hard, harder than Hannah's, so could she really blame the girl for wanting some relief? But still, it surprised her that even Evelyn's strength had its limits. Hannah was unsure if it was comforting to once again be understood or if it was a hard way to see the figment of the past she was starting to look up to.

Then a steady hand grabbed me and dragged me out of the water. I don't remember it all. I spit and spattered as everyone surrounded me, and the world was as blurry outside of the water as it was in it. But once my lungs cleared and my eyes focused, I saw who was holding me in his arms. The boy, the one I'd never seen before. His rich brown eyes were kind and smiling at me. My chilled skin warmed at his touch.

"I can't believe you did that," he said, as though we were the only two people there. I coughed, unsure if I'd be able to find my voice but wanting to say something.

"I told you . . . I wasn't . . . bluffing," I said, in the quietest whisper. As he leaned in to listen and his breath touched my cheek, smiling

at me as though I'd said something surprising, I felt like I was flying for
the second time that day.

And that is how I met Harry Westbrook
at the fairgrounds and how he grasped me
just in time to keep me from drowning.

I loved Harry almost immediately,
and I think maybe Myrtle did too.

Mother and Daddy would not let
Myrtle and me go with boys, so when
Mother asked how we had liked the fair
the next morning as Daddy sipped his
coffee and we set the table for breakfast, we dared not tell either of them
about him. But I couldn't keep him a
secret long. By the end of May, they
knew his name almost as well as they
knew my own.

CHAPTER 9

The number Hannah had written on a fluorescent Post-it and stuck to the side of her monitor stared back at her. It had a Memphis area code and ended with a 7233, which spelled out *SAFE* on a phone keypad. The Crippled Children's Hospital and School was now a full-service inpatient mental health facility called the Pines Wellness Center. She'd found out that much information through her online research. And it was still run by the same organization that founded the home in 1919 called the Safe Place, which was run out of a Memphis office park.

Who knew if the organization had any old files stored or kept historical information about the charity home that had occupied the building for the first sixty years of its existence? She gritted her teeth and grabbed the Post-it off the screen, yanking the phone off the hook and stabbing the phone number into the keypad before she could second-guess her decision.

"What the hell am I doing?" Hannah muttered to herself as the phone started to ring. She was following a lead. She was tracking down a story. She was doing her goddamn job. But this was the kind of vulnerability she'd been skillfully avoiding. It was weird to start feeling things again, like the pins and needles that would spread through her legs when she stood up after sitting funny.

"Hello, you've reached the Safe Place. How may I direct your call?" said a high-pitched, helpful-sounding voice on the other end of the line after one ring. Hannah took a breath to speak but found she didn't know what to say.

"Hi, I'm a reporter from . . ." She paused, not wanting to give the name of her small-town newspaper. If anyone called back and word reached Monty, her story would be ruined. "From the *Chicago Tribune*. I'm looking to get some information about a resident at the Crippled Children's Hospital or maybe the Home for the Incurables, which is now the Pines Wellness Center."

"I'm sorry, all patient records are confidential," the receptionist cut her off.

"No, it's not a current resident. This was a resident in the early 1930s. I only have a first name and the name of your facility. I was hoping—"

"Oh, the old Crippled Children's Home? I'm sorry, we don't keep any records like that here at the Safe Place. If you'd like, I can connect you with the Pines. Or I could take a message for Ms. Dawson. She might know." She said the name like everyone knew who Ms. Dawson was.

"I'm sorry, who?"

"Oh," she tittered, "Ms. Dawson is our president. If they don't have what you need down at the Pines, I bet she'd know better than anyone. Her family's been in charge for, like, ever. What's your name again? You said you work for the *Chicago Times*?" A rustling of paper on the other end of the line made Hannah suddenly aware of the trail she was leaving behind.

"You know what? I'm in town for some research. I think I'll just stop by the Pines and ask them myself. No need to bother Ms. Dawson just yet. Thanks so much," Hannah said in closing, wanting to hang up the phone like a kidnapper in a movie trying to avoid having their location tracked.

"I know she won't mind. She talks to reporters all the time—"

"I'll keep that in mind. Thank you so much!" Hannah said. She swore there was a little twang in her voice as she said her goodbye and hung up the phone, heart pounding. She crumpled up the sticky note and tossed it in the garbage can under her desk.

Hannah closed all the tabs on her screen that had anything to do with the Safe Place or the Pines Wellness Center. What would Dolores or Monty think if they happened to see a screen full of mental health information? Who knows if Monty called her references from the *Trib* and got the lowdown on her final days there? All the botched assignments, showing up late if at all, and when she did show up, she was still so blitzed on meds that she could hardly function. And the final straw, being let go after she went missing for two weeks; she refused to let her father call in about her stay in the psych ward. It wasn't technically legal to share that kind of information between former and future employers, but she wouldn't put it past Monty to get nosy.

At the last minute, she typed Facebook into the address bar. With her phone still dead, she'd avoided social media (and, as a result, Alex) for nearly twenty-four hours. Huh. She hadn't even thought about stopping to check in on him till this very minute, which felt—odd.

She still wanted to look, though. The desire hadn't somehow disappeared overnight. When his profile popped up, her chest constricted. His picture was different. It wasn't the one she took of him years ago in their apartment when life was normal and they'd planned to get married as soon as his residency was over.

No.

She clicked on the small, circular image in the top left of the screen. It was of Alex smiling, his fiancée's face snuggled up next to his, also laughing, in a professional photograph. Janie's hand was up against his face and casually displaying her engagement ring. Tears poured into Hannah's eyes, stinging as they accumulated. *Damn him.*

She couldn't bring herself to click on the nearly one hundred comments on the picture. At least half the "What a cute couple" messages would likely be from people who would have left the same message on a picture of Hannah and Alex a few years back. She did check her notifications and quickly read the messages in her inbox from Tricia, her college roommate, who was pregnant with her third child, and Alex's aunt Carrie, who still checked in occasionally. No big news. No "I made a mistake" message from Alex. An entire day had passed in the virtual world, and no one even noticed she was gone. Then an old question, similar to the one she'd just read from Evelyn as she contemplated drowning in the gap, echoed through her mind: *Would anyone notice if I were gone?*

Hannah closed the internet browser and Facebook along with it, a creeping chill crawling up her neck and tensing her shoulders, scared by her own thought. She shuddered and took a deep breath, remembering how Laura had taught her to center herself in her last session before she was released from the hospital and in countless sessions after.

"Breathe like it matters," she would say when encouraging Hannah to talk about the tough times instead of bottling them up or pretending they didn't exist.

"One," she whispered, after blowing out her first breath and before taking another.

Her mother would notice if she were gone.

"Two," she said after her second, her heart rate already becoming steadier.

Mamaw would notice.

"Three," she said after the final breath dissipated into space in front of her.

Her brother would notice.

Carla would notice.

Laura would notice.

Monty would notice.

Evelyn would notice.

Well, not Evelyn, but . . . The front door opened and shut with a swoosh-bang followed by Monty's heavy footsteps, snapping Hannah out of her thoughts. Back to reality, Hannah shoved the folders on her desk into her bag and collected the last few items she needed to take home with her. It was hard to imagine being away from internet access for another night, but at the same time it was better not to be able to pick the emotional scabs that were finally starting to heal.

Hannah turned off her screen and pushed in her rolling chair.

"'Night, Monty!" she called as she rushed out the front door without waiting to hear his response. Cold turkey might be the only way to get over her addiction.

CHAPTER 10

The clock above the workbench on the back wall of the garage showed 6:00 p.m. on the dot. She'd been gone from the house for almost twelve hours that day.

Evelyn's story gave Hannah a purpose, and while she worked on it, she could convince herself that she was still a good journalist who hadn't nearly offed herself six months ago after being dumped, or at least that's how her friends and work had seen it, she was sure. But it was hard to explain depression to someone who hadn't experienced it. It was like explaining salt without using the word *salty*—pretty much impossible. Worse than the embarrassment of her attempted suicide last May was that as she was trying to end her life, her father had been fighting for his. She used to wish there were life transplants—that she could just pass hers on to him, since she'd lost her ability to use hers to the fullest. She didn't think those things anymore, not often, not unless something brought her back to those bleak days steeped in depression and blurred with sleeping pills. The numbing properties of Senatobia, Mamaw, and her increased focus on Evelyn's life were much healthier than Ambien. No one ever overdosed on research, right?

The articles had finally caught up to 1929, the year Evelyn was shot, and the list of suspects was growing with each document recovered. Harry Westbrook. The first full name Evelyn had left in her bread-crumb trail of clues. There had to be a reason she revealed his name and no one else's. Could that mean he was the one who pulled the trigger? She tried to imagine what the love interest, or lead suspect, might have looked like, how old he must've been to be out drinking with the older kids, how he'd set his sights on the waifish Evelyn. Too many questions and too few answers currently, but with this bit of information, she had more to go on.

Up until his name showed up, Evelyn seemed like she'd been careful not to use full names. Hannah was still unsure whether Brown was even Evelyn's stepmother's real name before her marriage to Evelyn's father, after a search of the land records in Senatobia in the twenties.

There had to be articles about the shooting from 1929. In addition to the mass of random files, clippings, letters, photographs, notes, and references in the basement, Monty kept original proofs of every edition of the *Tate County Record*, even back to when it was the *Tate County Democrat*. The morgue. At the *Tribune* the morgue took up a whole floor, but here years of papers fit in a wall full of drawers. She'd seen Dolores take the top copy of a pile of papers each week and slide it into a plastic envelope that was then filed away in one of the massive metal cabinets lining Monty's office walls.

Hannah had no idea how to ask him to search through the files without telling him the whole story, and even then, she wasn't sure he'd let her ransack them without good reason.

Hannah slunk into the house at two minutes past six. Carla peeked her head out of the kitchen.

"There you are, dear," she said, with all the warmth Hannah could ever hope for when returning home after a long day. Then the smell hit her. The house reeked of fried fish, which made her nose wrinkle.

"Good evening, Carla," Hannah said, trying to hide her reaction to spare the housekeeper's feelings. Hannah wasn't a fan of seafood and had to do her very best to make fake "I love this" sounds every Friday. Why Carla, a Baptist, insisted on meatless Fridays Hannah would never know, but she'd given up trying to explain the Catholic origin of the tradition. She found it easier to choke down a few bites and then nibble on other leftovers in the middle of the night after Carla had gone home.

"I've put your Saturday dinner in the fridge, and there are plenty of eggs for breakfast. I picked up a roast at Piggly Wiggly today in case you wanted to try your hand at a Sunday dinner. I wrote out the instructions and put them on the refrigerator."

Carla didn't work weekends but had filled in for the first few weeks after Mamaw's accident. But now that Hannah was taking up new duties, Carla had decided she could be trusted with more responsibility. Hannah was eager to help, but any form of housekeeping, especially cooking, seemed so overwhelming that she usually ended up ordering takeout on the nights she was in charge of making dinner. Mamaw still didn't know she was eating KFC on Sundays and recently told Carla she should ask Hannah for her fried chicken recipe. She'd never seen Carla's eyes bulge quite so big.

Hannah was getting better at hiding the evidence of any fast-food meals and even attempted to bake the chicken Carla had left for her last week, which ended up overcooked and bland, but at least she'd tried. But this weekend, Hannah had other things on her mind than how to trick her grandmother and her grandmother's housekeeper into believing she'd made a pepperoni pizza with stuffed crust from scratch.

"Carla, can I ask you a question?" Hannah asked, sitting down at the kitchen table and hanging her bag over the back of her chair.

"I put all the instructions on the fridge, hun," she said, continuing to stir whatever she had cooking on the stove.

"No, not that. Something having to do with work. Your family has worked with Mamaw's family since you were a little girl, right?"

"Before me, hun. My grammy was hired to work for your great-grandpa, Calvin Patton, when she was sixteen years old, I think when he married your great-grammy Florence, and they settled on Camille Boulevard. My momma followed Miss Mable when she married, and

I took over when my momma got too old to keep up with your daddy and Sammy."

"Damn, that long?"

"Yes, indeed. But my Kami wanted to be a teacher, and it's not like you or your momma will be hiring a housekeeper anytime soon. So I'm the last in a long line."

"Have you ever wanted to do something else?" Hannah asked, tapping the space next to her at the table. Carla didn't take the hint and remained standing in the kitchen. She rarely let Hannah into her world.

"I'm happy with my life, hun. And I'm proud of my girl. Only wish I have is that I could see my grandbabies more often. But that is enough of that. I know you didn't set out wanting to ask me about my hopes and dreams."

"I like hearing them, though."

"Eh, you're a sweet girl, but I have work to do unless you have something more pressing to talk about."

"Well, I need some help," Hannah said.

"Now, that is something I'd like to talk to you about," Carla said, grabbing the iced tea from the refrigerator and bringing over two glasses, which tinkled against each other. Hannah had rarely, if ever, seen the woman sit down while working, but when Carla took the chair beside Hannah, she knew Carla was willing to talk. She probably thought they'd be discussing men, like Guy Franklin, or gossiping about the newspaper.

"Now—what's on your mind?" She placed a glass with a printed floral pattern on it in front of Hannah and filled it with the amber liquid. Hannah had not grown up with sweet tea and still preferred the half-flavored bite of a diet soda or the calming effect of a glass of wine with dinner, but in Mamaw's house, it was water, milk, or tea, and she was parched from her bike ride. She took a deep, long drink and licked her lips before starting into her questions.

"I'm researching an article right now about something that happened in Senatobia in the twenties. I'm having the hardest time fact-checking this thing. Did your grandma ever tell you about a shooting from when she was younger? A girl named Evelyn, shot in her home somewhere in town? I can't seem to find any actual records other than a first-person account of the incident, and . . . I guess she could be making it up, but . . . I don't know. It all feels so real."

Carla took a sip of her tea and then smoothed the doily at the center of the table with her fingertips. She clicked her tongue like she was thinking deeply.

"I don't know that story in particular, but one thing I learned from my grammy was that every family has darkness they face. My uncle Louis's wife shot him because she thought he was an intruder on a night when he was late comin' home from work, and Terrance, my little cousin, found his daddy's gun and shot the little neighbor boy he was playing with, and . . . well . . . that's in my family alone. If you look too closely at any life, you're gonna find tragedy. I think it only gets remembered if people tell stories. But people don't like sad stories, especially stuffy families round here, if you know what I mean."

Carla held Hannah's gaze for a moment. The cloudy brown of Carla's irises seemed to leak into the whites of her eyes, and Hannah did know what she meant. Carla had been the one to find Uncle Samuel in Papaw's office. She'd been the one to try to hold Mamaw together as she fell apart in her arms, and she'd been the one to bleach the walls and the floor and to buy the circular area rug that covered the bleach stain that was almost worse than the bloodstain that had once been there. No one from her father's family had ever said the word *depression* or *suicide*—Mamaw's tolerable fiction was an accident while Sam was cleaning his firearm, but accidents didn't usually come with a goodbye note.

"I know. Mamaw never wants to talk about what happened to Uncle Samuel." Hannah said it instead of tiptoeing around the tragedy. Even her own father struggled to talk about why his brother took his own life. If it wasn't for her mother's usually annoying bluntness, Hannah may never have known.

"It's hard to talk about such things, hun." Carla placed her warm hand over Hannah's and gave a squeeze. "Brings up all the pain again. But I think holding all that poison inside can be worse than how much it hurts comin' out, you know?"

Alex. Just the name in her mind rustled up the ache of loss in her chest and the image of him laughing with Janie. Indulging that pain had led her to disturbing places in the spring. She didn't want to get back to that place, so it seemed safer to lock away the pain and dole it out in nibbles of sorrow and regret rather than feasting on them to the point of gluttony.

"But this story is old. It shouldn't hurt anymore. I just need to find *some* hard evidence. Or at least someone who knows the girl's full name or has some recollection of the crime. Without a full name, it's difficult. And it happened so long ago that anyone who would remember is gone now. I do have a man's name," Hannah recalled, lost in her stream of consciousness, "and the name of the facility in Memphis where the girl in the story may have lived when she was paralyzed. I *might* be able to find her name there, but . . ."

Carla collected the empty glasses from the table and balanced them in one hand. Then she grabbed the glass pitcher with the other, and Hannah knew she'd lost her attention.

"I need to find a place to look up some old records. The town hall had a few, but I only have a first name. It was from so long ago . . ."

"You know, when Kami was doing a research paper for some history class at the University of Memphis, she found some interesting things down at the university library. They have these films with the newspapers copied onto them—"

"Microfiche," Hannah filled in the blank for Carla, perking up. "That's exactly what I need."

"Yes, micro-fish. That's right."

"That is good to know. And while I'm in Memphis, I could check out the old hospital. See if they have records or logs or pictures or *something.*" Hannah knew this was the next step in her research. She'd need to find a way to get to Memphis. It was only forty or fifty minutes by car, but it seemed like an eternity away to Hannah. She had work during the week and Mamaw in the evenings and on weekends. And though Mamaw often offered her Buick to Hannah for any "social calls," she hadn't taken her up on the offer yet. Hannah used to think that was because she hadn't made any real friends here in Senatobia. But every time she thought about venturing outside the comfort zone of the town, anxiety clamped down on her ability to make decisions, leaving her to wonder if the isolation the town provided acted as a protective buffer, an excuse to stay stuck exactly where she was.

"What pictures?" Mamaw cut into the conversation, rolling in from the back hall in her wheelchair. Her hair was fluffed up and held in place by what was likely half a can of Aqua Net. She had on a pair of blue slacks and a floral button-up, her nails painted a coral that matched the flowers on her blouse perfectly.

"Don't you look pretty? Mr. Davenport is gonna be speechless," Carla said, pushing Mamaw's chair into the living room next to her favorite armchair. Hannah had been so busy with her problems, she hadn't noticed the tray of appetizers there. How could she have forgotten? Mamaw's gentleman caller was coming for dinner tonight. It was his first official visit since the accident, though he'd snuck in a few "just in the neighborhood" hellos over the past few weeks.

The doorbell rang. All three women froze.

"Do I look all right, darlin'?" Mamaw asked Hannah, like she was a schoolgirl getting ready for an ice-cream social.

"You look beautiful, Mamaw," Hannah said as Carla went to the door, kissing her grandmother's cheek. "But I should go change."

She hadn't even taken the time to shower that morning, and her clothes were musty from dust and sweat after sifting through the archives.

"You know you always look beautiful to me," Mamaw said, patting Hannah's cheek before she stood up. "But . . ."

"But I should probably freshen up," Hannah added with a wink. Carla was greeting a sport-coat-clad Mr. Davenport at the front door, so Hannah grabbed her bag and dashed through the fishy-smelling kitchen without being seen.

As the murmur of polite conversation persisted in the living room, Hannah snuck into the hall bathroom to change, the anxiety of venturing to Memphis on her own pushing against the desire to keep the investigation moving forward. Completely preoccupied with the internal debate and planning her theoretical trip to Memphis, she quickly pulled on a clean shirt, brushed her teeth, combed her hair back into a fresh ponytail, and dotted on a thin layer of foundation and mascara. After applying a slather of lip gloss, she caught a glimpse of herself in the mirror. The red in the striped shirt brought out a light blush in her cheeks, and there was a touch of sparkle in her eyes that had been missing for a long time. She didn't look numb; she looked almost . . . happy.

Hannah rarely took selfies, but if Alex could look happy and like he'd moved on, she wanted to look like she didn't care anymore. And if she looked a little bit hot in the process, so be it. She grabbed at her back pocket for her phone when she remembered. *Damn it.* It was still dead, sitting in a Ziploc of rice in her bag.

Hands against the counter, leaning forward and biting at her glossy lip, she stared into the mirror, examining her reflection. There was something different about her, something bright that went beyond makeup or complementary wardrobe choices. Hannah let go of her lip and tried to smile with no teeth, the waxy flavor of lip gloss lingering on the tip of her tongue. Old Hannah was there. The one who could still call her dad on the phone and who chased a story like it was her calling. The Hannah that had imagined what it would be like to walk down the aisle and be called "Mom" one day.

With two swift tugs, she yanked a handful of tissues out of the crocheted box on the back of the toilet. The light-pink gloss came off in a few swipes, barely bright enough to stain the tissue paper. She talked to Laura endlessly about how hard it was to get over Alex, but she never wanted to actually get over him. As long as she still had her love for him, her hope that he'd come back, she didn't have to start over and truly accept that her life was going to move on without him.

She tried the smile again. It was good enough. Just a little of the old, happy Hannah. Just enough to give her hope of a future on her own, but not enough to make her give up all hope of ever seeing Alex's name show up on her phone again.

CHAPTER 11

Hannah sped north on Highway 51 toward Memphis. "Speeding" may have been an exaggeration in Mamaw's Buick, but she was going faster than she could on her bike, so that counted for something. She was still nervous about making the trip, the anxious side of her mind saying it would be easier to try a different day and kick the can down the road. But after a particularly interesting dinner with Mamaw and Mr. Davenport last night, Hannah had been handed a free Saturday and the keys to the Buick that morning, and the journalist inside her wasn't going to pass up the opportunity.

Dinner the night before had been more fun than Hannah ever could've guessed dinner with two senior citizens could be. Mr. Davenport had a subtle sense of humor that cracked Hannah up despite her attempts to fade into the background so that Mamaw could enjoy her pseudo date.

But when Mr. Davenport asked about her work at the *Record*, Hannah mentioned her need to visit Memphis to do research, and Mamaw's gentleman caller was brimming with questions and advice.

After a few basic "getting to know you" questions, Hannah could tell that the retired minister from Arkansas likely had very little first-hand information that could fill in the blanks of Evelyn's life. Mamaw was less inclined to indulge in any conversation involving Hannah's research. More clearheaded than when she offered her sleepy reference to the Crippled Children's Hospital, she'd lost her helpful attitude and kept trying to sway the conversation away from such controversial topics. Hannah cooperated in Mamaw's attempts to steer the discussion away from her work, but Mr. Davenport didn't make it easy.

"I agree that the university library is likely your best option," Davenport said at one point after a long sip of iced tea. "If you need a vehicle—"

"She has a car," Mamaw cut in, slightly rude for her usually tempered demeanor.

Hannah started at the sharp interruption and watched her grandmother closely. She clearly had tender feelings for Mr. Davenport, but what was she feeling right now? If Hannah were in her shoes, she'd be feeling like Mr. Davenport was overstepping, acting like he had some superior take on the situation because he was a man, but Hannah assumed Mamaw would like these attempts at chivalry.

"The Buick in the garage? I'm not sure that would get you to Coldwater, much less Memphis."

Mamaw stiffened. The Buick had been a gift from Papaw. Mamaw rarely drove anymore, and it was older than any of her grandchildren, but she thought it was the most beautiful car in existence and insisted on keeping her driver's license up to date.

"It's okay. I'm fine. If I need to go to Memphis, I will take an Uber." It would be expensive, but Hannah had a bit in savings and didn't have many expenses living with Mamaw.

"An Uber?" Mr. Davenport questioned, clearly not up on the newest trends.

Mamaw took the opportunity to show her modernity and, Hannah thought, pay him back a little for the comment about her car.

"They are the new sort of taxis. You can call one with a service on your computer."

"Well, your phone," Hannah corrected.

"Do we have those in Senatobia?" Mr. Davenport asked.

"Of course we do. I'm sure plenty of the college kids at the university use the driving service, don't you think, Hannah?"

"Oh yes. I'm sure of it," Hannah responded emphatically, as though she had long-held opinions on the driving habits of the youth in Tate County. She sat back and let Mamaw and her gentleman caller banter back and forth in a slightly flirtatious repartee as she thought through the logistics of getting to the University of Memphis and finding her way into the Crippled Children's Hospital without a phone or a car. If her phone didn't start working soon, she'd have to dip into savings or bulk up the balance on her credit card and buy a new one.

"Sounds like you are going to Memphis tomorrow," Mr. Davenport said to Hannah, tapping her elbow with his own. Even if she hadn't seen him wink, she'd have heard it in the playful way he made his statement.

"Wait. What?" Hannah asked, nearly speechless with anticipation.

"Your Mamaw is gonna spend the day with me and my granddaughter, Suzie."

"Oh my God. Seriously?" It was far sooner than Hannah had expected, but she wasn't going to pass up the opportunity. But then she paused, not sure how her grandmother felt about the change in plans. "But I don't have to, Mamaw. I can go another time."

"Oh, hush!" Mamaw waved her hand like she was batting away Hannah's concerns. "You can take my car, and I need an outing. Besides, I don't think Mr. Davenport will let me get a word in edgewise until I say yes to his offer. He can be such a persistent man, don't you think?"

It should've been awkward to see her grandmother use her womanly ways on a man, but it wasn't. It fascinated Hannah. She wanted to study the push and pull of this old-school dynamic, a kind of dance that was far too complicated for Hannah. Davenport's well-intentioned but exhausting helpfulness was suffocating, and she wouldn't even know where to start with the passive and vulnerable role Mamaw had perfected.

"So it seems," Hannah said, entertained by their method of flirting.

Mr. Davenport and Mamaw solidified their plans for the next day, and as soon as could be considered polite, Hannah excused herself to her room under the guise of an early bedtime to leave the two lovebirds alone.

She'd left at noon. Though the research trip was happening sooner than Hannah had expected, it felt right to be on the path to answers. She'd checked her email incessantly before leaving work Friday.

In the absence of her phone's GPS, she'd asked Mr. Davenport for directions. He'd presented Hannah with handwritten directions this morning when he picked up Mamaw. He advised her to go up US 51, a road that took her past Graceland and into the city. She knew from her brief tenure in traffic reporting that she could just as easily take I-55 to the city, but without the voice on her phone telling her every last turn, she was hesitant to make the trip without some guidance. So she decided to lean on Mr. Davenport's directions.

Once she was over the Tennessee state line and in the city proper, Hannah turned onto the parkway that was supposed to lead her to her first stop, the University of Memphis. She eyed the pawnshop on the corner and the train tracks parallel to the road. It felt a little like home this close to the city's center. She missed the neighborhoods of Chicago, the people, the houses, the small markets on every other corner. She even missed seeing bulletproof glass with names and gang signs etched into it.

A long freight train crept along beside her, graffiti offering a splash of color she was always secretly grateful for no matter where she lived. On the other side of the road were brick houses and shops, and occasionally a few almost-suburban neighborhoods sprouted up in between the patches of older-looking communities. She tried to imagine what the world looked like back when Evelyn might have visited. Were these houses here, or was it just farmland?

She continued up the parkway and eventually outpaced the train to her right. After crossing the tracks and managing a couple of tricky turns, she found herself in the parking lot on the outskirts of the University of Memphis. Usually, she would've looked at the campus online and found exactly where the university library was located, but today she was on more of a Choose Your Own Adventure kind of a trip since she hadn't had the opportunity to do any advance research.

She wanted to know what Evelyn's life felt like, and this was one way to find out. If she'd been alive in 1929, Hannah would have had to explore and discover her surroundings without any online guidance. The idea was a bit frightening but also exhilarating, like she was walking across a tightrope she'd traversed a million times but they'd forgotten to put out the net. She knew she could make it to the other side, but what if this time she slipped and fell?

Well, she wasn't going to turn back now. Hannah grabbed her bag off the passenger-side seat, its metal buckle scratching against the vinyl-coated padded surface. It took an extra-hard shove to get the door open. It creaked, like the joints of an old woman trying to stand for the first time in a long while.

She slammed the door hard to get it closed and then locked it with one of the tinkling keys Mamaw had handed her that morning. She wasn't sure who would ever want to steal the brown beauty, but then again, on a college campus, someone might think grandma's old car was "retro," so it was better to be safe than face Mamaw's silent look of disappointment.

After crossing both lanes of traffic and the train tracks without much difficulty, she reached the concrete path that led to campus. There was an energy there that reminded her of her days at Northwestern. She'd never been one of those exciting college students who had lots of dates or went to all the football games. She had never joined a sorority or had a one-night stand, and in all four years she had participated in only one game of beer pong—which she lost. Most of her time not studying was spent as a reporter and then as an editor for the *Daily Northwestern*. She'd spent many a late night in the third-floor office of the Norris University Center, researching, writing, and eventually editing the features section of the paper. Those years were the foundation of her career as a journalist, and she still could remember what it felt like to rush across campus to her next class or spend hours researching in the library. Life on campus always felt like it had a purpose.

Sure, there were stressful times. Once, right before finals, she'd been crossing Lincoln to get on campus. For a brief moment she considered if it would be better to let one of the cars zipping by hit her and remove all the items from her to-do list in one tragic second. But that upsetting moment thankfully passed quickly after scaring her enough to keep her from playing such what-if games again for many, many years.

"I didn't realize you have a history of suicidal ideations," Laura said during therapy when Hannah had, half-jokingly, told the story the week before Mamaw hurt herself and Hannah's mother gave her the strongly recommended option of moving to Mississippi. Hearing the phrase *suicidal ideation* made Hannah start. She cocked her head, looking at her therapist like she was the one who had lost her mind.

"Um, that's not what I was trying to say. It only happened that one time until everything fell apart with . . . you know," she explained. Alex caused this. If he hadn't left, she wouldn't have broken. If they were together still, she wouldn't have wanted to end things. That was the only narrative that felt right to Hannah.

Laura leaned in, only a few years older than Hannah and with a perky nose and styled hair that at first made her wonder if this woman could be of much help. But Hannah had learned that when her therapist got this steady, thoughtful look on her face and put her notepad to the side that insight beyond a certain age was about to be dispensed.

"Actually, it sounds to me like you've likely been dealing with some underlying depression and anxiety for some time now." She squinted like she was trying to see a picture better. "Stick with me here and I'll try to explain. Depression can be hereditary, and with your family history, I wouldn't be surprised if, once you lost the structure of your micromanaged childhood in college, the symptoms became more difficult to bear. And that is why you became so easily and fully enmeshed with Alex." Hannah flinched, not liking that line of reasoning. It made her feel even more damaged and unlovable, but she sat, speechless, reluctantly letting Laura finish. "You leaned on that relationship to give you that structure and stabilize your self-image. And then when that scaffolding was gone, poof, you were left to carry this preexisting condition without *any* coping mechanisms."

Hannah shook her head and changed the direction in which her legs were defensively crossed. "No. I've never felt like this before. This is because of him. Because of what he did."

Laura made the annoying hmm sound that always meant she didn't agree. Hannah braced herself.

"I know I say this all the time, but there are reasons and there are justifications. Just because you can find the reasoning behind a behavior doesn't necessarily justify it. Alex"—she said the name that cut like a blade—"and his behavior are reasons for your heartbreak, but not everyone who goes through the trauma you've experienced deals with the stumbling blocks you've been working through. At some point it isn't healthy to rehash trauma without working to heal it, to look deeper, Hannah. Beyond Alex. Beyond your breakup."

"I'm taking the medicine. I'm going to therapy. That's all I can do right now," Hannah had said, folding her arms so that her body was completely closed off.

Laura sat in that energy, leaning back into her armchair, letting the challenge to look deeper hang heavy for a moment.

"I understand. It's very painful, and with the trauma of losing your father so quickly, it can leave anyone feeling unsure, lost. I will gladly listen to you talk about anything that helps lift your grief, Hannah, but the way out of this pain is not inertia, it is forward motion."

" '*The best way out is always through.*' I get it," she snipped. "I've read Robert Frost." But at that time Hannah didn't want "out"—she wanted to go *back*. Laura shifted to a new topic, reassuring Hannah they'd explore the idea of moving on again soon. Hannah moved to Senatobia two weeks later and had let their weekly sessions drift away. But on days like today, when she was on a campus again, tracking down a story, she thought about telling Laura. Maybe when she got her new phone.

It wasn't difficult to find the Ned R. McWherter Library. The campus was nearly empty. According to Mr. Davenport, today was game day, but since it was an away game, that meant a quiet campus and everyone inside watching from the confines of their home. A few cheers echoed out of random windows as she passed through the part of campus where the student center was located. Then she followed the signage and took a glance at the large map by the clock tower. Hannah found her way to the front of the four-story library in under fifteen minutes.

After flashing her old ID badge from the *Tribune* and navigating through the spacious domed four-story entry, Hannah found a way to a resource desk. She said the words *reporter* and *Chicago Tribune* and was quickly assigned a petite and slightly nervous student assistant, who escorted her up to the second floor where the microfilm was held.

Maggie, a first-year graduate student in library studies, showed Hannah to the microfilm copies that could be viewed on large machines in a shadowy corner of the resource room.

"Let me know if you need any help," Maggie said with a sweet little twang in a whisper, like she'd grown up in a home full of secrets so that she'd only learned to raise her voice loud enough to be heard inside a library.

"Thank you. Don't go too far! I'm sure I'll have a million more questions," Hannah said with an overly helpless smile, taking Maggie's place at the computer. She'd given Maggie Harry's name and a few details when she offered to help with the search. It was better to keep the grad student close and busy. Hopefully, Maggie wasn't the suspicious type who would google Hannah's name as soon as she got back to the research desk.

Please don't be nosy, Maggie. Please, Hannah thought as she nodded and said a quick thanks for all her help.

Finally, alone in her element, Hannah started a familiar research pattern that had served her well as a student and journalist. Thankfully, she knew how to navigate the compact microfilm files far more efficiently than the mess that met her every day in the basement of the *Record*.

First, she searched the online database of historical newspapers. Still, without a full name for Evelyn, each search came back with hundreds of random suggestions even when she narrowed the search field to 1929 and only included newspapers from northern Mississippi and southern Tennessee. As the afternoon dragged on, she moved on to searching local papers. Nothing on the shooting of a girl. The more images that flipped by, the more Hannah felt like she was searching for a needle in a haystack.

She paused, pen cap between her teeth as she considered her seeming dead end. It was nearly impossible to find a singular fourteen-year-old girl with only a first name. She'd typed all the names she had written in the notebook, one at a time, into the online archive database. But Mrs. Brown, Evelyn, Mr. Brodick, the postman, and even Harry Westbrook brought up random links that led to the same dead ends she'd already met. Then she thought about her next destination—the Pines. The former home of the Memphis Crippled Children's Hospital and School. That place existed. There was no doubt.

She typed the name of the facility into the search bar, and four resources popped up. Two looked to be articles about the hospital's founding in 1919, one was about a lawsuit against the estate of a widow who wanted to retain the charitable donation left to the hospital in her husband's will, and the top hit was an archived box of materials. Hannah's ears rang as she focused on the description.

BOX CONTAINS ANNUAL REPORTS, BYLAWS, MINUTES FROM MEETINGS OF THE CHARITABLE BOARD, AND PHOTOGRAPHS—ITEMS DONATED BY MISS SHELBY DAWSON OF MEMPHIS, TENNESSEE.

The ringing in her ears turned into a buzz that covered her whole body. It was THE buzz, the one she felt the first time she read one of Evelyn's letters. It was not a flashing red arrow pointing to all the answers, but it was a solid lead and Hannah was going to follow it.

With Maggie's help, Hannah found the resource box. Even in the well-maintained library, there was a thin layer of dust on the top of the brown cardboard lid, and the documents inside smelled old, musty. Her eyes twitched with a familiar itch she had to fight nearly every time she touched the files at the *Record*.

Maggie returned to her desk, and Hannah settled on the floor to look through the documents inside. First was a typewritten log of what ended up being minutes to meetings held by the charitable board that kept the hospital running. The majority of the members were men through much of the twenties and thirties, but one woman, Shelby Dawson, took over during the war and led the organization until it was discontinued in the mid-1980s.

Dawson. The name was familiar, but Hannah had left her notebook back at the table where she'd been working. She'd remember the name and check for it later. Hannah continued shuffling through the items. There were a few digitized files on microfilm she'd have to pick through on one of the machines, but what she didn't expect was the small manila envelope at the bottom of the box, closed with a button and string. Whatever was inside was hefty enough to need several rows of stamps if it were to be mailed. As she unraveled the string that kept the top flap of the envelope closed, Hannah savored each loop, the anticipation, the hope that there might be something new and useful inside.

What she found was a pile of photographs. Most in black and white. Each labeled on the back in a neat cursive. On top was a postcard with a photo of a large stone building: *Crippled Children's Hospital and School, 1919.* It wasn't direct evidence of Evelyn, but it was a step closer to the world she'd become certain Evelyn lived inside. According to the bylaws and press releases included in the box, the hospital had been founded in 1919 by Dr. Jeffery Dawson, an orthopedic surgeon who specialized in "incurable" medicine. In those days, children who were born with a significant physical "defect" or who acquired one through disease or accident were often not cared for at home. This hospital and school had been organized to provide care for those children, away from home, at no cost to the family.

Of course, Hannah noted, all the faces that stared back at her in the first fifty years of the charity were white. She cringed. Sometimes it was hard to accept that this kind of open discrimination was deeply entwined not just in the history of her country but also in her own family's history. Though Patrick Williamson had had a difficult time discussing some of his family's secrets, like Sam's suicide and Papaw's alcoholism, he had always been open about the way he felt about his upper-middle-class white ancestors. Though his parents were involved in the civil rights movement, they were the first generation to not wholly embrace the systemic racism woven into the roots of his home state. He loved telling her and Brody stories passed down from their family history, but each one was spelled out with a half apology, explaining that he moved north hoping to find a more balanced outlook on diversity and inclusion. Growing up, Hannah wasn't sure if he found exactly what he was looking for, since the poisonous effects of discrimination turned out to be everywhere, even if the symptoms looked different. But as she settled into her life down here, she saw what her father must've been running from.

The other pictures in the pile included photos taken of the hospital's float in the Cotton Carnival parade, a rickety playground outside the living quarters of the Children's Hospital, and then several group photos of blurry black-and-white figures, some in nurses' uniforms, some in skirts and fluffy shirts, and a few men in tweed trousers with ties and metal-rimmed glasses.

Hannah flipped the first group photo over—*1921 faculty* was scrawled across the top with a list of names neatly printed underneath. She moved to the next one and repeated the inspection. Each subsequent photo was the same as the first—a date, often with chunks of years in between, and a list of names. Altogether there were about twenty-five faculty images, most in black and white, some in bleached-out color, but all well documented with names and dates on the back.

Hannah shuffled through the pile again, this time with the names and dates facing up rather than the photos. Some of the names from the faculty stayed the same for years on end; most rotated frequently. But one name showed up on every list: Dawson. That was the name of the woman who had donated the files and the name of the doctor who had founded the school.

Placing all the items carefully back in the box, Hannah stumbled to her feet, her right leg tingling with pins and needles from sitting on the floor too long. With a new purpose, she copied every photo, front and back, and started in on the microfilm articles that were stored inside the boxes, scratching down information, names, and potential leads in her notebook.

She jumped when Maggie touched her elbow as she sat at the microfilm viewer.

"Oh my God. You scared me," Hannah gasped, heart pounding in her ears. She could tell by the twitch on her assistant's lips that her shocked expression had been too loud.

"So sorry," she answered in an exaggerated whisper, as if she were trying to teach Hannah how to be quiet in a library. "It's just that we close in an hour and I need to go downstairs to help with the checkout rush. I found a few things that might be helpful, but nothing about your Evelyn."

Closing? Hannah wondered, glancing at the clock over the line of couches to her right. It was already 5:00 p.m. How had she gotten so wrapped up in her research that she'd lost track of time this massively?

"Oh shit," Hannah cursed, once again at full volume, immediately feeling like she'd sworn in church. "Sorry," she whispered, "I didn't mean to stay this long."

Hannah closed her research notebook and piled up the resources she'd been using. She'd promised to be back home by eight. The Pines was only fifteen minutes or so from the library, according to Mr. Davenport, but who knew if anyone from that facility would be willing to sit down and talk to her this late in the day. She cursed herself as she piled copies into her messenger bag. She had to try to get to the Pines; she didn't know when she'd have another opportunity to have a whole day off with a mode of transportation to keep herself going on this wild goose chase of a story.

"Here are a few things I found and printed for you about a Harry Westbrook. I'm not sure if it's your fella, but I hope so. He sounds . . . interesting." Maggie held out a manila folder about half an inch thick with printed materials.

"Seriously? That's fantastic." She grabbed the offered documents and went to peek inside the folder when she remembered the time as Maggie stood to leave.

"I'll keep an eye out for anything else. Oh, and I sent you a few links," she said, the colorful pins on her library credentials clicking as the fabric lanyard straightened into a V. "To the email on your business card."

She doubted that she could still access the mailbox Maggie had been emailing all afternoon. Thankfully Maggie hadn't tried the phone number, which would either lead to a dead end or some other random employee at the *Trib* who may or may not remember Hannah and be able to put two and two together.

"Here, let me give you my number and my personal email. That one can be kind of . . . sketchy." Hannah scribbled out the information printed in raised ink on the front of the card and wrote out her more up-to-date information on the back of it. "There you go. That should work better."

Maggie slipped the card into her ID holder at the end of her lanyard. "Sounds great. I'll forward everythin'. I don't have a card, but you can call me here." She pointed to a yellow Post-it on the front of the envelope Hannah still had clutched in her hands.

"My phone is toast. I'm waiting for a replacement." She tried to sound official, like she was anticipating the delivery of a new device from Chicago any day now.

"Email works fine too." She fiddled with her ID badge and took a step back, away from the desk. "Well, it was nice meeting you, Miss Williamson. Best of luck. You know, I started in journalism. I can't wait to read your story."

Hannah stopped packing for a moment and made eye contact with the young grad student. She wasn't sure, but Hannah thought she read admiration in the woman's eyes, like Maggie saw the reporter Hannah wanted to be in her. The look filled Hannah with shame. She looked away, finished filling her bag, and gave the best smile she could muster.

"Thank you for all your help."

And without looking back, Hannah rushed across campus, the slight fall nip in the air barely registering against her bare arms. She was getting too good at lying, and it was going to catch up with her if she didn't stop soon. But as she unlocked the Buick and used the push-button door handle to get the massive door open with a screech, she knew it wasn't possible to stop. Not yet.

She pulled out the sheet of Mr. Davenport's handwritten directions and started the car, the sun dipping lower in the sky than Hannah had hoped. She had one more stop to get to today and a growing list of questions, paired with a burning curiosity that wasn't going away. Being an entirely transparent, sainted journalist wasn't in her immediate future—she knew that. At the Pines, she'd likely need the business cards in her wallet and the set of outdated press credentials in her bag, as well as a great backstory and a few sleights of hand. But after that, she'd stop lying. Or . . . at least she'd try to.

CHAPTER 12

The sun was rapidly dropping as Hannah reached the black gates of the Pines Wellness Center. The facility sat nestled in the middle of an eclectic mix of nicely remodeled older homes and run-down shops and dilapidated houses that needed to be demolished and rebuilt before anyone could live in them again. A curved drive just past the open gates led to a two-story brick structure with a columned porch.

Even though it was past five, the building was buzzing with activity. Cars lined the drive, and the oak trees planted along the side of the road were strung with twinkling white lights that made it look like the stars had sunk to the earth as the night fell slowly around them. Mamaw's brown Buick stood out like a rusty nail in a line of shiny new bolts. A black Jaguar, silver BMW, and midnight-blue Tesla were in front of her. A Lexus SUV pulled up behind Hannah, making it impossible for her to have second thoughts about joining the queue. Initially, when Maggie had reminded her of the time, Hannah had been afraid that no one would be at the front desk of the treatment center, but she had not anticipated there would be a line out the door.

The parade of cars went up to the front porch, where it looked like there was valet service provided. Men in tuxes passed keys over to men wearing vests, while women in floor-length, sparkling gowns emerged from their vehicles like King Arthur's Lady of the Lake. Hannah looked down at her worn-out jeans and T-shirt. There was no way she was going to blend in among this cast of characters. Then again, if they thought she was a member of the press, that might explain her casual dress and would likely gain her some leeway to ask about the facility and maybe even gain access to records. Of course, that would mean more lying, but she might as well add "master manipulator" to her résumé at this point.

Wouldn't Dad be so proud? Hannah's guilt whispered.

One car remained before it was her turn to talk to the valet. Hannah ran her fingers through her hair, slicked on a new coat of peppermint-flavored ChapStick, wrestled into her flak jacket, and snagged her press credentials from her bag. Using the manual crank handle, she rolled her window down to talk to the valet without having to mess with the sticky door. Once the glass partition was gone, a sharp stench of burning rubber filled the interior of the car. She coughed and gritted her teeth to keep from gagging. Because she hadn't eaten anything since a piece of toast and a large coffee on the way up to the university, Hannah's stomach was already tight and overly sensitive. She wasn't the only one to pick up on the stench. The slender woman exiting her BMW in front of Hannah ran a jeweled hand under her nose like she'd wandered into a fish market on a hundred-degree day.

Hannah rolled forward, eyes drawn upward by four massive white columns and a sign that read THE SAFE PLACE: CHARITY GALA AND AUCTION. For a moment, she wished she were wearing something fancy and had an invitation to the party. These were the kinds of charity events she'd have gone to one day with Alex. He'd have a tux in the back of the closet in a dry cleaner's bag. She would've gotten a sitter for the kids and had her hair done and a manicure to match her gown. They'd take his stupid, sporty coupe because it was the only one without car seats surgically attached to the rear bench.

Hannah exited her rickety car, feeling out of place among the fancy vehicles and dresses but glad she didn't have to show an invitation to get past the valet.

"Don't forget your ticket!" A man wearing white gloves handed her a small square of paper with a handwritten number as he opened the oversize wooden front doors.

"Thanks," she said under her breath, rushing through the entry. The next fancy couple in line exited their vehicles, complaining loudly about the wait, and Hannah had no desire to meet them face-to-face. But she froze in place as soon as her feet hit the marble entry floor. The vestibule curved around the edges, and the darker marble pieces pointed inward to the middle of the room, where the bluish purple of the early evening cascaded in from a skylight. During the day, the sun's rays would've flashed off the tiny particles in the marble, making the floor glitter as if the starlight from the trees were embedded within.

The beauty in this place was palpable but also unsettling. Like the dripping trees and towering columns and marble floors and sparkles and skylights were all put there to make the ugliness of disease and disability dissolve into the background—a lovely mask that concealed a time in the world when it had been reasonable to send children away because their bodies were broken and to tell them their futures were broken as well.

The air sucked around her as the front doors opened again, like the room was taking a deep breath. Hannah moved through the vestibule into a dark side room, pretending to admire a line of photographs on the wall. She watched the newly arrived couples half-heartedly. They didn't seem to notice the skylight or the floor, and the only sparkles they seemed interested in were the ones sewn into the bodices of the middle-aged women's gowns.

Hannah took a step farther into the room, working on blending into the background. Perhaps she could be added to the list of unnoticeable things for now, at least until the stream of guests slowed and she could figure out the next step in this hastily thought-out plan.

As she lingered in her hiding place, the pictures she was pretending to look at started to come into focus as her eyes adjusted to the lack of light. She started. Could it be possible? Some of the photographs were the same as the ones in the research box from the library. Hannah drifted across the soft blue-and-white floral carpet to the other side of the room to examine another tall display of old photos.

On this wall were pictures she'd never seen before. All of them were of children, little forms settled in wheelchairs or walking with the help of crutches or braces around their legs. Several were what looked like class pictures, lines of sallow faces from toddler to teen. Goose bumps covered her arms under her heavy canvas jacket. She was closer to answers than she'd ever been.

She ran through the dates on the golden plaques at the bottom of each eight-by-ten-inch image. Not every school year was represented. It looked as though, when photography was far rarer, that the school had invested in professional photos every few years or that only a few pictures were selected for display in the lobby of the Pines to give some sense of history and dignity.

That's when she saw it, a photograph from 1930. Hannah scanned each face, confident that she'd be able to sense which one was Evelyn based only on the description in her letter and the connection Hannah was starting to believe existed between them.

She would likely be one of the oldest students in the picture if she'd been shot at fourteen. Hannah took a step toward the wall, lightly caressing the glass separating her from the aging photograph. The faces took on even less detail up close, like an ink drawing that had been left out in the rain, making the lines bleed into each other. But there, on the outer edge of the second row, was a young blonde woman sitting in a wheelchair. She wasn't smiling, but she looked like she *wanted* to smile, like the kind of girl who would swing over a river and fall in love with a boy at first sight. It *could* be Evelyn.

Someone cleared his throat behind her.

Hannah spun around, snatching her hand back from the photograph. A tall, dark-haired stranger stood there, arms crossed with a stern look on his face. His blue eyes, even in the gray of the room, were bright against his airbrushed tan. His hair seemed authentic at least— silver strands accented the darker ones at his temples. She scrambled for the press credentials hidden just under the flap of her bag. But before she could stumble through her half-assed cover story, the man started talking.

"Can you believe that was taken almost one hundred years ago?" he asked in one of those official-sounding, warm southern accents. He looked over her head at the photo with the golden 1930 plaque at the bottom.

"Well, not exactly. Ninety years is more like it," Hannah corrected, not glancing back at the picture, finding the stranger more interesting at the moment.

"Close enough," he responded, shrugging and putting his hands in his pockets, squinting at the photograph like it was a 3D painting he could make pop out at him if he looked at it the right way. In the few seconds his hands were visible she didn't notice a ring, though she did hate herself for looking. When was the last time she'd noticed a detail like that?

"Ten years is a long time to gloss over," she said, half under her breath, nervously checking the room for an approaching security guard or police officer. Really, she should shut up and not argue.

"I was rounding up," he said, simply.

"Well," Hannah said, ordering herself to be silent but also unable to stop, "which ten are you leaving out? The twenties, with Prohibition? Or the thirties, when the government was like, oops, never mind, hashtag Great Depression? Or the forties, when Hitler was defeated, and the US government dropped not one but two atomic bombs? Or . . . the fifties, with the baby boom and the Korean War, not to mention that DNA was discovered. Then, the sixties—I mean, if you skipped the sixties, we'd miss integration and JFK, Martin Luther King, Vietnam . . . and the moon and . . . well . . . you get the idea."

"Well, damn, that's a lot to pick from." He chuckled and scanned her face silently for a moment. Her stomach danced. "I mean, not the fifties, that's for sure," he said, finally looking away.

"Seriously?" she pressed, arguing so he wouldn't notice her nerves. The world of men was easier when Alex was her only focus. Sure, she used to notice guys, talk to them, maybe even tell a joke or two, but she never had to worry about the vulnerability of wondering what they thought of her. Or the deeper question any inkling of an attraction ignited: Would she ever find someone she could care about as much as she'd loved him? It was easier to push them all away. "Of all the decades, you *save* the fifties? What, are you all about housewives, or was your mom born in the fifties or something?"

"Ha. Well, yes, ma'am, she was, but that's not why." His speech patterns were slow and polite, like he'd practiced this exact conversation before.

"Well, then—why? I'm seriously dying to know." Hannah was starting to smile now, edging toward flirting, which was frightening as all get-out. This man was not just handsome but smart and had a touch of cockiness that could only be pulled off by someone wearing a tux he likely owned. This is when it would've been helpful to wear makeup or brush her hair or wear clothes that didn't look like a sack.

No, Hannah. Stop, she ordered herself. *Focus.*

He shrugged. "TV was invented in the fifties."

"Television?"

"Yes, ma'am. I was raised on *Teenage Mutant Ninja Turtles, Knight Rider,* and *He-Man.*" He popped a large peppermint in his mouth and tucked the crinkly wrapper in his pocket. "Did you know She-Ra was He-Man's sister?"

Hannah fought a begrudging smile she tried to hide with a swipe of her hand. This man needed no encouragement.

"That show was . . . before my time," she said, moving to another row of pictures to keep herself from giving in to the blatant flirting being tossed her way by this charming and handsome man who smelled a little too good for her liking. "Anyway, you have a point with the TV thing. They say that's why Vietnam was so unpopular. People got to see war up close and personal for the first time."

The man followed, and Hannah stopped paying full attention to the dates or images.

"Well, that and how the press reported it."

"What?" she asked, turning around, not sure if she should be outraged or laugh.

"You know, the Cronkite moment and the embedded journalist and—"

"And you think that was wrong?" Outrage it was.

"No, not wrong, just . . . fact," he said, nonchalantly, almost arrogantly, ignoring her indignation. Her opinion of him was turning south, rapidly. A free press was the safeguard of democracy, damn it.

"The way journalists documented and reported that war was revolutionary. Heroic. Arnett, Turner, Hodierne, Steinbeck . . ."

"Whoa. Was your momma a journalist or something?" He echoed her earlier joke about the 1950s.

She refused to laugh, still bristling at his comments. "No, I am," she said, chin up in defiance.

His smile dropped away and his hands came out of his pockets, and he stood to a full, dignified height of at least six one. The playful Romeo transformed into a no-nonsense businessman.

"Why didn't you say so sooner?" He took a step back and looked out into the main hall where the line of attendees had thinned to almost nonexistent.

"Because you were too busy sharing your opinions on He-Man." She followed him this time, his change in mood fascinating her. From flirt to recluse at the mention of her being a journalist. What was he hiding?

"Well, that was off the record."

Hannah sniggered, expecting a joke, but he still seemed serious. She stepped even closer to the jittery man, whose pulse was beating so hard she could see it pumping through his jugular. Seeing a powerful man in a vulnerable position only made her want to ask more uncomfortable questions. She kind of liked seeing him squirm—it made her feel empowered in a strange way. Before, he was the pursuer. Now she was.

"I'm not here to write a story about *you*. I'm here to write a story about this place," she said, gesturing to the hand-carved crown molding and the polished oak floors. "So your eighties TV fetish can remain a secret. What, does your wife not know you're here? Are you skipping work? Don't worry, you can trust me. We *are* off the record, after all."

He cocked his head, and the corner of his mouth turned up, which caused a little line to crease up his cheek in a sexy, actor kind of way. No wonder this man was cocky. He'd been born with lottery-winning genes, and he knew it.

"You don't know who I am, do you?"

Hannah did a double take. Did she know who he was? He didn't look like any famous person she'd been acquainted with. And if he were a local sports star, she would have zero chance of picking him out of a lineup. It didn't help that she'd been in a pit of depression and avoidance for the past year, so even if he was someone she *should* know, like an Olympic medal winner or something, she'd never be able to tell.

"Uh, should I?" She glanced around the room. "Am I missing something? Do you know *me*?"

"I don't think so, Miss . . ." He trailed off, giving her room to fill in the blank.

"Williamson. I'm Hannah Williamson." She put out her hand.

"Nice to meet you, Miss Williamson." He shook her hand. It was warm and a little damp, like his palms had been sweating inside his pants pockets.

"Call me Hannah. And I'm sorry, but who are you?"

"I'm Pete Dawson."

"Dawson?" The name in the box of records, the blurry faces. It couldn't be a coincidence. She walked over to the wall of pictures and pointed to a black-and-white framed eight-by-ten of a woman wearing a wide collared dress with a blaze, hair cut neatly into a short, swept-back hairdo with a tight smile and what was likely fiery red lipstick, though it was hard to tell in the faded photograph. At the bottom was another one of those helpful plaques. This one read, *Shelby Dawson*.

"Any relation?"

"Yes. That's my great-aunt." He joined her again, more reserved but seemingly no longer worried that she was trying to mine information.

"So, Jeffery Dawson was your great-grandfather?" she asked, putting the pieces together, fingers twitching for her notebook. She was finally making connections between her random dotted clues.

"How do you know all these names?" he asked, watching her with interest.

"I'm a journalist, remember?"

"Yes, I've caught on to that." He laughed at her again like he found her endlessly entertaining. He kept doing that. "But *why* do you know all these names?"

"Because I'm writing a . . . a piece about this place. The hospital and school for . . ."

"Peter, there you are." An elderly woman being pushed in a wheelchair by a young, studious-looking female assistant stopped just outside the darkened lobby area. The woman in the chair had her silvery hair tied up in a French twist, and she wore an understated bluish-gray gown that covered her legs and threatened to catch up in the wheels of her chair.

"Auntie Bee, don't you look lovely," he said, all graciousness and charm. He leaned over to kiss her cheek, and she kissed his back.

"Oh, hush now. I'm far too old to be considered lovely." She brushed away the compliment as she wiped away a smear of red lipstick on his cheek as he stood up. "Carrie and I have been looking for you everywhere, haven't we?"

"Yes, ma'am," the young woman confirmed on cue, like a doll with her string pulled.

"I'm sorry, Auntie. Carrie." Hannah watched Peter Dawson's face, like he'd been doing with hers since she turned around and found him behind her. He loved his aunt; she was sure of that. His eyes were soft, and he didn't seem annoyed by her rebuke. It reminded Hannah of how it felt to talk to Mamaw when she softly explained the rules of her house when Hannah had first moved in, including the curfew she'd never even come close to breaking and the rules about "gentlemen callers"—also not an issue. But Peter's auntie Bee was not the same as Mamaw in some ways, it seemed. She might have some of the polished, demure mannerisms of a well-bred southern aristocrat, but she gave off the power vibe of a businesswoman who knew what she wanted.

"Jim Strickland is here. I gave him your introduction, but he wanted to see you for a few minutes before your speech. And Mark wants to go over some details with you—you know how Mark is . . . but your father swears by him."

"Mark is here?" he asked, looking at Carrie like they had some shared understanding about how terrible Mark was.

"Yes, and you'll keep your opinions to yourself for now, if you please. Both of you," Auntie Bee said, pointing with a knobby index finger at the two much younger figures, who towered above her but also seemed to bow to her demands.

"Yes, ma'am," they both said in unison, and Hannah couldn't stop a chuckle. Auntie Bee's head snapped to the sound of her snort.

She recognized the seated woman now, under the wrinkles of age and frailties of time and the polish of modern makeup and fashion.

"You're Shelby Dawson, aren't you?" she asked with a touch of awe, reaching into her bag for her notebook, her brain exceeding its capacity to hold all the new information. She would have to be older than Mamaw, which seemed impossible, but Hannah knew she was right.

"Peter, who is this woman?" she asked her nephew pointedly, not nearly as much like Mamaw as she'd thought. Not one friendly note, or any attempt at a pleasant greeting in her tone or stare. But Hannah had interviewed drug dealers and heads of state; she'd even shaken hands with a sitting president and had always hoped to one day ask the hard questions to the hardest people on the planet. Bee's aggressive question only made the strong, journalist part of Hannah further ignite those low flames.

"I'm Hannah Williamson, from the *Chicago Tribune*. I'm writing a story about—"

"Are you talking to the press without Mark present?" Auntie Bee asked Peter with a quaver of anger in her voice.

"No, no, it isn't what you think. Hannah isn't here to talk about the campaign . . ."

The campaign? Hannah squinted at Peter, and then back at his aunt. Dawson. She thought she remembered a Senator Jack Dawson having some buzz for a potential presidential bid. Any press about him inevitably mentioned his father's political pedigree as the governor of Tennessee at some point in an equally long career, but this Peter Dawson, closer to thirty than forty, was a new face to Hannah and must be part of his nepotistic staff.

"Of course she is, Peter. You are too naive for your own good." She gestured to Carrie. "Move me forward, child. And Peter, be a dear and turn on some lights in this room, would you?"

Peter flicked on the lights, and the room, which turned out to be something of a museum or gallery, illuminated. Hannah tried to take in as many of the displays as possible. It was a history of the Dawson family's charity, the one founded by Dr. Jeffery Dawson, the Safe Place. It was responsible for the Crippled Children's Hospital and School and the Home for the Incurables during the polio outbreak that ravaged children and young adults through the greater half of the twentieth century.

"What did you say your name was again? Let me see your credentials. I know Palmer at the *Tribune*. He should know better than this."

Shit. No. Maybe Maggie and the friendly receptionist she talked to at the Safe Place the day before wouldn't call her ID in, but Ms. Shelby Dawson wouldn't hesitate. And if she were talking about Tom Palmer, the editor in chief of the newspaper, it wouldn't take much for him to share the truth about Hannah's breakdown and crash at the paper. Not to mention that using her outdated ID was technically fraud. She rushed to clarify her motives.

"Ms. Dawson, I'm here because I have questions about the Crippled Children's Hospital and School that was housed in this facility starting in 1919. I promise, I have no interest in your nephew or your gala—"

Ms. Dawson interrupted. "No interest in my great-nephew, huh? Do you buy that, Carrie?"

"No, ma'am," the young woman answered immediately, and Hannah couldn't help but glare for half a second, before addressing Mr. Dawson again.

"I swear. I don't even know anything about—sorry, what was your name again? Peter?" Hannah bluffed forgetfulness, trying to drive her point home.

"I guess I'm pretty forgettable, Auntie. Better tell Mark. Could be an issue with the constituents." It irked Hannah that he wasn't taking any of this seriously.

"Honestly, Ms. Dawson, I didn't even know this event was going on tonight. I was just down the road at the University of Memphis doing some research on an old story my grandmother told me, and while I was in town, I found this address, and I thought that I'd take a look at the hospital, ask a few questions, maybe look through old patient files. I'm looking for a woman who was a patient here in the 1930s. All I have is her first name . . . Evelyn—"

"I'm sorry. Patient files are sealed. Now, Peter, we must go." Shelby Dawson gestured for her assistant to move her chair toward the lobby.

Hannah, panicking at losing this opportunity now that one of her leads had finally paid off, followed close behind. "But surely this long after a patient's passing . . ."

"Sealed means sealed, Ms. Williamson." Shelby waved her off, and Peter Dawson sighed. His jovial nature became serious, like when he'd had the same suspicions about her intentions as his aunt. But this time, his displeasure was focused in a different direction.

"Auntie," he said, thoughtfully, following at a more measured pace than Hannah, "a story about the hospital could be beneficial in the long run, don't you think? For our family. For . . . the campaign. I mean, the hospital is in district."

Ms. Shelby Dawson, nearly as ancient as the walls that surrounded them, held up her hand, bringing the wheelchair to a halt. She considered his words and with trembling hands retrieved a small silver compact from her pocket and a tube of ruby-red lipstick. She applied it correctly despite the movement in her extremities. As she rubbed her lips together and returned the items to her pocket, she stared at Hannah like her glare was as effective as a lie detector. Speaking to Peter, Ms. Dawson never took her eyes off the perceived intruder.

"Peter, if you are so invested in this supposed story, have Ms. Williamson contact my office with her official information. We will confirm her identity and get her any other information or historical documents pertinent to the hospital. But no patient records. Understood?"

Peter smiled at Hannah like he'd won her a stuffed animal as a prize at the fair, not knowing that her offer was no good to Hannah. She needed patient records—specifically one patient's records. Besides, the need to confirm her identity was a requirement that would keep Hannah at arm's length from the truth.

"Yes, ma'am," Hannah said, crossing her hands in front of her body with her notebook clasped behind them, trying to look humble and resigned.

"Good. Now Peter, we shouldn't keep the mayor waiting," Ms. Dawson called and gestured in the direction of the door the partygoers had disappeared through. Carrie rolled her toward the room. Peter hesitated.

"Beg your pardon, Auntie, but can I have one additional moment with Miss Williamson?"

She stared at him and then snuck a glance at Hannah, looking her up and down with a sour expression on her face, like she couldn't see what a man might see in her. But then she sighed and muttered something about *men* before signaling to Carrie silently.

"Thank you, Auntie," he called out after her.

"Don't forget to turn off the lights in the museum, Peter."

"Yes, Auntie . . ."

When she was far enough away to not be able to see, Peter rolled his eyes playfully at Hannah, like badass Shelby Dawson was an adorable toddler, but Hannah was grateful he asked to stay behind. She had so many questions. She'd known the Dawson name had seemed familiar, but she hadn't expected to stumble into a political dynasty.

"So, you're a part of this family—the Dawsons?"

"Yup, born and raised," he said, falling in step with Hannah.

"So, wait—your dad is Jack Dawson? Like, Senator Jack Dawson?"

He ran a hand through his hair, bobbing his head. "Yes, ma'am. He is."

"Like, four-term senator, presidential hopeful Jack Dawson?" Hannah asked, not sure if she should be suspicious, intimidated, or reluctantly charmed.

"Uh-huh. You really didn't know about this event, about me, did you?" he asked, like he found the idea novel, compelling. He cracked the peppermint in his mouth between his molars, close enough that the calming scent was reaching her nose with each breath. She forced herself to stay focused.

"No idea."

"Hmm, well . . . that's interesting," he said, as they stopped by the door she'd entered not even half an hour earlier. He was watching her closely, like he wanted to memorize every reaction. It couldn't have been easy to grow up in the shadow of his father and his grandfather, to have the pressure of a political pedigree.

"So this is an event for him—the senator."

"I love how everyone calls him *the senator* like he's the only one who exists," Peter mused in passing as he rummaged through the inside pocket of his tuxedo jacket. "Here." He presented her with a business card, held between his pointer and middle fingers. Hannah took it and read the raised black letters on the front. The Tennessee state seal in gold was in the upper left-hand corner. It read:

PETER J. DAWSON
STATE SENATOR
DISTRICT 30

"Wait . . . so . . . this is . . . ," she stuttered, putting the pieces together. Peter, son of Jack Dawson, grandson of Fred Dawson, was in the family business. This wasn't Jack's party to raise money for his presidential candidacy, after all.

Peter cut in, confirming Hannah's suspicions.

"This is my fundraiser."

CHAPTER 13

"Back already?" the valet manager asked as Hannah walked out the front door of the Pines. It likely wasn't hard to remember the only person that night who'd dressed like a college student, driving a rattling Buick. The crew of three young men in vests who had witnessed Hannah's unfortunate arrival stood watching in the background.

Hannah's cheeks burned. She held out her valet ticket.

"Mike, make sure Miss Williamson gets reunited with her car, will ya?" Peter said from where he was standing behind Hannah, holding the door open with an extended arm.

"Yes, sir," he replied and took Hannah's ticket as one of the men ran off with her keys to retrieve her car.

"Thanks," she said, somewhat reluctantly, standing on the front porch, still not sure how to process everything that had happened inside and the usefulness of her new connection. He kept the door open, and the mix of stuffy indoor air with the crisp, chill fall sent a shiver through her.

"No worries, Miss Williamson. But I . . . I'm afraid I must go now. I feel sure that I've pushed Bee past her boiling point, and if I throw off the whole schedule, she might never forgive me." His accent deepened, and she wasn't sure if he'd been holding it back when they were in the museum or if he was coating it on with a broad stroke now because he knew how lovely his words sounded swathed in it.

"Of course! I'm fine." She waved him off, getting tired of southern men trying to take care of her. "I'll find my way home like the grown woman I am."

"Oh, I had no worries about that," he said in a hushed tone, like he was sharing a secret, his smile turning up one corner of his mouth in a way that made a dimple pop. "I'm just wonderin', are you sure you can't stay?" His body leaned toward hers like when sunflowers turned toward the sun. Part of her wished she could stay and watch his speech and have a cocktail. But it was getting late, and if she didn't hurry, she wouldn't make it home in time for Mamaw's bedtime routine, and she was sure to be exhausted from her day out and about.

Plus, she shouldn't push her luck any further than she already had. She had his card in her back pocket, and she'd given him a Post-it with her name and number, deciding that it was better to keep any phone number leading to the actual *Chicago Tribune* out of Peter's, or his aunt Bee's, hands.

"I'm sorry, I need to get back. Besides, I don't want to cause any issues with your 'auntie,'" she teased, her body drawing toward Peter's like a magnet, unwillingly, centimeters at a time.

He stared down at her, and Hannah expected one last attempt to charm her into staying, but instead he said, "I understand" and nodded at Mike. "I look forward to next time, Miss Williamson."

"Yes. Next time," Hannah echoed. Then, with a semi-bow, he backed away into the building, his final farewell getting lost in the swoosh of the door.

Wanting to tip the valet, Hannah handed off a clutch of folded dollar bills that she thankfully had stashed in some small corner pocket of her bag. She'd intended to use the money on vending-machine snacks or coffee, but her day had been too busy to find time for either, and her stomach ached as a result. The car's interior was warm and stuffy, reminding her of Mamaw's house, which only made her want to get to the safety of that world even faster. The car lurched away from the grand brick structure of the Pines, leaving behind all the fancy people and cars, the trees and floors made up of shimmering stars, and most of all—Senator Peter Dawson.

In the dark, Highway 51 was lined with reflective dashes in the middle of the road and dotted with occasional blasts of bright lights as she chugged through small town after small town. After seeing the modern version of what might have been Evelyn's post-shooting life, Hannah started to make a mental list of the next steps in her research. First on the list: get a new phone. How did anyone get anything done without those damn things?

"Oh my God," Hannah murmured, pressing harder on the gas pedal, counting the hours since she'd entered the library. She hadn't even thought of Alex one time. What the . . .

A loud whine rang in Hannah's ears. The car slowed, and Hannah guided it to the side of the highway and into what looked like an abandoned parking lot made of gravel and broken asphalt. As she rolled onto the uneven surface, the gas pedal lost its effectiveness, the engine cut out, and a burning rubber smell filled the car.

"Damn it," Hannah cursed, slamming her hand against the steering wheel. As the car went completely dead, barely responding to any of her efforts at starting the engine, the pitch-black of the road seemed to flood the car like water rising around her. Panic rushed in as well, making her ears ring to the same note as the whining of the car before it died.

She glanced around the interior of the vehicle. If she hadn't known better, it was almost like being tossed back in time—no GPS, no cell phone, and no OnStar. The only thing she had in Mamaw's Buick that didn't exist in modern dashboards was a cigarette lighter. So, if push came to shove, she could build a little fire on the side of the road and live there. She rolled her eyes at her joke.

She had to face facts. The last town was at least five miles back and over a series of bridges through a marsh that looked like it went on for miles. Unfamiliar with this road, she had no idea how close the next town was. It couldn't be too far, but in the dark and without knowing her location, trying to walk would be a considerable risk.

She glanced at her watch. It was only a few minutes past seven. She was about half an hour into her hour-long trip home and would've made it back to Senatobia before her 8:00 p.m. deadline, but the bad news with being on time was that no one would miss her there for an hour or even two, given her history of running late.

Hannah gathered her jacket around her. She could wait for a car to pass by; a Good Samaritan might offer her help. Then again, the car was a good ten feet from the road, so she'd have to flag someone down by the side of the highway. In Chicago, where she'd grown up, the idea of a single woman waving down a stranger in the forbidding night sounded more like the beginning of a nightly news story than a viable plan.

Irritated that she'd gone on an adventure without putting any contingency plan in place, she started digging through the car. Hannah popped open the glove compartment, where the original manual sat undisturbed, and spotted a folded map.

"Thank God." She sighed. Her shoulders couldn't relax, but at least the map would give her something to focus on other than the disturbing headlines that could result from this night. She rapidly unfolded the forty-five-year-old pamphlet and smoothed it out on the seat next to her, working on remembering how to read basic cartography.

"There is Memphis," she muttered, using the dim dome light to get a good look at the lines and words on the page. The overall road systems were different back then, but she was able to find most of the major landmarks. There was US 51, trailing right along next to I-55, in some places so close that the two red lines seemed to touch.

As she looked closer, she found the marshland she'd just crossed through. According to the poster-size map, there was another town not too far off from where she approximated she was stranded. There was no way to know for sure how far the city might be, but surely there was more development along this road now than in the seventies. She'd have to risk it.

After folding the map and returning it to the glove compartment, Hannah tore a page out of her notebook and scribbled a quick note with her name and her grandmother's name and phone number and included a date and time at the last minute. She put the note under the windshield wiper and locked the car, taking her bag with her after a somewhat lengthy internal debate about whether it would be safer for her research to sit in an abandoned car or risk being lost forever in the case of her incredibly unlikely abduction. She'd definitely watched too many true-crime shows.

"Gone . . . without a trace . . . ," she mumbled as her feet hit the dusty shoulder alongside the road. "*Terror in Tate County.*" She continued brainstorming the title of her mystery news program.

A pickup truck rushed past her on the highway, and Hannah swerved into the grass, overwhelmed by the power of the large vehicle's wake. It was chilly out but not cold, at least not to a northerner. She could see her breath as it clouded in front of her face with each puff, but her skin didn't sting and the wind didn't cut through her jacket. She counted herself lucky to be stranded in Mississippi, where it was cool enough in November to kill off the mosquitos and yet warm enough to not worry about frostbite.

"*November Nightmare,*" she added to her list, holding on to her sarcasm as the only antidote to the lonesome fear inside her midsection.

She'd felt alone a lot in the past year, and this anxious, dangling feeling reminded her of the isolation of depression after her father's death and Alex's betrayal. Both events made her feel like there was no one in the world she could lean on. Both left her feeling like she had limited options and none that she really wanted to take. Both reminded her that, in the end, she was the only one she could always count on.

"*Lost on the Trail to . . . Murder.* Oh, that one is good," she muttered. If there was a job that included naming episodes of crime TV programs, she should apply for it. She chuckled, jumping back in the grass after another car sped past her.

Sure, she felt alone again and kind of freaked out, but at least now she had a growing faith in her ability to take care of herself that would make Laura proud. Even just a few months ago, Hannah would've curled up in the back seat of that car and let the world go by without her. Every step she took in her thrift store Doc Martens was a sign of her growing strength.

Several minutes later, after exhausting all possible news program titles and just as she was seriously considering flagging down one of the drivers on the road to ask to use their phone, the top of a red sign glowed in the distance. Her pulse quickened, and she smiled as she picked up the pace. She couldn't help continuing the ironic narration in her head. *She thought she had found safety, but what she found at the gas station could fuel nightmares . . .*

The fear was still there. The loneliness was ever present. But she was making it.

CHAPTER 14

When Hannah heard Mamaw's sweet voice through the receiver of the gas station phone, she almost cried.

"Oh, sweetheart. I'm so sorry. I just knew I should've taken the car in for a tune-up. Your papaw was always so good about that, and then Sammy . . . I've been so forgetful. I'll never forgive myself."

"Mamaw, I'm fine! Please don't worry. I just don't have my phone, so I can't order an Uber. If you could call my mom, she could order me one. Or have her call me here."

Frank, the owner of the store, whom she'd just met and tried to sweet-talk awkwardly, stared at her with a judgmental glare. He'd told her she could use the phone as long as it was local, which made Hannah want to roll her eyes and explain that "long distance" wasn't a thing anymore. Instead, she punched in Mamaw's Mississippi area code so the man wouldn't kick her out.

"I don't know what that is, sweetheart. The oo-per?"

"We talked about it last night at dinner. The car service? Just tell my mom to send me an Uber," Hannah spelled out *U-B-E-R* and continued with an address for the gas station, slightly concerned Mamaw had forgotten so quickly. "I'll be waiting. If you have any trouble, you can call me here."

She mumbled the last bit into the receiver since she was sure Frank wouldn't enjoy getting random calls at his store, but there were few options left. When Hannah hung up, she added a cup of coffee, a questionable-looking ham sandwich, a bag of chips, a bottle of water, and a few candy bars to the counter and smiled as she ran her credit card to pay for the overpriced items.

"Do you need a bag?" he asked, scratching at a spot under his faded trucker hat, sucking back the juices from the chew tucked in his bottom lip.

"No. No, thank you, sir," she said, scooping up the items from the counter in her arms and carrying her lukewarm coffee cup. She sat at the only table and chairs set up in the "deli" area of the gas station.

Before she unwrapped her sandwich, she angled her chair so she could see both Frank and out the front window, where her ride would eventually show up. Finally settled, she took a long sip of her coffee, which was thick, stale, and low quality but would do for now. The sandwich, on the other hand, was made on soggy white bread that had all but fused with the slice of American cheese lying on top of the graying ham.

She dropped the poor excuse for food and cleaned her fingertips on the napkin included in the package. Forget healthy. The Snickers bar was meant for two people but would be Hannah's one meal of the day. It didn't bother her that much. She'd lived off caffeine and vending-machine food for much of her career at the *Tribune*, so this wasn't exactly new. It paired with her crazy day nicely.

With a few minutes to herself, Hannah took a bite of the candy bar and dug out a few items from her satchel to keep her occupied. First, she opened the baggie with the dry rice and her phone and unzipped it for the first time since she'd left the house that morning. First attempt all day. She couldn't decide if this new shift in focus was a positive or a negative, but it was at least movement, which was a change. Even with a long reset push-and-hold of the power button, the device remained lifeless in her hands. She needed to call time of death. This phone was never coming back.

After giving up on playing tech wizard, Hannah selected one of the labeled files she'd retrieved and opened to the first page inside. She'd reread all the letters over and over again, but this one kept running through her mind today, especially after her charged exchange with the handsome Peter Dawson. This letter told the full story of Evelyn's blossoming relationship with Harry and the havoc it brought into her home life. Adult Evelyn, who was writing the letter many years after her young heart had been swept away by the young man, who was only meant to be in town for the weekend as part of a traveling rodeo, seemed to have a mature outlook on the romantic interlude. But Hannah could see why Evelyn found Harry so exotic, so dreamy. She'd loved Alex in the instant way Evelyn did with Harry, even if he was just a premed student the first time they were assigned as partners in their speech class. Alex wasn't as much of a charmer, and Hannah was more shy and unsure of herself, but the frightening vulnerability of first love was relatable. Still, she could also see how quickly that kind of intense, immature love could turn dangerous, maybe deadly, even?

September 14, 1935

Dear Mr. Martin,

Harry Westbrook was only in town for the weekend of May 11, and little child that I was, I was desperate to see him again. I'd never before felt anything as wonderful as his arms around me, holding me while I shivered. I didn't shiver long, but I have to admit, I pretended to be as cold as an Eskimo in December so that he'd keep his arm around me as we walked back to the fair.

I found out as we walked that Harry Westbrook was a cowpuncher for the Dakota Max rodeo and had been traveling with them since he was sixteen. Nearly twenty, he said he was growing tired of mucking stalls and wrangling horses. I could see something in his eyes that looked like longing for a home of his own, just like I wanted. I could tell he liked me. It wasn't just the way his fingers held me tight around my waist, and he leaned in to smell my hair as it dried, but it was also the way he laughed at my gumption and how I stood up to Lucy and her crew.

"The girls I grew up with would never have been brave enough to do all that," he said, his voice so smooth and calm, like he was talking to one of his wild horses.

"I really shouldn't have done it either. My mother will throw a fit," I said, truly frightened of Mother but also wanting Harry to think my home and family were normal.

But then Myrtle added from behind us, "She's gonna whip you this time. I know she is."

"Oh hush, Myrtle," I said, trying to calm her before she ruined the magic between Harry and me, but it was too late. He stopped me in my tracks and turned me to look him in the eye again. I liked facing him this way, his breath warm on my cheek and nowhere to look but into his turquoise eyes.

"Does your momma whup you?" he asked me, all serious like. Like he was some knight in shining armor who would come protect me if I was in danger. He was a stranger, and we all knew it, but I liked feeling powerful enough to make a man want to take care of me. It was funny what a pretty smile and a nice figure could do to a fella.

"She's not our momma," Myrtle cut in again, and I gave her a hard look that made her wither almost as quickly as a glare from Mother could.

"She's our stepmother, and she doesn't whup us. She disciplines us for our own good." Even as I said it, I hated myself for lying. But I also knew that if a man knew you were from a bad family, he'd lose interest, and I would give anything to have Harry Westbrook stay interested in me at least a little longer.

"I don't like that," he said, with a far-off look in his eyes. We started walking again but had to part ways when we got back to the fairgrounds and a

tall man wearing chaps and a cowboy hat
yelled at Harry for slacking off.

Harry asked my name, and if he could
write to me, so I scribbled my address
on the back of an empty popcorn bag.

I didn't think I'd ever see Harry
again. As I drifted off to sleep after
sneaking my still-damp dress past
Mother, who was busy making bread in
the kitchen when we got home, I dreamed
of that boy. I dreamed of his eyes, a
home of my own, and a world where someone stronger than Mother would stand
up for me.

That desperation to feel loved touched a little too close to home
and too close to Laura's assessment of Hannah's own relationship, but it
was hard to blame the girl for wanting more. For wanting to be loved.
It was hard not to cheer for her.

I was beyond surprised the next
afternoon. Just as I was returning
the cold chicken to the icebox after
lunch, Harry Westbrook himself knocked
on the front door. Mother answered,
Daddy asleep in the wingback chair in
the front room for his afternoon nap.
She had her church voice on, all sweet
sounding and nice. Harry asked for me,
just like it was normal for a man to
knock on my door and ask, "Is Evelyn
here?"

"And who might you be?" Mother's "charitable soul" disappeared like the holy ghost in a whorehouse, and I knew I'd better find that horsewhip and hide it good.

Harry kept a cool head and asked if he could have permission to talk to me. I didn't hear the whole conversation, but my heart was beating around inside my chest like the time that sick raccoon got stuck under the house and went wild. I didn't know if I wanted to cry from joy or if I wanted to die from it so I wouldn't have to face Mother.

A few minutes later, she called my name with some level of politeness and let me talk to Harry on the front porch. She left the door open, and I knew she must be listening by the screen, but I didn't care. He told me that he was supposed to leave town in the morning, but that he couldn't stop thinking about me. It was the first time I'd heard a boy say out loud that he was sweet on me.

He touched my hand ever so lightly, and it made my heart stop feeling wild, and instead, it felt like it was melting, filling my chest with a warm, bubbly, glowing liquid like carbonite sunshine. I wanted that scrumptious feeling to last forever. But Mother cleared her throat inside the house, and Daddy's snore slipped out from one of the open windows, and I knew that burst of light was just the clouds parting momentarily on a cold, stormy day.

Harry asked if I could come to the fair again that night. I knew it was impossible and I said so, taking my hand away from his. He all but begged me, saying he hadn't slept or eaten since meeting me.

"Meet me by the cotton candy at ten, won't ya? Just to say goodbye," he begged, whispering so softly I was sure Mother couldn't hear.

"I can't," I said again, turning away so he couldn't see that I had tears in my eyes. I wanted to go. I wanted it more than air. But even though there were no bars or chains, I was in as much of a prison as Al Capone.

Mother stepped onto the porch, grim and silent in her gray dress and with clasped hands. Harry, giving me one last pleading look, said his farewells, placed the cap he'd been clutching in his nervous grip back on his head, and took off down the road that led to Main Street.

I wanted to run after him and beg him to take me with him and his rodeo.

I knew how to work and clean, and I'd even muck stalls like a farmhand. Mother put a firm hand on my forearm like she could read my thoughts.

"Did you let that boy touch you?" she asked, as she watched him turn the corner out of sight. I thought about him saving me from the river, holding me in his arms, keeping me warm, grazing my hand on the porch—

"No, ma'am" was the only answer I could possibly give. She whipped me around in front of her, twisting my arm till it felt like it might snap.

"If you ever speak to that . . . cowpuncher . . . again, I will . . ."

"Whip me?" I said with just as much sass as when I'd shown up Lucy at the gap. Mother's eyes widened. I winced as she dug her nails into my skin till I wanted to cry, but I didn't look away. She dropped my arm. I rubbed it, wondering how long it would be till she broke something inside of me that she couldn't hide.

Or shot her? Hannah pondered. Mother or Harry—those were her two suspects. Her father was too ill. Her sister loved her. Not enough mention of the stepsister. As far as Hannah could see, it was one of the two.

"No. I'll send you to the Convent of the Good Shepherd."

The force of that threat was harsher than any whupping. We'd all seen beautiful, vibrant Francine May, a cheerleader and the head of every social club in the senior high, be sent away to the home for wayward girls last spring and come back a frail, pious, broken thing who could barely hold a steady hand to sew a straight line, much less find a man to marry. To be sent away, just like my brother and my little sister. To leave Myrtle all alone. Leave Daddy all sick and eating whatever it was his wife put in his food.

I held my rebellious tongue and followed Mother's every instruction, pretending that my arm didn't ache. I willingly walked back inside my prison cell. I'd had my dose of sunshine. I thought it could keep me warm enough.

But then Harry Westbrook left the rodeo and moved in with some friends down the street. He'd walk past my house every day on his way to and from work at the railroad station. He'd smile and say hello. And soon, there were few places I could go in town without hearing him whistling some tune, coming down the street in the opposite direction.

I'd heard the preacher talk about temptation my whole life, but I never really understood until then. It doesn't look like a fast-talking snake or some fancy fruit seduction. No—temptation looks a lot like happiness, and I wanted it more than just about anything in this world, and I thought Harry Westbrook wanted to give it to me. But Mother was determined to stop that from happening—no matter the cost.

The bell on the door to the convenience store rang, bringing Hannah back to the present. A young woman carrying a baby on her hip paid for her gas with some crisp bills as the little boy innocently grabbed for the rack of lighters just out of reach.

Temptation, Hannah thought ruefully, completely understanding Evelyn's internal conflict.

She checked her watch. It had been longer than she'd thought. Rather than going through more of her research, it was probably best to pack up her belongings. If the car service wasn't there to pick her up in the next ten minutes or so, she'd need to beg Frank to make another call.

"Well, there you are," said a familiar voice coming from a tall figure casting a long shadow over her spot at the table. She scrunched her eyelids and held back a curse word. Of course Mamaw wouldn't call a stranger to come retrieve her stranded granddaughter. She'd call someone she knew and trusted and likely had on speed dial.

"Hello, Guy," Hannah said without looking up, the embarrassment from their first meeting resurfacing. She didn't need to see him. His accent would've been enough, but his outfit was nearly identical to the one he'd been wearing the first time they met. His somewhat dressy gray shoes with matching laces, the straight-leg, medium-blue jeans and tan belt with an almost-too-tight white T-shirt and an unbuttoned collared shirt with rolled-up sleeves all made it look like he'd picked his outfit out of a "hot handyman" catalog somewhere. For some reason, Mamaw seemed determined to make Guy her granddaughter's knight in shining armor. With an excruciatingly meddling mother, Hannah half wondered if it was a matchmaking attempt, but Mamaw had never seemed the type to meddle.

"Your grandmother—"

"I know. Mamaw sent you." Hannah cut him off, not meaning to be rude, but at the same time not daring to make eye contact. Why Guy Franklin was destined to be a witness to all the most embarrassing moments in her recent life, Hannah had no idea.

"Yes, ma'am. Said you'd had some car troubles. Asked if I'd give you a ride home. I said I'd be honored to help as long as you didn't run away this time. You don't have a bike here, do you?" he asked, acting like he was searching the inside of the market for a wayward bicycle.

Hannah ignored his teasing and stood up with her hands full of empty snack wrappers. "I asked her to get an Uber." She tossed the garbage and chugged the last bit of her lukewarm coffee without gagging.

"Oh, gracious, an Uber? That's what she was sayin'? Well, guess you'll have to settle for the next best thing, huh?" He smiled big, like the eight-year-old Cub Scout who won the pinewood derby she covered a few weeks ago.

She'd felt smart and vivacious when she was standing in the shadows bantering with Senator Peter Dawson, but here in the Gas Depot with Guy Franklin, Hannah felt like a bumbling idiot. But why? Peter was a well-traveled, experienced politician with a deadly wit. Shouldn't he be more intimidating than the overly polite carpenter from a small Mississippi town? She had no idea what it was about Guy that made her feel so out of sorts. He looked at her like he knew her, like he had a story in his head about little Hannah Williamson and he found it funny.

It left her feeling vulnerable, like a snail without a shell, far too easy to dissolve with a dash of salt.

She threw her empty-enough coffee cup in the garbage and then retrieved her full bag from the chair. Her breath was stale, and she didn't dare look at her reflection in the window, especially in contrast with the ruggedly handsome and just-put-together-enough Guy.

"Ready," she said, limiting the number of words she spoke.

"All right, then. Let's get this show on the road. Thank you, Frank!" Guy waved at the surly man behind the counter.

"Have a good night," Frank said and waved back like they were old friends. Was this man pals with everyone in Mississippi?

"Do you know him?" Hannah asked, stumbling after Guy as they left through the swinging front door of the convenience mart.

"Just about everybody around here knows old Frank. His family has run this place since the first car drove down 51." Guy dug in his pocket for his keys.

"Well, good ole Frank looked at me like I was trying to rob the place." Hannah followed him through the brightly lit parking lot of the gas station, looking for his truck but only spotting a compact car parked under a yellow streetlight.

"He doesn't always take to strangers well. But Frank's come a long way. Back when he was just a kid, this used to be a whites-only establishment. Let's just say that Frank's family was . . . reluctant to make changes."

"Oh my God, seriously?" she said, glaring at the convenience store. "Why would *you* still go there?"

"Why, 'cause I'm Black?" he said matter-of-factly and stopped by a silver Honda Civic. He hit the button that automatically unlocked the doors, making the lights flash and horn chirp. Hannah couldn't read his tone. Rarely, if ever, did southerners of any race bring up the topic of racism.

"No," Hannah squeaked, stuttering and trying to correct herself as quickly as possible, her neck and cheeks burning. She felt outraged as a human being, but she didn't know how to communicate that, unsure what would sound offensive coming from a white woman who hadn't been raised in Mississippi. "I mean . . . it should bother everyone . . ."

"As a Black man, of course it bothers me. But"—Guy skirted around her to open the passenger-side door with an extended arm—"if I didn't go places because of people's families' spotted pasts, I'd go nowhere." He gestured for her to get into the car and stepped away, crossing in front of the vehicle as Hannah responded.

"I get that, but shouldn't there be some . . . some consequence?"

"I'd like to think so, and there are plenty of places I won't give my business, but Frank's different than his daddy," Guy said thoughtfully, standing inside his opened door, leaning against the top of the roof, pausing like he was thinking. He tapped the roof with his keys and then pointed at Hannah. "He's made real changes since he took over. My daddy taught me to judge a man based on his actions, not his family. I think you'd be on my side with this one, anyway. I mean, I'm wonderin' if you've ever visited the Williamson plantation." He cocked his head, winked, and disappeared into the car, leaving the implications of his sentence to hang in the air.

A hot poker blazed through her conscience. She wanted to be different from her ancestors, better. She wanted to carry on the new path her father had forged by teaching his children to think and live differently than other Williamsons had. But Guy was correct: everyone had a past. She didn't fully know the right answers anymore.

But what she did know was that she was officially out of control when it came to conversations with this man. He had a way of twisting every word she said into something she didn't mean merely by using polite charm, a straight smile, and an electric wit as his tools of manipulation.

"No, you're right," she said, as she ducked into the car herself. "My family has its own Confederate skeletons in the closet—"

"And I still talk to you, don't I?" he cut in, starting the car.

"Unfortunately," she said, returning his slightly playful sarcastic tone, closing the door. "I'm kidding. But my father didn't try to hide that fact from us. It's nothing I'm proud of, but it's different actually being here. I know racism is everywhere. It's just crazy knowing it was so proudly displayed not that long ago."

"You found her!" a young female voice called out from the darkened back seat before Guy could respond to Hannah's contribution in the surprisingly deep discussion.

"Oh my God!" Hannah gasped, turning around with her hands up like she was about to be mugged. A petite girl dressed in a soccer uniform sat with an iPad on her lap. Eleven or twelve, maybe a little younger—Hannah wasn't very experienced at estimating a kid's age, so it was only a guess.

"Rosie, you're going to scare the poor woman to death," Guy chided gently, talking through the rearview mirror as he pulled out of the parking spot.

"I'm sorry!" she said, singsong, making her sound on the younger side of Hannah's age-guessing spectrum.

Hannah's heart was pounding faster than a hummingbird's wings. If she'd thought she was at a loss for words when talking to Guy, she was three times as confused by the kid in the back of the car. She glanced between the two figures, one focused on the road and the other entirely focused on Hannah's face.

"Are you all right?" Guy asked quietly, checking on Hannah before turning onto the highway.

"I think so," she responded, her nerves still rattled by her walk in the dark. *Walk in the Dark. Yup. Another good one.*

"Miss Williamson is doin' just fine, baby," Guy called into the back seat.

"Uh, Hannah. You guys can call me Hannah," Hannah said, addressing both the grown-up in the front seat and the miniature human in the back. "And you are . . . Rosie?"

The girl sat up as tall as her over-the-shoulder belt would allow and smiled. "Yes, ma'am. And I heard you are a reporter from Chicago and that you write stories for the *Record* and that Miss Mable is your grammy and—"

"Whoa, Rosie, where did you get my bio?"

"My daddy told me," Rosie said, clearly proud of her daddy and his vast knowledge of Hannah's personal and professional life.

"Your daddy?" Hannah questioned, looking at Guy with a raised eyebrow. He couldn't be more than thirty. She'd thought Rosie could be a niece or a cousin, but his kid?

"I may have slipped her a few details on the way over here," he joked.

"I was surprised he could tell me much of anything with how fast he was drivin'," Rosie teased her father, and Guy flinched.

"Oh, hush now," he said. "I wasn't goin' that fast." Rosie coughed. "All right, a little fast, but your grandma was very upset on the phone."

Hannah paused, her emotions swelling unexpectedly. She turned her body toward Guy, grateful despite herself.

"Thank you for helping her," she said, pushing through the warning bells in her body telling her to stop being nice.

"Your grandmother is a gem and has been close to our family for years. I appreciate any opportunity to help Miss Mable."

"Which is also very helpful to me, it turns out," she said, her own way of saying thank you for herself, which was even harder than the praise for helping Mamaw.

"Ha. I guess so," he said, glancing at her from the corner of his eye while keeping most of his focus on the road.

Hannah wanted to change the subject, feeling a little sick, either from the car or from opening herself up ever so slightly. "So, this is your daughter, then?"

"Yes, ma'am. I've been her dad for going on—what is it, 12.5 years, Miss Rosie?"

Twelve and a half years. Hannah did some mental math. Even if Guy were thirty, that'd mean Rosie had been born when he was still in high school. She'd thought about the concept of having children one day, but it was surprising to see someone her age with a child who was approaching her teens. At thirty-one her biological clock was starting to tick louder every day, which only added to her anxieties about the future.

"You know how old I am, Daddy. Don't let him fool you, Hannah."

"Miss Williamson," Guy corrected.

"Oh no, I told you—I prefer Hannah," she corrected. The only time she was called Miss Williamson before moving south was in the official letter she got relieving her of her position at the *Tribune* after Tom had broken the news on the phone a few days earlier. And then again, when the doctor came into her hospital room and told her she couldn't go home and would be put on a seventy-two-hour hold. She'd rather be Hannah.

"I'm sorry, I'm sure it is fine with you, but I think Rosie should show some respect for her elders. So, for now, if you don't mind, I think she should go on calling you Miss Williamson," he said, patting the wheel as he made his point.

"*Elders?* God, how old do you think I am?" Hannah scoffed, not sure if she should be insulted by the term.

"Some things are a little different round here. I'm sure it would be the same way if we visited y'all in Chicago. As I see it, there's no harm in respect, is there?" he said it like it was a casual, well-known thought. Hannah understood, especially after living with Mamaw and working at the *Record*, and she knew that little nurse Nancy would likely swoon at Guy's parenting style.

"That's fine," Hannah said, because ultimately it wasn't any of her business. Painfully bad at starting up small talk, she looked out the window during the lull in conversation, watching the murky patches of forest with occasional houses set far back from the road blur by. An awkward silence filled the car. When Rosie broke it, Hannah was almost grateful to hear her name.

"Miss Williamson?"

"Yes, Rosie?"

"What story are you working on? Miss Mable said you were writing a story and doing research up in the city and—"

"Rosie Mae, how did you hear any of that?" Guy asked over his shoulder, interrupting.

Rosie hesitated and then answered bashfully, "Your phone is turned up pretty loudly."

"You can hear my calls, and you never told me?"

"Maybe . . ."

Guy laughed at himself. "Well, dang it, no wonder you know my schedule better than I do."

"Sorry, Daddy. I can't help but listen. It's just so loud."

Hannah snickered, and Guy gave her a questioning look.

"What's so funny, Miss Williamson?" he asked, not at all perturbed. More like they were sharing some inside joke.

"Who's the elder now? Damn, Franklin. How loud IS your phone?"

Rosie let out a loud HA, followed by a trill of giggles.

"Hey now. When I'm working construction, I have to keep it loud, or else I can't hear a word. I guess I never thought of changing it. But I don't think it's nearly as funny as you two do," Guy explained, looking back and forth between Hannah, Rosie, and the road.

"It gets funnier the more you try to explain it," Hannah said, getting far too much satisfaction out of the exchange.

"How about you answer Rosie's question instead of riling up the guy who is giving you a ride home. Unless you want me to take you back to the Gas Depot to wait for that phantom Uber that was never going to show up."

"Oh my God, I think that was a threat. Rosie, did you hear that? Your father just threatened to abandon me on the side of the road. I am shocked. Completely shocked. I think someone as elderly as your father should be able to provide a better example for his daughter. Am I right, Rosie?"

"She's right, Daddy. That wasn't very nice," Rosie added, with an air of forced seriousness.

"Look at you coming between a man and his daughter. It's downright unnatural."

"Hey, you were the one with all the threats. I'm just an innocent little passenger." Hannah put up her hands and batted her eyes, even if no one could see it in the dimly lit cabin of the car.

"Innocent, my eye. You're a rabble-rouser."

"Did you just call your daughter a *rabble*? Rosie, I'd be offended if I were you," Hannah called out behind her and heard a giggle in response.

"Oh, hush, don't you go brainwashing my child with your 'Yankee ways.'" Guy put on an exaggerated, overly proper accent that was almost too spot-on.

"You don't even know how accurate that is," Hannah said, a real smile on her face, feeling a fleeting sense of belonging that was as uncomfortable as it was pleasurable. She sat back in her seat, letting the strap hold her. She'd let herself go for a second there, allowed herself out of the carefully constructed shell she hid inside, and she wasn't sure how she felt about it just yet.

"So, are you going to keep us in suspense? What story does Mr. Martin have you working on that has you driving your Mamaw's piece of junk into Memphis on a Saturday afternoon?" Guy asked, clearly as curious as Rosie.

Hannah bit her lip and considered her answer carefully, conflicted. She'd initially wanted to keep the Evelyn story to herself, and she knew Mamaw preferred to stay out of it altogether. But at the same time, if she hadn't let Mamaw and Carla and Mr. Davenport in on the story the other day, she'd never have gone to Memphis and met Maggie, seen the children's hospital, walked its halls, met Peter and Shelby Dawson, or gotten closer to finding Evelyn than ever before. Evelyn wrote to the newspaper because she wanted her story to be heard. What was the harm in telling it?

"Well, first off, it's not an assignment for Monty," she said, turning her body to face Guy and so she could see Rosie better. She'd put away her iPad and was sipping out of her water bottle in the back seat like she was ready to watch a movie.

"I guess that's not much of a surprise. I didn't think the *Record* was into much investigative journalism," Guy commented. Hannah liked that he seemed to know something about the paper.

"The story does start with the *Record*, but Monty doesn't know anything about it. I'm thinking about pitching it to the *Tribune*."

It was the first time Hannah admitted out loud that she planned to write and publish this article. Of course, the idea had always been there, but she was getting more and more sure that Evelyn's story needed to be heard, and not just by Hannah and the people she happened to talk to about it.

"Oh my Lord, woman. Are you going to tease us forever? What is the story about?" Guy prodded, and the anticipation from both Franklins was tangible.

"Wait, I do need to warn you that it is a bit violent. I'm not sure how you feel about that," Hannah said to Guy, not wanting to make the same mistake she had earlier with her name.

"How violent?"

"Like, *Dateline* or *48 Hours* mysteries violent," Hannah said, trying to find the accurate scale and still lingering on the fictional titles she'd been brainstorming earlier for her own potential episode.

"Oh, we love those shows, right, Daddy?" Rosie chimed in, which made Hannah like the quick-witted preteen even more than she already did.

"So, it's like a murder mystery?" Guy asked without responding to his daughter, maybe a little embarrassed by the fact that he let his twelve-year-old watch TV shows about true crime.

"Kind of. Not a murder, but a mystery for sure."

Guy shrugged, and his shoulders flexed under the fitted flannel he was wearing, which suddenly didn't annoy Hannah nearly as much as it had fifteen minutes ago.

"Why not?" he said. "I like a good mystery."

CHAPTER 15

"Then Rosie asked to see the letters." Hannah fluffed the pillows behind Mamaw and then helped her lie back into the strategically placed supports. "I'm going to let Guy read them first to see if they are suitable for Rosie, but I thought it was adorable."

"I am so glad you're home safe and sound. I have never been so worried in my whole life. What would I have told your mother if something happened to you?" Mamaw asked for the twentieth time that night. She'd been apologizing and comforting Hannah endlessly since she'd walked in the door at nine o'clock. Hannah was only one hour past her original ETA, but with all the drama that had happened in between, Mamaw was in a state of extreme anxiety. Mr. Davenport was holding her hand as she sat in her wheelchair, manicured nails digging into his skin.

Hannah, who'd been smiling to herself while walking up the front path to the house, had to reset her mood to match Mamaw's concern. But she couldn't hold it in forever. This day had been filled with all the emotional highs and lows, but overall Hannah was hopeful and full of purpose. It wasn't a big leap, but it was movement, and it was difficult to admit, but she was a little proud of herself.

Mamaw had not recovered as well. Even after Mr. Davenport said his goodbyes and Hannah helped Mamaw through her slightly tardy bedtime routine, she had continued to run through the same script of concern. Hannah kept trying to calm her worries and distract her from the exhausting emotional loop. Her sleeping pills would do the trick in a few minutes, but she hated the idea of drugging her grandmother instead of comforting her.

"I'm okay, Mamaw. I told you. I'm a city girl. I've been through scarier things." She kissed Mamaw's forehead and took in her smell like she did each night, pulling up the covers and tucking them around her body.

"Guy suggested that we go out to Bethesda Cemetery on Wednesday and take a look around for Evelyn's headstone. I thought that was a good idea. That's where Papaw and Uncle Samuel are buried, right? Daddy used to take me there, remember? Thought you'd like to come along. We could bring flowers and make sure everything is nice and tidy." Hannah sorted Mamaw's medication like she did each night, not even lingering on the familiar ones this time.

"That's nice, darlin', but I don't think I'd like to go," Mamaw said, sounding worn out, almost like she was half-asleep already.

"No? I mean, I guess it would be tough with your chair, but I think I could figure something out with Guy's help," Hannah suggested.

"That is thoughtful of you, dear, but I'd rather not, if that's all right."

Papaw Williamson had passed away of liver disease when Hannah was eight. She barely knew him, and from what her mother said, Papaw had been a mediocre dad and husband at home, a top-notch professor of chemistry at Ole Miss, and a spectacular, high-functioning alcoholic everywhere. Hannah's father rarely talked about Papaw, before or after his passing. And Mamaw hardly mentioned him to Hannah in the twenty-odd years since his passing, so it made some sense that she didn't want to visit his grave. And Patrick Williamson was buried back in Oak Park Cemetery, where her mother could visit his headstone as often as she liked. Hannah and Mamaw could talk about Hannah's father, but mentions of Papaw and Samuel were met with a polite hesitance that Hannah was starting to find irksome.

"Of course it's all right. I'll still take some flowers, I think. This whole Evelyn thing has gotten me thinking. I feel like I know this random woman, but I barely knew Uncle Samuel. You know?" Hannah brought over the miniature cup of water and another with Mamaw's pills and handed them over, working on autopilot.

Samuel she remembered far better than Papaw. He was musically talented, funny, and always up for playing a game of chess (which he always let Hannah and Brody win). She was in high school when the call came in, and her mom wailed while her dad cried softly in his armchair. It took Hannah's mother's lack of social filtering for Hannah to understand why Samuel's funeral was closed casket, but her father's admission of Samuel's suicide was far more subtle. Like, when he forced Brody to visit a therapist after a panic attack during finals his freshman year at Northwestern and made sure Hannah got to her therapy appointments every week, even after he was too frail to drive her himself.

Maybe that's what made her feel close to Samuel and what made her want to be here for Mamaw when her sons couldn't. Hannah made it out the other side of her depression, when Samuel didn't. Putting flowers on his grave was the least she could do for him.

As Hannah went to retrieve the empty disposable cups, lost in her thoughts, Mamaw grabbed at her, like she needed something desperately. She was shaking.

"Oh no. What's wrong?" Hannah dropped the garbage and took Mamaw's hands, sitting on the edge of the bed. Her cheeks were already wet with tears, her glasses dirty with the residue of face cream and a bit of the foundation Hannah missed when she washed her face.

"I just wish you'd leave well enough alone sometimes," she said in a small voice followed by a silent sob that shook her hunched shoulders.

Hannah didn't know what to say or do. She'd never, ever seen her calm, lovely, gentle grandmother break down. Not at either of her sons' funerals, or Papaw's memorial, or even when she was in physical pain. She was so practiced and honed in her pleasant southern belle persona that it had erased the vast spectrum of emotions most humans feel openly every single day.

"Oh, Mamaw." Hannah put her arms around her grandma and pulled her into her shoulder like a baby. "It's just part of my job. I'm sorry about your car, and I'm sorry I scared you, and I'm sorry I asked about going to the cemetery." She apologized for all the things she thought might be weighing heavily on the elderly woman, patting her rounded shoulders and back, bent by her years on this planet and so many hardships that Hannah couldn't even conceptualize.

In Hannah's embrace, Mamaw slowly regained control of her emotions, sniffing and then swallowing, like she was forcing down the sadness. She leaned back, blinking away the tears. "Heavens, I threw a little hissy fit there, didn't I?" She sniffled and wiped her nose.

Hannah watched her grandmother for a moment. From her father's stories and the brief glimpses of her personality during holiday visits, she'd always thought the woman was akin to a saint, that she'd mastered kindness and empathy and didn't fight with the twin demons of anger and regret that stalked Hannah daily. But that wasn't possible, was it? How had it taken Hannah so long to see that for ninety-one years Mamaw had been pretending?

"No, no, that wasn't a hissy fit. It's okay to be sad," Hannah said, not letting go even after Mamaw settled into her half-sitting, half-lying-down sleeping position.

"It was nothing, honey. Pass me a Kleenex, won't you?"

Hannah grabbed a few tissues from the crocheted Kleenex box cover. Mamaw took off her glasses, trembling like the homeschooled kid who won the county spelling bee Hannah covered for the *Record* three weeks ago. The winning word was *bougainvillea*.

"Does this story really bother you that much?" Hannah asked, as she watched Mamaw tidy herself up. She couldn't imagine giving up her pursuit. It gave her hope that she would be able to get her life back on track while doing a service for a young woman who didn't have as many options as Hannah did a century later.

But seeing Mamaw so shook up left Hannah conflicted. She could stop talking about Evelyn, but she didn't know how to stop pursuing the leads that were pouring into her life like an avalanche or riding the exhilarating and slightly dangerous wave.

"No, no, dear. It's nothing in particular about this Evelyn girl," Mamaw said, blotting at her face. "I only wonder if her family would want their secrets told in such a . . . public way. They must've had their reasons for keeping things so hush-hush." She twisted the mangled tissue around her polished pointer finger until it covered her arthritic knuckle and coral-colored nail.

Covering up. Yes. The real reason behind Mamaw's breakdown had nothing to do with the stranger, Evelyn. Mamaw had secrets she'd covered with nuanced phrases like *went off by accident* and *he'd been feeling blue* and *he'd had a little too much to drink*. And some of those secrets were buried in Bethesda Cemetery along with nearly every man she'd ever really loved.

"But *Evelyn* wanted her story told. *She* wrote to the newspaper. Someone overlooked her story or was hiding it for some reason—I don't know why yet, but I want to. I am trying to help her be heard." Hannah tried to explain as sensitively as possible, not sure if she would trigger another crash with a few clumsy words. Then again, she'd never stopped to think if Uncle Samuel had a story that needed to be heard. Maybe that's what Mamaw was truly afraid of, which Hannah could understand on some level, having insisted on secrecy when it came to her own attempt.

"I know, dear." Mamaw patted her arm sweetly, her emotions sealed back up into the expertly carved box inside her. "I'm feeling a bit foolish tonight. I need some beauty rest."

Mamaw's medicine was starting to kick in, to Hannah's great relief. With each of her grandmother's slow blinks leading to a swift and total slumber, Hannah finished the nighttime routine with the television, remote, lights, and tray removal, leaving the door open just a crack when she departed. Outside the bedroom, where the dissonance of Mamaw's suppressed emotions still hung like a dense fog on a fall Chicago morning, Hannah took a moment to lean against the wall and just breathe.

Even with the tray still in her grip, she needed to find that centering breath Laura reminded her of at nearly every session since Hannah had walked into her office after being released from the hospital. Laura would likely say that she was proud of Hannah for taking so many risks and making progress. But she'd likely also say that Hannah didn't have to do it all at once, that she needed to add stressors one at a time, building up her strength and resilience. But a story rarely waited. And even if this one had a longer shelf life than most, Hannah didn't have any desire to wait.

Ding!

A loud pinging sound called out from Papaw's office, where Hannah had stowed her belongings after Mr. Davenport had left for the evening.

Ding! Ding! Ding!

A string of notifications, the sounds too distinct and familiar to be confusing, echoed through the hallway. Hannah's jaw dropped. Her phone.

She put the tray down in the hall, flinching when the silverware clattered against the barely touched bowl of soup, and rushed to the office. The phone was now quiet. Hannah dumped the contents of her messenger bag on the leather couch, sending files and her notebook spilling out along with the gallon-size Ziploc bag of rice with her phone inside. She ripped open the zipper and retrieved her phone, trembling even more than Mamaw had during her breakdown.

She'd convinced herself that she didn't miss the device and that she could comfortably live without the technological umbilical cord. A very present part of her mind had been actively patting herself on the back for being so evolved. But as she held up the suddenly working phone and saw a screen full of notifications from various apps, Hannah knew she'd been full of shit. Once an addict, always an addict.

The first few messages were from her mother, but then, there it was, the thing she'd been waiting for, for more than nine months, whether she wanted to admit it or not.

Alex: Hey.

After months of silence, not one apology, not one call when her father died, not one email when she was in the hospital, no acknowledgment that she'd left town. Nothing. And then a hey from Thursday, three weeks before his romantic winter wedding, at least according to the link for his TheKnot.com registry that she'd found by stalking his Facebook profile.

Hannah's throat constricted. She couldn't breathe. It would be one thing if he'd left it at the nebulous Thursday night hey, but there were several more follow-ups over the past forty-eight hours. She read each one carefully, like there might be some subtle message in the spaces between the words or the placement of the punctuation. She took off her jacket and settled onto the floor, folding her legs up underneath her and leaning back against the bottom half of the couch, feeling like she must be hallucinating.

Friday morning:

Alex: I hope this is still your number. Stacey told me you moved. Can you let me know if my texts are coming through?

Friday at lunchtime:

Alex: Hello?

Friday at nearly midnight:

Alex: Maybe I'm blocked? If not, can you let me know?

Then two missed calls at 3:00 a.m. on Saturday.
Then at 9:00 a.m. on Saturday:

Alex: I really need to talk to you. Please answer me.

Then a call at lunch and a call around the time Hannah was exchanging numbers with Peter Dawson. Oh God—this time he left a message. She was full-on shaking now. If she were stronger, she'd swipe to the left on this notification and make it disappear. She'd block his number and delete his voice mail without listening. That's what she'd do if she wanted to stay healthy, if she wanted to continue her trek out of the inky pit he'd left her in. If she wanted to keep moving away from codependency and toward independence. But who was she kidding? Would a starving woman be able to resist a feast, even if she knew it might be poisoned? Maybe. Or maybe not.

Hannah touched the voice-mail notification and the phone opened, recognizing her face. Pressing play, she held the phone up to her ear, worried she might not be able to hear through her own labored breaths. But then his voice hit her, like a snowball to the face, an unexpected shock that takes your breath away and leaves you numb.

Hey. I don't know if you're getting any of my messages or if you are just still really upset with me, which I don't blame you. I really don't. I have a lot I want to tell you that I should've said last year. I know I have no right to ask, but . . . can I see you? I'm going to be in Memphis for a conference in two weeks, right before Thanksgiving. I saw on Facebook that you are living with Mamaw now, and I know I'll be only an hour away. I was hoping I could take you out to dinner. You know—for old time's sake? I'll send you an email with the details. I understand if you never want to see me again, but could you let me know one way or the other? Please? Um, okay . . . thank you. Talk soon. Bye.

His voice was a time machine sucking her back through the weeks and months since she had last seen him. She'd gone to work that morning, kissed him on the forehead like she always did before leaving.

"Have a good day," she whispered, sneaking a smell of his skin, her habit whenever he was close.

"You too," he said, turning his face to meet hers and kissing her, for what would be the last time, on her lips.

"I love you," she said, meaning it wholeheartedly. He was the man who'd held her in his arms while she cried over her father's diagnosis, when she called his doctor to get a better idea of the treatment plan; he'd comforted her as she heard the word *terminal*. She loved him. Endlessly.

"I love you," he said back, lying.

She never would've guessed that she'd never hear his voice say *I love you* again. After she'd found him with Janie, they were never alone in the same room. He moved out immediately, ignored her calls and texts, and fell into a new life without her like in his life story she was written in pencil and he'd decided to make revisions.

She dropped the phone, overwhelmed by the phantoms of her past. His voice brought back all that pain and loss, tears not just filling her eyes but flooding her face and mouth and pouring down her neck and soaking into the collar of her shirt. The kind of crying that hurt, not in some existential way, but also made her chest, shoulders, throat, and head ache.

"Damn you." She gasped, pushing her fists into her closed eyes till stars appeared. "Damn you. Damn you. Damn you!"

She was angry—beyond angry. She was furious at the audacity of his request. He wanted to talk now? Now that he'd decided it was time? Now that he wanted to see her, he was determined to make it happen? But she wasn't just angry at Alex . . .

Hannah used the bottom half of her shirt to dry her face and wipe her nose, taking in air through her nose and holding it, then letting it out slowly, trying to regain control before she spiraled too far out of control. She picked up the phone and opened her email, where she saw a similar message to the one in his voice mail.

Yes, she was angry at Alex. She was wounded beyond belief by his affair and the way he discarded her like a piece of garbage. But right now, she was also mad at herself—because she wanted to see him. Desperately.

And even though she knew she shouldn't, and even though she knew she couldn't tell anyone in her life that she was going to see him again, Hannah closed out of her email and opened her text messages. She ignored the new texts from her mom; her old roommate, Tricia, who'd just had a baby and couldn't stop sending pics; Brody, asking if he could borrow her password for Netflix; and even her therapist, asking if they could find a time to have a tele-appointment; and opened the messages from Alex.

Slightly nauseated, mouth dry and sticky from all the coffee and the lack of anything substantial in her stomach, she started typing. She'd often thought about all the things she'd say to Alex if she ever got the chance, and most of those words had four letters in them, but strangely that's not what she wrote as she typed her first message since she'd texted him about her father's death.

Hannah: Hey.

CHAPTER 16

"Hey!" a man said, knocking on Hannah's desk at the *Record* with his knuckles. She palmed her phone, rereading on Wednesday the series of texts she'd exchanged with Alex Saturday night, and looked up, surprised. Guy stood in front of her, holding out a coffee from Broken Cup, smiling.

The last time she'd seen that smile was when he rang the doorbell Sunday afternoon after helping to get Mamaw's Buick towed from its resting place halfway back from Memphis. He'd stood on the front porch bundled up for the chill in the air, finding Hannah in sweats and a T-shirt, not expecting company. She cursed in her head, determined not to look like a poor college student at least once when they met up. Saturday had been fun with Guy and Rosie, and she'd thought about it more than once since then, but even with their new friendly rapport she felt a touch like a charity case. Especially when he was dressed like an L.L.Bean model and she was wearing a cocoon of fabric.

"Won't you come in?" Hannah asked after saying hello, trying her best to sound like a hostess, but ending up seeming sarcastic instead. He shook his head.

"No, thank you, I gotta get home for dinner." He peeked around her shoulder and into the house, inhaling through his nose. "Though you're making me hungry. Is Carla here on a Sunday? It smells like her baked chicken."

Hannah scrunched up her face, glad he was only smelling the dinner she'd thrown together based on Carla's recipe and not tasting it.

"No, that's all me. So, better be glad you have dinner waiting at home."

"Ha." He chuckled. He laughed at her jokes a lot, which was rare for anyone to do lately. If she ever attempted humor at the office, Monty and Dolores usually looked at her like she was speaking Russian. It was fun to have someone who got her sense of humor at least a little. "You're a smart lady. I'm sure you figured it out."

"Smart has nothing to do with it. My dad used to say, *Baking is a science. Cooking is an art.*" She quoted her father without a single hitch in her cadence, holding up one finger like he always had when making a point, which startled her. She rarely brought up her father to anyone but family.

"Well, sounds like a wise man."

"Yes, he was." She wrapped her arms around her midsection, the cold afternoon air hitting her all at once. Guy seemed to notice.

"I won't keep you." He put his fists in the pockets of his tan canvas jacket and shifted his weight, like he might be nervous, though Hannah couldn't be sure since she'd never seen him as anything but self-assured. "I just . . . I didn't get your number. Thought it would be a good idea to have for our trip to Bethesda. I was going to call the house, but since I was here . . ."

"Oh yeah. For the research thing at the cemetery." It took her half a second to catch up to his reference. She'd convinced herself that his offer to comb through the graveyard for a random headstone had been a polite promise that would never materialize, so his follow-through surprised her. She'd latched on to the opportunity, unable to stop thinking about the story for very long since her Memphis trip.

"For sure, that would be great. Here, give me your phone. I'll put in my number. My phone started working again last night, believe it or not." She'd filled in Rosie and Guy on the state of her cell phone the night before, during their ride back to Senatobia. She left out the fact that she'd caused its demise with her stubborn bike ride in the rain.

"Well, guess you won't be needing anybody to rescue you from country gas stations anymore, then, will you?" He passed her his device with a "New Contact" screen open. She typed in her information and saved it under *Hannah*. Then, rethinking, she added *Williamson*, in case he had a plethora of Hannahs in his life.

"You'd think, but no. I'm sure I'll find a way." She gave him back his phone and returned to her self-hug stance.

"You know you don't have to wait for an emergency," he said, that winning smile and confidence returning. She felt that funny flip in her midsection and barely resisted smiling back. "Reach out anytime. About the Evelyn stuff, I mean. I . . . I'm sure Rosie would love it."

"For sure. I can send you guys the articles if you like," she offered, remembering Rosie's request to read them, but also remembering that she should pass anything for Rosie past Guy first.

"Yes, that'd be fantastic," he agreed enthusiastically. Hannah shivered involuntarily. She curled her toes up in her socks, becoming legitimately cold at this point. "I'm sorry. I'm keeping you out here in the freezing cold. I better let you get inside."

"I'll send you those files," she said, letting him retreat.

"Sounds good. I'll get all caught up before Wednesday." He took a step back. "Give my best to your mamaw."

"Sure," she responded, submitting to the natural flow of niceties, somewhat reticent to see the conversation end. "And say hi to Rosie for me," she added at the last minute.

"Will do!" he called back one final time before turning to walk down the front path toward his truck. She closed the front door once he seemed to be safe inside his vehicle, wondering how Guy Franklin had gone from someone she never wanted to see again to someone she looked forward to getting to know better.

She sent him all the image files with the pages of Evelyn's story later that night. He read through them over the next few days, and they'd been texting off and on ever since. It had grown into an easy banter that reminded Hannah of what it felt like to have a friend. She hadn't seen him since Sunday, but already it felt easy, organic.

"You just saved my life," she said, snagging the offered coffee and taking a sip without checking its temperature. The liquid was steaming hot and burned her tongue, but she could still tell it was some sweetened, nutmeggy version of coffee. Not her standard order, but it tasted like changing leaves, snow flurries, pink cheeks, and fall back home. Plus, it contained caffeine, which was the one ingredient she couldn't live without.

"I feel like I keep doing that," Guy said, taking a drink from his lidded cup. It had been four days since the low-key rescue from the Gas Depot. With Guy's help, they'd gotten Mamaw's Buick towed back to town and dropped off in her garage, where it still sat. Instead of selling the car or having a mechanic give it the death sentence, Mamaw had hired Guy to fix it up, only convincing Hannah even further that he *was* a handyman.

"You ready to go?" he asked after swallowing.

"Oh my God. I forgot!" Hannah checked the line of clocks on the wall. Half past noon on Wednesday.

"I should've been clearer in my text." He took out his phone and pretended to read. "*See you tomorrow at 12:30.* Oh, I can see why you were confused. I should've used an emoji. My apologies."

"Ha, ha, ha." Hannah rolled her eyes and collected her things. "I'm sorry. I'm a little distracted," she said, which was not exactly a lie. "Let me check in with Monty, and then we can head to the cemetery." She looked him up and down, really seeing him for the first time that day. "You look kind of fancy today," she said, trying not to feel like a slob next to his semi-casual but polished getup. Under his dark blazer, he was wearing a patterned collared shirt with a skinny tie and a pair of deep-blue jeans. There was no other way to say it—he looked handsome.

"Oh, this old thing?" he said with a heavy accent, the one that'd made her crack up when they were in the car with Rosie.

"I always feel underdressed around you," she said, a little annoyed that even though she was starting to like Guy, he still made her feel nervous. She put on her jacket, remembering the chill in the air on her bike ride to work that morning, and took another sip of the drink on her desk.

"I disagree. Rosie thinks you are pretty stylish. She's already asking for one of those." He pointed at Hannah.

"My flak jacket?" She rearranged the olive-green canvas material till it sat comfortably on her body. "I got this thing at a thrift store when I was at Northwestern. It's a million years old."

"I think that's called 'vintage,'" he said to her back as she walked to Monty's office.

"Vintage my ass," she said over her shoulder. When she turned back around, she nearly ran face-first into Monty. He stood in the doorway, the lines on his face deeper and sterner than she had ever seen them.

"Oh God, Monty. You scared me."

"Miss Williamson," he said in a way that could only mean "Watch your language, young lady." She dropped her shoulders and softened her facial landscape, adopting her new, pleasant-as-pie persona. "When you are finished with your visitor, could I talk with you?"

"Oh, I was going off-site for my lunch today. Do you mind?" she asked, wondering why in the world Monty wanted to meet with her. Unless it was to try to put her back in classifieds. No, that was the last thing she needed. When his features didn't soften, she added, "Sir."

Monty didn't respond to Hannah and instead looked over her head, focusing on Guy.

"Mr. Franklin. Good to see you again," Monty said, purposefully avoiding Hannah's question.

"Good afternoon, Mr. Martin," Guy responded, sounding friendly, though Hannah didn't turn around to check his expression.

"Your father is well?" Monty asked, as though he knew everything about the town. As he chatted with Guy, Hannah sized up the filing cabinets lining the back wall of his office, longingly. If only she could look inside them without having to get a pass from Monty.

"Yes, sir. He's finishing up his busy season. You know how that is."

Monty nodded, though it wasn't likely that he had any idea what it was like during the busy season in the construction business. Hannah stopped ogling the cabinets from a distance and tried to check back in with what the men were talking about. But it seemed Monty had completed his duty to be courteous. He looked back at Hannah.

"As always, your lunch hour is yours to do with as you wish, Miss Williamson. We can talk when you return." He put his thumbs through his belt loops and swayed a little. There was something off about his demeanor—like he was wearing a mask of himself, plastic.

"Thank you," she said, squinting, wanting to peek under the mask but also not willing to invest the time with Guy waiting right there. "We won't be too long."

"Have a good time," he said, not moving from his office door, watching them in a way that made Hannah shudder as she joined Guy at her desk and retrieved her coffee. How was she going to get out of whatever this new assignment was? She'd worry about it later.

"Let's do this thing," she said playfully, in an attempt to shake off the weird vibe she was still picking up from Monty.

"You don't have to get bossy," he said, following Hannah toward the front door.

"I feel like he's still watching us," she said between clenched teeth.

Guy glanced back and then murmured, "Yup, sure is."

"Ugh, that guy. What the hell is his problem?" They got outside, and Guy's silver Civic was parked along the side of the road right in front of the newspaper offices. He opened her car door. He always seemed to find a way to get to a door before she did. It was annoying but also a little endearing. She was starting to see why some women liked having a gentleman around. Perhaps the southern belle genes were finally having their moment. Gracefully she dipped into the car. When Guy climbed in the other side, she followed up: "We should probably get back ASAP. I feel like a kid with a curfew."

"What do you think, I'm made of time?" he said, dragging the last half of the word *time*, putting in *h*'s where there weren't usually any. "I have to be back at work in forty-five minutes."

They pulled away from the building, and Hannah had to steady the coffee cups in the car's shallow molded plastic holders.

"Damn, Mamaw is demanding!"

"Mamaw?" Guy quirked up an eyebrow. "You think me working for your mamaw is my full-time job?"

"Yes?" Hannah answered, the affirmation trailing up at the end like a question.

"No, ma'am. I help my daddy out before and after work, but I'd go crazy doing construction every day." He took a full turn onto US 51, south this time. They had to be close to the cemetery, but she hadn't gone this way down 51 since Uncle Samuel's funeral.

"So, what is the big secret? Where do you work?"

"I teach at Senatobia Middle School, down the street from the *Record*."

"What the hell? Why didn't you tell me this?" Hannah exclaimed, feeling like she'd just found out he was an undercover agent for the CIA.

"What?" he asked, glancing at her sideways, his eyes smiling and his mouth wanting to.

"How did I not know this?" she asked, surprised at how playful she felt around Guy. It seemed like he wanted to talk to the unfiltered part of her mind, not the one putting on a show. And she liked that.

"Because you didn't ask," he responded.

"Whatever. We already had the carpenter/handyman talk. I didn't think to ask. So, middle school." She turned her body to face him and curled her knees up. "You must teach a subject, and I'm guessing it's not woodshop. Let me guess . . ." She leaned back to take him in head to toe.

"So help me if you say PE . . ."

"First of all, PE? Do you guys say PE down here? It's gym. Just like soda is pop," she joked.

"You are stalling," he said, turning down a dirt road that Hannah would've most definitely missed. She knew they were close.

"Fine. Not woodworking and not *gym*. Science?"

Guy pulled the car up onto the berm next to an ancient-looking cast-iron fence with an arched opening where the name *Bethesd*a was framed and spelled out in twisted metal. Even as a child, Hannah had found it strangely romantic—like the setting for a wedding, not a place to lay your loved one in the ground. But after burying her father, she understood a little more—it was a sacred place you trusted to hold your father, mother, husband, child. It was meant to be beautiful. It needed to be.

"Language arts," he said, putting the car in park. "Like, creative writing and literature, poetry, and maybe a touch of journalism." He took the key out of the ignition, and she thought she detected a touch of shyness in his answer when he stared off into the distance like he was checking out the cemetery gate.

"Wait, were you at the spelling bee in Coldwater last month?" Hannah put her phone in her pocket and decided to only take her notebook and a pencil on their expedition. "And you teach journalism? Dang. I'm learning so much about you."

"Yes, ma'am, I teach the heck out of journalism. And I sure was at the spelling bee." He opened his door, and a cool breeze cut right through the collected heat of the car. She shivered and braced herself for the cold, putting the pencil behind her ear.

"I was there too! I covered it for the *Record*." She shook her head at the coincidence, not just at their first interaction but also the journalism connection. No wonder he wanted to help with Evelyn's story.

"Yeah. I know," he said. "I saw you." He got out of the car, and Hannah followed him from her side.

"You saw me? That is . . . hilarious," she said. "What else do you know about me?" she asked, catching up with him.

"Oh, you'd be surprised. I know you worked for the *Tribune*."

"Everyone seems to know that."

"You want to know the nitty-gritty?" he asked, glancing back at her over his shoulder. After talking to Monty every day, she could probably guess what Guy had heard.

"Let me guess, you heard that I went through a bad breakup, then had a mental breakdown, after which I lost my job at the *Tribune*, just in time to live in my parents' house to watch my father die of cancer?" she said, finding it impossible to keep the bitterness out of her response. Or at least that's what she'd assumed people said behind her back. She knew that's what people said about her in Chicago. She had friends, obviously, but after being in a long-term relationship, many of them were surface level and shared. They sided with Hannah at first, after seeing Alex cut and run with a new woman, but when the depression made her pull away and her grief was no longer novel to them, nearly everyone faded away or she pushed them away, knowing they'd tire of her eventually. Maybe that's why she blurted it all out to Guy like that. Even if he hadn't already heard all the gossip, she'd rather tell him up front and let him bow out now.

"Whoa," he said, breathing heavier than normal as they walked up the hill toward the cemetery. "I definitely didn't hear all that. I knew your daddy passed away. I hadn't heard about . . . the rest of it," he said gently, slowing as he approached the archway entrance into the Bethesda Cemetery. A historical plaque, green with raised brass letters, stood just outside the gates. He stopped in front of the sign, suddenly somber, studying her.

"Welp, now you have," she said in a low voice, wishing she'd kept her mouth shut. "Looks like we're here."

Talking about her father outside the cemetery that held the rest of his family hit her in an odd way. He'd buried his grandparents, father, and brother here. She'd walked under this archway as a child after Papaw died, holding her father's hand, wishing she could make him feel better, but already knowing that bringing back the dead was beyond her innocent pleadings with the divine.

Guy took the hint and let the subject drop, examining the entrance alongside Hannah. The carving of a magnolia flower sat at the top of the sign, above a brief history of the cemetery. A Presbyterian minister had created it in 1848. It took special note of the veterans of various wars buried there, and the victims of yellow fever and smallpox outbreaks that decimated the area at the end of the nineteenth and beginning of the twentieth century. But Hannah knew from personal experience that the stories buried here went beyond wars and pandemics.

Hannah took a picture of the sign with her phone.

"Are you ready?" Guy asked, pulling the collar of his blazer up around his ears. Hannah's phone buzzed in her hand. She glanced down and saw Alex's name. Her heart fluttered the way it used to when they'd first started dating and she couldn't believe the smart, handsome, popular frat boy was interested in her out of all the girls who flirted with him in her dorm. She couldn't help but smile before dismissing the notification and putting the phone in her pocket.

"Beyond ready," she said, the grin lingering on her lips.

Guy glanced away quickly and then gestured toward the worn path walked by mourners for the past 170 years.

Guilt hit her in the gut. Alex was engaged to another woman and he'd broken her heart; he shouldn't be able to make her smile. But he did. And she'd let Guy see her weakness, even if he didn't know it. She'd be stronger, she told herself. She wouldn't let Alex take over her brain again. But even as Hannah followed Guy through crumbling headstones, half covered in moss, with names and numbers carved generations ago, she couldn't stop wondering if Alex loved getting her texts too.

CHAPTER 17

"Over here!" Guy called from behind a row of shrubs. They'd been combing through the headstones, using an online directory set up by the local historical society to search the cataloged memorials. Without Evelyn's last name, they'd checked all gravestones with names starting with an *E*, but so far there were no good options. They'd looked at all the Browns and searched for any Westbrooks, but nothing matched the dates that would line up with Evelyn's life. Evelyn's family was not in this cemetery. But that didn't stop Hannah from being mesmerized by the names and dates on the headstones, especially in this older section of the plot. And when Guy called to her, she had to actively slow her steps to keep from running in what should be a solemn place.

"What have you found?" Hannah asked, a little out of breath from her speedy walk. It was still cool out, and when the wind rose, it cut through all her layers, but it was only her hands that were cold.

"I think I found your family," he said, pointing to a line of headstones, some sunken into the ground and overgrown with moss and crabgrass, others part of a curved white monument with fading names carved into the limestone that read *Williamson*.

"Oh my God, that's amazing." Hannah took pictures and read through who rested there. Dates went back to the 1840s when the cemetery was first founded. She knew her father's family had helped settle Senatobia, but seeing their actual resting places made it even more real. She was surprised her dad had never shared this with her on one of their visits. She knelt to get a closer look at some of the nearly buried headstones that were harder to read.

"There are more over here too," he said, stopping by a tall obelisk that looked newer or quite possibly was made of better materials than the other ones that seemed to be melting away with time. But Hannah barely heard him. She'd found Mamaw's mother and father: Calvin and Florence Patton.

Guy left his discovery and stood by her side as she knelt in the grass to get a better look.

"This is my great-grandma. Mamaw's mother," she said, tracing the family tree in her head. "She died before I was born. Mamaw and Papaw didn't talk about her much, but my father had some stories, let me tell you. She was a hard woman—cold, I guess. My dad used to tell this story about Papaw voting for JFK. Grandma Patton wouldn't let him in the house for a year. Broke Mamaw's heart that they couldn't visit."

"Sounds like your papaw was headstrong. I'm guessing it runs in the family," he said, making a joke, but Hannah was too lost in her thoughts to pick up on it. She spoke half to herself and half to Guy.

"I don't know what he was," Hannah said, not sure what to think of him anymore. The longer she lived in Tate County, the harder it was to know how to judge her ancestors. "To be honest, I don't know much about anyone buried here. We barely visited, and my dad didn't tell us much, you know? From what I could piece together, I think Mamaw Patton liked her little bubble of a world. She couldn't see the need for any change. My dad used to call it brainwashing. He said it's the reason he never moved back here. He was afraid of it. Afraid of it for us."

She didn't understand how to find the balance between pride and shame, something she'd not been taught as a child. Even while loving his family, her father had rejected his roots, and his southern heritage was easy to vilify and condemn from the suburbs of Chicago. He spoke of the Klan that ran rampant in Senatobia when he was a boy and the way his grandmother would speak about people of color. What was it like watching people he once respected in his town do despicable things, like their neighbor Joe Nearwad, who tried to stop the integration of their elementary school by forming a barricade? Even his own grandmother was an open bigot who banned Mamaw and Papaw from their home because they voted for JFK and wore black when Martin Luther King was shot. He'd explained that it was one thing losing respect for your neighbor; it was another thing losing respect for your family.

And here she was, the woman, the myth, the legend, the villain in many of her father's stories about why he left Senatobia and never moved back. But here, seeing her buried six feet in the ground, a cold, fading stone the only reminder of her existence, Hannah wondered how such a beautiful and loving woman like Mamaw had come from such a hardened woman as Florence.

"Did you see these?" Guy asked, pointing to a trail of small headstones, some so buried by debris that she could barely make them out. Each one read *Infant Boy* or *Infant Girl* with a single date underneath or, on a few, a dash between two dates that were horrifically close together. Hannah had known that Mamaw's brother was nearly a teenager when she was born, but she didn't realize such sorrow had preceded her birth. Hannah counted: one, two . . . four . . . seven, eight. There were eight infants buried next to Mamaw Mable's mother. Eight.

"What the hell?" The grief was immediate and inexplicably real. They'd seen plenty of headstones marking the short lives of infants and children, but nothing like this parade of painful memories. Hannah used a stick to dig out the last two rectangles, almost in disbelief. The dates ranged over a dozen years. "She must've been pregnant or recovering from childbirth for more than a decade."

"I can't even imagine losing one child, much less . . ." Guy stopped, like saying the number would be too much, and Hannah swore the words caught in his throat at the end. Hannah understood that emotion.

She felt it also, but there was another feeling that was rising inside her and taking over the sorrow of those lost little children.

"Why didn't I know about this?" she asked, frustrated. "These are Mamaw's siblings, and she never even mentioned anything about them. Why does everyone hide from sad things down here?"

She tossed the stick and stood up, frustrated. All the strata she had to go through to get to even the top crust of the true story when it came to anything in this town made her want to scream. She'd just told Guy her whole breakdown story, and they'd spent a handful of hours with each other. This detail from her family history meant nothing when it came to the real reason she was at the cemetery—Evelyn—but it did matter if there was some genetic issue that caused the stillbirths. Did Mamaw lose any babies? Hannah didn't even know. No wonder it was so hard to find out information on a stranger when she didn't even have the full story about her own flesh and blood.

"It's just the way it is round here." Guy followed Hannah as she moved away from the plot holding her great-grandparents and their children.

"Exactly," she said, feeling defeated. She checked the time—they still had a few minutes left before her self-appointed deadline, but she was done with this wild goose chase. "We'd better get back."

"All right," he answered, pausing. "Would you mind terribly if I took a minute—alone?"

He checked his watch and then gazed out over toward the newer part of the Bethesda Cemetery. Hannah's eyes followed his. She knew she should go too, find her grandfather and uncle, pay her respects. She'd been filled with curiosity and wonder at the exploration of her family history and becoming acquainted with the people who had made it possible for her to be in this world. But when it came to visiting the graves of those she knew, and mourned, who reminded her of her father's headstone in a cemetery in Illinois, which she hadn't visited since his funeral—she didn't want to do it without someone to hold her hand. She'd only visited her papaw's and Samuel's graves with her father by her side.

"Yeah, I'll meet you at the car," she said. He tossed her the keys, and she turned her back on him before she could see which direction he went.

He tumbled into the car, shivering but smiling, five minutes later. Hannah glanced at her phone one more time. When the text buzzed through, she assumed it was Alex, but peeking at her phone she saw Peter Dawson's name instead, following up on Hannah's trip to the Pines. She quickly wrote and sent a response, then stowed her phone.

"Oh, it's nice and warm in here," Guy said, pressing his hands to the heating vent and bringing just enough of the fresh air in with him to make Hannah shiver.

"Yeah, I'm pretty proud of my car-warming skills. Comes from living in a tundra." She avoided asking about his little solo walkabout and talking about her stupid emotional outburst or the fact that even with Guy taking time out of his day to drive her around town, they'd come up with nothing helpful for her Evelyn story.

"Well, I'll return the favor when summer hits. You haven't known hot till you know Mississippi hot. It's like walking around in boilin' water."

Summer. Would she still be here in the summer? She'd planned to stay until Mamaw got back on her feet, but that was before the plans for the extension on the back of the house and the job at the *Record* and discovering Evelyn. Staying in Senatobia would be easy enough—no rent, a built-in job, less pressure from her mom, and no constant reminders of the way things used to be. But staying here still felt like giving up on the goals she'd always had for her future. She wasn't ready for that just yet, especially now that her engine was no longer totally idle.

Guy took a U-turn, kicking up dust that surrounded the car in a whirlwind, and headed back to the main road. It was already 1:25 p.m.

"Damn, I didn't realize it was so late. You're not gonna make it back in time for your class," she said, wishing they hadn't tried to squeeze in this failure of a trip.

"It's okay. I have a planning period after lunch. I can be a few minutes late." Stopped at a red light, he wiggled out of his blazer and expertly tossed it onto the back seat without leaving one wrinkle.

"That's right, you are apparently an English teacher, per our conversation before traipsing around a graveyard and finding absolutely nothing." She tried to be playful again, but it fell flat. There was a weird vibe in the car, and Hannah knew she was the cause of it, but she didn't know how to change her emotions like changing the gears on a vehicle, as Mamaw did.

"You have a strange definition of nothing. We found out a whole lot of something if I do remember correctly."

"About *my* family, sure. But that doesn't help with my story. No one cares about the Williamson family line, and it wasn't worth making you late."

They made it back to the *Record* offices in what seemed like half the time it had taken to drive out to Bethesda. Guy positioned the car as close to the stairs as possible and then turned his full attention to Hannah.

"Calm yourself," he said, touching her shoulder gently with his fingertips. The phrase threw Hannah off enough to stop her from responding immediately. "I chose to come with you, and I thoroughly enjoyed myself. And if anyone made me late—I did. I wanted to see my grandma."

He enjoyed himself. She liked knowing that. She liked it a lot. Then the time caught her eye again.

"Shit, it's late. You need to go." She pointed at the clock and gathered her things while Guy watched her. He always kind of smirked when Hannah swore. She wasn't sure if it was a criticism or respect. As she was about to pop out of the car, Hannah reached for the pair of coffee cups. "I'll toss these."

Guy placed his hot-to-the-touch hand on top of hers to stop her, and it did the trick. Instead of making her nervous this time, his sure demeanor calmed her.

"I'll take care of it."

"Okay," she said. Her breath caught in her throat, and she didn't pull away. "Well, um, thank you for going with me and driving and, you know, the coffee. Next time it's on me."

"You're welcome." He took his hand back and placed it on the wheel. "Thank you for the good company. If you ever need a ride somewhere, let me know. I won't even charge ya."

"Yeah? I'll take you up on that offer. Thank you. But, seriously, if there's anything I can do to repay your way-too-generous help, you'll tell me, right?" She had a feeling that Guy Franklin would be a priceless resource with his knowledge of the town and what seemed to be a natural instinct for story and research. It didn't hurt that she was starting to enjoy his company.

"I might need your assistance when my journalism unit comes around in the spring," he said, once again opening a tiny window into what her life would be like if she decided to stay here past Mamaw's recovery period. The view wasn't as terrible as she'd expected.

"That sounds fun," she said, starting to exit.

"Hey, Hannah?"

"Yeah?" She turned back, her feet already on the grass.

"I'm sorry about your dad," he said, putting the car in drive. He said it in a way that didn't sound hollow or fake.

Her ears rang as she fought unexpected tears. Guy would've gotten along with her dad; she was sure of it. Both intellectuals. Both soft-spoken yet strong-spirited. Both excellent fathers.

"Thank you," she said as he rolled up his window and waved as he pulled away. She waved back, shell-shocked. Why did Guy make her feel so many things?

She watched his car as he drove off toward Senatobia Middle School, where she'd just learned that Guy taught a bunch of eighth graders about all the beautiful things she was passionate about in life: writing, poetry, journalism, literature. And nearly six weeks ago, it had also been the reason Guy saw Hannah for the first time—whether she had known it or not.

CHAPTER 18

When Hannah returned from her outing to the cemetery with Guy, she was windswept and distracted. Adventure suited Hannah. She liked being out in the field, and she loved spending time with someone who had caught the same itch for investigation that she'd been scratching. It was invigorating and inspiring and left her ready to get to work.

She made brief small talk with Dolores and found out that Monty was still out for lunch, his door locked and the lights dark. He'd seemed intent on having a conversation when she got back, but it must not have been that serious, which meant she could get back to work. First she needed to respond to Peter. She reread their conversation from earlier that day.

Peter Dawson: Hey there! Pete Dawson here. It was great meeting you on Saturday.
I know you had some questions about the Pines. Any way I can help?

Hannah: Mr. Dawson—thank you for reaching out. It was an interesting night, that's for sure!
I do have questions about the Pines. Maybe I can give you a call?

Peter Dawson: Call me Pete. How about over drinks?

She pondered this offer. Drinks in exchange for information. That wasn't unusual. But what kind of information would Peter Dawson bring to such an exchange? She needed access to files. She wouldn't get that over drinks.

Hannah: I would love to talk, but I'm looking for some specific information.
Would you be able to help me out?

Hannah hit "Send." Peter Dawson might be trying to get a date, but Hannah wasn't interested in the flirty "playboy," as he'd been called by the *Daily Memphian* in an article about his father, prior to the start of Peter's own political career. But she'd let him help her keep the investigation moving forward. No text bubbles showed up, so Hannah flipped over to another message she needed to answer—this one from Alex.

Hannah: I'm up for dinner on Wednesday. I'll clear my schedule. Aren't you lucky? ;)

The winky face was a bit much; she knew it as soon as she'd hit "Send." Hannah tamped down her guilt with all her carefully crafted excuses, the main one being her search for "closure." But she wasn't sure that was true. There was no guarantee that the visit would bring closure, but she'd missed his face and craved his voice for so long that she couldn't deny herself the opportunity to experience it again one more time.

Then again, their meeting would be right before Thanksgiving. From her extensive online research, it was clear that Alex was getting married in December, so Hannah held no fantasies of a romantic connection. Truly, she also wanted to see Alex out of a hope that her feelings for him had faded, that the magic of his smile and touch had waned during their time apart, leaving her strong enough to let him go.

Her phone dinged.

Alex: So lucky ;)
I'll give you the details in a few days. I'll find someplace with some local flair.

"Local flair." Hannah snickered. He remembered. Every time they were trying to decide where to go for dinner, when they found time for a rare date night and Alex would ask where Hannah wanted to go, she always said, *I don't care as long as it has some local flair.* Alex would always say, *We live in Chicago. What do you mean "local flair"?* She never was able to articulate what she meant in those moments entirely, but Alex would inevitably find something new and fantastic that they'd try out together.

She forced herself not to respond, not even a smiley face or a laughing emoji, and put her phone in her desk drawer. Those stupid little things kept her feeling in control, like she was doing this on her terms, even if deep down she knew she was lying to herself.

Monty picked that exact moment to return from wherever he'd gone during his lunch hour that day. He didn't say a word, just walked past Hannah's desk and gestured for her to follow. He looked stormy and severe, and quiet little Dolores gave Hannah an accusatory look. She shrugged in response and followed without question. Even when Monty had been bossy or annoyed in the past, he still had an overarching air of joviality. But not today. Today he had something serious on his mind, and she knew it.

When Hannah walked into Monty's office, he was already sitting. He pointed to a chair, and the gesture made Hannah swallow loudly, wishing she had had more for lunch than the nutmeg coffee. She had no guesses as to what had her editor so on edge.

He sat behind his desk, tie loosened a bit at the neck so it made an open triangle, revealing the top buttons of his dress shirt. He steepled his fingers and leaned his lips against them as Hannah settled into one of the chairs. She'd freshened up since the cemetery and had her hair brushed and pulled back into a high ponytail, and though she was missing the protection of her oversize jacket, she hoped her V-neck blouse and nicest pair of jeans helped her look at least a little professional.

"Miss Williamson, welcome back," he said, as though she'd been on some trip instead of on an hour-long lunch break. She didn't see the somewhat humorous caricature of a southern gentleman she often found humor and fault in. Today he looked like an editor. An angry editor.

Hannah tended to ramble when she was nervous. It was either talk incessantly or argue, and she didn't know what to argue about until he came out and said that he wanted to change her assignment. So instead, she let her nerves take over and started overexplaining her afternoon activities.

"Thanks. Sorry I got back a little late. I wanted to do some . . . uh . . . family history, and Guy offered to take me to the Bethesda Cemetery down on 51. We have a family plot there. My papaw and my uncle and a whole bunch of others. It was kind of cold but really interesting and—"

"I'm not concerned about your lunch activities, Miss Williamson." Monty cut her off.

Hannah stopped speaking immediately. It was better to let him talk and find out what was going on than to waste time trying to guess. She held her breath, put her hands under her legs, and waited for Monty to find the words he was searching for.

"Can you tell me why I have a call from Ms. Shelby Dawson asking about you? She said you used your press credentials to get into one of her nephew's fundraising events."

Damn it. Of course Shelby Dawson had taken it upon herself to search her out. That curmudgeonly old battle-ax. In the days since her visit to the Pines, Hannah had been tempted to reach out to the Safe Place organization, as Peter had suggested, and search for more information on Evelyn, but there was something about Shelby and the way she had looked at Hannah like she was the enemy that kept her from taking the risk.

"I wasn't trying to get into the event, and they weren't press credentials—it was just my old ID badge. I visited the Pines to do a little research on a side project I'm working on. It was on a Saturday during my free time, and I didn't know there was a fundraiser that night. I just showed up and was looking through the pictures in the lobby, and then this man came up to me, and you'll never guess who it was." Hannah tried to make herself sound as innocent as possible.

Monty did not seem entertained. He removed his fingers from his lips, where they rested anytime he wasn't speaking.

"Enlighten me," he said, not playing into her narrative. She couldn't get fired again. What would she tell her mother? Or Mamaw or Guy, even? And beyond her hurt pride, if she lost access to the archives, how would she ever finish Evelyn's story? Hannah rushed to explain.

"It was Peter Dawson. State senator Peter Dawson. As in US senator Jack Dawson's son." Hannah paused for a reaction from Monty, but he just stared at her. "But I didn't even know that. So we had this whole conversation. It turns out he's a pretty interesting guy. But then Miss Dawson came up, and she thought I was trying to get information about their family, and she made me leave. But I swear Peter didn't care. He gave me his phone number and everything. I can show you. The number is at my desk. *He* texted *me*."

Monty put up his hand to make Hannah stop talking. "So let me get this right. You snuck into a fundraising event to work on a 'personal project.' And then used old credentials from the *Chicago Tribune* to fraudulently get information from a state senator?"

"ID. Not credentials. I swear. And no! No, I wasn't there to get information from Peter Dawson or Jack Dawson or Shelby Dawson. I don't give a shit about the Dawson family." Monty flinched at her curse word. Hannah corrected herself, wanting to stay on Monty's good side. "Sorry, I don't give a crap about the Dawson family. I wanted to know more about the building. There used to be this children's hospital there, and I wanted more information about one of their patients from the 1930s. That's all."

Monty put his hands on the paper-covered desk and sighed, making the random pages rustle like they were alive. "You fail to explain why you thought it was acceptable to use unethical methods. You were not on assignment. And this story you told Ms. Dawson about? I need you to kill it. Immediately."

"Kill it?" She didn't know how to "kill" this story, and she didn't want to. Monty wasn't exactly a journalist, but he'd have to see the potential in this story. Guy and Rosie were interested, and Mr. Davenport wanted to know more badly enough to push Hannah into her weekend research trip. So far the only uninterested party was Mamaw. There was no promise that this story would end up in print, but with her new leads, how could she give up now?

"Yes, kill the story and keep to your approved assignments," Monty said, rummaging through a stack of files on his desk, searching for what was likely a new busywork assignment to keep her occupied.

"But it's not for the *Record*, it's for . . ." She hesitated, sure she shouldn't admit that she was planning on pitching the story to a bigger newspaper than the *Record* if she ever found all, or at least some, of the missing puzzle pieces. "I don't know yet, but it has a lot of potential news pegs, with potential true-crime tie-ins and angles on child labor and abuse laws. I'm not settled on one just yet, but as I keep researching, I know I'll find it—"

"Miss Williamson," Monty interjected, clearly not interested. "If the project is not for this newspaper, I must ask that you cease and desist your investigations while in our employ. Your actions over the past weekend have put a black mark on the *Record* and harmed our relationship with the Dawson family, and to be quite honest, your story sounds like a mess. You don't even know what makes this thing current. You can't have ten pegs—you need one. And it needs to be significant."

Hannah narrowed her eyes at Monty, scooching to the edge of her seat, something off-putting striking her about his statement, and it wasn't his critique of her pitch.

"What do you mean, our 'relationship' with the Dawsons? How does a small Mississippi county newspaper have a relationship with a political figure in Memphis?"

Monty's chair squeaked beneath him as he shifted in his seat. A few nerves seemed to transfer back to the other side of the desk. He took a moment to slip out of his suit coat and stood to hang it on the coat hanger in the back corner of his office, right next to his line of diplomas and awards.

"The Dawsons are an old family and, as you found from your research, are involved in many causes. This newspaper would never have made it financially if it weren't for their charitable efforts. We would have had to close our doors years ago."

He returned to his chair, more like himself, almost like he'd forgotten to be outraged at Hannah for the moment while he was on the defensive himself.

"Are you saying that the Dawsons own this newspaper?" Hannah asked, more confused and disturbed with every layer of this conversation. Never mind that she'd been caught. Never mind that Shelby Dawson apparently called the *Chicago Tribune* looking for her and ended up being pointed to the *Tate County Record* instead. Those things didn't even bother her at the moment.

"No, of course not. They don't own it." He cleared space on his desk and made a pile of random pages and envelopes on either side as if Moses parting a sea of paper. "This newspaper is dedicated to community news and has been supported by charitable grants for decades. Shelby Dawson sits on the board of the SVC Group, which just happens to make my salary—and your salary for that matter—possible. Surely you didn't think those piddly little ads for Anne's Greenhouse or Piggly Wiggly were keeping us afloat."

It made sense. Hannah knew it was happening more and more often, especially with small local newspapers. The *Salt Lake Tribune* had sent shock waves through the newspaper business when it was approved for nonprofit status with the IRS, and even the *New York Times* took funding from foundations. But this wasn't how it was supposed to work.

"But you can't give the Dawsons special treatment just because they fund your newspaper, Monty. Killing articles because a donor tells you to? Talk about unethical . . ."

At the mention of ethics and the *Record* possibly being on the wrong side of them, Monty sat up straight as a rod and stopped messing around with the disaster on his desk.

"Unethical? You were not on assignment for the *Record*. You made me and this organization look unprofessional. I am of half a mind to send you out that door and never let you back in." Monty's voice crescendoed as he spelled out the potential consequence for her, and any confidence and fire Hannah had gained was immediately doused. She couldn't lose another job. She couldn't lose her access to Evelyn's story. She couldn't fail—yet again.

"No. Please, no." She clasped her hands together on her lap, tears pooling on her lower eyelids, willing to do anything to make it all better. She could research the story without Monty—or Shelby Dawson— knowing. It would be hard—but possible. One day she'd have to get his permission to use Evelyn's rejected articles, or perhaps build up enough of an appetite for lying that she could invent a different origin story, but those were not today worries. Today, she was facing failure just when she was starting to taste success again, and anything looked preferable to that low. "I am so sorry. I overstepped, and I made a big mistake. I promise that I will just stay in the basement and do my work."

The silence in that moment was like the two sides of a vise closing slowly, squeezing Hannah from every direction. Monty made that smacking sound that usually made Hannah feel sick, and a rebellious tear ran down her cheek, unveiling more emotion than he probably ever knew she possessed. He let out a rattly breath, his answer rumbling in his chest as he proclaimed it.

"All right. One more chance." He slapped the bare spot on his desk and then leaned as far forward as he could manage. "But listen here: If you get yourself into trouble even one more time, there won't be a warning. You'll be let go."

Hannah wiped at her cheeks and put on her best impression of a pleasant face. She sniffed, and Monty continued to soften right in front of her eyes.

"Yes, sir, I understand."

"And . . . and I'm gonna need that ID you've been using. I'll keep it safe if you want to put it in your scrapbook one day, but for now, it'll be safer in my desk."

Hannah nodded and blinked away the last traces of her emotional moment.

"And . . . and . . ." He stuttered again, going through a list he must've created inside his head but also seeming to find it difficult to stay angry at a tearful young woman. She should be offended, but she was grateful for the one time misogyny was working in her favor. "This project you've been working on, does it have anything to do with Guy Franklin?"

"No! Not at all." At least that was the truth, though it was the only bit of honesty she could afford at the moment. She'd literally just promised to be a straight arrow and was already about to break that vow. "I am just trying to compile an accurate family history for my grandmother. It seems that her father took some charitable interest in the children's hospital, in particular one patient, who I mentioned to Ms. Dawson, and I thought she would like to have a picture or something if they happen to have any."

Monty clapped his giant hands together thunderously. "Well, why didn't you ask me? Then we could've saved ourselves all kinds of difficulties. I don't exactly have any pictures of your papaw at the children's home, but I have every single proof of every single edition of the newspaper since my great-granddaddy founded it in 1881. Why, I could find you stories about the Williamson family going back to when the *Record* was still the *Tate County Democrat*."

"Oh, you do?" she asked innocently and hated herself just a little bit for manipulating Monty's weakness for frail women. If she could look in those files, there was no doubt she could find more information about Evelyn, maybe even her last name, which would open up all kinds of doors when it came to tracking down the truth.

"I sure do. Just tell me what you want, and I can get it for you."

"Well," she hedged, "maybe I could just take a look?" She added a flutter or two of her eyelashes. Overkill or not, it didn't seem to faze Monty either way. He shook his head.

"No. Nobody goes through those files but me. Wouldn't want them to become a mess like those archives, am I right?" He grabbed a stack of Post-its and a large fountain pen, then he scratched off a note and stuck it on the number pad on his desk's phone. "But I have a memory like a jackrabbit even if my bones are creaking. Don't you worry. I have got you covered."

She gave him a tight smile. "Yes, thank you."

He beamed at her now as though she'd gone from a problem student visiting the principal's office to valedictorian in one meeting.

"Well, dear, I feel a whole lot better. It sounds like this was an innocent mistake. I'm sorry to be so dramatic, but the Dawson family is pretty important around these parts. It's always better to stay on their good side."

Clearly, Hannah thought to herself, wanting so badly to roll her eyes. She didn't like a political candidate's family controlling any part of the news media in the area, and she wondered what other newspapers were editing their stories based on their support.

"I'm sorry I put you in that position. I promise it won't happen again." She stood up, hoping that this close call was officially over.

"I know it won't, hun. Now you head on outta here. I'm sure you've got some work to do, and I've got plenty to fill my time till I go home to Momma."

Ugh. Grossed her out every time.

"Yes, sir," she said, taking the opening to escape without faltering. She was halfway to her desk when she heard Monty call in Dolores to take a memo, Hannah's ears burning from the stress of that exchange. She'd come so close to losing the very fine strands of life she'd started to weave together, all because of that stupid ID badge—and Shelby Dawson. But Hannah had some ideas about how to get her information and how to do it in a way that would circumvent Ms. Dawson.

Ding!

"Damn it," Hannah cursed, the sound of the notification in the quiet office making her jump. She covered her mouth even though no one was around to call her on her language. It had to be Alex. She'd found a way to stop herself from responding to him earlier, but after the drama with Monty, the idea of a text from her ex was too compelling to pass up. With a yank, she opened her top desk drawer.

"I should put a lock on this," she muttered to herself, cursing her lack of self-control but also relishing the anticipation, the rush of seeing his name glowing on her screen, the hungry way her eyes devoured every syllable. Ugh. She was pathetic, but there was an involuntary nature to the whole thing. Sometimes she couldn't help it—

Guy Franklin: Thanks for letting me tag along. Rosie is going to be so jealous.

Hmm. A text from Guy was not exactly what she'd been bracing for, but there it was—and she didn't hate it. Hannah picked up her phone and opened her messaging app. Even if his name didn't give her exploding fireworks, at least she didn't have to hold off from texting him back, which was—nice.

Hannah: She should be. Tell her that next time she's invited.

Guy Franklin: Sounds great.

Thinking bubbles trembled on the screen as he composed another message. They stopped and started a few times. Then his message came through. She watched with curiosity, still trying to figure out this man and what was going on behind his intriguing eyes and charm.

Guy Franklin: Can you tell Miss Mable that her part came in and I'll be stopping by later to work on the Buick?

Hannah: Oh good! She will be so relieved.

It was her turn to hesitate. She didn't know what it was about Guy or even Rosie for that matter, but they felt comfortable, safe. And bantering with them in the car over the weekend and exploring the cemetery with Guy was the most fun she'd had in a long time. Mamaw always told her she needed to be more social . . . She started typing again.

Hannah: Why don't you two come for dinner? I'm sure Carla won't mind.

As soon as she hit "Send" and the message went through, Hannah wondered if she'd made a mistake—jumped the gun. Maybe it was too early for an invitation according to whatever weird etiquette rules everyone else seemed to know and live by. The bubbles danced again, this time making her a little nervous, but when his answer popped in, she felt immediate relief and started typing quickly.

Guy Franklin: We'd love to.

Hannah: I'll get the details and text you in a bit.

Guy Franklin: Sounds great. See you tonight.

Hannah: See you tonight.

He didn't make her heart pound and palms sweat like Alex, and there were no butterflies when she saw his face or when his name came up on her phone, but she did like the steady way being around Guy made her feel.

CHAPTER 19

Hannah looked out over the landscape of the archive room, hands on her hips. In three weeks, she'd made her way through nearly two-thirds of the filing cabinets, and it showed. Last week, Monty started moving the metal storage units out once their contents were fully scanned. The room was beginning to feel cavernous in comparison to when she'd taken her first tentative steps into the chaotic basement.

When she'd started the assignment twenty days earlier, it'd seemed like a purgatory equal to one of Dante's seven terraces. But there was a fascinating satisfaction to recording history—making it permanent in some way. And with each drawer she completed, the motivation to continue had begun to escalate beyond the desire to find more of Evelyn's story.

Hannah made her way back to her portable workstation, which included a stool, notebook, pencil, and a few other supplies. She opened another drawer, almost finished with her second row of cabinets that week. The large pink Post-it pad sat by her side. As soon as she cleared out this drawer, Hannah would write *Storage* on one of the sticky notes and place it on top of the unit. The other seven filing cabinets in the row were similarly marked. Every time another line of metal towers disappeared, Hannah felt a sense of satisfaction but with an aftertaste of anxiety. It'd been an eternity since she'd opened a filing cabinet and known a piece of Evelyn's story was inside.

Usually, Hannah could sense when a lead related to her was close. She wasn't all New Agey, but there was an energy to a story that she could zero in on like a sixth sense.

But she hadn't felt so much as a goose bump since her trip to Memphis. There had been a few leads that came out of her journey to the university and Maggie's research skills, but most of them were dead ends. One would entail an overnight trip to Kentucky to look into a possible link to Harry's life. She'd go check it out after the Thanksgiving holiday, hopeful that it was the same Harry she'd been pursuing.

Thanksgiving. More time off from work, which normally she'd be happy for, but not this year, when it meant less time digging for answers and more time hanging out at Mamaw's house with her mom, who was coming to visit after turkey day, which would be spent in California with Brody and his two boys. Who could blame her? Brody and his wife had invited Hannah to join them, but there was no way she'd leave Mamaw alone, even though her grandmother was finally mobile enough to navigate her house with her walker now.

Hannah hauled out a stack of files and took them over to the computer. She shuffled through them quickly, having gotten pretty good at scanning a document with her eyes and knowing if it was from Evelyn. She was looking for the thin, cheap typewriter paper. It would likely be several pages long, single-spaced, typed, and written in a clear, first-person narrative. Most pages she could pass over just by the feel of the paper between her fingers. She used to look at every file with optimism and think, *This one is it. This time I'll find her.*

But that Pollyanna outlook had disappeared after a week without any discoveries and had never come back. She sighed. Nothing again. Along with hundreds of others she'd picked through, this pile was bereft of anything helpful. It was difficult even to muster up disappointment anymore. She organized the pages by paper size and scanned them one by one.

The trail wasn't totally dead. There was information at the Pines, and she was so close to finally gaining access to their files while avoiding any run-ins with Shelby Dawson. It turned out her great-nephew was far more helpful than Ms. Dawson herself.

A few texts and one phone call later, Peter had promised to find a way around his aunt to get Hannah the records she wanted if she'd meet him for one drink. It felt a little skeevy trading a drink for information, but Peter was fun to talk to, crazy charming, and a great potential contact for her journalism career. They'd arranged to meet up when she was in Memphis on Wednesday before her probably-a-bad-idea dinner with Alex. But pairing Alex's visit with a legit reason for making the trek to the city took the edge off her guilt.

Hannah wasn't used to using her womanly wiles on a man, but if Peter Dawson found her grouchy reporter look attractive, she wasn't beyond buttering up her source. But since the files for the children's hospital were organized by surnames, it would take considerable effort to look through each folder and ascertain which one held Evelyn's secrets—time and effort a state senator in the middle of a reelection campaign didn't have. She had to find a last name for Evelyn, which was where things got tricky. Hannah had used LexisNexis, Newspapers. com, and Ancestry.com, as well as visiting the records room at city hall, to no avail.

She knew, absolutely knew, that if she was going to find Evelyn's last name somewhere, the *Tate County Record* likely held that secret, but Hannah had still not found a way to get into Monty's files. Especially after Shelby's call.

Hannah dropped down onto the stool and replaced the documents, the folder crowned with a green Post-it that read *Scanned*. One more row and she'd be done for the day. Carla was making ribs again, and Rosie and Guy were coming over to finish the last few touches on

Mamaw's car. The first visit went off without a hitch, and they'd become semi-regular callers over the last week. Hannah had come to look forward to their visits.

Rosie liked to tell Hannah about school and, when her daddy wasn't around, boys. And Guy, when he could get a word in between Rosie's stories and Hannah's questions, talked about teaching and carpentry and his dream of going back to school to become a principal, which Hannah thought he'd be great at, but it made Rosie scrunch her nose up.

The last item in the drawer lay flat, wedged between a partition and the rear, almost creating a false floor. It was difficult to find an edge to grasp. Hannah wiggled her fingers around the perimeter of the manila envelope, trying to find her way between the packet and the metal walls. After a few minutes, she pried the oversize rectangular packet out of its hiding place. It was old. The flap didn't have adhesive. Instead, it had a string that looped around two cardboard buttons. She turned it over in her lap, and the word *Rejected* was written on the front of it in red wax pencil.

This time, no otherworldly warnings tipped her off as she unwound the red string that kept the envelope closed. Inside were several hastily folded documents. None of them in their original pocket and every single one shoved roughly into the small space without any seeming concern for possible damage.

Hannah selected one cluster of pages, crumpled together, and unfolded the thin paper. She gasped and nearly dropped the whole stack.

It was from Evelyn.

There was no mistake. Besides the familiar technical aspects, like the paper type and the quality of typewriter, Hannah would recognize that voice anywhere. Her eyes stung, and this time not from the dust in the air. She had missed this voice. She didn't even know how badly she had wanted to find out the rest of Evelyn's story until this very moment.

It felt like talking to an old friend. Or like seeing her brother, for the first time in too many years, at her father's funeral. It felt like picking up where they had left off. It felt like texting Alex.

She dumped out the remaining artifacts. One. Two. Three. Four. Fewer than she'd expected, but each installment was longer than the previous one. She was shaking now. The other submissions Hannah found had been filed at random. These three had been collected intentionally over the course of—Hannah checked the dates at the top of each message—six months. Someone back in 1935 had caught on that every few weeks a letter would show up, giving the next installment of this dramatic tale like it was a serial on the radio. Maybe they were collected for personal entertainment, or maybe another journalist thought they smelled the same story that Hannah did. Or maybe someone didn't want this story told at all. Well, she wasn't going to let that happen. Hannah flattened the pages to the best of her ability and put them in order.

The sound of the front door creaking leaked through the floorboards down into the basement. Usually, Hannah didn't notice such minute details. Most of her day was filled with murmured conversations or the tromp of Monty's footsteps or the click-clack of Dolores's low heels. But today she knew what that creak meant. It was closing time. Dolores was heading home, and soon Monty would stand at the top of the stairs and call her name. There was no time to catch up now.

In the past, Hannah had scanned the Evelyn letters and then taken the copies home, storing away the originals to keep them safe. But she didn't have time for that today. And she wasn't going to wait. The neatly arranged papers slid easily into the manila folder.

She closed the flap and secured it with the button and string closure, quickly wrote *Storage* on a pink Post-it, and slapped it on the end of the row. Hannah cleaned up her station, making sure every drawer was closed and locked for easy transport. She flew up the stairs with the envelope of letters clutched tightly by her side.

"Hey, I'm heading home," she called out from across the room in the direction of Monty's open door.

"Miss Williamson, one moment, please!"

Almost, she thought, looking at the exit only a few feet away with longing. Her jaw clenched, but she responded sweetly and calmly as she pulled on her stocking cap and gloves for the ride home. "Yes, sir?"

"Oh, there you are," he said, rounding the corner and meeting her by the door. "Where are we on the files in the basement? Mrs. Tonya Sellers is lookin' to start renovations beginning of December. Lots of engagements around Christmas, you know how it goes."

She literally did not know how "it goes" and wasn't exactly in the mood to think about engagements, weddings, deadlines, or pretty much anything other than the story in her bag. But her ability to *pretend* to care had grown exponentially.

"Yes, I'm sure." She grinned, but then shifted to an "I regret to inform you" scowl. "I do think it will take two or three weeks at least to get the rest of the room scanned."

"I was afraid of that." He sank his hands deep into his pockets and rocked back on his heels. "I think I'm going to have to cut your project short, hun. I'll have Terry clear things out down there over Thanksgiving, and he can finish this grunt work of scanning and filing at the storage facility. Then you can get back where you belong—on assignment. What do you think about that?"

"No, thank you," she said, rushing to reject his offer as soon as he stopped talking. It made sense why he'd expect her to be overjoyed at the change, just like when he'd suggested taking her out of the archives a few weeks earlier, but the idea made her panic. It wasn't only because of her dedication to Evelyn either. She wanted to finish what she'd started, complete something that she could be proud of, and not hand it off to Terry to toss together in his spare time. She wasn't inching forward anymore. Her momentum was building, and it felt fantastic to be successful again, even if it was by sorting files in a basement.

"I was worried you might say that." He took out his handkerchief and used it to wipe his head and then dab at his nose, which normally would make Hannah gag, but today it made her impatient. "I know it can be frightening to get back on the horse, dear, but you can't keep hiding from it anymore."

"I'm not worried about . . . the horse . . . whatever that is a metaphor for." Hannah tilted her head, wishing she had a translation guide for Monty. "I like my assignment, and I've put in a lot of hours down there. I want to see it through."

"Well, no matter the reason—I'm sorry, but I need you elsewhere." He drove the handkerchief back into the recesses of his pocket and shrugged. "When you get back from break, you'll be back on traffic and education."

"Oh, come on, Monty. This is ridiculous . . ." Hannah stomped and clenched her fists by her side, helpless.

"No, dear, this is business, and I have to make decisions that keep this newspaper working. If you want to continue your tenure at this establishment," he said, getting formal in his speech like he always did when he was getting worked up, "I advise that you do as you are told."

"But—" She pushed one more time, knowing that the soft, friendly Monty couldn't be too far under his gruff, no-nonsense exterior.

"Have a good evening, Miss Williamson," he said, cutting her off before she could form a sentence and walking away, putting a solid end to their conversation.

"Whatever," she muttered, feeling like a teenager as she huffed out of the office and roughly wrestled her bike to the street. As she sped through the black roads, the nip in the air bit at her cheeks. It was a nostalgic feeling that reminded her of childhood and autumn in Chicago. It also helped cool the resentment that was boiling up inside her. Outside the rumble of her tires and the wind in her face, Hannah's only comfort was knowing that she carried with her four new letters. Maybe they held the answers she'd been searching for, or perhaps they didn't, and she'd never find out who shot Evelyn.

CHAPTER 20

Hannah's legs ached as she made the turn into Mamaw's slanted driveway. The light was on in the garage, which meant Guy was inside doing whatever he needed to do to Mamaw's car. Gliding to a stop inside the garage, Hannah jumped off her bicycle and lifted it onto its holder on the rear wall, just over Papaw's old workbench. The sound must have gotten Guy's attention because he peeked his head out from underneath the propped-open hood of the Buick.

"Hey there, speed demon! Didn't know you'd headed home," Guy said, rubbing his clean hands on a white rag that didn't show even a smudge of grease. He'd clearly changed after work but still looked as put together as ever with his dark-blue jeans and a maroon T-shirt with matching unbuttoned flannel. His sleeves were rolled up, probably for necessity, but also in such a precise way that it looked like it must have been on purpose.

"Damn it," she cursed. She'd forgotten to text Guy and let him know when she was on her way home so that Rosie could set the table. Guy put a finger to his lips. Hannah lowered her voice and whispered, "I mean—damn it."

He laughed. "You know you could just not curse, right?"

She looped her bag's shoulder strap over her head, where she'd been wearing it across her body like a seat belt, and placed the whole thing on the workbench. "You know that you could like me for who I am and not try and change me, right?" she tossed back, playful but also tapping into her more negative emotions.

"I mean, who would want to change such a charming, delightful creature as you?" he said, joining her where she stood elbow deep in her bag, digging through her belongings.

"Don't you try and charm me. I won't fall for that trick again," she said, trying to keep up the banter and locate the envelope of letters before she exploded from anticipation.

"Wait, what do you mean *again*? Are you saying you fell for my charms at some point? Why was I not made aware of this?" He flashed his most winning smile and leaned on the counter with one of his elbows.

"Here it is!" she exclaimed, ignoring his quip and slipping the manila envelope out from the clutch of items she'd started taking with her everywhere she went. She was nearly as excited to share the new articles with Guy as she was to read them herself. He had a pretty good journalistic instinct, and he definitely understood the hunger a good story could build inside a reporter. He'd been helpful and interested and provided some great insights as someone who grew up in the area. Plus, it was nice having somebody to talk to about . . . everything. She'd lived inside her head alone for far too long now.

"Here is what?" he asked, eyeing the package in her hand.

"I finally found more." Hannah quickly unraveled the string that separated both of them from the next chapter of Evelyn's story.

"Wait. More *letters*? As in, more than one?"

Chatting with her mom now and again wasn't the same as having someone she could text when a thought came to her at ten o'clock at night. Last week, he'd even taken her to the spot on the river where Evelyn fell in while trying to swing the gap, which was still a summer tradition in Senatobia. Hannah had threatened to try out the tradition the whole hike, making Guy grumble and Rosie laugh.

"It's not safe," Guy argued with both females following him down the worn backwoods trail.

"I'm a big girl, Guy. I can decide what is safe and what is not safe," Hannah pushed back, enjoying his willingness to debate and finding it invigorating to be a strong example for Rosie.

"Yeah, Daddy. She's a grown woman," Rosie chimed in, and Hannah's chest filled with a warm pride.

"You two can't gang up on me," Guy said. "I'm just the voice of safety."

They continued like that, ducking through low-hanging branches, and Hannah worried that every shift in the underbrush was a snake, which Guy found hilarious, reassuring Hannah that snakes went into hibernation once it got colder. When they got to the gap, some wise parent or Good Samaritan had removed the rope for the winter, shutting down further jokes about daring deeds. Hannah wasn't sure if it was the hike or connecting another real place to Evelyn's story or her growing friendship with the little Franklin family, but she fell asleep that night easily, without remembering to check her phone.

Hannah waved the envelope triumphantly. "Yes! Four letters!"

"Well, that is the best news I have had all day," he said, tossing his still-extremely-clean rag onto the counter.

"Yeah, no *s-h-i-t*," she whispered, checking over her shoulder to make sure that the door to the house was closed. "Me too. By a lot."

At some point, she'd have to share about Monty's new business decisions. But for now, she'd let the excitement of discovery hang in the air for a little bit longer.

"Should we read one before we let Carla know I'm home?"

"Hell yeah, we should," he blurted out, making Hannah's eyes widen.

"Mr. Franklin! Watch your language." She feigned shock and horror, trying on the overly exaggerated southern accent Guy liked to use when he was making a point.

"Oh, I'm sorry. I meant *hell yeah, we should*," he whispered, mimicking Hannah's ridiculous attempts to hide her swearing.

"Oh, shut up and listen." She hit him with his rag, and he recoiled as though she had tossed a grenade. Guy crossed his arms and then put a finger to his lips in a silent promise to stay quiet. Once she was satisfied that he'd behave, Hannah started reading out loud.

```
October 10, 1935

Dear Mr. Martin,
I have not heard back from your insti-
tution, and I have not seen my letters
published in your newspaper, so I am
assuming that you have not found my
story compelling enough for publica-
tion just yet. Please do not give up on
me. I promise I will get to the point
the best I can.
    Writing to you has brought a light
back into my life that I thought was
gone forever. When I was shot, everyone
thought I would die. I stayed in the
hospital for a year. I had operations,
blood transfusions, the flu, pneumonia,
heart trouble, a dislocated kidney, and
I took enough medications to kill a
dog. But at some point, I and everybody
else decided I was going to live.
```

"Oh my God, I love that," Hannah said, pointing to the first two paragraphs. Writing her story brought a light back into Evelyn's life, just like researching her story was starting to do for Hannah.

"But I'd kind of like to know who shot her, though. Am I right?" Guy asked, kindly moving her finger out of the way.

"Okay, okay. Read for yourself," Hannah said, offering to share the letter. He moved in closer, their shoulders touching. She could hear him breathing but also felt each rise and fall of his chest as his arm pressed into hers briefly with each inhale. The soft touch of his flannel and the heat that permeated through from his skin made Hannah want to lean in as they both started reading again.

> I lived in the Home for Crippled Children as a student until I was eighteen and then was transferred to the Home for the Incurables once I became of age. I have been here for just over two years. I told one of the other girls here, Diane, about writing these letters to you. She didn't like it one little bit. She told me that this was my world, and I would have to make my life accordingly. She said I needed to stop thinking about things outside of this place because I was going to live here and die here. I could go out there and visit, and the people out there could come to see me. I could bring them happiness, and they, in turn, could make life more complete for me. But she warned me not even to think that I could go out there to live, for I would never be happy in their world.
>
> "They belong to that world, you to this one, so make your life to fit

in here." Such was Diane's advice. I
couldn't see it that way—I still don't
see it that way. I think that the world
belongs to me as much as to Myrtle or
Vivian or anyone else for that matter.
So I'm going to keep writing these letters to you. And maybe one day you'll
see fit to put them in the newspaper.
But I won't give up and settle for the
small, sad world Diane wants for me.

"She's so fierce," Guy added, his breath on her cheek when he
spoke, distracting Hannah momentarily and adding to the heady feeling she already got whenever she read Evelyn's words.

"I think she's my hero," Hannah added, not even joking this time.
She wanted to get this story out almost as badly as Evelyn had when she
typed up the first article. And she was starting to see Guy as an integral
part of that process.

I will now pick up where I left
off the last time I wrote to you. I
think I was telling you about Harry
Westbrook, the nineteen-year-old cowpuncher I thought I was in love with
that summer. He was braver and more
handsome than any of the boys I'd met
in town. Harry officially moved across
the street with people who were good
friends of ours so that he could be
near me.

One morning, from across the street,
he heard Mother screaming at me. He

came rushing over, burst in right through the front door without knocking, which stunned and frightened me because I knew Mother wouldn't like it. She'd retired to her bedroom already.

He said, "Evelyn, where is your mother?"

"Harry, please don't go see her. It would only make matters worse."

"I'm going to see her whether you tell me her location or not. So you might as well tell me where she is." He was stubborn, and I knew I couldn't stop him because even after I begged him and tore at his arm to keep him from going upstairs to search for himself, he still insisted. So I gave in and told him that she was in her room.

"Is this it? Is this when the guns come out?" Guy asked, leaning over Hannah's shoulder even more pronouncedly, pointing to the sentence on the page.

"Shhh. I'm reading," Hannah scolded. She risked looking up at him but had to stare back at the yellowed article as soon as she'd caught his eye, the sleeping butterflies in her stomach waking up a little more than she'd like.

They stayed in a room for two hours, and what I went through while that door was shut was plenty. When they came out together, Harry and Mother were the best of friends. I don't know what he said to this very day, but Harry became my first boyfriend.

It was a strange sensation having a boyfriend. Mother was still stringent and kept us apart as often as possible. But Harry was allowed to sit and talk with me on the front porch after dinner most nights. One evening after Mother went inside to put Daddy to bed, he took my hand in his and kissed it. I thought my heart might explode. I had never felt more beautiful in my entire life.

If Mother had left Harry and I alone, I really do think he would have married me. But that is when Mr. Fred came to stay with us. His place in this mixed-up story of my life started when Mother noticed Mr. Fred's keen interest in me. He was twice my age, I fourteen, he twenty-eight. I thought then that he was ancient. I was a rather good-looking girl with a nice figure and a smart appearance, who realized it even then. I remember once I was walking down the street with a girlfriend, and several men were working, and as we passed, one stuck to me and said, "You are a very beautiful girl."

I said, "I know it" and went on.

"Who is this asshole?" Hannah asked herself under her breath, adding a Mr. Fred to her suspects list.

"Shhh, I'm reading," Guy teased, repeating her earlier complaint, bumping into her side lightly. Hannah pushed back playfully.

"Fine. I'll keep all my comments till the end." She straightened the page and reread the line she'd been stuck on.

"You don't need to make comments. Your facial expressions say everything," he said, the touch of his eyes on her face tangible. Hannah pretended to keep reading, hoping he wouldn't notice the blush she was sure must be visible on her neck and cheeks.

Mr. Fred seemed to think I was just about as beautiful as anybody. He was from Memphis and staying in Senatobia for a little while, looking for some farmland. I could always feel his eyes on me. Somehow Mother and Daddy liked Mr. Fred and wanted me to go with him. Well, Mother wanted me to go with him. Daddy was getting sicker and sicker every day and was far too ill to understand what Mother was trying to do.

"He has money and can take you the places you want to go," she'd say. "He's not just some silly boy who wants to be necking all the time. He has sense. He's a grown man. He can take care of you."

But I didn't want Mr. Fred to take care of me. I wanted Harry to take care of me, but my mother told me that she would take away her permission for

Harry if I didn't start to entertain
Mr. Fred.

It started with sitting together in
the evenings. He would read to me.
Sonnets from Shakespeare. Poems by
Lord Byron. Sometimes it felt like I
was in a schoolroom the way he would go
on and on about stories and poetry and
even politics, which I had less interest in than all the other things. But
I thought I loved Harry.

So, I sat with Mr. Fred, and I
smiled at Mr. Fred, and I made sure
that Mr. Fred got the best piece of
meat at the dinner table, and I smiled
at him as he walked up the stairs to
his room every night.

I still had not been allowed to go
on a single date with Harry, but Mother
told me as long as I let Mr. Fred take
me riding that she'd allow me to go to
the movies alone with Harry. Of course,
I didn't tell Harry about any of this.
What fellow would like to know that his
girl was going out with another guy?
But I thought about that old saying.
You know the one? The one about what
you don't know can't hurt you. So, I
agreed to go riding with Mr. Fred. It
was a decision I would soon come to
regret.

I hate to be a bother, but I must leave the story there for now. I will write again as soon as I'm able. Please continue to consider my submission for publication if you do please, sir.

I am eternally in your debt,
Evelyn

CHAPTER 21

Hannah lowered the papers in front of her, the lighthearted vibe gone. Evelyn wasn't perfect. She was rebellious and more than a touch vain, yet Hannah couldn't help but respect her bravery and resilience.

"I can't believe they forced their daughter to go out with a man twice her age," Guy said, the first one to talk. "It makes me sick to my stomach. That girl was barely older than Rosie is right now. How in heaven's name did anyone think that was a good idea?"

"It's pretty mind-blowing *now* but normal back then, maybe?" Hannah asked, equally stunned and offended by what was just the newest atrocity in Evelyn's life they had learned of.

"You know what else was 'normal' back then? Prohibition. Segregation. Jim Crow laws. Lynching. Normal for 1929 doesn't mean it's okay."

Hannah glanced over at Guy. He was angry. She could tell in one look that this most recent submission had touched a very tender nerve.

"Oh, I'm not defending it. I mean, add to your list sexism, sexual harassment, little access to birth control, rape culture, women treated as second-class citizens. The list goes on. Just looking at the historical context."

"Screw the historical context. I have a daughter. Who the hell could sell off their kid like that?" Guy asked, slamming his fist down on the

counter and sending a surprised jolt through Hannah, scattering all the
tingling, warm feelings they'd been exchanging during the reading of
the article. He blew out a long, hard breath and scratched at the stubble
on his chin. Noticing her stunned stance, Guy rubbed a hand across his
mouth, looking a little embarrassed that he couldn't get his emotions
entirely under control.

Surprised at his outburst, Hannah also found she was feeling something different from shock. She wasn't going to say it out loud, but she
kind of liked seeing Guy lose it a little bit. He was always so calm and
focused, and he spoke like a teacher who had the instructions for every
moment in life written in front of him. But Evelyn's story had touched
him in a way that made him look up from his sheet of directions and
ask questions. And that was more attractive than his charming smile or
flattering words.

"You okay?" Hannah asked, almost tempted to reach out and put
a hand on his shoulder but holding back, willing to acknowledge the
effect Guy had on her but not interested in indulging those feelings.
Not yet, at least. Not until after she saw Alex, heard what he had to
say, figured some things out in her own life. She held on to the papers
tighter, keeping her hand in check.

"Yeah. Yeah, I'm okay." He pushed away from the workbench,
where he'd been leaning, and headed back toward the still-open hood
of the Buick. "I guess it just hit a little close to home. You know?"

He searched through a tray of tools on the ground in front of the
car. It seemed like Guy didn't want to talk about his reaction, but that
only made Hannah want to ask more questions. That predilection made
her a good reporter but a terrible friend. She hadn't figured out how to
separate the two yet.

"I feel it too. It makes me sick reading about all the things that hap-
pened to Evelyn, but you know what makes *me* furious? It wasn't just
Evelyn, right? I think that's why I want to tell this story so badly—for
Evelyn, sure, but also because I think it makes something inside all of

us ask some hard questions," she said, following him to his spot on the other side of the garage.

"Being a parent is never easy, but stories like that, I don't know, it does make you worry."

"Yeah, when I was Rosie's age, I barely even wanted to talk to my dad about anything going on in my life. Felt weird that I was getting boobs and my period and . . ."

Guy grimaced, and Hannah stopped her train of thought before it went too far. If swearing was frowned upon, then talking about puberty with a member of the opposite sex was probably downright taboo.

"Rosie's still pretty good about talking to me. And my sisters said they would help her when the time comes for"—he waved his hand in the air while holding a wrench—"all of that."

"So." Hannah stepped even closer to Guy now, not just for proximity's sake but because she didn't want Rosie to hear her next question if she happened to walk into the garage during their discussion. "Rosie's mom is completely out of the picture, then?"

It was a bold ask, and Guy kept working for a second like he hadn't heard her, making the blush return to Hannah's cheeks. She was about to go along with his fiction and excuse herself to go inside and check on dinner, but Guy spoke up first.

"Megan and I met our sophomore year. We dated all through high school, but senior year she got pregnant." He checked Hannah's reaction out of the corner of his eye. She was more than invested—she was wide-eyed and riveted. She tried to tell herself she was listening like a reporter, unbiased, interested in a good story. But she knew that was all BS. She'd been wanting to ask for a long time, to know more about Rosie, of course, but also to know more about Guy. He was a good father, a remarkable father, a father to Rosie in the way that Patrick Williamson had been a father to Hannah. But what led to this smart, charismatic, attractive man doing all of this alone?

Biting on her pinkie nail, she tried to be patient and let Guy work his way through his own story. It was an old trick she'd been taught about interviewing: sometimes not talking can get a reluctant source to open up.

"Now, that likely sounds scandalous to you, but I assure you, it is more common around here than one would hope." He twisted the wrench with great effort, working on loosening something that Hannah couldn't see from where she was standing. "I tried to marry Megan, but her family thought she was too young, and in retrospect—they were likely right. Rosie was born three weeks after we graduated from Senatobia High School. If you think she's adorable now, God, you should've seen her then. Just the most attentive little thing, like she was taking in the whole world, you know?"

"I don't think that's exactly changed," Hannah added, perfectly able to imagine a bright-eyed baby girl resting in Guy's arms. With a little hop, she lifted herself onto the workbench, putting a fist under her chin, supported by her knee.

"No, no, it hasn't, has it?" he agreed and swapped out the wrench for some other tool Hannah didn't recognize. "But Rosie's momma wasn't ready for a baby, and I don't blame her. Megan had always been a beautiful dancer. She'd done all kinds of workshops and summer programs in all kinds of places before getting pregnant, and I wasn't exactly ready either. I had a baseball scholarship to Ole Miss, full ride and everything. So we planned to put the baby up for adoption. But then I saw her, and I can't explain it." He rested his hand on top of the grille of the car and stared off into space like he was experiencing the memory in real time. "I saw her, and I just couldn't sign those adoption papers."

Hannah swallowed and blinked rapidly. The look on Guy's face, the love and devotion to a child, the captivation with his daughter's vigor and intelligence—it was the way her father used to look when talking about her. Guy went back to the task he was tinkering with, and Hannah cleared her throat so she could speak without sounding emotional.

"So, did Megan change her mind, then?"

Guy shook his head. "Nuh-uh. She signed off her parental rights and moved to New York. She's done pretty well too. Went to Columbia, been in some Broadway shows, and made a real name for herself."

"And you . . ."

Guy put the tool back on the tray with a clang and slammed the hood shut. This time his hands were actually dirty. He wiped at them and then grabbed a set of keys off the counter.

"Let's just say I haven't played baseball in some time," he said with a wink, spinning the key ring around his pointer finger. "So, should we try this thing out?" he asked, knocking on the hood.

That was as much of Guy's backstory as she was going to get for that moment, but it was enough. Just like Evelyn's puzzle was snapping together piece by piece, so was Guy's.

"Absolutely," she said, hopping down to the cement floor, dusting herself off in case any sawdust had clung to her clothing. Then she remembered her conversation with Monty. She held up both her hands. "Wait for just a second. I forgot to tell you something super important."

Guy palmed the keys and came to stand next to her, half sitting on the workbench next to where she was standing. He folded his arms in mock seriousness, close enough that she could feel his body heat and smell the traces of motor oil on his fingers.

"I'm all ears."

The anxiety about Monty's decision was coming back full force. She put her hands in her pockets and shrugged.

"Monty is moving me back to the traffic and education sections. He doesn't want me to finish the archives. Terry is moving the filing cabinets out over Thanksgiving break."

Guy's head bobbed ever so slightly as he took in the information. "So, you'll be writing again?"

"Uh, I guess. But I don't count blurbs about old ladies getting into car accidents and coverage of school spelling bees as hard-hitting journalism." She'd expected outrage, anger, frustration, just like she'd felt when Monty broke the news. Or gosh, at least one *Damn it*, but he seemed calm and unfazed.

"Neither is sitting in a basement, scanning files," Guy said, and it cut a little too close to a nerve that was still very tender and barely starting to heal. How did he always seem to find her bare spots and irritate them?

"Uh, yeah, it is. I'm researching an important story that goes beyond the *Record* and Monty and this little town. It takes time and footwork and"—she lowered her voice—"effing dedication."

"I get that," he said, not taking her bait when she slighted his hometown. "I'm not trying to minimize this particular story, but you don't know what you have in these new articles. And whether you want to admit it or not, you've been under Monty's heel down there in that cellar. I know it doesn't look like it, but he's doing you a favor, shoving you out of the nest, if you will."

"I thought you cared more than this. Five minutes ago you looked like you were ready to get into a fight over Evelyn's love life," she said, roughly pushing away from the plywood surface they were both leaning on and loading up her belongings. Who was Guy Franklin, anyway? Just some man she'd met a few weeks ago. What did his opinion matter?

Guy watched her without moving, like she was a toddler throwing a temper tantrum over a piece of candy. This was why she used to think he was arrogant. He was. Once she had her things put together, Hannah donned her bag and turned to face Guy again before heading inside.

"Oh, and one more thing. I can't even find any more information until I have Evelyn's last name, and I can't find that out without the files from the *Record*. You *know* that. So excuse me if I'm a little bit frustrated."

"This is your definition of 'a little bit'?" Guy responded, turning her anger into another joke.

Hannah bit her lip and gave him a tight, fake smile.

"I know women down here aren't supposed to express real emotion, but yeah, I'm upset and—gasp—angry. I have a graduate degree in journalism. I worked for the *Chicago Tribune* for six years, and I was this close to transitioning into feature writing." She held her thumb and pointer finger so close together that no light could pass through. "And that all fell apart for me because . . . well, because of some personal things, but . . . this story—Evelyn's story—could change all that. Do you think reporting about traffic patterns on I-55 and the minutes of school board meetings is writing? No, Guy, *this* is writing."

She patted her bag, stuffed to the brim with research, notes, and leads. It had been empty when she walked off the plane into the Memphis airport three months ago, but now it was so heavy that the strap left a mark on her neck when she was biking to and from work.

"Whoa, hold on one second, now," he said, reaching out and resting a hand on her shoulder. "Will you just listen for a second?"

She stared up at him, hoping he couldn't feel the frantic pounding of her heartbeat or see the line of sweat that was gathering at her hairline. She wanted to toss his hand off, run inside, and slam the door in his face, but she was worried about looking childish yet again. Showing her feelings was one thing. Acting out of control was another.

"Yeah, okay."

"I wasn't talkin' about you writing some fluff piece for the *Record*. I was talkin' about you writing for yourself," he said, his voice soothing and serene. She opened her mouth to respond, but he put his other hand on her opposite shoulder and didn't let her get a word in. "And if you read these new articles and they don't tell you enough, then we *will* find a way to get you what you need. I promise you."

"How? It's impossible without her name. Without the rest of her story," she said, softening but still on edge.

"Then we'll get her name. We will get her story," he said. His eyes spelled sincerity, and he didn't seem bothered by her skeptical gaze. She licked her lips and tapped the thick sole of her boot on the garage floor, feeling the heat of her outrage escape from her like steam off the asphalt during a summer rainstorm.

"So I think this means you *do* care, then. Just to clarify." She raised one eyebrow.

"Don't push your luck," he said, giving her shoulders a gentle squeeze but not letting go.

"Why are you helping me, Guy Franklin?" Hannah asked, meeting his warm gaze, the connection just as physical as his hands on her shoulders.

"Because I like how your brain works," he said, grazing her forehead with his hand. "And, despite your Yankee stubbornness," he joked, "you seem to have a good heart." He lightly pressed his palm against her chest, just under her collarbone. He had to feel it, her racing pulse, the way her skin warmed wherever he touched it.

The door to the garage squeaked open. Guy dropped his hands and took a giant step in reverse. Rosie called out her name and took Hannah by the hand, spouting information about school, making dinner with Carla, and setting the table at such a rapid speed that it all started blending together. But even after Hannah went inside, making conversation and helping with dinner, and even while Guy was saying grace, she could feel the memory of his hands on her skin, and she wondered what would've happened if Rosie hadn't interrupted.

CHAPTER 22

Carla left after dinner was on the table and had been delivered to Mamaw's bedroom on a tray. Hannah filled Rosie in on the latest developments with Evelyn, with some careful editing, and promised to send the rest of the new pages to Guy as soon as she had a chance to review them that evening.

After dinner, Guy insisted on helping with cleanup and gave Rosie a pass for once, since the sixth grader had a project due the next day and still was not finished. As Hannah and Guy cleared the table, Rosie poured every ounce of her artistic creativity into the paper bag she'd brought from home to transform it into an "Indian vest."

"I know. I know," Guy said when Hannah rolled her eyes at the concept of a traditional feathered-headband-and-golden-buckle type of Thanksgiving depiction. Hannah collected the dessert plates and put them next to the sink to be rinsed.

"I wrote an article a few years back about this push by educators in Chicago to teach the real narrative of Thanksgiving," Hannah said, low enough that Rosie couldn't hear them in case her thoughts would hurt the girl's feelings.

She ran the water and washed off the residue of cake crumbs and frosting before placing the dishes in the sink full of lemon-scented bubbles and warm water. Guy filled the other sink with warm water, set a collection of silverware beside her, and then took up the position to her left and started to roll up his sleeves.

"A few of us have talked to the administration. It just takes some time for things to change down here. But they do change . . . eventually."

"I guess, but I don't know, how does it not drive you crazy?" Hannah asked, referring not just to the Thanksgiving inaccuracies but to all the microaggressions against anyone seen as different.

"I wouldn't assume that it doesn't. I mean, my momma taught *me* not to assume . . ."

"I know you've told me this one. I think it's your nice way of calling me an ass," she said, remembering the joke from one of their first conversations.

"Not an ass," he said, dropping his volume and getting sober, maybe more severe than she'd ever seen him. "But you act like you know what it is like being a person of color, and as well-meaning as you are—you don't know. And I appreciate your outrage. I promise I do, like I've said before—it's refreshing in some ways. But it's *exhausting* always taking care of your outrage when I have enough to be outraged about."

Hannah didn't respond immediately, letting his thoughtful rebuke settle in. Since getting to Mississippi—and, if she was honest with herself, even before—every discussion on racism had somehow become about how it made *her* feel: embarrassment at her family history, guilt at her "privilege," desperation to be different, confusion about how to counteract the damage done.

On a much smaller scale, it reminded her of when she'd found out about Alex's affair and her relationship ended. Brody, who'd been close friends with Alex in the years he'd been a part of their family, had a sudden urge to fly in from California just so he could punch his former buddy in the face, which felt good to Hannah at first. But when Brody started calling the hospital where Alex worked, trying to get him fired, and found the name of Alex's new girlfriend and called her family to tell them she was a slut—his anger stopped being about Hannah. It made her feel lonely and isolated, and eventually made her stop talking to Brody altogether.

"I'm sorry," she said, wishing he'd been wrong but knowing he was spot-on. "My father had a saying growing up, like your momma: *silence is complicity*. I learned to speak before I think, sometimes. But you're right, this is your life every day, and there is zero way for me to understand even half of what you experience."

"Let's put aside the fact that many individuals don't have the means to just up and move their whole lives." He made an invisible ball with his hands and placed it on the counter. "As for me, this is my home, and my family is here and community and . . . You know there are things wrong with Chicago too." He picked up the sponge and wiped down a plate in circular motions as he spoke. "The first time we met, you looked at me like I was gonna rob you blind. Can't tell me that's because it's some utopia up there in the Windy City."

"Well, yeah, but you can find crime anywhere." Hannah pointed as she made her argument, water running down her arm.

"Sure, but discrimination is everywhere too; it just wears different masks," Guy said, dunking Hannah's rinsed plates into the sink of warm water.

Chicago was not some bastion of equality, and she knew that even when she spent years of her teens and young adulthood disparaging the South and confounding her racist roots. But somehow she'd always seen the South as "the worst" bad guy in the fight, which was making her start to wonder if that heated focus on a faraway villain made her overlook the ones at arm's reach. When Hannah didn't respond with some quip or quickly formed opinion, Guy spoke up with an attempt to lighten the mood.

"But I do see why you love it up there so much—not every city can be the murder capital of the country. Been meaning to ask. Did you guys get a medal for that?"

"No." Hannah chuckled, splashing a few drops of water in his direction before plunging another plate into his side of the sink, trying to snap out of her deep thoughts and play along. "It is just one medal. We pass it around, like the Stanley Cup."

"Oh, I see," he said, snickering.

"You think I'm a bit much, don't you?" Hannah asked, feeling vulnerable, a youthful tremble to her question. He gave her one of those out-of-the-corner-of-his-eye looks that she wondered if he practiced in the mirror.

"No, ma'am. Not too much at all." He continued with his part of the chore, nearly finished with all the plates they'd used. "But I also don't totally agree with your daddy's way of doin' things."

"My daddy?" she asked, trying not to allow herself to fall into a repeat performance of her outburst from the garage. She turned off the water on her side of the sink and picked up a towel to start drying the stack of clean dishes in front of her, listening before lashing out this time.

"You said he moved y'all north because he didn't want you growing up around all the same things he did?"

"Yeah, that's right." The dry plates stacked up next to Hannah, like every conversation with Guy, one layer at a time. She was determined to listen this time, really listen.

"So this is how I talk about it with my kids at school." He stopped and rolled his eyes up toward the ceiling, like he was trying to find the right way to explain what he wanted to say. "When I was a kid, we had this big old magnolia tree in my yard. It was huge, bigger than the one by the courthouse down the street."

Hannah tried to imagine the scene in her head. The tree in the main square had branches that touched the top of the two-story building and spread out over a massive stone courtyard. She rode past it nearly every day on her way to and from the *Record*, and she'd recently started wondering if the lightly tinted autumn leaves were ever going to fall.

Guy continued, pulling the plug from the sink, drying his hands, and beginning to unroll his sleeves.

"The property line goes right through that tree, and at some point, before my daddy owned it, when two neighbors were fighting or something, they hacked into that tree and put a metal fence right through it." He slashed his finger through the residue of bubbles that hadn't made it down the drain.

"By the time I was a teenager, the business picked up steam, and we bought the land next door. So my daddy wanted to take down that fence, make it all one big yard. We spent a week digging the posts out from the ground and hauling the chain-link to the dump. Then we refilled the holes with dirt, till after a while you couldn't even tell there had been anything separating the two pieces of land . . . except for that tree. The tree had grown around that fence, and they'd become all intertwined." He linked his fingers, weaving them together like a basket.

"It'd made that magnolia tree grow all crooked on one side, and half the branches didn't even have leaves or flowers anymore. My grandpa wanted to cut it down, plant a new tree. But Daddy loved that tree. Said I'd learned to walk under that tree and that my sister Lacey had played house by its roots. He thought it was unfair to cut down something so beautiful because some angry man decided that his problems were more important than that tree."

"What ended up happening?" She liked seeing the world from Guy's steady but firm outlook. So often, she felt like she rode swells of passion or impulse that took her to the highest of highs but then tossed her into the watery depths nearly as often. He reminded Hannah of those freight trains she'd seen in Memphis, unhurried but centered on a track that kept him focused and would eventually lead him to his destination.

"My daddy kept the tree. Took him a while, but eventually, he dug that fence out of the flesh of the tree one piece at a time. He'd dig and carve and then let it heal and then start over on another spot." Guy shrugged. "I still can't say who was right, but I do know that Rosie took her first steps under that tree. And she climbed it for the first time when she was eight. And last April, my brother was married under its branches, which are startin' to bloom again."

Hannah hadn't ever been in Mississippi when the magnolias bloomed, but she could only imagine what the tree by the courthouse would look like covered in bright, fragrant blossoms. And for a moment, instead of dreading a timeline that kept her in Mississippi any longer than necessary, she hoped she was still here in the springtime so she could see it.

"In my way of thinking—there's no use hiding from the fact that there was a fence stuck in that tree, or even yelling about it if you're not willing to stick around and do your part to make it better. I love my home. I want to help it bloom again," he said firmly, a deep passion vibrating through his words.

"Damn, that's really beautiful," Hannah said, her eyes moist with realization. She could see it, the tree and the fence growing into its bark and the temptation to destroy the good parts along with the bad. She usually avoided looking into Guy's face, his eyes a deep brown she felt immersed in far too easily, but she wanted to see him clearly in that moment. The metaphor was lovely, poetic and meaningful, but the strong man behind those opinions—he was a story she wanted to know more about, wanted to be like.

"Eh, it works in lots of ways. It's easy to run away, you know. Staying and fixing—that's the hard part." He turned his body to face Hannah's, and she didn't break their eye contact, the connection charged with electricity. Guy was using the metaphor in reference to the systemic racism that was embedded in the flesh of his state. And pointing out that Hannah's father could've chosen a different avenue by staying and investing in Mississippi in order to do his part to better the world he came from. And maybe even referencing the way Rosie's mom walked away from her daughter twelve years ago.

But it also reminded Hannah of how embedded Alex had been in every part of her body, mind, and heart. Dangerously so. Deathly so. And instead of doing the work to cut him out, she'd run away, first with Ambien, then with dreams of death, and finally by escaping to a small town in Mississippi. But maybe there was a different way. A better way.

"Done!" Rosie chimed in from across the room, and the electrical current was interrupted when they both looked toward the kitchen table where she sat. She held up the crumpled Piggly Wiggly bag cut to fit like a vest and turned inside out. On the blank space on the back of the creation were figures drawn in a line like they were sentences.

At the top was a little girl stick figure with curly hair. Next to her was a tall man with short hair and a big smile. Rosie and Guy. Underneath was a house and what looked like a cat and a rainbow heart that joined them all together. Then two more rows of stick figures, a soccer ball, music notes, paper with a pencil next to it, and finally, at the bottom, a simple drawing of a tree with flowers on it.

"I have a feeling someone was listening to our conversation," Hannah said out of the side of her mouth, like she was trying to hide her comment but speaking intentionally loud enough for Rosie to hear.

"She always has had excellent hearing," Guy whispered back, mimicking Hannah's exaggerated style.

"How do you ever keep anything a secret?" she volleyed back, Rosie putting one hand on her hip like she was too mature for the childish back-and-forth.

"Who says I can?" Guy said, ignoring his daughter's attitude.

"Would you two act like grown-ups and tell me what you think of this thing?" Rosie huffed in feigned annoyance and placed the assignment on the table.

"Well, fine, when you put it that way," Guy said, drying his hands on the dishrag from the counter one last time before heading over to assess his daughter's work. She watched them there, Guy giving his glowingly positive critique and Rosie taking it all in like she was learning from Socrates himself, and her thoughts drifted to the cartoonlike tree at the bottom of Rosie's family story. She was glad that Guy and his father believed in sticking around and making something better instead of running away if such beautiful things could come out of it.

CHAPTER 23

Once Rosie and Guy said their farewells and headed home for the night, and Hannah finished the last few chores to make the kitchen presentable for Carla's sharp eye, she was finally able to settle in and think about Evelyn again. She'd been dying for the opportunity.

With minimal effort after setting up the pullout bed every night for three months, Hannah unfolded the thin mattress and metal frame and tossed on the pillows and blanket she used. Soon, the suite in the back of the house would be complete, and she would move into a brand-new bedroom, private bathroom included, with a private entrance out the side that would give her some autonomy as Mamaw was more able to care for herself again.

The idea of having her own space had been compelling when Hannah first moved in with Mamaw, but after spending so much time in her papaw's study, she knew she would miss the slightly musty smell of his old books lining the walls and the scent of pipe tobacco that had sunk into most of the furniture over the years. It was the closest she'd ever been to her grandfather.

They'd visited for most Thanksgivings, making the long drive the day before the holiday. But she was only eight when he passed, and during the few visits she could recall that predated his death, she'd been scared of the seeming stranger who wore tall socks with slippers and puffed smoke like a steam engine. It was one of the things she'd missed out on because of her father's decision to distance himself from his southern roots. And no matter how she tried, she couldn't stop thinking about that tree that Guy and Rosie seemed to love so much.

Hannah quickly changed into a pair of soft flannel pants and an oversize, worn Northwestern shirt that was starting to fray at the neck. She and Alex used to fight over who owned that shirt first. He insisted that it was a present from his parents when he got his acceptance letter, but Hannah could remember picking out the shirt on her first day of freshman orientation while her parents were still there helping her get settled.

After Alex moved out and Hannah was packing up her things to move back in with her parents, she found a second, identical shirt crumpled up and hidden behind one of the drawers in her dresser. It seemed almost brand-new, stiff to the touch like it had never been worn. Hannah didn't know which shirt belonged to her and which one belonged to Alex originally, but she wore both of them, and they both made her remember. She didn't fully understand why she liked to sleep in such a painful memory, but like most things having to do with Alex, she would rather have proof that they had once been happy than to let his most recent mistakes erase those years.

Hannah sat on the bed and laid out the letters in front of her, each in a separate pile. There were four of them, dated October 10, 1935; November 12, 1935; January 8, 1936; and March 17, 1936.

```
November 12, 1935


Dear Mr. Martin,
I hope this submission finds you well.
I know it has been some time, but I
write as regularly as my situation
allows. Diane thinks I'm taking too
```

long to tell you my story. But what she doesn't understand is that there are so many pieces that come together, and I only remember some of them at some times and others of them at other times. I will write down my story in my journal as often as possible until I have the chance to put it all together for you.

I am eternally devoted to finally sharing the truth of my story. I hope from the deepest parts of my heart that you will find pieces of my account that might help another girl in my position. Life isn't very fair to very many of us—that's a universal truth—and I know it gets harder every single day with this Depression going on. But I've learned that to give up hope entirely is to throw away your ticket to a better tomorrow.

Back in the summer of 1929, I was still full of hopes and dreams. Harry was my beau, and his mother lived in Kentucky. She hadn't seen him for a while, so out of the blue Harry asked me to go with him to see his mother the next month for the Fourth of July.

"Harry, you know Mother and Daddy aren't going to let me go, but you may ask them." Harry had magic over Mother because after sitting down and talking in the evening one night, Mother said it was okay as long as the lady across the street and her daughter and son were going too. But as soon as Harry left, I found out the real reason Mother was all right with me going.

She took me up to her bedroom and sat me down on the edge of her and Daddy's big four-poster bed. She patted the space next to her and took out a brush and asked me to take the comb out of my hair. Mother had never paid any sort of individual attention to me before. I felt unnerved but didn't dare stand against her since she'd been so sweet about Harry and the trip.

"You can go with Harry and Mrs. Strong if you like, Evelyn," she said, raking her stiff-bristled horsehair brush through my short blonde hair. The bristles stung my scalp every time she set it down at the top of each stroke. "But first, I need you to do something for me."

I don't know how I was surprised. Mother had never been one to do something out of the kindness of her heart. As she brushed my hair with little tenderness or care, I remembered the straps on my back from the horsewhip and the scar on my belly from the appendicitis I never really had.

239

"Mr. Fred has taken a fancy to you. You know how your father and I feel about the situation. I know that you think you love Harry, and he is a fine young man. But he is only nineteen and has been a cowpuncher since he dropped out of high school. You will be poor with Harry. If you want to go to Paducah to meet Harry's mother, you must let Mr. Fred take you out on a date first."

I started to protest when Mother took the hairbrush and slapped it against the top of my head, making the horsehairs feel like little daggers in my scalp. I chose my words wisely.

"But I love Harry," I said, remembering not to cry, though I wanted to.

"I'm sure you think you do," Mother said. "But Mr. Fred is a very successful gentleman. You're lucky that he's taken a liking to you. You have expensive tastes, Evelyn. Mr. Fred can give you those things. Harry will give you nothing but babies and swollen ankles."

To me, I had no other choice. If I met Harry's mother in Paducah, he might be able to propose. Then I'd never have to do one thing Mother told me to do again. I knew how to smile and flirt. And Mr. Fred, quiet as he was at the dinner table, had lively discussions with the other boarders in the sitting room most evenings. And he had a Ford that was a silvery green and made me think of frost on the grass in December. Part of me did like that a rich older gentleman found me beautiful and exciting. So I couldn't see the harm in letting Mr. Fred take me on a drive the next Saturday afternoon. But little did I know how wrong I could be.

"Oh God," Hannah said, nearly ill at the slowly developing sacrifice of this girl's future and happiness. How, at fourteen, she saw herself as a commodity to be traded for a better life. Just the idea of it made Hannah think of the discussion she'd had with Guy in the garage earlier that evening. She spread the document out on the bed and took pictures of each page, then with a flick of her thumb she shared the images in a text, adding a quick note, and hit "Send."

Hannah: Mr. Fred is such a creep. Just moved to the top of my suspects list.

Almost immediately, thinking bubbles did the waiting dance that always made Hannah, at least mentally, hold her breath. His message came in, and she let out a loud "Ha!" and responded in a flurry of typing.

Guy Franklin: Just got Rosie to bed—will read ASAP. And agreed—super creep. But I still think it's Mrs. Brown. #guilty

Hannah: Did you seriously just hashtag guilty?

Guy Franklin: I'm just trying to fit in with the cool kids.

Hannah: Good luck with that . . .

Her thumb hovered over the keypad, ready to respond to whatever he sent next, but no bubbles appeared. *He's probably reading,* she thought, wanting to not seem so eager, the warmth of his touch still at the front of her mind.

Focus, Hannah. She shuffled to the next letter, but instead of reading it, Hannah took pictures of all the pages and forwarded them to Guy. Then she picked up the next submission.

January 8, 1936

Dear Mr. Martin,
I am genuinely sorry I cut my last submission so short. The memory of this
time in my life can be quite overwhelming now and then. I know my story has
a disquietude to it. But you must know
that I have changed Mr. Fred's name.
I genuinely believe his influence was
the reason my story never made it much
further than a tiny little note in our
local newspaper. But it needs to be
said. Just because you're rich and a
man doesn't give you the right to ruin
some poor girl's life.
When it was time for my date with
Mr. Fred, Mother lent me Louisa's best
dress and let me have pin curlers in
my hair overnight. When she said I

might wear some of her red lipstick, I thought I had died and gone to heaven. It felt so good to have Mother treat me kindly. And when I saw how beautiful I looked with my hair all done up, and my lips so kissable and ruby red, I hoped Harry would get to see me even though I had gone through great pains to make sure he didn't find out about my outing.

When I got down the stairs, Mr. Fred took a long breath in through his straight white teeth, and I knew that he saw what I had in that mirror. Mother let me wear her hat, so I didn't get too much sun, and Mr. Fred held the door to his fancy car. I climbed inside, feeling a bit like the Queen of England. A part of me wanted to like Mr. Fred. I wanted to like him. My youthful beauty was a fistful of dollars that would blow away with time, and I knew it. But I loved Harry. And Mr. Fred made me feel nervous and funny. I didn't like the way he looked at me.

We drove around some dusty roads for a while. I lost track of where we were going with the sun beating down and not having any breakfast. There was a big picnic basket in the back that I knew Mother had packed for us, and I longed to know what it was like to eat the first serving of something from my father's house instead of the last.

After an hour or so, he parked his car in a big meadow, driving nearly down to the shore of a small pond with a dock built out into it.

Mr. Fred spread a blanket that I had washed with my own hands too many times to count. We sat under a large willow tree and nibbled on sandwiches and strawberries. He told me all about his family and his job and his plans for the future. I said all the right things to make him think I was listening and that I cared a whit about his dreams of power and glory.

"I feel like I can tell you anything," he said to me, scooting closer to my corner of the picnic blanket, my heart beating in my chest. There had been three bottles of beer in the basket, and he had drunk every single one while I sipped on my soda pop. But now his eyes were glassy, and the nervousness that kept him quiet before dissolved into nothingness. I knew what was coming, somehow. He reached his hand out to touch my hair, and I jumped off of that blanket like it was filled with electric shock. Then I remembered Mother. I knew she'd be angry if I were rude. So I slipped my shoes and stockings off, Mr. Fred taking great interest in my bare legs, and ran down to the water.

"What in heaven's name are you up to?" he asked me, taking off his shoes and socks and rolling up his pants to his knees. I stepped into the water, the muddy bottom seeping between my toes. He splashed in behind me, sending dirty slashes of pond water up the skirt of the dress I'd borrowed from Louisa. I'd come down to the pond to escape, but having Mr. Fred wrapped beside me and nothing but water out in front made me feel more trapped than ever. He was breathing heavily, smiling all big like I was playing a game with him. He clasped his arms around my waist and pulled me in tight against his chest.

"I'm far too hot," I said, pushing away. I could see now why good girls were never supposed to be alone with a man. And I wondered desperately why Mother had let me go so far away with him.

"Just one kiss?" he asked, reaching for my hand again. I tucked it away and ran up the shore back to our picnic. He followed quickly behind.

"Do you want to learn how to drive, Evelyn? Then you can have this car and everything else you want."

"No, thank you." I rushed to put my stockings back on, but he grabbed my arm to stop me. I tried to wrench away, but his fingers hurt as they clamped down on my wrist. I said no again, which only made him hold on tighter.

He said I was a tease, which made me fight back against him like a tiger. But he didn't let go. He knelt next to me, a glassy flame burning in his eyes.

"Can't you see that I love you, Evelyn? You will learn to love me . . ."

And he tried to kiss me, and I wasn't strong enough to stop him. Somehow I didn't mind Harry kissing me, but this man? I just didn't like it. I took my mind away, somewhere I could forget what was happening with Mr. Fred, hoping I'd never have to remember it again.

We drove home as it was getting dark. Mother never made me go on a date with him alone again, never even mentioned the mud on my dress or the smudge of red lipstick that stained the collar. And when Harry came to pick me up for our trip three weeks later, she stood on the front porch and wiped at the corner of her eye with her hanky as though she'd miss me.

"Holy shit . . . ," Hannah whispered. It was becoming clearer and clearer why Evelyn's story had been rejected in 1936. She'd been sexually assaulted at the age of fourteen. The horrors depicted in her simple retelling were many, but they also weren't unique. An older, powerful man making moves on a younger, beautiful girl. Her inability to protect herself. Her experience being glossed over and ignored because the truth was inconvenient. Hannah reached for the next pile of pages, eager to know what happened next, when her phone buzzed again. Guy must've gotten to the end of the second submission.

Alex: You awake?

Hannah's pulse whooshed in her ears, and a sweaty flush broke out on her neck and chest. Guy's text came in on top of Alex's notification, followed in rapid succession by three more, but Hannah couldn't stop staring at Alex's simple *You awake?*

She opened the app and swiped Guy's name to the right and touched "Hide Alerts" so they weren't distracting. A little crescent moon appeared, and the notifications for his communications went silent. Then she touched Alex's name, fear and anticipation a sweet cocktail of emotions that rushed through her veins, halting every other thought process that didn't have to do with that one sentence: *You awake?*

Hannah: Yeah.

Hannah responded simply, still not sure how safe it was to open up.

Alex: There you are.
I just got to my hotel. It's official. I'm in Memphis.

Hotel. In Memphis. This was real. He was actually following through. She'd been counting down in the back of her mind but not letting herself believe he would really come—that she would really see him again.

Hannah: Where are you staying?

Alex: The Peabody. Full of local flair. Did you know they have ducks in here?

Hannah's lips twitched, wanting to smile but so very afraid of letting it happen.

Hannah: Yeah, I've heard.

Alex: I mean, I knew things were backward down here, but poultry in the lobby was surprising, even with all the stories your dad used to tell.

Hannah wasn't sure what hit her harder—Alex's casual mention of her father or his snarky comment about a town he'd set foot in just an hour earlier. Part of Hannah wanted to say: *Don't talk about my dad. You didn't even come to his funeral.* Or: *If you want to see backward, look at how you started your new relationship*—but she didn't want to fight. Not today, not when she was about to get the one thing she'd been craving since she walked into her apartment and saw an unknown pair of women's running shoes piled up at the front door. A chance to see him again and maybe find a way to make sense of what went wrong.

Hannah: It's not so bad here once you get used to it.

Alex: Seriously? I never thought I'd hear you say that.
So—does that mean you're going to stay here long-term?

Long-term? Three months ago she'd never, ever considered staying longer than it took to get Mamaw back on her feet and for Alex to get married without her around. But now, with her new room nearly finished, and the Evelyn story coming together, even with its bumps in the road, and not to mention how much she'd miss Mamaw and Carla and Rosie and even Guy . . .

Hannah: Undecided.

Alex: Damn. You're serious.

Hannah: Yeah, pretty serious.

Thinking bubbles started and stopped several times. When his next message came in, the tears that she'd stopped at the end of Evelyn's last letter came back, wetting her cheeks and sending a little sob through her chest, like she was trying to get air but couldn't.

Alex: I can't wait to see you tomorrow.

And then, when she didn't respond:

Alex: I miss you.

There it was, right in front of her eyes—the words she'd hoped to see every time she picked up her phone and checked the lock screen for messages. Every time she checked her email or direct messages on social media. *I miss you.*

But now that she saw them, all she could think was: *How dare he miss me?* He'd chosen to leave and destroy their stable and happy life. She knew she should tell him off, say all the swear words, and then block him everywhere. But she couldn't go back to the despair, couldn't douse that place inside her that only lit up when he was in her life. She knew she might regret it; she knew she was being disloyal to the woman he'd hurt without so much as an explanation, but she couldn't help herself. She typed her next message quickly and hit "Send" before she could change her mind.

Hannah: I miss you too.

CHAPTER 24

Running late, Hannah rushed past Mamaw as she ate her breakfast at the kitchen table like she always did, slowly and in phases that started with coffee and proceeded through toast, bacon, and eventually some variety of eggs. But today, Hannah had helped her out of bed early and gotten her dressed in slacks and a baby-blue blouse before leaving her sitting at her vanity to do her makeup.

Usually, Mamaw's mornings were slow and assisted by Nancy, but Mr. Davenport was coming for breakfast today, and that changed everything. He now sat at the chair beside her, wearing a sport coat at eight thirty in the morning.

"Good mornin', darlin'," Mamaw called cheerfully from the table. Now that Mamaw was more mobile, her sweet, melodic twang, which blurred the sharp edges of life, would seep into her overloaded mind and calm it when she least expected it.

"Hey! Good morning, Mamaw!" Hannah said, kissing Mamaw's cheek as she chewed her second-to-last bite of her breakfast, pretending that she hadn't spent the morning helping her prepare for her boyfriend's visit. "Mr. Davenport, you're here early."

"Your grandmother invited me for a good ole southern breakfast, and how could I refuse?" Mr. Davenport was a nice gentleman, as far as Hannah could tell. Most important, he made Mamaw happy and treated her well.

"Mamaw, look what I've got for you!" Hannah dug around in her jacket pocket and dangled the keys to the Buick in front of Mamaw.

"Oh! My sweet girl! Thank you so much." Her eyes lit up in genuine excitement. "Would you be a dear and put them on the hook by the back door? I probably won't be needing them anytime soon, but I'm such a loon I'll lose them otherwise." She pointed an arthritic finger at a row of small hooks screwed into the wall by the door to the garage. Hannah already knew of the key graveyard that existed there and gladly replaced Mamaw's set on the only available hook.

"Don't let her fool you, Mr. Davenport. She'll be taking that monstrosity for a spin once she gets these boots off, won't you, Mable?" Carla exited the kitchen, faded apron already tied in place, with a giant plate of food in her hands, addressing Hannah. "Why don't you try eating a real breakfast for once?" she asked, placing enough food to feed three farmhands on the table at Hannah's usual spot.

"Sorry, Carla, I don't have time this morning, I'm running hella late," she said, snatching a piece of bacon and not even taking the time to apologize for swearing. "And Mamaw, you shouldn't thank me, you should thank Guy. I don't know how to unclog a toilet, much less install a carburetor and whatever kind of belt he put in there."

"Yes, of course. Let me know how much I owe him, and I'll write a check. Carla, can you make sure the check gets to the Franklin child?" she said, sounding very official. Hannah liked seeing glimpses of what Mamaw must've been like in her younger years. She'd become so timid in her old age, a sweet old grandmother, but there were times when Hannah could see the spunk that had been there before the years and the grief in her life dragged her down.

"I don't think he's gonna let you pay him, Mamaw. I asked him last night, and he said it was 'on the house.'"

"I knew that boy was sweet on you," Carla said, shoving the plate toward where Hannah was standing. She took another piece of bacon and then pushed it back.

"Guy? Oh God, no." Hannah rejected Carla's suggestion, not because there wasn't a part of her that also wondered if it was true, but because with Alex coming into town she didn't have space in her life for another confusing situation with a man.

Carla's lips smacked at the name of the Lord being used in vain, before taking the plate back into the kitchen.

Hannah still hadn't figured out what everyone's problem with swearing was. "I mean, goodness, no." The sarcasm was so thick that even sweet little Mamaw would be able to pick up on it.

"He is, I'm sure of it," Carla said.

"Carla! Stop!" Hannah said, not only out of embarrassment at the discussion of her nonexistent love life but because when she finally looked at his messages this morning, she found that she'd missed ten or so texts about the pages she'd sent before getting distracted by Alex.

"His little girl is darling," Mamaw said to Mr. Davenport.

"She is beautiful and so, so smart," Hannah said, filling an empty glass with the orange juice. Hannah had always wanted kids of her own one day and loved her rowdy and snuggly nephews, but the experience of getting to know Rosie was entirely different. She was excited to see her and hear her worldview, and found it impossible not to cheer for everything she did. Hannah was starting to wonder if this was what it felt like, in some tiny way, to be a parent.

"I think the feeling is mutual. She thinks you hung the moon and the stars," Carla agreed, her voice echoing out of the kitchen, where a ceramic scraping made Hannah cringe at how much food she'd just wasted.

"She truly is adorable. She brought me my tea yesterday, and I am always surprised to see how very light-skinned she is. Her daddy is mixed," she said to Mr. Davenport, "but she must take after her momma. She could almost pass for white if she got her hair straightened."

Hannah's hands paused midpour. She knew it wasn't fair to assume that a woman born in the 1930s in Mississippi would develop without some of the prejudicial brainwashing Hannah's father had moved north to avoid, but, to be honest, Hannah had never heard Mamaw say a nasty word about anyone, regardless of race. It made her feel like when Brody would jump onto her side of the trampoline, shaking the surface and making her fall down.

"Mamaw, that's not an appropriate thing to say," Hannah murmured low, hoping Carla hadn't heard.

"What, dear?" she said, sipping at her glass of juice, seemingly ignorant of the underlying prejudice in her assessment of Rosie's whiteness. Mr. Davenport was uncharacteristically mute.

"Guy and Rosie don't care about looking white. That's not a thing anymore. And what if Carla hears you?"

"Oh, I'm sorry, hun," she said, putting down her glass and licking her lips, looking sincerely surprised. "I meant no offense. She's a lovely girl, either way. And Carla doesn't mind. She knows who I am."

"I know, Mamaw," Hannah said with a touch of compassion. Mamaw was ninety-one years old. She and Papaw had voted for JFK and other pro-integration candidates when segregation was a hot-button and revolutionary topic. Mamaw was the first teacher to volunteer to teach in an integrated classroom at Senatobia High. And Hannah's father had always said that their quiet stance against the rampant injustices of their time was what sculpted his outlook on life.

But the idea of what looked progressive had changed in the past since she was young, and some things that were revolutionary in her time were outdated nearly three-quarters of a century later. But then Hannah remembered the tree, Guy's magnolia tree, and that fence that was stuck inside it and his reminder that it wasn't about her feelings or even Mamaw's. It was about what was right.

"But he's my"—she searched for the right word—"he's my friend. So I want you to get to know him."

"Oh," she said passively, chewing suspiciously slowly. She swallowed and spoke unhurriedly, as though she were picking out words one at a time, like weeds. "That's sweet of you, dear. I'm glad you are making friends, but I think you might be careful about giving him the—the wrong idea."

"The wrong idea? Mamaw, we are just friends." Hannah repeated Mamaw's phrasing, feeling like she was fourteen-year-old Evelyn being scolded for liking a boy and threatened with being sent to a convent. "And you asked him to help me."

"When I asked him to help you those few times, I didn't know you two would hit it off. Then again, you are a pretty girl, and he seems to prefer white women, probably because his mother was white, God rest her soul. Good woman. Friends with your father growing up—"

"Mamaw!" Hannah shouted, making the frail woman jump in her seat, hands shaking like she was being held at gunpoint. Carla walked in from the kitchen, her features hardened like when Hannah tracked in mud after riding through a puddle.

"Didn't you say you needed to get to work?" Carla snapped, and Hannah couldn't figure out what she'd done wrong. Guy was her friend, and Rosie was a perfect little person if she ever had met one. Wasn't this the right time for outrage? Hannah checked her watch—it was past 8:30 a.m., which meant Monty had already been in the office half an hour, and Hannah was wasting precious minutes of her last day in the archives. Mamaw had recovered from her shock, and Hannah dipped down to give her another kiss on the cheek.

"I love you, Mamaw," she said, not knowing what else to say at that moment.

"I love you too, darlin'," she replied, caressing Hannah's face and giving her a sideways air-kiss in return.

Hannah rushed out to the garage, pushed the button that opened the automatic door, and was wrestling her bike off the wall when Mr. Davenport peeked his head full of white hair outside.

"I'm supposed to be telling you about dinner tonight, but Hannah"—he stood on the top step of the wooden stairs, grasping the doorknob to steady himself—"be nice to your grandma. She's a good woman who's done lots of kind things in her life. She's sitting in there crying after you scolded her."

Hannah dropped the bike onto the cement floor, where it bounced back at her, cracking her hip with the handlebars. She winced, annoyed at her misstep with the bike, annoyed that she was running late because she'd let herself stay up past midnight pretending she could still be friends with Alex, annoyed that she never did anything right in anyone's eyes.

"I'm sorry, Mr. Davenport. I don't mean her any disrespect, but if it hurts Mamaw's feelings, how do you think Guy or Carla feel hearing little things like that?"

"She's an old woman. She has love in her heart, not hate. Carla knows that, don't you think?"

"Carla does, I agree." She knew better than anyone that Mamaw was good to the core. "But I'm sorry, I don't think it's right for me to say nothing. Guy and Rosie are important to me. Mamaw is important to me. Carla is important to me. I don't see the issue." Hannah got on her bike and adjusted her center of gravity until she could balance without wobbling.

"I can see that Mr. Franklin and his girl have found a special place in your life, and often you need to use a stone to quash such situations. But other times a feather is just as useful," Mr. Davenport professed like he was quoting a proverb.

"Maybe," Hannah said. Mr. Davenport didn't move, like he was waiting for Hannah to say more. He was a retired minister and seemed to have a heart that matched Mamaw's in patience. She straddled her bike, not wanting to have this conversation with this new man in Mamaw's life. "Goodbye, Mr. Davenport."

"Oh, Hannah?" Mr. Davenport called after her. Hannah used the hand brakes to slow her descent down the driveway and called back over her shoulder.

"Yeah?"

"Carla told me to ask if your young man will be joining you for Thanksgiving?"

Hannah let go of her brakes and sped away from the house, her only answer to Carla's question getting lost in the wind.

"He's not MY young man!"

CHAPTER 25

"Okay, I'll see what I can find in regard to her last name. Her first is Evelyn," Hannah said into her phone, keeping her volume to a minimum outside the *Record*.

"And you'll get me that information before I head to the Pines tomorrow?" Peter Dawson asked. He'd called to set up the final details of their meetup. She was supposed to see him tomorrow before meeting up with Alex, and she had promised to get him the rest of Evelyn's information in time for his visit to the Pines that same day.

"I'll do my best," Hannah said, whispering now. Monty could pop out from any corner, and if he found out about her ongoing investigation, she'd likely be fired.

"Sounds fun. I can't wait to see you again," he said, in a low voice. Hannah cringed at the compliment, not because she found Peter distasteful so much as she hated how often he attempted to smooth-talk her.

"Talk soon. Goodbye," was all she could force without feeling like she was accepting his compliments, which would've been weird. Then again, everything felt slightly off after her somewhat tense conversation on her way out the door, and getting to work late, where the final nail in the "this is going to be a shitty day" coffin was finally getting ready to dig into the archives for the last time and finding the door to the basement locked.

"Damn it," she cursed between clamped teeth, pounding a fist on the hollow metal door, resting her forehead against the rough green paint. "Has Monty been in?" Hannah shouted over her shoulder to Dolores, who was sitting dutifully at her desk like a good little secretary.

"No, no. I haven't heard from him just yet."

"Do you happen to have the key to the basement?" Hannah asked, without turning around, her shouts reverberating off the door and back into her face.

"No, dear. It's in his desk."

"Do you have a key to his office, then?" she called out.

"No, dear," she said again.

"Figures," she grumbled, catapulting herself across the room and tossing herself into her desk chair, defeated.

Her mug was empty—again. She'd already had three cups that morning, and even with the slightly metallic aftertaste of Dolores's best coffee-making efforts, Hannah was ready for another. She'd stayed up far too late texting with Alex last night, and in the light of day she still wasn't sure if it was entirely a good idea or not.

They'd caught up on the basics of the past several months—his job advancements and new apartment—while skipping the details of his relationship and upcoming marriage. And then covered her move to Mississippi and the loss of her father while leaving out the debilitating depression, job loss, and stint at the psych ward. It had been the filtered Facebook version of her life and his, which left Hannah feeling anxious about meeting him face-to-face. She couldn't live up to the "normal" person she'd been in the past. It was impossible.

Hannah had fallen asleep, phone in hand. She'd woken up three hours later with a sick feeling in her stomach that had to do with regret. She'd let her chat with Alex keep her from reading Evelyn's letters and, worst of all, pushed her actual friend, Guy, out of her mind.

She still hadn't read his messages. Hannah had never been one to read the last page of a book first or search the internet for TV show spoilers, so she didn't want to find out anything about the end of the story that didn't come directly from Evelyn's mind. Hannah's focus on Alex always found a way to take precedence. She checked the line of clocks on the wall. It was past ten, and Monty wasn't in his office—*maybe he took an extra day off for the holiday,* she thought, reaching for any explanation. If she wasn't getting through that basement door anytime soon, then she had time to read the only remaining clue in her possession.

March 17, 1936

Mr. Martin,

I have been wholly under the weather for some time. I am nearly recovered, and thank you for your patience. I have decided to put considerable effort into telling the rest of this story as con-cisely as possible, which is not always the easiest of tasks when speaking of one's life, but I shall do my best. Soon you shall know who was responsible for my injuries, as will the rest of your readers. I promise.

On July 3, at about midnight, we started out for Paducah, Kentucky. At that time it was Harry, me, Mrs. Strong from across the street, and her daugh-ter, Lilly. Mother insisted the Strongs accompany me and Harry, talking about propriety and such, which steamed me up after what she'd let Mr. Fred do.

We arrived there at about ten in the morning. I was a sick piece of humanity; we had eaten hot dogs at three in the morning, and that was more than I could stand. Harry's mother was quite different than I had imagined her—tall and slender, and a bit stylish.

She looked younger than Louisa, even with a grown son. His family was quite well known in those parts and doing well despite hard times. He introduced me as his girl, and that did not please his mother at all. She pinched her glossy lips and wrinkled her perfect powdered nose and said Harry and I were too young to think of such things.

Harry and his brothers went to town, and the girl visitors and I went to lie down. I slept for some time but still felt nearly as sick as when the doctor thought I had appendicitis. I snuck down the back staircase and stopped when I heard Mrs. Strong talking with Harry's mother.

"How old is that girl you came with?" she asked, not even using my Christian name, although I know Harry told it to her. Mrs. Strong said to her that I just turned fourteen in the spring, and Harry's mother tsk-tsked.

"I wish she wouldn't be so pally
with Harry. They are too young for such
things."

Mrs. Strong agreed, and that's when
I heard that Harry was only sixteen.

What? Only sixteen? Hannah felt the echo of betrayal Evelyn must've
endured. Harry lied. He was a strange man she'd met at a carnival, who
worked his way into her life and lied about his age. And in order to
date him, she'd been put in a terrible position and been assaulted by a
man twice her age. Hannah suffered outrage on her behalf, the pages
waving in her grip.

You see, he had told me and everyone
else in Senatobia that he was nineteen
and ready to settle down. It was all a
lie. I was so sick that I just went out
the back door and through the alley and
went looking for the boys. I needed to
talk to Harry. I wanted to know if what
his mother said was the truth. I went
all over town. At one point there were
three men following me, and I was so
scared and sick enough that I thought
my insides were going to turn out.

Finally, I went up on a porch
and asked an older lady and man sitting there if I might use the phone.
I couldn't find the number, and they
asked if they might do anything to help
me. When I told them Harry's name, they
knew exactly where his mother's house

was. The old lady suggested that the man might take me there. So we piled into his big old truck, and I held my head out the window so the night air could settle my stomach.

When we got to the Westbrooks' home, Harry scolded me terribly. He said that they looked everywhere for me throughout town and thought that something awful might have happened. He called me a silly little girl and told me to stop crying like a baby. He said I'd embarrassed him and that he'd never felt so angry in his whole life. I was shocked that he could be so changed, but I also wondered if I ever really knew him. Could I know someone after only a few short weeks?

His mother, who sat at the table smoking a cigarette in her dressing gown, glared at me. I knew I must look like a little girl to her. My heart was broken, and I went out on the back porch and cried until I couldn't cry anymore.

Harry decided that we had better leave in the morning, with me being so sick and upset and all. He called Mother long-distance and told her the plans. I hated causing such a fuss, but I couldn't imagine sitting in a car for hours feeling as sick and low as I was at that moment.

At six the next morning, we started back to Senatobia. I didn't dare bring up any of the horrible things I'd witnessed and discovered during our trip, so I sat silent, watching life pass me by. And was I glad to get back? Yes, but for such a short time.

The next time I write, I will complete my tale and answer the question that everyone had on their tongues seven years ago: Who shot Evelyn? The answer surprises even me to this day.

Sincerely,

Evelyn

What the . . . ? Hannah flipped over the pages, scanning them with her eyes, to make sure she hadn't mixed something up, but no—there were no more words or pages, just a terrible cliff-hanger that had no resolution and left her with the sickening knowledge that there must be more of Evelyn's story orphaned in one of the basement files. Why did it seem like doors Monty had shut and locked were the only things keeping her from putting together the last few pieces of Evelyn's puzzle?

This mystery ending must've been what Guy was texting about the night before. Hannah read through his messages hastily, able to tell where he was in each article by his comments.

Guy Franklin: This is getting so much creepier.

Are you reading?

Hello?

You must've fallen asleep. I'll send you my reactions for later.
Warning—text bomb . . .
No, Evelyn! Don't go with him.
Oh man, I really don't like that Mr. Fred.
I think her stepmom is evil.
Oh my God—did what I think happened happen?
Hot dogs at 3:00 a.m. sounds amazing right now.
Harry is 16?!?!?!
Wait—he's mad at her? Huh?
Happy to be home, but it didn't last long—what is that supposed to mean?
You'll tell us the truth in the next letter, Evelyn? What next letter?
Okay, not kidding this time, I don't have another letter. Do you have it?
Send it when you wake up. I'm on the edge of my seat.
Sleep tight!

She didn't know what she felt worse about—the fact that she'd ignored Guy's text chain so she could talk to a man who'd ignored her for ten months now or that she didn't have another article to pass on to satisfy Guy's request. With no idea where to even start apologizing or explaining, Hannah put her phone away, pushing her response off to later.

"Hannah?" Dolores called from her desk, putting down the receiver to the landline she answered on behalf of the newspaper. Hannah hadn't heard it ring, but that didn't mean it hadn't; she wasn't the best at noticing anything outside her bubble of influence lately.

"Yeah?" Hannah called back as she continued organizing her Evelyn files, nothing else to fill her time while she was stuck in the empty space between two locked doors.

"That was Monty, hun. Some bad news. His wife had a heart attack. She's at North Oak and going into surgery."

"Oh my God. Poor Monty," Hannah said, sitting up straighter, the papers she'd been shuffling slipping from her fingers. She might not be the biggest Monty fan, but he loved his wife as much or possibly more than any other man. Hannah didn't envy anyone who had to sit by their loved one's side as they fought for their life. Her father's end was too fresh a memory to make her numb to what Monty must be going through.

"Yes, dear. I know." Dolores worked a tissue up under her glasses and dabbed at what must've been tears, though Hannah couldn't see them from where she sat. "Monty said it would be all right if we started our holiday time early. No need to sit around here doin' nothing."

Oh no. If Monty wasn't able to come in today, then there was no way for Hannah to get into the archives to search for the missing final installment, or for her to make another attempt at getting into the proofs filed away in his office to attain Evelyn's last name once and for all.

"You almost ready, hun?" Dolores asked, somehow already dressed in her coat and gloves, likely anxious to get home and get an early start on her Thanksgiving dinner preparations for her husband and six children, their spouses, and all thirteen of her grandchildren.

"Almost," she replied, gathering her belongings, not ready at all but only in ways that she couldn't express to the elderly woman who was beyond loyal to her boss. Hannah glanced around the room, half-frantic. She didn't know what she expected to find, a Post-it with Hannah's name? A big, flashing arrow pointing at the key to the basement? A neat stack of paper tied with a bow that told all of Evelyn's story, filling in all the big, mysterious blanks? No such luck. All that stared back at her was Monty's darkened office, Dolores's tidy desk, a few files, and desks for the random part-timers who rarely, if ever, came into the office anymore. But no arrows or bows or keys.

Defeated, she followed Dolores to the door, Hannah's hope and drive shutting down with every light switch Dolores flipped. Going through the motions, Hannah wrestled her bike out of the vestibule and set it down at the bottom of the cement stairs, a task that had once seemed impossible and was now second nature. Finishing her shutdown routine, Dolores closed the inner office door and then joined Hannah outside.

"Have a good day, dear." Dolores waved to Hannah, while burying herself in a wool coat, clearly not used to the chill in the air.

Hannah waved and was about to get on her bike when she saw something. Instead of heading to her car, parked on the street right next to the *Record*, Dolores remained standing at the top of the stairs like she was a lost child in a department store. Then, when she thought no one was looking, she attempted to stand on her tiptoes and reached up toward the top of the door trim, until a box was settled in the palm of her hand.

Dolores slid the box open and retrieved a metal key from the compartment inside. With a few quick twists, she secured both of the locks and then returned the case to its proper location. Hannah turned away quickly for plausible deniability.

With an official holiday farewell and a few more polite words about Monty's poor wife, Dolores climbed into her car, the seat pulled nearly all the way up so she could reach the wheel, and left with a wave. Hannah let out a sigh of relief. It hadn't been an arrow or a bow or an alarm or a trapdoor, but the universe, or whatever it was keeping her sane, did give her one thing—a key.

It would get her inside before the files disappeared and let her search without needing to hide from Monty's watchful and judgmental eye. But she'd need help—and Hannah knew just the person to call. She took out her phone and opened the messages she hadn't known how to respond to just half an hour ago. But now she did.

Hannah: Guy—can you meet me at the Record tomorrow at noon?

She hit "Send" and was about to close out of the application so she could get on her bike to ride home when a return text vibrated in her hand.

Guy Franklin: Absolutely. Dare I ask why?

Hannah: Probably better if you don't. Oh, and bring tools.

CHAPTER 26

"You said to bring my tools," Guy said, tilting to one side, weighed down by a giant silver toolbox, heading straight toward Hannah, who had already retrieved the key and unlocked the front door. Carla was with Mamaw, prepping for the holiday, but would be leaving to get home to her own family and turkey stuffing, which left Hannah a little nervous. Even with Nancy's visit in a few hours, Hannah was certain Mamaw would be alone for her bedtime routine. Thankfully, last night when Mamaw heard that Hannah was meeting with a state senator, she insisted she was ready to stay on her own for a few hours and Nancy agreed. Hannah knew it was time to let Mamaw start taking on some of her own self-care again, so she went along with the plan.

During their evening together, they'd both played the game of "nothing happened / everything is fine," ignoring the argument from earlier in the day. Hannah planned to revisit the conversation when Pam arrived the day after Thanksgiving. Maybe she'd be able to explain better than Hannah.

"Wanna tell me what we're doing today?"

"I'll tell you inside. Come on." She waved him up the stairs and into the safety of the office, keeping an eye out for passing cars as they slipped inside, unseen. Guy wore a gunmetal-gray canvas jacket, dark jeans, and a ball cap and smelled lightly of cologne as he walked past her in the vestibule. He hadn't been able to make it at noon after all. Still, after dropping Rosie at his parents' house and finishing a few items for his side job with his father's construction business, he'd texted that he could meet Hannah at the *Record* at 2:00 p.m., which would tighten her timeline, but it appeared to be the only way to get what she needed.

"This is a little more covert than I feel comfortable with," Guy said, scanning the dark interior of the room.

"I know, but I was afraid if I told you my plan ahead of time, you'd say no." She gave him a forced, cringing smile that admitted her guilt.

"I don't think I like it when you call something your 'plan,'" he said, following her instructions, and then turned around to face Hannah. His mouth was open like he was about to finish a thought; instead, he stopped and took a good, long look at her instead. His eyes were tracking over her hair, flowing white blouse with a fitted leather jacket that she'd bought years before at a consignment shop, fitted jeans, and heeled booties. It was the one "professional-looking" outfit she'd brought from Chicago. She'd worn it only one time, during her interview for the newspaper position.

"Uh, you look nice," he said, swallowing loudly and then taking off his jacket and holding it in his arms.

"You can put that on my chair." She pointed at his jacket, her neck hot under her lengthy hair, especially after his compliment, afraid if she acknowledged it that she'd be back in that place where she wanted to be close to him.

"Is this how you always dress for dabbling in espionage?" he said, adjusting his belt at his hips, a loose-fitting button-up hanging open over an orange V-neck. He looked a little more rugged than usual; the outfit was like something an actor in a movie would wear to go to Thanksgiving dinner with his big, loud, but also oh-so-amazing family.

"This is not espionage. You don't even have to do anything—I'll break all the rules. You can just stand there telling me to stop the whole time if it makes you feel better."

"Reminder—I still don't know what we are doing, and you still have not told me why you are dressed like that," he said, squinting like he wanted to see her better.

"I'm dressed like this 'cause I have a meeting with Peter later," she said, mumbling the confession a bit. Hannah had told Guy about their first run-in. Plus, if she told him about drinks with Peter, then she didn't have to mention her more embarrassing appointment for the evening with Alex, whom they had not discussed yet. Peter was a business contact, but Alex . . . maybe it was Hannah's guilty conscience, but she feared Guy would judge her for meeting with him. Likely because she judged herself for doing it.

"As in Peter Dawson?" he asked, hands in his pockets, shoulders raised, trying to look casual. "You two are on a first-name basis now?" he asked. Hannah swore that there was a slight edge to his question, making it sound like an accusation.

"I guess," she said, hating the touch of hurt in his voice. She tried to explain. "I finally caved and I'm meeting him for drinks. He can get me files from the Pines but only with Evelyn's last name. So . . . here's where you come in. Question: If one were to need to pick a lock that looked something like that one over there, how might he, or she, do it?"

Her timeline was insanely tight. Hannah would need to contact Peter immediately once they found Evelyn's information so he could have time to retrieve the proper files from the Pines before their meeting. That would give Hannah and Guy a little over an hour. Hannah had an Uber set to pick her up at three thirty.

"Damn it, Hannah, you intend to break into Monty's office?" Guy asked, his voice louder than what felt comfortable in the dim room. He didn't seem to find her humor very interesting this time around.

"Maybe?" she said sheepishly, her heart racing just enough to let her brain know that deep down she thought this was a bad idea, but she also knew that people did insane things when they were backed into a corner.

"This is a little risky," he said, shaking his head. "I love this story—seriously, just as much as you do, but breaking and entering and going on dates with strangers is just insane."

"Is it risky, though?" Hannah liked Guy a lot, but she didn't like it when he tried to tell her what to do. "As long as I don't scratch the door, there's no way he will even know I've been here. I'm not *taking* anything. I'm only looking at documents that should be open to anyone. And it's not a date. It's a professional meeting."

"You're gonna get yourself in trouble, Hannah. I don't like it. There has to be another way." Guy leaned down to pick up his tool chest and made an oof sound as he lifted it off the creaking floorboards, taking a step toward the exit.

"No! Please don't go," she said, panic turning on her fight-or-flight reflex. She needed him here—not just to help her, but . . . She didn't know how to finish that thought. She needed him . . . period. In some way, she needed Guy Franklin to be on her side. She rushed across the room to stop him from leaving, grasping his forearm, his muscles taut from the resistance of the heavy toolbox. At her touch, his momentum wavered and then stopped as he stared down at her.

She'd never noticed how tall he was until that moment—stronger than she'd expected too. She could tell by the way he leaned into her warmth as she stood next to him and by how easily he met her gaze that he didn't really want to leave, which felt like an invitation to keep talking.

"I can't do this without you." Her grip tightened, willing him to stay. She didn't just say the words, she meant them.

Staring down into her eyes, Guy's resolve faltered and quickly dissolved. He let out a reluctant groan. "Fine," he said, relaxing into her firm hold, fully surrendering. "What do you need?"

"Thank you!" Hannah blurted, flooded with relief like she'd swallowed an antidote. If there hadn't been a giant toolbox in the way, she would've hugged him, but there wasn't time for any of that with the quickly impending deadline, so Hannah forced herself to focus on the task at hand.

"I watched a YouTube video on how to get this door open, but I'm afraid I'll make a mess of it on my own," she said, leading him to Monty's door, where she gestured for Guy to place his toolbox back on the floor. He knelt on one knee and inspected the doorknob from all angles and then unlatched the lid of his chest.

"This is a pretty standard indoor lock. You're lucky there's no dead bolt." He started to pick through the neatly sorted collection of tools. Hannah knelt beside him, watching him search.

"I think I need a paper clip and a flathead screwdriver and a Phillips-head screwdriver," Hannah listed, retrieving a large paper clip from her pocket and showing it to Guy to prove that she'd done some research.

"I don't think we'll need that." He took out a tool with a wooden handle on the end and a long, thin, pointed metal shaft, and without a second thought, he pressed it into the neck of the doorknob, popping off the handle.

"Hey, I was going to do that!" Hannah said, squinting, not sure how he found the vulnerable spot on the lock without a flashlight.

"Eh, I'm already over my head in this thing. Might as well make sure it's done right," he said, lingering on her face a beat longer than she'd expected. Yeah, it did feel like they were getting in over their heads. He looked away first, switching tools until he could pop off the base of the knob and then unscrew the internal workings with a smaller screwdriver. The knob fell off, and the door opened like he'd said a password.

"Oh my God, you're magic," she said, touching his back as she stood to either find what she was looking for or leave knowing that it wasn't meant to be, at least not today. Guy didn't respond, quietly collecting all the pieces of the doorknob that he'd need to replace, not as satisfied with the successful break-in as she was. She'd make it up to him, she promised herself that. It was difficult to know that a man she was coming to respect found fault with her decisions, but the squeak of Monty's door opening teleported those concerns right onto the back burner of her mind.

It was dim inside, but somehow a little brighter than the rest of the darkened office. To the right were the files, and to the left, Monty's desk, which held the keys to the basement. She wanted to get to both, but the paper's proofs were at the top of the priority list. The filing cabinets here were different from the ones in the basement. The basement cabinets were tall, with four square drawers, making her think of a morgue, where bodies were stored headfirst.

The ones here in Monty's office took up a whole wall and consisted of long drawers, rectangles that opened up to massive rows of filed newspapers, the tallest of which she'd need a chair to examine the insides. More like what a morgue looked like if bodies were stored sideways, which was likely where the name for the storage of old newspaper files had come from in journalism. The drawers were filled with once-living information that lay forgotten, so pretty apropos after all.

Hannah opened one of the most easily accessible middle drawers. Folded newspapers encased in sturdy plastic bags were filed away inside, pressed together into one giant row without any dividers or numerals to guide her.

"Welp, here goes nothing," she whispered to herself, before picking a random spot in the middle of the drawer and wedging her hand in between the pages. She wiggled the newspapers apart, making enough space so she could get a look at the dates on the top right-hand corner.

July 5, 1968.

Too late. She skipped down the line and checked again.

October 1973.

"Okay," she whispered to herself, quickly getting the lay of the land.

"Are they in there?" Guy asked from the doorway, standing now and watching Hannah's search as he leaned against the doorjamb.

"I think so. I just need to find the right drawer," she said, making sure every paper was back in place. She closed the row she'd been working on and knelt next to the lower two rows.

"Anything I can do to help?" he asked, taking a step inside, his hands shoved into his pockets like he was nervous. Distracted by the new supply of newspapers she was itching to explore, Hannah could only halfway pay attention to Guy's anxious request. She pointed over at Monty's desk.

"In the middle drawer—you know the thin one where they keep pens and pencils and stuff like that? There's a key chain with a yellow elastic band on it. That's the key to the basement. Could you get that door unlocked for me?"

"Sure, that sounds easy enough," he said, seemingly more comfortable with their search-and-recover mission. "I found them. What now?" he asked just as she pulled out the first newspaper to the right in the current row to check the date. The sound of Guy closing Monty's desk drawer set off a nervous shiver up Hannah's spine.

"Uh, I mean, if you really don't mind—in the basement there is a desk in the back corner. In the bottom drawer are some files with all the original documents. Could you bring all of them up?"

"Yeah, no problem," he replied. She gave him a nervous thumbs-up and returned to her search as he left the room.

November 1945.

Still too late. If there was a consistent filing pattern used on these papers, that meant they were in chronological order from right to left. She double-checked her theory midway and then at the end of the line, finding her conclusion was correct. That meant she was close. There was one more drawer left. It sat nearly flush with the floor. She dragged it open, sat cross-legged on the thin carpeting, and took out the first newspaper all the way to the right.

January 29, 1881.

Tate County Democrat—the original title of the newspaper—was visible through the clouded plastic sheeting that protected the ancient artifact.

It was here, in this row. It had to be. July 1929. That was the month and year—she was sure of it. She skipped great chunks of time at first and then made fewer and fewer hops down the line until she found the 1920s. She could feel it coming closer. It was here—the story. This buzzy, alive feeling that went along with catching the next thread in the tapestry of a story was more intoxicating than anything in her life, and she wanted to savor every damn moment.

When she reached July 1929, Hannah retrieved all four of the newspapers from that month and laid them on the ground, marking their spot with a June newspaper turned on its side. July 5, 12, 19, and 26. Evelyn could be in any one of them.

Hannah removed the July 5 paper from its plastic sheath and carefully unfolded it. This edition was the least likely to hold any answers to the mystery shooting since, according to Evelyn's last missive, she and Harry had returned from their trip on that same day. News moved more slowly in those times, and even if Evelyn had been shot on the fifth, it would be a whole week before it hit the local newspaper, but Hannah couldn't risk it.

Each page was a tightly packed sea of words, hard to navigate at first. The article titles were barely more substantial than the stories themselves, and each column was separated by a few centimeters of space on the sides and a slight dash above and below. The first few pages held all the big news items, including patriotic pontifications, and each additional page was filled with more socially focused items, ads, and classifieds. As expected, there was no mention of a girl being shot in her home.

Hannah carefully folded up the July 5 paper and moved on to July 12. This one she looked through a little more purposefully, searching not just for Evelyn's name, since there was no possible way to know if she was using a pseudonym, but also keeping an eye out for anything that sounded similar. After going through the pages twice, nothing stood out, and she started to worry that maybe she had her timing wrong, or maybe Evelyn did. According to Monty's clock—it was a little past 3:00 p.m., and her car would be arriving soon. This whole thing was taking longer than she'd expected.

On to the next paper, Hannah unfolded the July 19 *Tate County Democrat* and scanned the articles and headlines until she saw it. She had to read the headline twice—but there it was. It read like an odd, formal short story, a totally archaic form of journalism that made Evelyn's articles seem more normal. Hannah read eagerly.

```
Girl Fights for Life So She May Marry
Cowpuncher

Senatobia, Miss., July 19, 1929—
"Evelyn darling, if you'll only get
well, you and Harry can get married
right away."

And Evelyn Kensley, 14, who was found
shot in her bedroom, groped for her
stepmother's hand and smiled content-
edly, on the edge of consciousness.
    Harry Westbrook, 19, a clean-look-
ing boy with a beardless face and sleek
```

hair, smiled at Evelyn from the other
side of the bed and nodded his head in
vigorous assent.

Dr. Shields Abernathy, who has
been making a desperate fight to save
Evelyn's life ever since she was found
with a .25-caliber bullet in her spine,
is not so sure the wedding bells will
ring for the schoolgirl. Evelyn already
has had one blood transfusion.

Harry, whose head is in a whirl over
the events of the last 24 hours, was
initially held by the police for questioning. Once cleared of all wrongdo-
ing, he now only thinks of one thing—he
wants his sweetheart to live. He stands
ready to give the next blood transfusion if it is necessary.

(continued on page 5)

Evelyn Kensley. There she was in black and white, real as day. Evelyn
Kensley. The two names went together so naturally that it seemed like
Hannah had always known it. The article was strangely casual, though,
focusing so much on Harry, who also ended up being real. Nothing yet
about who may have shot the poor, paralyzed child, and not even an
ounce of suspicion cast on her doting stepmother. Hannah couldn't get
to page 5 fast enough.

(continued from first page)
He has not left her bedside long enough
to drink a cup of coffee and vows to

stay with her until the gun-wielding culprit is apprehended.

"I was at work when it happened," Westbrook said Friday of the crime. "Everyone thought it was my doing, but it was love at first sight with Evelyn and me."

Harry, nearly exhausted, sat on the chair outside of Evelyn's door at Methodist Hospital. Any moment, he may be called upon for a blood transfusion.

Evelyn's stepmother, too shaken to give an official comment, told the police that she'd found Evelyn on the floor of her room, shot on the afternoon of July 17.

"It is a terrible mystery," Harry explained.

And this slim boy cowpuncher, who drifted into town last May with Dakota Max's rodeo show, straightened his shoulders and signified his intention to find the assailant himself if necessary.

The notification on Hannah's phone buzzed—her car was on its way. *Shit.* She was running so far behind. Unable to fully process the significance of what she'd read, Hannah took pictures of the article, refolded the papers, secured their plastic coverings, and put them back into place where they belonged. She could think through it all on her way to Memphis.

It didn't take much to return Monty's office to its original condition, leaving no trace of their break-in. Hannah rushed to the basement, the door left ajar. She stood at the top and shouted for Guy. He came up the stairs, arms loaded with files.

"That place is overwhelming," he said, as he met her outside the door. "Is this what you were looking for?" She tried to decipher what exactly he was holding but knew whatever it was she didn't have time to make a trip down into the basement to retrieve any additional items, so she just said yes and stashed the files in her bag, preferring the originals to the scans for fact-checking purposes.

Her phone dinged again, announcing her car's arrival.

"I'm so sorry to do this, but I have to go," she said, kicking herself that she was cutting it so close.

"Wait, you're going *now*?" he asked, looking at her empty hands like she'd been slacking.

"Yes, I'm sorry, but my ride is here. I have my meeting—"

"With Dawson, yeah, I remember." He sighed and took in the room while Hannah got ready to leave. Guy quickly locked the basement door. His tools were in their box, and nothing else had been disturbed. "You go ahead and get out of here. I'll lock things up."

"You will?" she asked, in the middle of texting her driver that she'd be out in a minute, so filled with anxiety that her head was pounding along with her heartbeat.

"Yeah, there's nothing left to be done, really. I'll just add it to the list of things you owe me for." He gave her a sideways look and half smile that, when not already in pre-heart-attack mode, sent her heart a little flutter every time. She put her phone away and went on her tiptoes so she could wrap her arms around Guy's shoulders. He stumbled back a half step, but once he got his footing, he wrapped his arms around her waist gradually, like he wasn't sure if he was invited to return the embrace. But once they were firmly in place, Hannah thought she felt him pull her in a little closer until their cheeks pressed together. His skin was smooth as the corner of her mouth grazed it, and she tightened her clasp as well. If she hadn't had a car outside waiting, a meeting with Peter, and a reunion with Alex, she would've held on longer. But she had to let go.

"You are the best," she whispered in his ear and then planted a quick kiss on his cheek before stepping away. His arms slipped off her as she stepped back, and neither of them seemed to know what exactly to say.

"I'd better go."

"Oh yeah. Well, you don't want to keep good ole Pete waiting, do you?" Guy said, that twang of bitterness returning to his voice, almost like . . . like he cared about her. No, she took a step back. She couldn't think that way with him. Not today. Not when she was about to meet up with Alex.

"I guess," she said, taking a few more steps backward, needing desperately to leave but also wanting to stay in a way that was hard for her to wrap her mind around. "Oh, don't forget to put Monty's keys back in his drawer. And the key to the front is on top of the door trim."

"Yes, ma'am," he said, touching his fingers to his forehead like he was taking orders and waving goodbye at the same time. She waved back, and he headed off toward Monty's office. She was about to make her final exit when she realized she hadn't even told him about Evelyn and the article.

"Oh! Guy, wait," she called out as he turned the corner. He reappeared at the mention of his name.

"You need to get out of here, missy," he scolded. "I know I'm enthralling, but you've got places to go. People to see," he joked, his accent always making anything he said in mock seriousness that much funnier to Hannah.

"Shh. Listen."

He pretended to lock his lips.

"I found her—Evelyn. I'll send you the article, but she's absolutely real," she said. The only way those words would feel any more significant would be when she sat down to type them out when she finally wrote the entirety of Evelyn's story.

"Well, damn. This was all worth it, then." She knew he meant the B&E she had just conned him into, but it wasn't the only way that statement applied to her life. This whole search made her life feel worth it.

"Yeah, I guess it was."

CHAPTER 27

Hannah felt massively underdressed, sitting in the swanky Peabody Hotel bar. Most of the women were wearing high heels and skintight dresses, with hairdos that looked like they'd been put together with a curling iron and cement. And Hannah's best efforts at doing her makeup paled in comparison to the lashes, blush, and lip color that populated the room. She hid her jeans and booties under the bar and took another sip of her gin and tonic. It had been a while since she'd had alcohol of any kind, but with the night she had lined up, Hannah needed something to take the edge off her nerves.

She was going to take the night one man at a time, focusing first on her meeting with Peter Dawson rather than lingering on her appointment with Alex. But it was getting difficult not to lose focus. It was half past five and Peter was a little late, but she couldn't blame him. She'd texted him Evelyn's last name as soon as she'd jumped into her hired car, but that was only a little under two hours ago. She finished the last few drops of her drink and gestured to the bartender for another, feeling zero percent less anxious.

She didn't mind waiting, even though she felt a bit like a hobo next to the boobs and diamonds pressing in from all sides. Her only concern was with any possible overlap for her reservation with Alex. When she'd texted to confirm their meeting that morning, he'd responded with a simple Yes. See you tonight. She'd been worried all day that he might be having second thoughts, and showing up late would make it far too easy for him to back out.

"Hannah?" She recognized the voice immediately.

"Mr. Dawson," Hannah blurted, spinning around on her barstool, the gin possibly softening her jagged, nervous edges minutely.

Peter Dawson stood next to Hannah, dressed in a pair of perfectly fitted slacks, a white collared shirt, unbuttoned at the neck, a sharp blazer that looked both casual and dressy, and shoes that had to cost more than Hannah's entire Mississippi wardrobe. Now, this man looked like he belonged here.

"I've told you three times now to call me Pete," he said, taking the stool next to her, setting his leather messenger bag—the only thing that made him stand out from the masses—at his feet.

"I'm sorry. You're right," she apologized and started again. "Let me buy you a drink . . . Pete." She lifted her glass and took the last sip of her second drink, welcoming the warmth that she'd been craving. The bartender took Pete's order, an old-fashioned, and then looked to Hannah expectantly.

"And you?"

"Oh, I couldn't. I've already reached my limit," she said, tipping her empty glass as evidence.

"You're not going to make me drink alone, are you? What if someone saw us? What would that headline be? *Senator Pete Dawson, Alcoholic?*"

Hannah had forgotten how very charming she found Pete Dawson.

"When you put it that way, how can I say no?"

"I agree, it would be cruel. Here, let me surprise you. Then, if you don't feel like drinking, you can blame it on me." He rested his chin on his closed fist, knowing he'd charmed her. She nodded and rolled her eyes, wishing she'd been better at resisting.

"She will have a blackberry Tennessee mule. Green Label, if you have it."

"Sure do," the bartender confirmed, mixing their drinks while Pete turned his attention back to Hannah, taking her in.

"You look nice tonight."

"So you *are* an alcoholic," she said. The twenty-something tattooed bartender snorted at her joke and then cleared his throat and went back to pretending that he was not listening.

"No, I'm sober . . . for now," he said as he took his drink and passed Hannah hers, without acknowledging the bartender, who smirked at Hannah as he walked away.

"To sobriety," she said, raising her glass.

"Never," he said, feigning shock and then raising his glass to the same height. "How about to . . . new friends."

"To new friends," she echoed, clinking glasses, and took a sip, the burning-sweet taste of whiskey and blackberry liquor filling her senses. Pete drank his whiskey in three mouthfuls and gestured for another, running his damp fingers through his hair. Hannah shifted in her seat, trying not to be impatient but wanting to check her phone to see the time. Pete noticed her disquietude and, taking a more judicious swig of his freshened drink, turned the conversation to the topic at hand.

"As you know, I made a little visit to the Pines today," he said. Hannah leaned forward and put a cocktail straw in the corner of her mouth, chomping down on it. "And after you finally sent me that name and I flirted with the girl at the desk, just a little"—he held his fingers close together and then widened them a little when she gave him a skeptical glare—"she took me to the file room and . . ."

Hannah took the straw out of her mouth and rotated it in a circle, uninterested in hearing about any potential dalliances that led to Pete's perusal of the medical files of injured and disabled children and young adults. "Go on . . ."

"I'm kidding. They know me there and let me right in. Good news—I think I found your little Evelyn." He hefted his bag off the floor and onto his knees and yanked out a thick, oversize envelope that he plopped onto the bar and slid her way. "I didn't take the time to dig through her whole file, but the basics seem to match."

Hannah picked up the parcel and opened the top flap; inside were thirty-odd pages of paperwork, and likely doctor's notes and perhaps even the answer to Hannah's ultimate, burning question of who put Evelyn in a wheelchair and changed the course of her life. She wanted nothing more than to delve into the riches that were encased in that envelope, but Hannah used every ounce of self-control she had left to close the flap and place it back down on the counter.

"This is absolutely amazing. Thank you," Hannah said, finding it difficult to resist the emotion tugging at her heartstrings. She took two long sips of her blackberry-flavored beverage, the burning barely noticeable this time, blinking back unexpected, and likely alcohol-induced, tears.

"My pleasure, truly." He put his hand over hers on top of the file. Reflexes slowed ever so slightly, Hannah slipped her hand away after a brief delay.

"What can I do to repay you, Mr. Dawson?" she said, lingering on her return to formality in an attempt to regain any sense of professionalism, finishing her beverage so she didn't have to look at him. She appreciated his help but didn't want to fall into his crosshairs of attraction. He withdrew his hand and tossed the rest of his drink back with a flick of the wrist, placing the glass down with an exaggerated clink.

"How about this, Miss Williamson?" he said, emphasizing her last name as payback for her return to proper etiquette. "If you publish this story, or make a podcast—or whatever people are doing these days—mention that good ole Pete Dawson helped you out of the kindness of his innocent little heart," he said, hand resting on his chest like he could hear "The Star-Spangled Banner" playing in his head. "Not to sound too self-serving, but this would play well with my female constituents. And promise me that next time we meet up it will be for dinner."

"Yeah, not self-serving at all," she teased, trying to keep him close without letting him take over the situation. "But that sounds like a fair enough trade," she said, stowing the envelope in her bag and passing her credit card to the bartender. "And I should probably leave the whole 'alcoholic' thing out of it, don't you think?" she asked, winking.

"That was a joke, and you know it." He pointed at her, eyeing her in that half-suspicious way he did when she first met him, staring at her mouth whenever she talked. She had to get out of there, or a first move was going to happen. Guy's jokes and touches were tender and innocent in comparison to Pete's bold moves, and she didn't like it.

"Maybe I do, and maybe I don't," she said, signing the bill and then sneaking a glance at her phone. It was 6:05 p.m.; alarm bells rang in her head and overpowered her subtle buzz.

"What about dinner to go along with these drinks? I'd love to hear more about you and your story. There is something about you that I can't help but like."

"I'm sure it's my sparkling personality," she sassed back, the alcohol in her bloodstream making her brave. "But I'm sorry, Mr. Dawson, I have a reservation next door. I must be on my way." She shook his hand and let go quickly. "Thank you again."

She brushed past his knees before he could answer. He was able to catch her hand just before she was out of reach, but her fingers slipped out of his easily.

"My name is Pete," he called after her, and Hannah just smiled.

CHAPTER 28

Hannah left the busy bar and rushed over to the Capriccio Grill across the hotel lobby. Every step she took reverberated through her body, shouting to her soul, "He's here."

Would he be waiting by the entrance to the restaurant, or maybe he'd thought to meet her outside the hotel, so she didn't get lost? Or maybe . . .

Self-conscious that she was already ten minutes late, Hannah decided to try the restaurant first and then worry about other options. Alex had always been extremely punctual, and Hannah's perpetual tardiness was one of the primary sources of contention in their relationship, which just put her more on edge.

"Hi. I'm here to meet a friend. He may have checked in already. The reservation is for Alex Penbrook." Hannah checked in with the young hostess, who was all teeth and hospitality.

"Looks like you're in luck—he's already seated and waiting for you. Give me a moment, and I'll take you over there." Her accent was thick like it was an elixir she'd swallowed whole and it was coating her throat and mouth. As the hostess disappeared behind a partition, Hannah retrieved a tube of lip gloss from her bag and slathered on a quick, fresh layer.

Rubbing her glossy lips together, she took in the people around her, trying to distract herself and look calm and collected, which she was not. She was about to see him for the first time in a long time and maybe the last time. Soon he'd be another woman's husband. And she'd have no excuse to not move on. God. That was as scary as seeing his face again.

There was a middle-aged couple snuggled up on benches off to the side of the restaurant's entrance. A family with young children bustled around close to the restrooms; one girl with a big smile made her think of Rosie and—as a result—Guy. Why did thinking of Guy make her feel so guilty? He was a great guy and an amazing friend, but . . . what else was he becoming? No, that was the whiskey talking.

"Miss, if you'll follow me." The hostess and all her impossibly white teeth were back. Hannah tried not to look around the room. She didn't want to see Alex before he saw her, sparing Hannah from any looks of disappointment at her current appearance. She knew she'd never been beautiful, but she couldn't bear for Alex to be able to pick up on just how broken she still was by his rejection.

"And here we are." The hostess pointed to a table and walked away.

In front of Hannah was the man she'd tried to stop loving after he stopped loving her. Six feet tall, dark hair, green eyes like ocean glass, and a smile that had always made her blush. *Alex.*

"Hannah! It's so good to see you!" He didn't wait for her to take her seat. Instead, he rushed over and put his arms around her before she had any chance to react. Already slightly unsteady from the three drinks she had consumed with Pete Dawson, Hannah wobbled and nearly fell over, the weight of her bag shifting her center of gravity. His embrace felt the same. He smelled the same. She stumbled back, not finding the reminder of the past comforting. It was disquieting.

"Well, oh my goodness. I'm so sorry. I got a little carried away." He was acting like she was an old college buddy and they'd lost touch after moving away, getting married, and having 1.5 kids each instead of the woman he'd promised to marry but didn't, and his cavalier attitude threw her off as much as his overly exuberant embrace. Still unable to find the right words, she placed her bag on the back of her chair and removed her jacket as Alex returned to his seat, slightly more solemn than before.

"I can't believe it's been so long," he said, as though she had been complicit in the decision not to see each other anymore.

This is going to be harder than I thought. Hannah willed herself to say something, anything, her mind and body empty. "How was your conference?" She decided to focus on the most mundane details possible, hoping it would keep her from stumbling into hurtful questions before they even had a chance to order an appetizer.

"It was fine. But that's boring. I want to know how you're doing." His eyes were dancing like they always did when he got excited about something. She couldn't remember the last time they danced for her. It was the temptation Evelyn talked about. That sparkle when he stared at her felt a lot like the promise of happiness. "You look amazing. It seems like going back to your southern roots has been good for you."

She knew the compliment was close to meaningless—both Guy and Pete had mentioned her slightly above-average effort at looking normal today. But somehow, the words sounded special in Alex's voice, and the brick wall inside her started to dissolve just a little.

"It's not nearly as terrible as I thought it would be," she said, taking a drink of her water and glancing at the menu. She needed to get some food in her stomach soon.

"I hope you don't mind, but I ordered a few things. Just appetizers. They have calamari here, and I know how much you like it. And some candied brussels sprouts like the ones we used to get at the Publican."

Every time he spoke, he mentioned another memory from their past together, as though it didn't cause him any pain. She finished her water and looked around for a busboy so she could get a refill.

"I don't eat calamari anymore," she said. What she should have said was *I don't eat anything that reminds me of you anymore,* but she wasn't nearly intoxicated enough for that level of honesty.

"Oh, no problem. More for me, I guess."

They sat in an uncomfortable hush for a few minutes as the busboy refilled their water, and the waitress took Hannah's drink order—plain seltzer water. She needed to slow the effects of her first three drinks, the attempt to numb herself backfiring. Hannah snagged a roll from the basket in the middle of the table and tried to stomach a few bites as Alex continued his attempts at small talk about his work, asking about Mamaw and living in Senatobia, and even about her job at the *Record.*

"Excuse me, are you Hannah Williamson?" A different waitress from the one who had taken their order and brought Alex his cocktail held a tray with a single drink in the middle of it.

"I am," she said, grateful for the interruption but also confused how anyone but Alex would know her full name here.

"This is for you," she said, placing a deep-purple drink on the table next to Hannah.

"Oh no, I didn't order anything."

"No, it's from that man over there." She pointed across the room to a table where Pete Dawson sat dining by himself. He held up his drink to her and winked. Hannah smirked back and raised her glass.

"Who the hell is that?" Alex asked, looking over his shoulder at Pete, who had gone back to eating.

Hannah's ears perked up. She'd known Alex long enough to be able to pick out when he was feeling a little jealous. She liked that he felt that way. He deserved to feel that way.

"Oh, that's just a friend of mine. We met at a charity event I was covering. His name is Peter Dawson. You may have heard of his dad, Jack Dawson. You know, he's running for president." She didn't feel even one bit guilty, stretching the truth about her first meeting with

Pete. She took another long drink from her blackberry Tennessee mule and felt as fancy as all get-out.

"That was a bold move. How did he know we weren't on a date?"

"I don't think he cared," Hannah said, appreciating Pete Dawson's personality more by the minute.

"I don't like it." Alex shifted in his seat, his slightly wrinkled blue dress shirt looking shabby next to Pete's classy fashion choices. "You're not dating that guy, are you? Because that's pretty possessive if he couldn't let you go out on your own."

Hannah cackled and then reined herself in, knowing she was getting a little too tipsy for her own good. "Alex, you don't need to take care of me anymore. I've been taking care of myself for a long time now."

Alex's face was starting to turn pink on his cheekbones, which meant he was getting upset. "It's a real jerk move if you brought your boyfriend with you to come see me, Hannah."

"Not that it's any of your business, but Pete is not my boyfriend. He and I had a business meeting before I was supposed to meet you. I don't get to Memphis that often, so when I do, I have to try and kill a couple of birds with one stone."

"Oh," Alex said, his shoulders dropping from a defensive posture and the tint of red quickly draining from his face. "Damn. Why did I want to fight that man?"

The question made Hannah's stomach turn. She wasn't sure if it was from too much blackberry syrup or too many alcoholic beverages in less than an hour, but whatever it was, she was tired of beating around the bush while Alex acted like her boyfriend.

"What the hell are we doing here, Alex? This sucks. You come to Memphis, and you talk to me like nothing even happened, and now you want to fight some guy like you're my boyfriend?" Her voice trembled, and her eyes grew moist. "Something did happen. You cheated on me, and now you are about to marry that woman instead of me. And I can't sit here and reminisce about old times and put up with you getting jealous when you were the one who left me. I should never have come here tonight. This was a huge mistake."

She shoved away from the table and tried to grab her things, tipping over her chair in the process. It fell with a monstrous crash, drawing the attention of every diner in the room. Storming out of the restaurant, Hannah knew she'd made a scene and that everyone was watching her pathetic attempt to escape. Trying to get as far away from Alex and the Capriccio Grill as she could, she took out her phone to order a car that would take her home.

"Hey, you okay?" Pete caught up to Hannah, putting his arm around her and guiding her to a bench by the giant fountain in the lobby.

"I don't want to talk about it," she said, forcefully, working through the steps on the app that would help her to summon her ride, which was proving to be a little tricky since her brain was working against three and a half alcoholic beverages.

"Was that your boyfriend? Did I make him angry by sending you that drink? If so, I'm very sorry. It was meant to be a joke," he explained, his arm loosely behind her, feeling more like a protective move than a flirtatious one.

"He is not my boyfriend. He is my ex-boyfriend, and you did absolutely nothing wrong. I just want to go home."

Hannah hated allowing anyone to see her be weak, but especially Pete, who seemed perpetually strong and confident. After losing her job at the *Tribune* after her breakdown, it pained her to think of anyone in her professional life seeing her this way. But she couldn't hold it in. Her lower lip trembled, and she broke down—hard—sobbing.

"I will order you a car. Don't you worry about it for one more second." He rubbed her shoulders with one hand and typed on his smartphone with the other, and she let him, trying to count down like Laura had taught her to. *One . . . two . . . three . . .*

"I had a feeling I'd find you out here," Alex said, approaching Pete with a scowl.

"I think Hannah would like to be left alone now," Pete said, defensively, putting his body between Hannah and Alex, his deep-seated southern beliefs about protecting women and children on full display. She bristled at all the male posturing, but her head was spinning.

"I'm fine," she protested, holding her head.

"I think you should stop speaking for her." Alex then spoke to Hannah as though Pete didn't exist. "Hannah, please. Can I talk to you for five minutes? Alone."

Pete started talking again, and then Alex, but Hannah couldn't focus on any one train of thought, all the words and arguments swirling around her already spinning head.

One. Two. Three. Four. Five. She counted, but no clarity came bounding into her clouded mind. *One. Two. Three. Four. Five.* She tried again, but still nothing. When Pete stood up and the volume of Pete and Alex's discussion grew loud enough to attract attention from bystanders, Hannah spoke.

"Pete, I'm fine. You should go," she said, her voice barely audible over the rush of the fountain.

"What?" he said, turning his back on the angry Alex, and still acting as a bodyguard. He leaned over to hear what she said more clearly.

"You should go. I can take care of myself," she said, looking up at him with still-damp eyes but at least some lucidity. "Before someone calls the cops or realizes who you are and gets a video."

Pete looked around the crowded lobby, more than a few eyes focused on the altercation he was now a part of. He straightened his blazer, wiped his hands on the tops of his pants legs, and straightened his already perfect hair.

"Come with me," he said, below what could even be considered a whisper. Hannah looked past Pete and focused intently on Alex, arms folded, biceps bulging like they used to after he'd worked out.

"You go—I'm okay," she said, using her head to gesture toward the exit. Pete gave her a pleading look that almost convinced Hannah to change her mind, but she didn't. She needed to have this talk with Alex, even if it was a mistake. But it was her mistake to make.

"I'm going to be at the bar. If you need me . . ." He held up his phone.

"Yeah. I got it. I'll call if I need to. Now, get out of here," Hannah said, touched by his sincerity but unwilling to be at the center of a scandal that could ruin his political reputation, or hers as a journalist. When he disappeared into the crowd, Hannah could breathe a little easier.

Alex took Pete's spot on the bench next to her and laced his fingers in between hers. She knew she should pull away as she had with Pete at the bar, but she didn't.

"I'm so sorry," he said, the lines around his eyes more profound than she remembered them, a new scar on his right cheek, making her wonder how he'd hurt himself. But he smelled the same, that was for sure, and his touch was still the one thing that could calm her in an instant.

"Alex, why did you come here?" she asked quickly before his scent and his smile and his touch worked their magic and made her forgive him. He'd ignored her for ten months now—she needed to remember that.

"For work . . ."

"No, don't give me that BS," she said. "You never go to this conference. You came because you knew I lived here, didn't you?"

"Yes," he admitted, his arm around her shoulders feeling so different from Pete's, less like comfort and more like the cocktail she'd been drinking—a sweet, intoxicating burning. "I needed to see you before . . ."

"Before you get married," she finished the sentence, already knowing it was true.

"Yeah, at first, that's why I wanted to come, but then . . ." He let go of her hand momentarily and ran his thumb up the curve of her neck and across her collarbone, like he was strolling down a path that he knew well, making her shiver. "Janie and I broke up two weeks ago."

The words took a few seconds to sink in. During those fleeting moments, Hannah's heartbeat seemed to pause for more beats than were humanly possible, and she blinked, blood rushing to her head.

"And the wedding?" she asked when she remembered what words were and how to say them.

"It's canceled." He removed his arm from her shoulders and touched her earlobe and jawline, making it harder to think than it already was when hearing such unexpected news.

"What . . . what happened?" she asked, shifting away from his heady touch so she could make sure she understood everything clearly.

"You happened, Hannah." Alex picked at a spot on his jeans. "I never stopped loving you, and Janie knew it. And I know you've built a new life here with your grandmother and a new job and, apparently, senators, and I know I don't deserve it, but—would you ever consider giving things another try?"

It was like the dream she used to have when she'd take Ambien, the same one every night. Alex would come home from work one day and tell her he'd made a colossal mistake. All he wanted was to be with her, and in the dream they'd get married and have babies and live nearly a whole lifetime in one night of dreaming, and the best part of it was that every second felt real, almost more real than her daily life.

Then she'd wake up the next morning, and in the few moments it took to transition between dreamland and real life, she'd experience the profound, gut-wrenching loss of the breakup all over again. That dream was why she started to prefer sleep over real life. It's why she ultimately thought she wanted to fall asleep and never wake up. But this wasn't a dream. This was real life, and Alex was sitting next to Hannah, offering her the one thing she thought she'd literally die for. She turned her hand over so their palms were touching and filled the space between his fingers with hers.

"You broke my heart," she said, the definition of *brokenhearted* not even close to efficient to describe what happened after he left.

"I know. I've regretted it every day since." His voice was thick with emotion and regret. Temptation. So much temptation. Hannah took in every angle of his face and slightly different twist of his features. His eyes. His nose. The crinkle around his eyes. The scar above his lip . . . the scar above his lip. That was the same scar she'd stared at in a Facebook picture while he ignored her. The one she'd obsessed over when her father was dying, when she ran away to another state to escape the pain of his abandonment. That scar didn't remind her of good times anymore, and she definitely didn't want to kiss it.

"Alex, why didn't you answer my text when my dad died?" she asked, that scar reminding her of how empty she felt, worthless when he discarded her. Dumped her. Ignored her. Looking at him live and in person didn't bring peace—it made her angry.

"I . . . I was confused. Janie was jealous of you. She told me I couldn't . . ."

Hannah snatched her hand back. "Janie was jealous of *me*?"

"Yes. She's crazy. I made such a huge mistake, Hannah. Please." He was begging, now.

She'd begged. She'd cried. And he'd ignored her.

"You used to call *me* crazy, Alex. You made me feel crazy." The same cloudy, heavy, gaslighty feeling was moving in like a low fog. Hannah stood up, wobbling ever so slightly. "I can't do this."

Alex grabbed her arm. "Don't. Please."

She yanked it away. Alex no longer looked like the antidote to pain. He *was* pain. And that was all he would ever be.

"Go to hell, Alex," she said, grabbing her things and forcing one foot after the other, heading toward the women's bathroom fifteen feet away. She'd be safe there. He couldn't come in and spin his stories of love and missing her. She was crying even harder now. She had to proactively block out Alex's voice by focusing on the echo of her footsteps instead.

When she shoved her way through the restroom door, she let it go and fell into a stall, yanking out long strips of toilet paper. Hannah's phone buzzed in her bag. Over and over, ringing and ringing. She reached in and pressed and held the button on the side without looking, avoiding temptation. The phone went quiet and the relief was instant. She'd stay in the bathroom stall all night if she had to, but she wouldn't face him again. She leaned her cheek against the cool aluminum of the stall and let herself feel. The pain was intense, and it was old but fresh at the same time. But as it burned through her and poured out of her, as she sat doubled over on the edge of the toilet in the stall, she could feel a lightening at the loss of her fantasy.

CHAPTER 29

Exiting the bathroom after a few staff members had knocked on her stall because of complaints from another visitor about her crying, she'd been worried she'd find Alex. But instead, Pete was waiting on a couch in the lobby.

"There you are. I was worried you'd found an escape hatch in there," he said, concern etched in the fine lines on his face.

Why does this guy give two shits about me? Hannah thought, baffled.

"I'm all right," she said, covering her puffy eyes with her palms for a second. "I need to get home. Could you . . ." She hated asking for help, but she didn't want to turn her phone back on and risk talking to Alex. Not while he was still in Memphis. "Could you get me a car? I just need to get home."

"For sure," he said, guiding her to a spot on the bench where he'd been waiting. He took out his phone and began to type.

"Thank you," she said meekly and sniffled in what turned out to be a very unladylike fashion, then used the edge of her sleeve to wipe up the snot and tear residue from her upper lip. She was empty of tears but full in a different way. She rejected Alex. *She* rejected *Alex*. It all still seemed only half-real.

"Okay, your car will be here in fifteen minutes. You really feel up to it? I mean, my place is around the corner. You could sleep this off, and I'd be on my best scout behavior," he said, holding up three fingers like he was saying the scout motto.

She gave him a skeptical look and rolled her swollen eyes, almost able to laugh. Almost. "No, but thanks for the offer."

"I like you, Hannah Williamson, crack reporter. There is just something about you that I can't put my finger on, but I like it a lot. You don't let me get away with my shit. I don't run into a lot of women like you."

Hannah rubbed her nose with her sleeve again, past caring if she was disgusting. "I've been told I'm one of a kind," she said, attempting humor, but her voice cracked and she sounded nearly as broken.

"That's for damn sure," he said, resting an arm on the back of the bench behind Hannah, but not actually touching her. They sat in silence until his phone announced the arrival of her ride.

He escorted her to the car and helped her settle into the back seat and then went to talk to the driver. She swore she saw him pass a cash tip of some kind, but she chose to turn a blind eye, already owing Pete Dawson far more than money. He leaned in through the back window.

"It was quite the night, Miss Williamson. You stay safe now, you hear?"

She semi-chuckled through her snuffly nose. "You too," she said, growing shy, perhaps sobering up a touch.

"And call me if you need anything, okay? I mean it. Anything."

"We'll see," she pushed back, unable to resist challenging him one more time. He waved and the car drove away. Hannah settled into the back seat, half-awake, but her brain was too active to cooperate with her tired body. As she drove away from Memphis, two things hit her: First, she didn't miss Alex, and she didn't regret telling him off. Walking away felt powerful; it felt like the opposite of being discarded. It felt like strength, like it was something Evelyn might do.

And second, Alex had chosen not to be in her life for the past ten months, and had been pulling away for months prior to Hannah's discovery of his affair. But tonight, two men who were not Alex put themselves on the line to help Hannah. Alex, on the other hand, only wanted to take. It was starting to look like her future didn't end the moment Alex walked out that door—maybe that's when it really started. Her chin rested on her chest, and Hannah let herself doze off in the pine-scented hired car, looking forward to climbing into her pullout bed and falling asleep alone.

"Miss, we are almost there." The driver tapped Hannah's knee and she jumped. They were about five minutes from home, and after her nap, Hannah's mind was somewhat clear. Hannah took out her phone and turned it on, thinking that she'd better warn Mamaw that she was headed in through the front door. But her screen was filled to the brim with notifications. Hannah didn't take the time to read them—the first few were clearly from Alex. She dialed Mamaw's number, but the phone rang and rang and rang, Mamaw the one person on the planet without a cell phone or an answering machine. *Huh.*

Hannah tried texting Guy and was surprised to find she hadn't had a message from him since she'd left for Memphis that afternoon. Hannah called his number, and it went straight to voice mail. *Shoot.*

First she checked her texts. There were three from Pete, asking her to send a message when she'd made it home okay. She responded to those right away with a gracious thank-you and assurance of her well-being.

Then there was one from her mom, sending Hannah her flight times for Friday, asking her to FaceTime with her nephews the next evening. She wouldn't tell her mom about Alex just yet, she'd decided.

She switched to voice mail, remembering a notification for it on her touch screen, which . . . was full?

Three messages from Mamaw, one from Guy, one from an unknown number, and one from the *Record*. Hannah started in chronological order.

> *Hey, Hannah. Guy here. So, I'm here with a police officer. He said there was an alarm going off at the* Record, *and he found me locking up when he came to check on it. I told him that you work here and asked me to come out and help you with a project. He said he'd need to talk to you in person. Could you give you a call ASAP, please? Thanks.*

The police? Oh no. Oh no. Oh no. Oh no. Hannah touched the next message.

> *Miss Williamson, this is Officer Allen from the Senatobia Police Department. I have a Mr. Guy Franklin here. He claims to be doing some work for you down here at the* Tate County Record. *A break-in was reported here this afternoon when a silent alarm was tripped, and I need confirmation that he had permission to be inside of the building at this time. Thank you for any information; my number is . . .*

How had she been so wrapped up in her reunion bubble and subsequent fight with Alex that she hadn't heard any of these messages? She felt ill, and it wasn't just from her alcohol intake. She knew who the next one had to be. *Monty.*

> *Miss Williamson, I would like to meet with you as soon as possible. It seems that there has been a break-in here at the* Record, *and I've been told you might have some information. The perpetrator was caught in the act and has been arrested, but he insists that you will be able to shed some light on this*

*situation. This crisis on top of the emergency with my dear
wife has left me deeply saddened. I will be spending the holiday with my family but will be back in the office for a few
hours on Friday. I hope to hear from you soon.*

Arrested. Guy had been arrested. Guilt flooded in, demolishing any
positivity from the night. No. Monty knew Guy—knew his parents.
Why would Monty let the police stop Guy when he was using a key?
Hannah knew the answer. If this had been one of Monty's friend's kids
jimmying a lock and helping out a pal, the officer or Monty would've
taken him at his word. But because it was Guy . . .

She slammed her bag with a closed fist, furious at her thoughtless,
selfish nature. She'd basically forced Guy to help her break into Monty's
office, not even considering that he was taking on ten times more risk
than she had. White woman who works at the *Record* gets caught trip-
ping an alarm on a day off—straightforward explanation, laughed off
as an accident. But when a young Black male is found with a giant
toolbox, setting off an alarm in a place where he's never worked and
doesn't have any reason to be—arrested.

The next two messages were from Mamaw: wondering where
Hannah was, asking if she needed a ride, pleading for her to check
in. The third was from 10:34 p.m. and made Hannah wish she could
teleport home in the blink of an eye:

*Hannah, darling. I'm so anxious about you. I called the
Franklins to see if Guy knew where you were, and they told me
that Guy had been arrested for breaking into your newspaper
office. I was speechless. He seemed like such a nice young man.
I was worried you might be all wrapped up in that situation,
but when I called the police department, they said you weren't
with him when he was arrested and that no one knows where
you are. If I don't hear from you soon, I'm going to drive on*

over to the police department to fill out a report. I can't stop imagining you dead on the side of the road somewhere. I don't want to bother your dear mother with more worries, but I'll be forced to call her if I don't hear from you soon. I love you, my little Hannah girl. I don't know how I'll live with myself if something has happened to you.

Her fear, panic, and self-hatred were so entirely out of control that Hannah was sure the car would explode if the emotions were made solid. The only way to manage was to make plans. She'd go home and check in on Mamaw first, let her know she was okay, and then go directly to the police department to give her statement, clear things up, and make sure Guy was no longer sitting in the county jail. If anyone should be there, she should. And if at all possible, she was going to fix this.

Hannah was halfway out of the car before it'd even come to a full stop. She ran up the front steps of the house, twisting the doorknob and finding it still locked. Mamaw had given Hannah a key when she'd moved in, but she'd never once had to use it, either because the door was open with someone at home or because she entered through the garage door each evening. But the door in from the garage would also be locked, so Hannah searched for the key. She fished it out of the interior zipper pocket of her bag and let herself inside, walking into a pitch-black house, the only light on in the kitchen and all the blinds drawn like Mamaw liked them in the evenings.

"Mamaw?" Hannah called out, taking off her shoes by the front door like Mamaw would want her to. All the worst thoughts went through Hannah's mind, and for a moment she wished that she had a lousy imagination, because with every call into the house that had no echoed response, Hannah created a new and even more terrible reason that the house was so quiet. Her heart pounded and her head swam. Hannah fought the explosion of worry in her midsection that felt like an alarm. With intense trepidation, she forced herself to walk down the hallway that led to Mamaw's bedroom, her head still woozy from the alcohol but also from the deafening whoosh of blood in her ears. Reaching Mamaw's bedroom, Hannah tapped lightly on the slightly ajar door that opened fully under her light touch.

"Mamaw, you in here?" she called into the room, hoping for a relieved hello or even an angry scolding. But when Hannah finally caught sight of Mamaw's bed, what she found was more disturbing—it was empty. *Hell no.* Worry morphed to panic, her ears ringing and feet moving uncharacteristically fast.

No more tiptoeing or gently calling, now she ran through the house, room to room, searching the bathrooms in particular, the new back suite, Papaw's office, the kitchen, the front room leading to the garage.

There, by the door to the garage, she saw it—or didn't see it would be more accurate. The row of hooks where the keys for certain things like the shed or the lawnmower were kept had one empty hook where Hannah had placed the key for the Buick just a few days earlier.

"Oh no." If Mamaw had tried to drive with her casts on, no one here to help her . . . Hannah swallowed back the rise of bile in her throat. If she had crashed on the side of the road somewhere, looking for her granddaughter, it was all Hannah's fault. Everything was her fault.

Hannah swung the door to the garage outward toward the set of wooden steps that she'd walked up and down countless times, day after day for the past several months. The car was there—she saw its outline immediately, thank heavens. But that respite from worry lasted only half a second because as the ancient garage door opened one inch at a time, Hannah's focus left the car and zeroed in on the small lump of floral material on the garage floor, boots sticking out from underneath.

"Mamaw!" Hannah screamed, horrified, dashing down the steps that must've tripped her as she tried to make her way to the car, the keys to the Buick still clutched in her knobby fingers. *She's dead,* a voice screamed inside Hannah's head. *You killed her! She's dead!*

No idea what to do, shaking and ready to vomit, Hannah knelt by Mamaw's head and checked her breathing. She wasn't sure, but there seemed to be just the slightest of breaths going in and out, weakly, which Hannah confirmed with a hand on Mamaw's still-warm back. She was alive.

"I'm here now, Mamaw. I've got you," Hannah said, taking out her phone. She dialed 911 and rubbed her grandmother's back, the only action she could do without worrying about hurting her further.

"Nine one one. What's your emergency?"

"My grandmother fell in her garage. I think she's been here a while. Uh . . ." Hannah scanned Mamaw for injuries, a pool of blood on the floor coming from a mystery source. Hannah's whole body was shaking out of control. This couldn't be the end. She'd come here to take care of Mamaw. To make sure things like this never happened. *Damn it.* "She's bleeding, but I don't know where. Do I move her? What do I do?" Hannah asked the operator, but the question was also meant for herself and God, in case He was listening after all.

The emergency operator ordered an ambulance and then took Hannah through first aid, step by step. She wished that she could take back everything she'd done in the past twenty-four hours as quickly as Mamaw's blood soaked into Hannah's jeans where she knelt. She'd give up everything she'd learned about Evelyn and her connection with Pete Dawson. She'd even give the closure she'd found with Alex back if it meant saving Mamaw and keeping Guy safe. But it wasn't that easy, and there were no take-backs in real life, and sometimes one person's mistakes set off a shock wave of devastation in the lives of those around them. And she was the author of these mistakes.

By the time the ambulance arrived, Mamaw's breathing had become ragged. The paramedics allowed Hannah to climb into the back of the ambulance with Mamaw. Hannah couldn't watch the things they were doing to her, knowing that they were saving her life but feeling each intervention as though they shared a body. Once the ambulance arrived at the hospital, Mamaw was rushed back behind double doors for immediate attention. It was bad—really bad, and it was all Hannah's fault.

Covered in her grandmother's blood, Hannah sat in one of the ER waiting room chairs, eyes hazy with shock and fear. She sent a brief text to her mother, asking for a call, and then sent Brody a similar directive. Pam sounded almost as concerned for her daughter as for her ninety-one-year-old mother-in-law.

"You okay, Hannah? Is there someone who can stay with you? I'm worried about you," her mother asked at the end of a series of impossible-to-answer questions. Hannah wasn't okay. Not even close to okay. She'd been strong for a moment tonight, and she was starting to make progress toward escaping from her inert state, but all her gains were canceled out by this failure. She was a failure. No wonder she was alone. No wonder her mother tried to run her life. No wonder her friends had dumped her during her depression. She was a shitty human. Alex was better without her. Pete too, and Guy . . . Oh God, Guy.

Hannah called the police department, her voice small and childlike when she asked for Officer Allen. But he was officially off for the night, home for the holiday. The receptionist would only take her name.

"But this is an emergency!" she yelled into the phone. "I need to speak with Officer Allen. Call him at home. Or put someone else on. Please!" She begged, but the receptionist calmly refused, only disclosing that someone had posted bail and Guy was no longer behind bars. She hung up and called him immediately, but there was no response.

"Guy, I'm so sorry. I will fix this. I promise. Call me if you can. Mamaw fell down and we're at the hospital. I hope you're okay." She hit the button to end the call. It wasn't okay. It couldn't possibly be okay if he'd been arrested. Oh God, she wished she could disappear.

The timeline solidified in her head, and she understood—he'd been in jail. She flinched at the thought of Guy sitting in a cell because of her carelessness, angry at herself mostly, but also angry at Monty and the police department, who should know better. A swirling whirlpool of regret and guilt dragged her down deeper by the minute, inflicting physical pain she'd only experienced with abandonment and her father's death. She'd pay Guy's father back the bond money. She'd reason with Monty. She'd go to the police and admit everything.

The world was a blur for the next few hours. A sweet nurse brought Hannah a pair of scrubs to change into and showed her to a bathroom where she could wash up. In the locked, oversize restroom, Hannah popped her phone out of its blood-coated case, pocketing the device and tossing the sheath in the garbage can.

Someone must've contacted Carla, because she came rushing into the waiting room at some point, crying and wringing her hands, asking a million questions. And then Mr. Davenport hobbled through the sliding glass doors soon after, and Hannah told her story of what had happened for the fifth or sixth time that evening.

"I'll make this right," she chanted, never running out of tears or regret. Hannah collapsed into her seat, feeling lost.

Carla tried to comfort her. Her mother had tried to console her over the phone, and even Mr. Davenport gave some words of wisdom, though he was as much of a mess as anyone and ended up getting emotional and trailing off.

"Oh, baby, come here. It's okay." Carla unbent Hannah and forced her into an embrace, thinking her melancholy was only about Mamaw and not her long string of sins. She buried her face deep into Carla's soft shoulder, and instead of faking a smile or holding back tears or making a snarky comment or finding a reason to be annoyed or offended in order to avoid feeling . . . everything, Hannah let go and sobbed against the scratchy fabric of Carla's holiday sweatshirt.

And when Carla muttered what were intended to be sweet, comforting words, saying everything was going to be okay, Hannah listened, but she didn't agree because she knew something no one else did—that was a lie people told when they knew it would not be okay. She had no control over whether Mamaw would survive, and she had no way of turning back time and leaving Guy out of her ill-planned reconnaissance at the *Record*. Whether Hannah listened to the truth in that statement or tried to believe the lie—it didn't really matter in the end. With so much out of her grasp, she *could* help make one thing okay again, and that thought held her as tightly as Carla's arms and calmed her more skillfully than some well-intended platitudes.

CHAPTER 30

"It was my fault, though," Hannah said to the prosecutor for the fourth time in their meeting. "He had no idea I didn't have express permission to be there—I swear."

"But he used tools to break into Mr. Martin's office?" William Grant, middle-aged with a ring of salt-and-pepper hair half circling his scalp, asked half-heartedly, like he could hardly care about the actual facts of the case.

"Yes, but . . . I asked him to do it. He didn't know it would be a problem. God, I didn't even know it would be a problem. I thought the worst thing that could happen is Monty would get mad at me and maybe I'd get fired, but—burglary? No. Never. A charge of burglary means there was intent to commit a crime, right?" Hannah had done some research and tried to get her mother's help until Pam realized what she was doing and insisted on Hannah getting her own representation rather than playing armchair social justice warrior.

"This will all be addressed by Mr. Franklin's attorneys in front of a grand jury." It was like he was bored. Hannah held up her phone in front of his face, trying to wake him from his apathy.

"Here . . . look . . . you can see in my texts. Two weeks ago I asked him to meet me there, and I didn't tell him why I needed his tools. This was entirely my fault," she said for the fifth time now. She hadn't seen

Guy since the day she turned him into a criminal. He'd been distant via text and had turned down every suggested meetup. Hannah was disappointed; she missed him so much, but she understood. She hated herself too.

Mr. Grant sighed in the way Monty used to when he found her petulance childish but also wished to act like a gentleman. It made Hannah want to throw her iPhone at him, though, little good it would do looking as crazy as she felt right now.

"Yes, I read your police interview in the file, Miss Williamson. But I can't go off of your word on this matter. Mr. Franklin was found in possession of burglary tools, inside the *Record* offices after hours where files were found to be missing."

"I was the one going through Monty's files—not Guy. I told him to go into Monty's desk. I asked him to bring up the files from the basement. Me. Not Guy Franklin. Why won't you all listen to me?" Hannah, on the edge of her chair at this point, slammed her fist on the desk, making the gold pen perched in Mr. Grant's fancy holder jangle and nearly fall. He stabilized it, eyeing Hannah cautiously.

"Miss Williamson, you seem like a well-intentioned young woman, but you are going to find yourself in trouble if you keep this up."

Hannah resisted rolling her eyes. She'd heard this enough from her mother, who was wholly against Hannah's willful confessions.

"Exactly! If anyone should be in trouble, it's me." She leaned in, the tiniest glimmer of hope stirring inside her heavy, tired heart.

Mr. Grant squinted, suspicious. "A false confession helps no one."

Outrage boiled inside her at the accusation.

"I'm not lying. I swear."

She didn't break eye contact, even after it had gone beyond the polite length of social norms. The statement seemed to mean something to Mr. Grant. He leaned back in his padded leather chair and spoke more thoughtfully than before.

"If Mr. Martin could corroborate even one of your claims, I would gladly listen. But for now my hands are tied. I'm sorry." Hannah grunted in frustration, and Mr. Grant rushed to address her aggravation. "Don't worry, dear. I've found that the truth seems to come out in these cases. If Mr. Franklin is as innocent as you say, I'm sure it will come to light."

Dead end. Another dead end. *Damn it.* Hannah shook her head, her voice heavy with sarcasm. "Yeah, I'm sure Guy will get treated fairly—in Mississippi. No way he could face any kind of prejudice."

"Now now." Mr. Grant stood suddenly and stared coolly at her. "Let's not bring race and such into this. This has nothing to do with discrimination—"

Hannah cut him off, refusing to stand. "Doesn't it? Then why aren't I facing the same charges as Guy?"

"I'm sorry, Miss Williamson. There is no proof you were there. Now"—Mr. Grant opened his office door—"I have another appointment. I'd like to ask you to leave."

"I bet you would," Hannah grumbled, leaning over to retrieve her bag. She took her time standing, shifting her weight so the heavy bag on her shoulder, packed with research, books, and notes, didn't make her tip over.

Mr. Grant stayed by his office door, holding it open even though a stopper kept it in place. The fury inside Hannah demolished any self-control she'd built up over the past four months in Senatobia. No friendly goodbye or half smile would cover her outrage today. Hannah stormed out, fueled by a fury that was becoming commonplace in her life.

"I *will* be back," Hannah said, storming past Mr. Grant. Once past the waiting room, she yanked out her phone with a new idea playing in her head, but the screen was filled with texts.

There were four long texts from Pam Williamson, asking where Hannah had gone and when she'd be back, and then tersely reminding

Hannah that she wasn't to just take the rental car without permission since she wasn't on the rental agreement.

But she'd had to leave without telling her mom, or else Pam Williamson, attorney-at-law, would insist on coming with her "unstable" daughter.

Yes, she felt a little out of control; the whirlpool of depression and sadness nibbled at her toes each day Mamaw stayed unconscious and each day Guy's charges were not dropped. The whirlpool was getting stronger, pulling her deeper into the murky depths, waterlogging every exposed bit of her heart and soul. She was holding her head above it this time, but that didn't mean it wasn't a daily—no, hourly—struggle.

But it wasn't too late to get out of the spiral. There was one man who could fix it all, one man who had no reason to prosecute an innocent man: Monty Martin. He'd been ignoring her calls and emails, and as far as she could tell, he hadn't been back to the *Record* since his wife's heart attack, leaving it to poor, trembling Dolores to fire Hannah. But thanks to Google, Hannah knew where Monty lived his quaint little life with Momma and his two cats and a chicken coop full of hens, and today he'd have an unexpected visitor.

CHAPTER 31

Hannah slammed the dust-coated door to her mother's rental car, squinting down the dirt driveway to see if she could make out the highway from her parking spot. No luck. She turned back to examine the blue-and-white turn-of-the-century Victorian farmhouse. The faint whooshing of cars rushing by was the only indication that she hadn't traveled back in time a century.

Monty had spoken of his home before; the house itself was built in the early 1900s after the old plantation home had burned down from being struck by lightning. Soon after, the Martins parceled out to smaller farms, got a big payout when I-55 snaked its way down through the heart of Mississippi, and finally sold off the last tidbits to housing developers, until eventually the only part the Martins still owned was the acreage this house sat on and the dusty road that led up to it.

It was a beautiful relic; Hannah couldn't deny that. The fascia looked like icing on a carefully constructed gingerbread house, the bright red of the door like licorice, the round stained glass window under the roof gable and vent like a whirling peppermint. Inside wasn't a witch waiting for hungry children, but even without cages and ovens and a pointy hat, Monty wasn't exactly the Pillsbury Doughboy he seemed to be.

Hannah collected her bag full of evidence from the passenger seat and closed the car door with her best attempt at stealth. Her stomach turned, and she coughed to clear her dry throat, her tired eyes gritty from lack of sleep and likely some of the dust from the road, trying to decide how much to tell Monty.

She'd kept Evelyn from Monty on purpose—he couldn't be trusted with her story. He'd have killed it from day one if Hannah had walked up the stairs of the *Record* and presented her findings to him when this all started nearly two months ago. Then the story never would've had a chance, and Evelyn's voice would've been ignored forever.

She stopped at the bottom of the porch stairs, the rumbling in her stomach turning into what felt like a deep fissure. It was easier to tell herself that she'd played all these secret agent games of hide-and-seek with the answers for purely altruistic reasons, but that wasn't really true. She wanted to break Evelyn's story out from the rejection pile, to give her tumultuous life some grander meaning, but Hannah's true motivations were not exactly pure. Hannah wanted to be a real reporter again—have her words mean something. Maybe he'd see her vision. Maybe he'd listen and change his mind, not just about Guy but about Evelyn too.

A cool breeze broke through Hannah's reverie. She shuddered, held her flak jacket closer to her torso, and forced herself up the steps. She was reaching to ring the doorbell when the front door swung open unexpectedly. A petite woman with bobbed hair and wearing purple scrubs stood on the other side. Hannah let out a small "Eep!"

"Sorry! I didn't mean to frighten you. Mrs. Martin saw you on the doorbell camera," the young woman said in a half whisper through the top half of the screen door. "How can I help you?"

"I'm looking for Mr. Martin. My name is Hannah. I'm one of his employees . . . down at the newspaper. I know he's busy with a"—Hannah searched for the term, needing to sound professional and polite—"family emergency, but I have an urgent matter I need to discuss with him."

"Oh, I see," the nurse-like woman responded, seeming to buy Hannah's introduction. "I think he mentioned you. I'm Katie, by the way. Come on in. I will see what I can do for you."

She held open the screen door, which screeched ever so slightly, making Hannah imagine an occupied porch swing on a warm summer night with sweaty glasses of iced tea resting on one of the side tables as crickets hummed away in the tall grass surrounding the house.

"I'll let Mr. Martin know you are here." Katie smiled and exited into one of the side rooms. The foyer was just as quaint as the porch, with a curving staircase made of a rich walnut with a white-and-stained-wood banister trailing all the way up on one side, making a sort of balcony at the top of the stairs. Plenty of blushing debutantes had likely stood at that precipice looking down on their shy prom dates, or daughters in wedding dresses awaiting their futures, or grandparents greeting babies in mothers' arms. It was strange to see inside Monty's world. It made him more human—harder to hate, but hopefully not harder to stand up to.

"Right this way," Katie said, returning almost immediately. Hannah followed her into a large living room area, with a grand fireplace using gas-burning logs and surrounded by stones, wood floors accented with richly colored burgundy carpets, and an off-white upholstered sofa and chair set that looked like it was from a movie. In the corner of the room was a circular table positioned under a picture window overlooking the side yard and a grove of trees that blocked any view of neighbors or the distant highway. Seated in a wheelchair next to the table was a sixty-something woman with blonde hair that was closer to white than yellow. A teacup with an amber liquid sat in front of her, and she was in a tasteful velour bathrobe with a zipper up the front and a steaming pot in the middle of the table. Monty was nowhere to be seen.

"You really do look like your daddy," the woman, presumably Mrs. Martin, called out to Hannah as she crossed the room. Her voice was soft and dainty, reminding Hannah of Mamaw's gliding vowels and measured tone, which made Hannah's heart hitch. A lovely sensation touched her skin, like a familiar caress.

"Oh, well . . . thank you," Hannah said, taken off guard by the mention of her father. She'd been thinking about him a lot lately—how strange it felt to be glad he wasn't alive to see how shameful she'd become.

"I take it you knew my father?" For some reason, she didn't cringe at this like she did when Monty brought him up. Momma pointed to the chair on the other side of the table, and Hannah took it as Katie wandered off into another room, leaving them alone.

"I sure did. We were in the same graduating class. Even back then we knew he was a math genius. Sure made your mamaw and papaw proud when he started teaching at the Columbia College, even if it did mean him living so far away. Monty put a little piece in the *Record* about it. I don't know if you knew that."

"No, he never mentioned it," Hannah said, settling into her seat and laying her phone on the table, finding that she wanted to hear more. It was a strange urge after pushing away any mention of her father since his death, finding that the only memories and grief she could bear were her own. "What was he like back then?" Hannah asked.

The older woman picked up the silver spoon resting on the edge of the saucer and stirred her tea, the metal making a soothing swooshing sound as it lightly scraped the cup bottom. She put it back in place with a delicate tink and lifted the drink by the curved handle, but as soon as it left the plate her hand started to shake, spilling the liquid out the sides. Hannah reached out instinctively and placed a steadying hand under the cup.

"Oh, aren't you a dear," Mrs. Martin said after taking a sip and replacing the cup with Hannah's help.

"I'm sorry, I didn't mean to overstep . . ." Hannah shoved her hands under her thighs, embarrassed that she'd tried to caretake a stranger.

"Oh, never. I'm still wobbly after my little incident, and you are such a kind young lady to want to help. Monty is lucky to have someone like you around at the office. He's always said such kind things."

It was difficult to hear so many positive comments about herself, especially right now. No wonder Mrs. Martin was willing to let Hannah in—she didn't know . . . everything. Her ignorance wouldn't last long, and then the terms of endearment and hospitality would disappear. She cleared her throat and set her face in stone.

"Speaking of Monty, is he here?" Hannah glanced around for signs of Mrs. Martin's other half, thinking that she might as well get the confrontation over with. Bonding over tea with "Momma" would only make this harder.

"Yes, Katie is checking on him. He's been such a worrywart that I sent him to his room for a nap a bit ago." She laughed but then winced, leaning back in her chair like she was trying to position herself just right so she could escape the pain.

Hannah's next sentence came with a tightness she recognized from watching her father after surgery and Mamaw when Hannah had first come to town.

"I can come back another time. I feel like I'm intruding." Everything she did right now felt wrong. If only Hannah could make one thing, one single thing, right, then maybe the dominos would stop crashing around her. But seeing the distress on Mrs. Martin's face made Hannah regret ever turning down their unpaved driveway without giving advance warning.

"Don't be silly. I like having you here. You can give me the good newspaper gossip." She winked like Mamaw sometimes did when she was telling a joke.

"I . . . I don't work there anymore, actually. That's why I'm here." Hannah stirred Mrs. Martin's tea like she'd observed moments earlier, even tapping the spoon when she'd completed the task.

"Oh my, I had no idea. I'm so sorry, Hannah. I can't imagine what my husband was thinking letting you go—a real journalist from the *Chicago Tribune*. What was that man thinking?" she huffed, her cheeks flushing, which made Hannah worry about the state of the elderly woman's newly stitched-up heart.

"No, no. It was my fault. I got carried away with a story and went too far to get information and . . ." Without asking, Hannah took the handle of the teacup and asked Mrs. Martin silently with one raised eyebrow if she'd like help again to take a sip, hoping it would aid in calming her.

"What's it about? This story you're writing."

There was an innocent excitement in Mrs. Martin's pale face that made Hannah want to spill the story she'd kept from the woman's husband for so long. If Mrs. Martin saw value in the story, maybe she could help convince Monty. It wasn't the *Tribune*, but she'd gladly trade her chance to get back into the *Tribune*'s good graces for Monty's cooperation in Guy's case. Plus, she didn't know what it was about Mrs. Montgomery Martin, but Hannah felt sure that she'd like Evelyn almost as much as Hannah had the first time she read her words.

"All right, I'll tell you. It all started when I found this rejected article in the basement of the *Record*." Hannah wrestled a stack of files from her messenger bag and set them on the table, opening to the first typewritten page with a red *R* circled in the corner. "It started with the words *My name is Evelyn* . . ."

Hannah summarized the story for an attentive Mrs. Martin, reading a few clips from the original articles, ending with the cliff-hanger she was still dangling from:

> The next time I write, I will complete my tale and answer the question that everyone had on their tongues seven years ago: Who shot Evelyn? The answer surprises even me to this day.

After those last words hung in the air between them, Mrs. Martin, hand over her heart and slightly breathless, asked, "Well, who did it?"

Hannah put the final page down and licked her lips, hesitant to tell the whole truth about her lack of answers.

"I don't know yet," she said, fully aware of the sealed envelope on her desk at home that Pete had delivered. It possibly held the end to Evelyn's story, but since she'd been completely wrapped up in her guilt over what she'd done to obtain those answers, Hannah hadn't opened the packet. "That's the information I was looking for when . . . when I messed up so badly."

Emotion clamped down on Hannah's throat, and the tears that came more often poured into her eyes quickly, as if weepy were her body's new natural state. The drive to find a conclusion to Evelyn's story had been muted by the aftermath of her tunnel vision and the real-life drama she'd authored. She tried to pin her current state on a couple of things: Alex, her obsession with getting her job back, and her overinvestment in Evelyn. But truly, for all this time, her focus had only ever been on one wholly self-serving thing: escaping her pain.

"It can't be as tragic as all that," Mrs. Martin said, reaching toward Hannah like she'd comfort her if her body would let her, no way to know all the events that informed Hannah's emotions.

Hannah blinked, and a few tears fell like raindrops onto her hands as she stared at them.

"I'm sure Mr. Martin will understand when he hears the whole story, dear. Please don't cry." She rummaged through the pocket of her robe and was offering a ball of tissues, likely unused but worse for wear, when Monty's familiar drawl filled the room, bouncing off the tall ceilings and polished floors.

"Momma, what are you doing up and out of bed?" Montgomery Martin crossed the room, wearing a pair of baggy lounge pants and a long sweater over what looked like a plain white undershirt. It was the most casual thing Hannah had ever seen her former boss wearing, and it felt a bit like seeing him naked. Katie followed swiftly behind Monty, also beelining for Mrs. Martin's resting spot.

"I was just keeping Hannah here company for a few minutes." She glanced back at Hannah, beaming like she expected this to be a good surprise rather than one that would likely piss her husband off.

When Monty finally reached his wife, he was out of breath and damp with perspiration, but Mrs. Martin didn't seem to mind. She patted his face affectionately as he placed a gentle kiss on her cheek and then the top of her head. He loved his wife, that had always been clear, but seeing their tenderness touched Hannah's already vulnerable heart. No. She had to resist any softening of her resolve—Monty might be a good husband, but that didn't mean he got a pass for the other asshole parts of his personality, which he promptly put on full display.

"Miss Williamson," he said coolly, resuming his full height, all warmth vacant from his demeanor.

"Hey," was Hannah's weak reply, her anxiety levels shooting through the roof, tensing her shoulders and raising her heart rate. He glowered down at her as his wife tried to play peacemaker the best way she knew how.

"Hannah has been telling me all about a very interestin' story she's been working on." She paused to regroup, very clearly worn down by her efforts at entertaining. "It's about a girl from our town from a long time ago. She was shot in her bedroom, and there are all these suspects and—"

"Katie," Monty spoke over his wife, clutching her shoulder lightly. She immediately stopped talking and watched his face, quietly confused.

"Would you make sure Mrs. Martin gets her afternoon snack? I have a business matter I need to tend to."

"Yes, sir," she said, unlocking the wheelchair brake with her foot.

"I'll join you in a minute, dear," Monty said, releasing her shoulder, keeping his eyes on Hannah, who was starting to squirm in her seat, not only as a result of her impending confrontation with a man who had fired her but also due to Mrs. Martin's state of turmoil. With a nearly imperceptible shift, Momma accepted his directive and made apologetic eye contact with Hannah, who mouthed the words "It's okay" before the older woman was helped out of the room.

Monty turned all his focus to Hannah, his skin turning a bright red even in the cool house.

"You have gone too far," he snarled, making Hannah gasp. He was angry, not "disappointed in you" angry or "I don't understand your quirks" angry—this was pure fury, far beyond what she'd thought him capable of displaying. She recoiled, surprised. No, shocked.

"I'm sorry, but you left me no choice. I called you and emailed you and sent you texts—everything I could think of. This is important, Monty"—she corrected herself—"Mr. Martin. The life of an educator and father and incredibly good man is on the line." She set her shoulders and started at the beginning of the speech she'd prepared for her visit to Mr. Grant's office. "This is all my fault. I was working on that story, and I'd reached a dead end and—"

"Get out," he spit, making Hannah blink and recoil.

"Please, you have to listen. Guy had nothing to do with this. He was just trying to help me. If you'd just listen, you'd understand. Please," she begged, standing up, hands involuntarily clutching in front of her.

"I don't want to hear it. I told you to drop that story the first time Ms. Dawson called me, and you persisted in this foolhardy pursuit."

The first time? Alarm bells rang in Hannah's head.

"You mean she called you again?" Hannah asked, trying to focus on Guy but also wondering what the hell difference this story made to Shelby Dawson.

"Yes, after her nephew made a fool of himself in some hotel lobby doing favors for you and this obsession. I killed the story, Miss Williamson. You should've let it die." He slashed at the air.

"Wait, is Pete okay?" Hannah asked, sidestepping the Evelyn topic for a moment. Did someone post a video after all? Did she need to add Pete to her list of victims? He'd called her the day after Thanksgiving. She didn't pick up, but did find the brain space to respond to his concerned message with a text briefly explaining about Mamaw's accident. He'd sent his best wishes, but not much else, which she'd taken to mean that he wasn't interested in remaining close after she kindly but firmly rejected his advances. But maybe his distance meant something else.

Monty nodded his head.

"Yes, Ms. Dawson and her team took care of the situation."

Hannah, getting distracted from her intended purpose of prostration and reconciliation, clenched her fist at the idea of this wealthy family using their influence to secure their power and—what? What else were they trying to preserve?

"Shelby is good at throwing money around, isn't she? Just like she's thrown money at you and your paper for who knows how long. Why are you so afraid of Shelby Dawson, Monty? What does she have on you?"

She stepped closer, aware of his slight body odor and the trail of sweat glistening on his neck. There was more to this situation than a few articles in the basement of a small-town newspaper, but what was it? And why did everyone want it hidden so badly? And why did those articles even exist if they could bring down this house of cards that someone—Monty or Shelby or some other mysterious figure—had been building for generations?

"I have no idea what you are talking about," he said, but Monty was a bad liar, and the fuzzy picture of why he was going after Guy was starting to come into focus.

"Yes, you do. Shelby Dawson has something on you or the paper or . . ." She glanced at the pages on the table and then back at Monty. "Oh my God, it's not about something you've done. You're blackmailing her, aren't you?"

"You've lost your mind," Monty said, huffing like he was laughing, but she didn't let up.

"The money from the Dawsons, your reaction to this story, Shelby Dawson's involvement in . . . everything. Why are you all so afraid of Evelyn Kensley?"

"I'm not afraid of anyone."

"No, but the Dawson family is. And you know the paper can't survive without their support. They 'donated' to the *Record* so your father would keep some scandal under wraps, and your father held on to the evidence, you know, just in case."

"You are letting your imagination get the better of you, Miss Williamson. I refuse to let you hustle me and the paper like you did with Peter or . . . or . . ." He stuttered, and the white crust at the corners of his mouth started to foam with built-up spit. "Or turn me into a criminal like you did Guy Franklin."

She bristled at his pointed insult, and the fury that was once on Monty's face flamed inside Hannah this time. She'd done a lot of things wrong, and it was true that she'd caused irreparable damages in far too many lives, including her own, but this was too much. This was a cover-up, and Guy was the most recent scapegoat.

"Are you shitting me, Monty?" she asked, rushing toward him, tapping a finger on his pliant chest. "The shady shit going on at your newspaper isn't his fault. Shelby Dawson pulled a few strings and slung a little cash to get Pete's indiscretions to disappear, but Guy doesn't have any of that, and you've decided to let him burn."

"No, little missy, you don't get off that easily." He didn't try to remove her accusatory finger; instead he towered over her, his eyes full of condemnation. "You use people, and when you are done with them, you blame everyone else for the rubble you left behind. Do I feel for Mr. Franklin? Yes, in a way, I do. Does it excuse his criminal activity or yours, for that matter? No. Now, if you'd kindly get out of my house before I have to call the police."

She glared at him, his insult slashing at the frayed remnants of her self-worth. She wasn't the only one reeling from the aftereffects of a raw, exposed nerve. If he wanted to protect his career, his family's good name, his home and everyone inside it, apparently he had to keep Hannah silent and minimized.

"I *will* find out what you're hiding." She retreated from her position and collected her jacket and bag, reaching for the files she'd been showing to Mrs. Martin.

"Leave those," he said with a cool finality.

"I have other copies," she shot back.

"Use them and I will sue."

"I dare you to." Hannah set her jaw and glared.

He put his hand over the stack, claiming them. "Publish these or any of your theories, Miss Williamson, and I will not lift one finger to help your Mr. Franklin."

Hannah had run out of words. It was like the air had been sucked out of her lungs. In the silence, Monty gathered the original documents into his arms and she could see it all slipping away.

"Please don't do this." Hannah's hand dropped to her side, her shoulders slumping, chest feeling like it was about to cave in. She wanted to fight, but that would mean sacrificing Guy—again. She couldn't, but how could she let Monty and Shelby Dawson get away with whatever scam they were playing? This was far bigger than a sweet little feature article about an unsolved crime. This was the modern hook she'd been looking for.

With one arm full of Evelyn's life story, Monty took out his phone and started to dial what Hannah assumed was 911. She put up her hands like he was taking hostages.

"Fine, I'm leaving." Hannah backed away, eyeing Monty, unsure what he was capable of after all his threats and with some kind of big secret riding on the guarantee of Hannah's silence. The rest of the room was the same as when Hannah was escorted in an hour ago. The vases and fancy rugs, lovely wooden floors, and marble fireplace mantel were only a few of the elegant accents that made the farmhouse unique. The position of the sun through the windows was a bit lower, darkening the corners of the space in a way that increased the dramatic focus on Monty's tense figure.

When she reached the threshold of the room, Monty was still holding the phone midair like a weapon but had not finished his call, which she took as a good sign.

"Goodbye, Miss Williamson," Monty said, his officious tone echoing through the room with ominous undertones of finality.

She couldn't bring herself to respond. Instead, Hannah tipped her chin in the air, turned on one foot, and walked away. She had to get out. After holding in a torrent of feelings, her efforts to plug up all the holes in the dam that kept them at bay were failing in rapid succession, and she could feel the collapse coming. As soon as she was out the front door, she ran down the porch steps and across the partially frozen clay driveway, choking on the tears that had become so commonplace. Nothing was better. Everything was worse. Monty was wrong about a lot of things, but right about one very important fact: intentional or not, Hannah destroyed people.

Leaving a trail of dust behind her as she sped down the Martins' driveway back toward town, she had to wonder what the hell she was any good for. Speeding into the sunset after turning west on Highway 4, Hannah had one last idea, but this time she wouldn't be asking Monty to lift a finger to help. It was time to see Guy—whether he liked it or not.

CHAPTER 32

The Senatobia Middle School building was an impressive structure. Hannah had admired it during her bike rides to and from work for the past few months. The former high school was built as part of the New Deal, and limestone carvings of muscled men donned the front of the auditorium, welcoming all who passed by. A tarnished copper sundial with art deco details sat between the two figures with an engraving that read *Time Flies* at the top. Rather than a whimsical saying that applied to the temporary nature of childhood, it read to Hannah as a warning, rushing her out of her car and toward the office doors to the right of the theater.

Even though it was past his normal school hours, Hannah knew Guy was here; his car was parked out front in its normal spot. She shivered while running across the pavement, eager to be out of the December wind, but when she reached out for the brass handle on the doors at the top of the stairs, she heard her name shouted from the parking lot.

"Hannah?"

It was Guy. She turned on her heel, making her coat spin out ever so slightly, letting the little bit of stored heat that had been building up underneath escape. When she finally laid eyes on him, there was a painful swelling in her chest, and her vision clouded with tears she was glad he couldn't see from a distance.

She'd known she missed him; she knew it in her mind and because of the ulcer-like hole in her heart when he turned down all requests to meet up. But seeing him right there in front of her caused a physical reaction she could never have predicted, her mouth suddenly dry and a tightness in her throat that she couldn't swallow down.

He was standing next to his car with a filing box in his hands and a stack of papers on the lid. His top button was left unfastened and he looked tired, no . . . he looked exhausted. His cheekbones stood out more prominently than she remembered, and worst of all, as soon as Hannah met his confused gaze, he immediately averted his eyes and turned away, opening his rear car door.

"Guy, hey!" Hannah finally managed to shout across the parking lot before running toward him, worried that if she gave him too much of a lead that he'd climb in the car and drive away before she had a chance to say a word. He emerged from the back seat and closed the door before turning to face Hannah, his now-empty hands shoved in the pockets of his fitted jacket. There was no smile, no spark of welcome in his eye. She hadn't realized it till it was gone, but Guy used to be alive when he was with her, his energy, interest, and fascination turned up to a ten. So now, the deadness in his glassy eyes and how he leaned away, ever so slightly, made his emotional shift even more obvious.

"Hey! I'm so glad I caught you," Hannah said, huffing out great clouds of fog into the space between them, the cold air sticking in her lungs and touching each breath with pain.

"Yeah, I'm kinda running late so . . ." He took a step back, but Hannah interrupted his excuse to leave.

"I know you don't want to see me," she said, strands of hair blowing into the corner of her mouth as she spoke. "But I need to talk to you. Here." She pulled an envelope out of her pocket and held it out to Guy. He didn't make an effort to reach for it. "Please, take it."

Guy met Hannah's gaze briefly, and a momentary and sudden softening melted the hardness there. He looked away with some effort and took the offered envelope, opening it to peek inside. Immediately, he folded down the flap and shook his head.

"I don't need your money." He held out the envelope like it was filled with fire ants.

"Don't be stubborn. It's to pay your dad back for the bond money. Please take it. Please." It should cover the bond money, yes, but also help with some of the attorney fees. She'd pay those back too, one day. It was the absolute least she could do. She stared at his downcast eyes, hoping that he'd look up again, that she could see him remember their connection, their friendship, even for one additional second.

"Fine," he said, folding up the check and putting it in his pocket along with his hand, resuming his caved-in, defensive stance. "I'll give it to my dad."

"Thank you," she said, a tiny dose of relief letting her breathe deeper, not even noticing the cold this time. "Also," she added quickly, knowing his patience was running thin, "I talked to the DA today."

Guy flinched and took another step away, pushing his fists deeper into his coat pockets. "Hannah, I know you're trying to help, but you gotta stay out of this now. My attorney says it makes me look bad."

"Why does everybody keep saying that?" Hannah groaned, stomping her foot. "I just want them to know the truth. I want them to listen to me. I want to fix this. I *need* to. I talked to Monty, and you gotta know—this whole thing is a big cover-up that is so freaking old, and he's taking it all out on you to keep me quiet. But if we publish this story about Evelyn *now*, it would take away his power and her story would finally be told. She needs us to tell it . . ."

"Evelyn?" Guy's measured calm broke as explosively as an icicle falling off the top of the Hancock Building in January. All the words and plans in Hannah's brain dissolved, and she stood, stunned, staring as Guy finally looked her in the eyes. But she was the one to look away this time, not able to face the disappointment and judgment there.

"Seriously, Hannah, Evelyn? Could you just listen to yourself for a minute? Evelyn is dead. She doesn't *need* you. I needed you, Hannah. Two weeks ago when the police called you and you ignored them, that's when I needed you. When you were off flirting with Pete Dawson at a bar in Memphis, that's when I needed you." He pointed north like he could see the city from there. Then, he took the first step toward her that he'd made in weeks, but it brought her no comfort. He lowered his voice to a trembling, angry whisper. "You're worried about Evelyn, and when it comes down to it, you're worried about you. You are so deeply involved with you-you-you-you that you can't seem to see anything outside of it. Not me, not Rosie, and not even your own goddamned grandma."

His words stung like a slap in the face, and Hannah cringed. It was one thing to hear them from Monty or to think them about herself, but to hear them from Guy? She sniffed, determined to hold back the tears. He continued, but his tone was more measured this time.

"Don't you get it? I'm going to lose my job. I have a child, Hannah. What's going to happen to her if I go to . . ."

His voice cracked, and he didn't finish his sentence, but she was sure they both knew what he was going to say. *Prison.* She snatched his hand into hers, and shockingly he didn't pull away. They stood close, inches between each other, their breath clouds mingling, taking in each other's exhales.

She'd painted Guy as ever enduring, ever giving, ever steadfast, ever patient, but what he really was . . . was human—a deeply frightened human. She stared up into his eyes, the well of shame she'd been digging for herself growing deeper by yards. His breath hitched; he licked his lips and then moved away from the pulsing heat of connection that they both knew was far too easy to ignite.

Hannah let his hand slip from hers. Usually full of retorts and arguments, she had none. She'd always had a hard time admitting fault, giving up on an argument, dropping a story, letting go of a lead even when she knew she should—an inherent obstinance she'd been born with. When she and Brody would fight as kids, her father would always sit them down across from each other for forced apologies and say, "There is no shame in admitting you're wrong."

But this time there *was* shame. This wasn't a tussle with a little brother—this was Guy's life she'd taken for granted. She'd thought by "fixing" things with Monty or the DA that she could erase the damage done as cleanly as his record could be erased. But seeing the hurt carved into Guy's body made Hannah think of the men carved on the side of the building. There was a mark on his soul that would always be there to remind him of a time when, because of the color of his skin, he was abandoned by a world that he'd done nothing but try to improve and she'd been complicit in that injury.

"I'm sorry I wasn't there, okay?" she said, her voice wavering, meaning this apology down to her core, unlike the forced, fake ones she'd mustered through as a child under her father's instruction. Her wrongs poured out, carried toward Guy by the wind. "I'm sorry I was a bad friend, and I'm sorry I put you in that situation. I'm sorry I used your friendship for my personal gain. I'm sorry I was so deeply selfish that I couldn't see anything else but my wants and my pain, and I will be ashamed of *that* for the rest of my life."

Guy stood facing his car door, holding the handle, and nodded, staring at the glass in front of him. She didn't wait more than half a second for him to respond, that stubborn streak flashing hotly for one brief moment.

"But I'm not sorry for trying to help now. It's all that I *can* do, Guy. I can't change the past. And you don't have to forgive me, or like me even, but I will find a way to balance this scale. I promise. I *swear* it to you on . . ." Hannah ran through her mind for something of import.

The Bible or God held little weight, and her own moral compass had been proved less than reliable, but when her gaze landed on the sundial and the ninety-year-old school building where her father had walked, learned, and lived, it felt as though he were near once again, that he was waiting for her to grow into the woman he'd hoped to raise—strong but also compassionate, resolved but also kind. "I swear it to you on my dad's good name."

Her promise lingered between them.

"Hannah, you're right. What's done is done. Can't change the past," Guy said, while opening his car door and then letting his rich brown eyes meet hers, sending curtains of heat down her shoulders and back. She hung on his silence, his next words having the ability to calm or crush. "But if I were you, I'd stop making promises you have no power to keep. Some mistakes have consequences, and unfortunately I'm suffering *your* consequences right now," he said, simply but with a sharp edge that slashed a deep wound into Hannah's conscience. Guy didn't wait for Hannah to respond. He ducked into the driver's seat, politely adding, "Give your mamaw my best," before closing his door with a muffled slam.

As he drove away, the exhaust from his car trailed behind him, and Hannah stood frozen in place, with no other option but to watch him leave. It seemed that she'd become far too accustomed to watching the men she cared about leave her.

She blinked, the comforting ghost of her father gone, likely a figment of her highly agitated nervous system. Left alone, frozen and heartbroken, she heard an old voice inside her mind whisper a thought she'd kept away for months, a voice that had once been a common companion shouting the same phrase over and over again: *They'd be better off without you.*

And at that moment, Hannah agreed.

CHAPTER 33

Hannah got all the way to Mamaw's empty room without anyone in the house seeming to notice. In the past weeks she'd spent a lot of time in that room with the TV on a low murmur in the background. The hospital bed was comfortable and made for a good place to hide.

She shed her outerwear, shoes, and bag, leaving a trail behind her as she stumbled toward the bed, as though it were a lifeboat in her stormy sea made treacherous by her fight with Monty and the hard truths from Guy and weighty guilt that she couldn't seem to escape. Lined up next to Mamaw's bed were her prescription bottles. Hannah hadn't had the heart to move them yet, plus there was one particular bottle that gave her comfort, that she took in her hand most nights and cradled as she slept. Ambien.

Ever since leaving the psych ward at Northwestern Hospital seven months ago, she'd taken her prescribed antidepressants, avoided sleep aids, and tried to start her life over after her emotional crash. But she knew that bottle full of pills could suck her into a calm, sleepy place that held no anxiety or guilt, and that was a beautiful temptation to hold in her hands.

She snatched the bottle and held it, enjoying the sound of the tumbling pills inside. Hannah needed a dose of peace right now, and there were two things that could provide that kind of artificial calm: Ambien and Alex. With her other hand, she did the one thing she'd been avoiding for the two weeks since he'd asked for another chance. She opened up Facebook on her phone and typed in Alex's name on the search bar, and his profile came up immediately.

As the page loaded, the air sucked out of the room. Tagged in a photo from a random friend's page, there he was—Alex, smiling broadly with his arm around his supposed ex-fiancée with the caption "The Love Birds."

Hannah gulped for air. She shouldn't care, hadn't cared, but seeing them together made so many old feelings pour into her overflowing whirlpool. She clicked on the picture in search of the date on the image, hoping that it was an old memory that somehow ended up on his wall. But investigating further only made it harder to breathe. Yesterday. It was from yesterday. She scrolled to the line of comments below the picture and read the words that felt like a bullet to her gut.

Janie! You'll be a beautiful bride.

You two look so in love!

Party! Party! #WeddingBells

With an old swell of jealousy taking her emotions even lower than when she'd stumbled in, she touched various spots on her screen. Hannah found the button with three little dots on the top of his profile and without hesitation hit "Block."

Then he finally disappeared.

Filled with grief and relief, Hannah pressed her phone into her midsection, where the pain originated, and then doubled over, resting her head on her knees. She wrapped her arms around her legs, trying to squeeze the pain out like juice from an orange, the bottle of Ambien still in her hand, rattling with each sob.

It was all too much—and she'd run out of actionable ways to fix anything she'd broken. Like the image she'd seen as a child of a man crawling through a desert crying out for water, she'd been living life one inch at a time, trying to survive off the hope of a nearby oasis. But her salvation had turned out to be a mirage, and after exerting so much effort, she was too tired to move one more centimeter.

The bottle rattled again, and she held it up to the light, a strange peace falling over her as she assessed the cluster of pills. There had to be fifteen or so tablets left inside. That would be enough to—

She didn't complete the thought but did unscrew the child safety cap and dump the contents of the bottle into the palm of her hand. Nineteen. They wouldn't be difficult to swallow, and she'd just fall asleep—fall asleep forever, no more pain, no more sorrys, no more rejection and failure. It would all go away. She would go away, just like last time. It had all gone to black, and she'd almost found her way out of this world of struggle.

Hannah closed her fingers around the pile of pills, and her fantasy of disappearing evaporated as quickly as her breath had while talking to Guy by his car. *I'd stop making promises you have no power to keep . . .* His warning stuck with her, burrowed into her as the pills dug into her palm.

The first time she took a handful of pills, she wanted to go back. Back to when she was with Alex and her father was her cushion, when life seemed simple. But today "back" didn't seem as compelling to Hannah.

She'd built a life here. A weird, messed-up, confusing life, but it had a purpose. Right now the purpose of this life was to fix all the things she'd messed up, but under that was far more. If she went quietly into the dark night, it would be her final attempt at running away. And even if Guy never talked to her again, she'd never forget his story about the tree. *Staying and fixing—that's the hard part,* he'd said. And he was right.

She opened her fist and looked at the pills, a new idea forming in her mind, when the door to Mamaw's bedroom swung open. Hannah froze as her mother stormed into the room, clearly prepared for a fight.

"Hannah! Where have you been? I've been worried sick. Please tell me you didn't go to the courthouse and . . ." Pam's slate-gray eyes landed on the collection of pills in Hannah's hand, and she gasped. Hannah could read the terror on her mother's face and became aware of what the scene must look like to her.

"I just wanted to hold them," Hannah insisted, staring up at her mother. "I swear. I'm putting them away."

"Hannah!" Pam said mournfully, carefully crossing the room, treating the handful of pills like Hannah was holding a loaded gun and any sudden movement would make her daughter pull the trigger. She spoke in a higher-pitched voice, like she was comforting a child scared of the dark. "Honey, listen. I found an attorney in Memphis who thinks he can help you and Guy. And . . . and . . . I called up Larry, and he said that job is still available if you are interested. I know it's not the same as a newspaper, but . . ."

"Mom, stop," Hannah said, pleadingly, but Pam didn't stop her rambling solutions to Hannah's mess of a life, getting closer to the bed with every suggestion.

"And . . . I know you feel bad about Mamaw, but she is an old woman, sweetheart. She fell. It's not your fault," she crooned, hand outstretched like she was asking for the medicine.

"No, it *is* my fault," she insisted. "Mamaw is my fault. And Guy, that's my fault too. If I hadn't been so focused on Alex—"

"Alex?" Pam said his name, and even though she was just repeating what Hannah had spoken, hearing it made her wince. "What does Alex have to do with this, honey? I thought we'd moved past Alex."

Hannah blinked, and tears fell into the brown pills in her hand. No use in keeping secrets now.

"I saw him the night before Thanksgiving. Um." She licked her painfully dry lips, tasting the salt from her tears. "He wanted to get back together. That's why . . ." She swallowed again, bringing the pills closer to her body. "That's why I wasn't here when Mamaw . . ."

"Oh." Her mother had more to say on that matter, Hannah could tell, but she held back, still focused on the deadly pile of prescription medicine her daughter was holding.

"Don't worry. It's not happening," she said, knowing what a fool she must sound like.

Pam shook her head, like Hannah had finished a sentence she'd started in her mind. "I'm sorry, sweetheart. That's so hard, but I'm proud of you. I know it hurts, but it's probably for the—"

"Don't say it's for the best," Hannah snapped. "You always say that. Like when dad died a whole year before the doctors said he should, you said, *Well, it's probably for the best. At least he's not in pain anymore.* Screw 'the best,' Mom. None of what has happened in the past year is 'for the best.'"

Pam crossed the last few feet of mauve carpet and sat gingerly on the edge of Mamaw's hospital bed.

"You're right. Not very much that's happened to you has been fair." She reached out to touch her daughter. Hannah flinched at first, but then let her mother run her fingers through her unkempt, greasy hair. "But I can't lose you, Hannah. You're my little girl. I used to be able to give you an ice pack or a Band-Aid and feel like I'd done my job as your mother, but as you got older, it got harder. I knew you and your father were close, and I thought, *Well, she has Patrick. Why does she need me?* But then he had to leave us." Pam's voice caught, and she sniffled herself into her state of maximum control. "And you're right, that wasn't for the best. But baby, your daddy didn't choose to leave you. You weren't old enough to see it, but when your uncle . . ." She stumbled, wiping at her eyes. "When Samuel took his own life, it nearly broke your father. And Mamaw . . . all dressed in black walking behind the coffin of her baby . . . oh God." Pam sobbed at the memory. "Hannah, please don't make me bury you."

Pam Williamson rarely showed true emotion, at least not that Hannah saw, but she'd been through a lot—widowed, living alone, dealing with a daughter who had fallen to pieces. Just like with Guy, sometimes Hannah forgot that her mother was human.

"Oh, Mom." Hannah held her arms out to her mother, dropping the pills onto the bedspread. Pam held her daughter tighter than Hannah could ever remember being held. And they both cried at their helplessness as Hannah explained everything that had happened that day.

Pam kissed her daughter's forehead and stayed close, like she wasn't ready to trust that Hannah's moment of crisis had passed. "First of all, let me help you."

It wasn't easy for Hannah to accept help, especially from her mother and especially when she'd caused so many of these problems herself, but she clearly wasn't able to do it all by herself right now.

"I'll try," she said, leaning into Pam's warm side.

Her mom, tonight with the pills, had been the safe place she needed to find when she was falling. Hannah was willing to attempt to trust her.

"I think I know how to get Guy's charges dropped," she said, snuggling into her mother's embrace.

"Wait, what?" Pam sat up as straight as the soft mattress would let her, checking her daughter's features to see if she was being sarcastic.

"I just need to check one thing first." Hannah sat up straight, collected the pills off the bed, passed the bottle to her mother willingly, and then slipped off the mattress. "Come with me?" she asked, reaching out for Pam's hand.

She took it.

CHAPTER 34

The unopened envelope she'd gotten from Pete two weeks ago sat on the desk in front of Hannah. After showing it to her mother, she'd asked to be alone for a few minutes as she examined the contents. It seemed only right that it happen this way, that Hannah's final moments with Evelyn should be one-on-one.

She opened the flap and slid a hefty stack of copy paper out and onto the oak surface. In these pages she hoped to find the leverage she was looking for, the weight that would tip the scales of justice in the right direction. But even if the file led to more dead ends or tempting leads, it was worth looking, and either way, this was Hannah's necessary farewell to the woman whose life she'd come to care about so deeply.

On the top of the stack was a small envelope, sealed and addressed to the *Record*. Unsent. Hannah opened it eagerly.

April 3, 1936

Mr. Martin,
Every good story must come to an end.
I hope that you have found some interest in my tale of woe. If you can find
it in your heart to publish it in any

form, whether fiction or non, I would feel my pain has been for some important reason. I will let my readers be the judge of that.

I returned from Paducah with more than just a stomachache. Mrs. Strong, the lady who had gone with us and had been speaking to Harry's mother so ferociously, came to talk to Mother and Daddy. She told them everything about Harry being sixteen and about me running away. She talked about Harry and me something terrible, like we'd done something wrong.

But Harry and I had never done anything wrong, and the accusation made my blood boil. Mother said I could no longer see Harry. She said that she never trusted me and that I was a waste of money and space in her house. She said she couldn't see why I was complaining all the time and why I would do this, and I shouldn't have done that, or I took too many baths, or always something.

She hated me just as much as she had the day she left scars on my back with that horsewhip. Or the day she tried to poison me to death. I knew it. I knew the only way out was with my name on a marriage certificate, but Harry was too young and had been cruel to me. And as desperate as I was, I couldn't stomach the thought of marrying Mr. Fred after what had happened between us. I told Mother how he'd taken advantage of me, but she seemed nearly pleased, saying, "He'll have to marry you now."

But I didn't want to marry that disgusting Mr. Fred, who was twice my age and talked of boring things like taxes and elections, and who hurt me and didn't stop even when I screamed.

I got worse in both spirits and health. Daddy was getting worse too. Mother kept nagging and was becoming frantic at my condition. I did not have clothes like other girls, nor could I go places I wanted to. I felt terrible, always sick, though nobody thought I was really ill. But I was.

I started to think it would be so much easier to die than to go on living, making such a mess of things. In my mind, I thought, if there weren't any Evelyn, there wouldn't be any reason for Mother and Daddy not to get along. And I decided Myrtle could have my clothes and Harry could find himself a girl who wasn't sick like I was.

So, on July 17, 1929, at about 2:30 p.m., I took the gun that was in my own mother's room, and I shot myself in the right breast.

The bullet hit my spine and paralyzed me from the waist down. And that,
my dear public, is the reason I am in
this chair. It wasn't because of my
love for Harry, and no intruder had
come to shoot me, and Mother, who hated
me enough to want me dead, had not
pulled the trigger.

I shot myself.

Hannah gasped and reread the line again. Evelyn . . . Evelyn had been her own assailant. Hannah's hero had—shot herself. Mr. Fred and Mother and Harry were the ones who loaded that weapon. Hannah understood Evelyn's seductive reasoning for pulling that trigger. She knew all too well. She also knew the shame of—after.

When I woke, I tried to explain
why I tried to end my life, but no one
wanted to listen. Everyone had their
own idea of who shot me, and after
months of speculating, no one wanted
to believe a young woman would feel so
desperate to end her suffering that
she'd turn a gun on herself. But it
was true.

It's been almost seven years since
that day in July. Nobody thought I
would live this long, but I guess I'm
just stubborn. My little sister came
home in May of 1932, and she didn't
even know I had been shot, but she soon
learned about it and was rather sweet.

Daddy was sick most of the time, and in December 1932 he died, carrying a part of my heart with him. Nobody expected me to live through that, but I did. The brother with whom Vivian had lived took her back with him and offered to take Myrtle too, but she didn't go. Vivian would marry in January of '33 to Jimmy Shackelford. She ended up with everything she wanted, and it didn't bring her happiness. I'm still not entirely sure what does bring happiness after all.

Sincerely,

Evelyn

Hannah reread the last few sentences, feeling them more deeply than any words of literature she had ever experienced: *Vivian had everything she wanted, and it didn't bring her happiness. I'm still not entirely sure what does bring happiness after all.*

Hannah still wasn't sure what brought happiness either, but she was starting to see what didn't. Pills, guns, hiding—didn't bring happiness. It didn't even bring peace. For both Hannah and Evelyn, it brought paralysis. For Samuel, the end of a bright and lovely life. And it spread the pain like an infection. *The only way out is through.* She'd hated Laura the first time she suggested letting herself experience the deep and unending pain of her experiences, but maybe that really was the only way out—facing the pain head-on. Doing instead of experiencing. Choosing instead of submitting.

Fourteen-year-old Evelyn Kensley, abused, used, and battered for many years, had thought to escape this world with a bullet to her heart. And in all the terrible irony that could only come from real life, she hadn't found a way out at the end of a gun's muzzle—she'd found herself more trapped than ever. And even more ironic—more than once in Hannah's life, Evelyn's words could've been her own. She folded the letter and replaced it in the envelope, wondering why it'd never made it to the *Record* when all the others had.

She turned her focus to the remaining pages. These were not letters and, other than the article she'd found in Monty's office, were the only real evidence she'd uncovered that proved Evelyn's existence. The first looked like an official hospital intake form, the blanks filled in with handwriting. Evelyn's name was at the top.

Name: Evelyn Kensley

Date: July 17, 1929

A few more lines with what must've been her home address and next of kin. Hannah didn't see anything new here, other than the interesting coincidence that the home she'd shot herself in was less than a mile from Mamaw's house. She continued to the handwritten portion that described her injury as a self-inflicted gunshot wound to her right breast and the details about her surgery and damage to her spinal column.

Then, at the bottom—

Complications: Pregnant

"What the . . . ?" Hannah squinted and then brought the page closer. There, in perfect cursive letters, it was easy enough to decipher.

Evelyn was pregnant when she shot herself. Hannah thought back to all the times she'd mentioned being ill and what she seemed to imply happened with Mr. Fred on the shore of that pond in the middle of nowhere. And how Harry, despite telling his mother and the whole world in a newspaper article that he was ready to marry Evelyn, disappeared from her story faster than he'd plunged into it.

Hannah flipped to the next page. The three sheets all seemed to be part of one document. An adoption record. Evelyn and her far-too-young age were listed at the top of the report. The baby was a girl, born March 23, 1930, somehow surviving not only Evelyn's spinal cord injury but also all the interventions that took place after that incident. It was a scandal that even Evelyn didn't want published in the newspaper, a family secret that had to be protected, an ugly truth that needed to be covered up by a beautiful fiction.

A baby.

This had to be it—the cover-up. Harry could potentially be the father of the child, but if that were true, why didn't the lovebirds just get married? In Hannah's mind the father had to be the boarder who had sexually assaulted Evelyn at the young age of fourteen. Hannah searched for the other handwritten insertions on the document when she ran into one that stood out.

Father: Fred Dawson

Hannah's heart was thrumming in her chest, exhaustion replaced with anticipation. She read the name again. Fred . . . Dawson.

Everything immediately made sense. She skimmed the rest of the pages, most of which contained standard language on the form, until she reached the signatures approving the adoption of the child. Evelyn's pretty signature on one line. Fred Dawson's on the other. There was no mistaking it, Fred was a Dawson. As in Jack, Pete, and Shelby Dawson.

"Mom!" Hannah yelled at the top of her lungs. "I need you!"

A crashing sound from the living room was followed by pounding footsteps, then Pam burst through Papaw's office door, phone in her hand, ready to call in some emergency.

"Oh my God, you nearly killed me," she said, out of breath. "What in heaven's name is the matter?"

"I found it. Look." She pointed to Fred's signature on the last page of the document. "Dawson, see? These are adoption papers. Google 'Fred Dawson.' He *has* to be related."

Pam typed the name into the phone as Hannah worked through the scenario in her mind. Fred Dawson got a fourteen-year-old girl, Evelyn, pregnant, and didn't marry her, and then she shot herself out of desperation. So the Dawsons hushed up the family by caring for the girl. She wrote to her hometown newspaper, and the family bought them off. The newspaper then kept the letters as insurance against the Dawsons to keep them paying and . . . boom.

"Hannah," Pam said, awe in her voice, holding up the device to her daughter's face. It was a Wikipedia page with a black-and-white headshot in the right-hand corner and the name *Fredrick Dawson* at the top of the page. "He was the governor of Tennessee."

"What?" Hannah snatched the phone and speed-read past his origin story and schooling to his political career. After a swift rise through local government in his thirties, at fifty-one he became the governor of Tennessee.

"Holy shit, Ma. Governor? His son, Jack Dawson, is running for president. You know what this means, right?"

Pam's eyes were alight with the possibilities. "You found that modern-day hook you were looking for. You should call Tom at the *Tribune*."

It really *was* everything she'd been looking for, and during an election season there was little doubt this story would run. Hannah gave the phone back to her mother, put the pages down, and then arranged them into a neat stack, knowing what had to happen now.

"Yeah," she said, deadpan as she slid the pages back into the manila envelope, "but I have to kill it."

"Wait, what?" Pam asked, cocking her head and staring at Hannah like she'd lost her mind. "Hannah, this is what you were looking for."

"I want to write this story more than just about anything, but I can't, Ma. Did you really think the leverage I was looking for would lead to a tell-all in a two-page spread? The only way this information gives me any power to help Guy is if I . . ." She struggled to say what she knew was true. "I have to promise to make it disappear."

Hannah expected Pam Williamson, who normally had a plan for every moment of Hannah's life whether she listened or not, to rush in with an opinion. Likely it would be the opposite of what Hannah wanted to do, but now she just gave Hannah's shoulder a gentle squeeze and said, "I respect that."

She glanced up at Pam, almost expecting to see her father standing there in her place. But looking back was still her tight-lipped, strait-laced, nearly perfect mother. Hannah pretended to examine the brass fasteners on the envelope, but really she was blinking back tears. After taking a moment to collect herself, she cleared her throat and said, simply and quietly, "Thank you."

"I know I can't fill in all the cracks your dad left behind, but I'm here for you. And I love you." She kissed her daughter on the top of her head, and for once it didn't feel forced.

Hannah returned the gesture by pressing her lips to her mother's smooth knuckles, whispering something she felt but very rarely said, "I love you too, Ma. I love you too."

When Hannah told the story to Laura during their e-therapy session the next day, she felt the weight of her growth. She'd called her at Pam's insistence the Monday after Thanksgiving, when Hannah was finding it impossible to get out of bed. They were on a twice-a-week phone-session schedule until Hannah and her mother made it back to Chicago. She'd almost forgotten how healing therapy could be.

"I have to tell you, Hannah, when you left for Mississippi and I didn't hear from you, I was worried. I thought there could be backsliding. And it sounds like there were struggles, but that overall you've grown so much. I'm proud of you. Well, can you say it? Are you proud of yourself?"

Hannah used to find it uncomfortable when Laura would express feelings about Hannah's work in therapy and when she'd be encouraged to say positive things about herself. She still had so much to work on, but Hannah could acknowledge that she was making a hard but good choice to help correct an error she'd made that hurt Guy, rather than hiding from it. She'd left Alex and effectively cut off her addiction at the source by blocking him electronically on every platform imaginable.

She'd found a connection with her mother, who still drove her absolutely insane but also turned out to be a really great shoulder to lean on. And she'd found the inner strength to make the most important decision of all, to change the path of her life story so it could be different from Evelyn's. She'd made the choice to live.

It wasn't easy to say out loud, but today it felt okay to agree.

"Yeah." She nodded, looking at herself on the small frame in the corner of the screen. "I'm really proud."

CHAPTER 35

"Here, you can use mine." Monty passed Hannah a golden fountain pen that he produced from the inner pocket of his suit coat. It was disturbingly warm to the touch when she took the writing implement from him across his desk. An eight-page document sat in front of her, flipped open to the last page, where a blank signature line stared up at her.

Hannah rubbed her eyes. She knew what she had to do, but that didn't make it easy. God, just sitting in the same room as Monty after their disgusting confrontation the week earlier was nauseating, but she was doing it.

"You will work with Mr. Grant to ensure all charges against Guy will be dropped, right?" The tip of the pen hovered over the line that was meant for her name.

"It's a standard NDA. But you have my word that if you sign it, I'll do everything in my power to get Mr. Franklin's name cleared." Monty spoke to Hannah like a disappointed parent who was going to let his teenager work off the cost of repairs for a dent in the family station wagon. With assistance from the attorney Pam had acquired for Hannah and a little tough love from Mrs. Martin, Monty had agreed to settle the issue out of court. And though it was painful to give up on Evelyn's truth, it was an easy sacrifice when it came to choosing between a story and a human being. Especially when that human was Guy.

"Fine," she said, then signed on the blank line and placed the pen on the desk, watching the ink soak into the paper and dry. It was done. The ball of tension in her chest let up a notch or two. Guy was safe, and so was Rosie. And now she could look him in the eye again without shame.

"And I'll need all of the files you stole from the *Record*." She cringed at the word *stole*.

"You have everything." Hannah wasn't going to tell him about the most recent discovery she'd made. At least one of Evelyn's letters wouldn't be destroyed. "I didn't take anything else home with me."

"And the copies?"

"The NDA doesn't say anything about copies."

Monty cleared his throat and steepled his fingers like he always did when he was being stern, pressing them to his lips, the crusty white at the corners of his mouth thicker than ever.

"I don't know what you are planning, but let me be clear: I will follow through on the consequences of this nondisclosure agreement in regard to official terms with the $100,000 penalty as well as more unspoken terms in regard to Mr. Franklin. So, if you are holding on to any hopes of publishing *any* files acquired in these offices, or any theories based on those files pertaining to the Dawson family and Evelyn Kensley, my lawyers will be contacting you."

"You should be ashamed of yourself, Monty"—she leaned forward, glaring—"and your father for this cover-up. I'm signing this bullshit agreement because you have given me no other choice, but you did it for money. I don't know how you sleep at night."

"Hannah." Monty used her given name for the first time in their interactions together, momentarily seeming nearly as tired as she felt. "My daddy had nothing to do with that sad situation."

"Maybe not, but he made sure no one knew what really happened, and Fred Dawson got to enjoy his life and make his money and run for office and be elected governor of Tennessee. Governor, Monty," Hannah pressed, the NDA signed, the deal made, and nothing else to lose. "And Evelyn was the collateral damage. She was pregnant with his baby, did you know that? He raped a fourteen-year-old and left her pregnant and so desperate she shot herself in the chest."

"I can neither confirm nor deny those accusations," Monty said robotically, and Hannah couldn't tell if he already knew those details or was surprised by them. She wanted to believe that he was kept naive of the more upsetting elements of his father's agreement with the Dawsons, for Mrs. Martin's sake and because she'd thought there could possibly be a good man inside his privileged body.

"I can confirm those accusations, Monty. I won't, but I can. If your conscience ever gets the best of you and you want to do what you know is right, please contact me." Hannah wrote her cell number and her mother's address in Chicago on a Post-it, then added it to the collection around his computer monitor.

"I have no idea what you are speaking about. Thank you for coming, Hannah. Now, would you kindly leave?" Monty was finished with the conversation now that he had what he wanted, so he stood up and walked to the edge of his desk, a gesture meant to encourage Hannah to go. Catapulting out of her chair, Hannah passed Monty on her way out of the office and narrowly avoided glaring up at him. Instead, she stormed past her desk where all her Post-its and pens sat untouched. She slammed the front door of the building as hard as she could, but the shock wave was absorbed by the dense brick structure, which let out an unsatisfying thunk.

Hannah climbed into the passenger seat of her mom's rental car. Pam Williamson sat at the wheel, her short blonde hair carefully styled that morning, sunglasses on the bridge of her nose.

"How did that go?" Pam had requested to go in with Hannah while she met with Monty, and though she'd let her mother help wordsmith the NDA along with a Memphis attorney her mother knew, she'd felt strongly about doing this last task on her own.

Emily Bleeker

"He's an asshole," Hannah said, still fuming.

"Sounds like it. I'm glad you let me help you get some proper counsel," she said, pulling out into the road.

"Yes, Ma. Me too." Hannah refrained from dropping in any snarky or defensive comments, one of the small ways she was attempting to show her continued gratitude.

"What about your friend? I hope he's properly represented. Even if Mr. Martin holds to his side of the agreement, that doesn't ensure that the prosecutor is going to drop all the charges."

"He said he doesn't want my help, Ma." Hannah leaned her forehead against the window, her breath steaming the glass so she couldn't watch the scenery go by for what would be the last time.

"I think you know something about not letting people help, huh?" Pam hadn't changed overnight; she still knew how to get a little dig in now and again.

Hannah didn't respond.

"Well, did you still want to make that second stop before the hospital?" she asked.

Mamaw had woken up the day after Hannah made the choice not to take that handful of pills. She'd been groggy and forgetful at first, but as the days went on, and much to Hannah's relief, she was starting to regain her memory and personality. The decision had been made once Mamaw woke up to rent out her house and use the monthly income to pay for a room at the Sunrise Nursing Home down the street. It killed Hannah that her grandmother would never go home again because of her.

"Yeah, I probably should."

Hannah's mother followed the directions on her phone to the pre-programmed address Hannah had given her.

"I think this is it," Pam said, pulling up in front of a large workshop with a sign out front: "Franklin and Son Construction." This is where Carla said that Guy spent most of his days since being put on administrative leave. Hannah and Guy hadn't talked since that day in front of the middle school. She'd decided to wait until she could tangibly show that she was keeping the promise she'd made.

Leaving without seeing Guy had been a tempting option, but it didn't fit with the hard, action-based choices Hannah was trying to make now. She didn't want Guy to know she was coming, or to give him a chance not to be there. Even now, Hannah was unsure if she'd be a welcome sight. The final thing Hannah might have to give up forever was Guy's friendship—and she knew she had to be okay with that.

But she needed to see him one last time before Mamaw's new tenants moved in and Hannah and Pam went back to Chicago. Brody had promised to take some time off work to fly in and check on Mamaw so that Hannah could go home and "get some rest." Chicago was home, always had been, but for some reason it felt strange to be leaving Senatobia, even if it was the only option that currently made sense.

"I'll be right back." Hannah opened the car door and stepped onto the gravel driveway leading to Guy's family's business. She held a package, wrapped in brown paper, to her chest. A set of large garage doors stood open, and an electric saw buzzed in the background as she approached.

When Hannah set foot inside the workroom, she saw him immediately—protective glasses, headphones on, and sawdust covering his arms. Those arms had held her once, and though she hadn't wanted to acknowledge it at the time, they'd fit in a way that made her feel safe. But it wasn't just the way he held her body against his, or the sideways smile he used to toss her way when he was teasing her—she missed having him in her life, and that was something she'd have to get used to. She pushed away the memory and continued her pilgrimage into the workroom.

Guy hadn't noticed her yet, and Hannah's old instinct was still there, urging her to run away. But she'd learned to calm that aggressive voice, so instead of taking the option to escape, she waved in his direction, hoping to get his attention.

The saw whined to a stop.

"Hannah?" Guy said, taking off his eyewear and headphones, patting at his dusty clothes and skin like he was trying to improve his appearance for her. He looked more surprised than angry, and that let Hannah's jaw loosen so she could speak.

"Hi," she said, knowing it sounded lame.

"Hey, I was just thinking about you. How is Miss Mable?" he asked, like he had run into an acquaintance at the grocery store, which was easier to stomach than his hard exterior from their last meeting but still cool enough to make her shiver. She scraped her foot on the dirt, drawing a line on the ground with the toe of her boot.

"Better. She's awake. Pretty lucid. The doctors are feeling hopeful."

"That's good news," he said, taking off his gloves and moving in Hannah's direction. "We sent her flowers. I hope she got them."

Hannah nodded. She'd cried when she read the card even though all it said was *Best wishes, Guy and Rosie.*

"Yes, she saw them. They were beautiful. Thank you." Hannah kept her sentences short and to the point so he didn't think she was here for a lengthy discussion that would likely be too painful for either of them. She might as well get to the point. "I talked to Monty today. You should be getting a call later, but he's not going to move forward with the charges. I . . . I just wanted to let you know."

"Damn it, what did you do now?" Guy's brow furrowed, and his gaze dropped as soon as Hannah mentioned Monty.

"Nothing bad. I just, I signed an NDA, and he agreed to make sure your charges were dropped. My attorney will be calling your attorney later to explain it all. But it's over. It's finally over," she said, hoping Guy could feel some sense of relief even if Hannah hated the double meaning of her last statement.

"You signed a nondisclosure agreement?" Guy asked, glancing at the parcel in Hannah's arms. "What for?"

"My Evelyn story." It was an easy decision—Evelyn's story for Guy's freedom. She'd make that trade any day. Hannah held out the package. "This is for you and Rosie. It's the information I got when I was in Memphis. I thought you guys deserved to know how it ended. You might want to look through it first. It's . . . um . . . sad."

"You gave up your story?" he asked, staring at the package like it held answers to more than just a wild goose chase.

"It was just an old story. My whole value system was so out of whack about this thing." Hannah shrugged her admission, shivering, the December breeze too cold for her light jacket.

"I can't disagree," Guy said, placing the package on his workbench, an obvious weight lifted from his shoulders as he glanced back at her, a tiny hint of his old crooked smile curling up into a partial dimple. "But I'm not surprised you figured it out. I'm sorry if I seemed harsh last week, but—"

"It was completely justified." She shut down his explanation. She wasn't here for Guy's thanks or sorrys. No one thanks you for fixing the vase you were responsible for breaking. This, she thought, should be no different. "It's honestly a relief. People down here are too nice. I'm sorry you had to call me on my shit, but I'm glad you did."

"I'll gladly call you out on your shit anytime, Hannah Williamson." The playful smirk she'd been missing was back for sure this time, and a rush of sunshine flooded the barren spot in her chest.

"Great. I've created a monster," she answered with a touch of friendly sarcasm, like old times. They both laughed, and the sound filled the workroom, surrounding the pair before dissolving into the air like a sugar lump in hot tea. In the sweet silence she shivered, and he gently took her by the elbow and pointed to a space heater installed in the ceiling.

355

"I can't stay," she said, freeing her arm from his light clasp, remembering her mom sitting in the car. "If you don't hear from Mr. Grant by the end of today, let me know. Right now I need to get to the hospital and then I have to pack."

His smile dropped.

"Oh. You're leaving Senatobia." He stated it so firmly it was like he was ordering her to go rather than asking about her plans. Hannah uneasily spewed the details of her departure.

"I'll be back in a few weeks to help Mamaw move into Sunrise," she said, staring at her toes again, wishing she still had her line in the dirt to focus on. "But yeah, I'm moving back to Chicago. There is a job at an online magazine. My mom knows the guy who runs it. Hey, it's a job."

"I see." Guy's hardness came back like he was a turtle engulfing himself in his shell, and his whole posture changed, standing tall, crossing his arms, his chest puffing out. Even with their tiny moment of connection just now, Hannah was surprised by his reaction. He'd been ignoring her for weeks.

"There is nothing here for me, Guy." She didn't mean to raise her voice, but her response echoed in the cavernous room and made it sound like she was talking into a megaphone.

"Nothing?" he asked with an edge of sincerity, shifting the tone of their conversation with one word that made the deadened space inside Hannah shudder like it'd been hit with a defibrillator.

"Mamaw is going to a nursing home because of me. And her house is all but rented. I don't have a job anymore. And I've been a terrible friend to you and Rosie. You are better off without me . . ."

"Shouldn't I get to decide what makes me better off?" he asked in a low, comforting voice, moving in close enough that Hannah could smell the sawdust on his skin. The conversation had slowed to a trickle, more being said in the silences than in the sentences. Guy didn't hate Hannah; he cared about her. Staring up into his vibrant, dark eyes,

Hannah knew just how badly she wanted to explore what he was offering her.

"Of course, but I mean besides last week . . . we haven't talked since that night."

"I know. I know. But I was hurt," he said, and his warm breath touched her forehead and cheek like a kiss. His face was soft, vulnerable, like he'd just taken off a plate of armor before heading into battle. "About the arrest and the living hell my life became, yes. But also . . . when you didn't answer the phone that night and then you didn't come back from that meeting with Pete Dawson, I just assumed . . ."

"You thought I was with Pete?" She choked, eyes wide. "God, no."

They'd been in touch, but she was in no place for flirting or going out for dinner or drinks. And with Mamaw and Guy on the top of her mind, there was no room for helpful but superfluous Pete.

"That's a bit of a relief," he teased, stepping closer and touching a strand of hair that had fallen over her shoulder. He really cared about her. Like, really really. A different brand of guilt hit Hannah in the gut. As close as she felt to Guy, he didn't really know her. Not the broken her.

"I need to tell you something," she said, picking at a rough spot on her palm, knowing the only way to be open with her story was to not look up and get distracted by Guy's reactions. "I know you've probably heard rumors, and I kinda told you about it, but—over six months ago I tried to . . . kill myself." She paused, working through the shame of saying those words out loud, remembering the moment she'd shoved all the pills in her mouth, the fear and relief that went along with that decision. Hannah made a fist, wishing she could wipe that moment out of her memory forever.

"I'd been through a bad breakup, and my dad was diagnosed with cancer, and I was losing my job because I'd become addicted to sleeping pills, and I was riddled with depression and I nearly died. My dad, um, my dad saved my life." Emotion overwhelmed Hannah as she recalled the patched-up door she'd come home to after the hospital and the newly replaced handle. "And that's why I came here after he died. I came for Mamaw, yeah, but I also came to hide away from all that pain. But then I found Evelyn's story and I met you and Rosie, and everything changed. I started to want to live, not just be alive, you know?"

"Then why do you want to leave that?" Guy asked, grazing her shoulder and elbow with his touch. If she was going to tell the truth, she had to tell Guy everything, and that meant telling him the real reason she didn't pick up her phone three weeks ago when he needed her most.

"I met up with Alex that night. My ex," she whispered, ashamed. "He was the reason I went to Memphis and everything happened. He was there."

"Oh," Guy said, his face falling and jaw going taut when she checked his expression. She hated hurting this man. But he needed to know. "So, you're back together now? That's why you're leaving?"

"No," she said, correcting him quickly, hurting a little less every time she owned that it was over with Alex. "But with everything that happened with you and Mamaw as a result, I nearly ended up back in that scary place emotionally, and that's not good. I need to get stable again. I need to be able to stand on my own two feet for once."

Hannah had always been independent in spirit, but she was coming to see that her bold nature didn't translate to not being dependent. Until she found her worth inside herself, instead of from outside sources, she'd be susceptible to the slings and arrows of life. And discovering that would take time and work and sacrifice.

"You think you need to be in Chicago to do that?" Guy asked, his passionate plea diminishing rapidly.

"Yeah, I think maybe I do. At least for a little bit," she said, nodding. "I tried running away from it, and you see how that turned out." She couldn't muster a laugh, but at least Guy was a good sport and faked one for her.

"I get that," Guy said, with a touch of admiration in the tilt of his chin and compassion in his gaze. Which didn't surprise Hannah; he was the one who taught her about staying and fixing, rather than running away. "You'll keep in touch?" he asked, hopeful.

"Absolutely," Hannah agreed, hating every word out of her mouth but knowing they were the right things to say. "Tell Rosie bye too. I'll make sure to take her to lunch when I'm back in a few weeks."

"She will love that," he replied, and Hannah took a step backward, broadcasting her intention to leave, knowing every minute she stayed made it harder to walk away. "Hey, don't go yet," he said, giving himself one final dusting. Hannah waited under the heat lamp, a faint buzz humming in the background.

"A goodbye isn't complete without a hug." He put out his arms.

She leaned into his offered embrace, resting her head on his chest, right where his heart was. His arms completely encompassed Hannah, and she melted into the smell of sawdust, deodorant, and sweat, feeling safe, wanting to never be away from the security she felt there, even though she knew it was impossible.

When he kissed the top of her head, Hannah shifted so that she could see Guy for one last time. Their faces inches apart, Hannah licked her lips, her breath quickening. Guy watched her and then leaned down, touching his lips to hers. She tilted her chin to the side, raising onto her tiptoes to press her mouth more firmly against his, running a hand up the back of his neck. He responded to her willingness, grasping at her waist, clutching the fabric of her shirt in his fingers and deepening their hold, his tongue grazing her bottom lip, sending a shiver of longing through Hannah's body.

"Hannah!" Pam shouted from the end of the driveway, barely audible over the whoosh in Hannah's ears. She grudgingly pulled away.

"Is that what the kids are calling a 'hug' these days?" she asked, smirking with her tingling lips, wanting more.

Guy rested his hands on her hips with an impish smirk of his own, holding her body against his like he didn't want to let her leave. "I wasn't exactly planning for that to happen, but I'm glad it did."

"Me too," she said, craving another kiss, about to hitch up on her tiptoes to retrieve it, when she heard her name for the second time. "I have to go," she said, and moved away from Guy's reach, removing herself from further temptation—not only the temptation to make out like teenagers but the temptation to stay in Senatobia for him. But temptation only *looked* like happiness, and so far succumbing to that draw had brought disaster, whereas resisting had brought strength. Staying and numbing herself with a new love interest would only fix her problems for so long. Grief was patient, and until she truly mourned her losses, it would sneak in and sabotage any happiness she attempted to build for herself. If her future was with Guy and in this town, she'd find the right way back. The healthy way back.

"Yeah, you'd better." He wanted more too; she could see it.

She took another step away, knowing she was running out of self-control. She kept backing away, her resolve firming with each step.

"Goodbye, Hannah. It was lovely getting to know you."

"Goodbye," she said, running down the driveway and jumping into the car at the bottom of the hill, slamming the door behind her so she didn't have a chance to change her mind.

CHAPTER 36

Mamaw's new hospital room was less scary than the ICU. Fewer machines beeped in her private room, and fewer numbers were illuminated on little monitors. Plus, Mamaw was awake now, which was far less frightening than when she'd been lying in bed practically lifeless with bandages encompassing her head.

In the past week she'd made so much progress, sitting up in her bed now, wearing her own nightgown (she'd insisted) and a fresh coat of nail polish (one of the ladies from the salon volunteered to make a house call). Now that the arrangements were made with Sunrise, Mamaw's discharge date had been moved up to the following day, and she was talking excitedly with her nurse about how Mr. Davenport was planning to visit in a few hours for dinner.

When Hannah and Pam entered the room, the nurse excused herself and Mamaw grinned, half her right eyebrow hidden by a band of gauze but the rest of her face as beautiful as ever.

Hannah had started every visit since Mamaw awoke the same way, and today followed the same pattern: "I'm so sorry."

And today, like all the visits before this one, Mamaw scolded, "Oh, hush now."

Hannah rushed across the room, and Mamaw's eyes lit up as Hannah leaned in for a kiss on the cheek. It would take a long time for Hannah to "hush" about not being there for Mamaw, but that was as far as Mamaw had allowed the conversation to go, and Hannah was working with Laura on moving forward with action more regularly rather than always looking behind with regret.

"Y'all packed?" Mamaw asked once Hannah was settled by the side of the bed, their fingers intertwined. As much as she used to long for home, it was difficult for Hannah to think about leaving Senatobia right now with so many things unsettled. But with Mamaw moving to Sunrise, and with her house rented and Hannah's job gone, there was no reason for her to stay.

"Almost. The renters will be moving in at the end of the week, and then we will be out of here," Pam interjected from the end of the bed. "If you two don't mind, I'm going to head back and do a few chores. Hannah, text me if you need a ride, okay?"

Pam was clearly glad her mother-in-law was returning to health, and Hannah was almost certain she didn't begrudge the time and effort spent on the transition into a nursing home. She was not a sentimental woman, and sitting around chatting seemed less important than finishing all the items on her to-do list, which Hannah was starting to think was her mother's way of saying *I love you.*

"Thanks, Ma," Hannah said. Pam kissed Hannah and waved to Mamaw before heading out. North Oak Regional Medical Center was only a little over a mile away from Mamaw's house, an easy walk that Hannah was used to making, finding the chill in the air invigorating and reminiscent of home. Once the door shut behind Pam, Hannah let out a sigh of relief. Things were better with her mom, but their personalities would never fully mesh. Pam had been giving her more space, and that felt like a good sign that they'd succeed at temporarily living together back in Oak Park.

Mamaw gave Hannah's hand a squeeze.

"How you doin', Hannah girl?" She sounded strong but looked tired despite her efforts to keep up with her self-care routine. Typical

Mamaw—in the hospital after being in a freaking coma and her first instinct was to care about someone else. Hannah used to deify her grandmother's patience and self-sacrifice, but lately she was starting to wonder if it was both a blessing and a curse.

"Mamaw, you gotta stop worrying about me. I'm here to take care of you, like I should've been before."

"Sweetheart, I can care about you and you can care about me. That's what family is all about. I used to pray that God would take me after I lost Sammy. Patrick had Pam and you kids, and I was tired of watching all the people I loved leave. But darling, I'm so delighted I had the chance to come to know you. You and Brody and my great-grandchildren are the only family I have left."

In general, Hannah was tired of crying. But the tears brought on by Mamaw's unconditional love were welcome, cleansing tears. It didn't take going to the right school or getting good grades or having an important job or following the juiciest lead to be enough in Mable Williamson's eyes. Just being was enough, and that was the ultimate soft place, where falling wasn't crashing but diving into a waiting embrace.

"I love you, Mamaw," Hannah said, so grateful that she could say that to her grandmother while holding her hand after being faced with the potential of her being gone forever.

"I love you too, Hannah girl." Mamaw kissed the back of Hannah's hand, and then held it to her chest, where Hannah could feel her heartbeat. Hannah's phone started to buzz in her back pocket. Probably her mom, but when three more texts came in rapid succession, she excused herself to take a peek, not willing to ignore her phone for too long anymore.

"Oh, it's Guy." The screen was filled with several messages in a row, surprising Hannah. He had been so quiet lately. But then again, her visit and that kiss . . .

"Well, what did he say?" Mamaw asked, like an impatient schoolgirl. Hannah blushed, remembering her grandmother's racially charged comments about the potential of a romantic relationship with Guy. If Hannah and Guy ended up together one day, which was a huge *if*, Mamaw would have to face those long-standing prejudices that held her hostage. But Hannah didn't want to fight with Mamaw while she was lying in a hospital bed.

"Oh, nothing." Hannah put the phone screen down on the bed and took Mamaw's hand again.

"That smile wasn't for nothing. Don't be shy, darlin'. I can tell you are sweet on him."

"I'm not 'sweet' on anybody. I will check later. I'm here to focus on *you*." The phone buzzed again and Mamaw sighed heavily.

"You're avoidin' your young man because of me."

"No. I'm not."

"Yes, you are. I know you think I'm old-fashioned, and sometimes I say things that come out wrong. I have nothing against Guy, and I thought it best to explain my comments the other day, but then . . ." Mamaw steered clear of mentioning the accident when referencing Hannah's heated response at breakfast the day before everything went to hell.

Hannah took the pause as an opportunity to speak up. "We'll have plenty of time to talk about such things."

Mamaw wasn't having it. "I'm an old woman, Hannah. Now is the only time I have to talk about such things."

The monitors in the room seemed to blink their agreement, evidence of how fragile Mamaw's promise truly was. Hannah nodded and vowed to let her grandmother tell her what had been on her mind, hoping it wouldn't spark conflict again.

"When I was your age, if a black man and a white woman took up together, it wasn't safe for either of them. When your daddy was little, there was a married woman in town whose husband claimed he'd found her with a black man from the wrong side of the tracks. He tried to take away her children when she divorced him for beating her. I saw the consequences of that accusation with my own eyes, hanging in the field next to the courthouse and burning in a yard down the street from your papaw and me. It made me sick. I wish I could say that was the first time in my life I'd seen the same situation, but it wasn't."

Hannah's stomach rolled as she tried to imagine what she would've done if she'd witnessed such injustices. She'd like to think that she would've called out the wrongdoers and joined anyone who wanted things to change, but it was easy to think that from the safety of hindsight. Maybe she would've been just as silent and privileged as so many others. Hannah shuddered at the thought as Mamaw continued.

"I think what I'm intending to say is—when you're taught something is dangerous for so long, it's hard to unthink it. You know? But I've been considering something. I don't believe in the bogeyman anymore, and I don't check under my bed for monsters, so I don't know why at ninety-one the idea of a black man and a white woman should frighten me so very much. I know your young man is a good person, a kindly father, and a steady provider. You'd be blessed to have such a man care about you."

Hannah patted her grandmother's arm, not sure of the exact thing to say, but she was touched by her grandmother's self-reflection. It was hard enough to change anything about herself as a thirty-something with only a third as much life under her belt. Some people avoided change because they said that you couldn't teach an old dog new tricks, but from what she could see with Mamaw, she was trying to teach herself new ideas.

"Thank you for sharing that story. I really don't have all the right answers." Hannah shrugged and bit her lip, finding her most honest words. "But I do know that I respect the *hell* out of you for being willing to try a new perspective. Also," she added, playfully rolling her eyes, "he's not my young man."

"Not yet, he isn't. But you both have eyes for each other, and I'm sure he's sending you sweet nothings in those texting messages."

The memory of his lips on hers flashed through her mind. And the memory of his arms releasing from her waist so reluctantly.

"Fine!" she said, blushing. "I'll check. Gosh, you're persistent sometimes, you know that?"

"I call it helpful," Mamaw said, waiting patiently as Hannah checked her messages.

Sure enough, they were all from Guy.

Guy Franklin: I know you're busy but—I just read through that file you gave me. Do you know what's in here? It's here! Her last letter. I'm sending it to you. You will NOT believe this. Oh, Hannah. There is more. So much more.

"Nothing romantic, just some stuff about work," Hannah informed her grandmother, feeling a bit disappointed that Mamaw had been wrong about Guy's motivations and that it was all about Evelyn.

There were at least ten image files attached in the text message. Hannah sent him a quick reply.

Hannah: Yeah! I read them last week. How far in are you?

Guy Franklin: Evelyn shot herself. She was PREGNANT.
But was it Harry's baby or Mr. Fred?
And now I'm looking at the adoption documents.

Hannah: Did you see it?

Guy Franklin: What? That Mr. Fred = Fred Dawson? Yeah I saw it.
Hannah, this is huge!

Hannah: I know, right?

Guy Franklin: Well, yeah. Crazy, I know, but . . . what about the other names?

Hannah: Other names? What do you mean?

Guy Franklin: I might be losing my mind, but . . . just look at the other signatures and tell me what you think.

Hannah went back to the signature page she'd been zooming in and out of, checking Fred Dawson's signature. This time she shifted the virtual page to the right, focusing on the only two unknown names remaining. The first one seemed to be from a woman: Agnes Clarmont, the adoption facilitator. Her name rang absolutely no bells. Hannah swiped the page to the right and zoomed in on the only remaining signature, that of the baby's adoptive parents.

Calvin Patton.

Hannah read it again and again. She tried to think back to the names on the headstones she'd taken note of at the cemetery last month. Patton was definitely a family name, but it had to be a coincidence. Right?

"Mamaw, when I was at the cemetery I thought I saw your daddy's name was Calvin. Is that right?"

"Yes, dear. Calvin August Patton. The kindest man I ever did meet. Why do you ask?"

Hannah read the name again, gathering the courage to ask the next question on her mind.

"I'm not sure, but bear with me if I ask a crazy question. Do you know if anyone in your family is adopted? Like, a cousin or something like that? I thought I remembered my dad telling a story about someone showing up in the middle of the night with a baby. Was that a true story after all?"

"We didn't talk about it much, big family secret and all that, but that story sure was about my daddy."

"Oh my God, are you sure?" Hannah asked, dazed and sitting on the edge of her chair. If the monitoring machines had been hooked up to Hannah's vitals, there would be a crash cart in the room at any minute. She had to find a way past her grandmother's natural defenses, which would be fairly easily triggered if Hannah prodded for scandalous information, to hear the rest of the story about Calvin Patton and the mystery baby. "I know it's unpleasant to talk about things from the past, and I hate to ask it of you, but it's important to know."

Mamaw considered it, her reactions slowing like she was getting tired from all the stimulation. Hannah promised herself that she'd accept whatever answer Mamaw gave her, even if she didn't want to talk about the past. Goodness knows it was taking Hannah long enough to deal with her past traumas; she wouldn't try to force a frail elderly woman to face hers.

But sleepy or not, Mamaw answered thoughtfully, "I don't think I mind telling it now. A brush with death is good for my courage," she said, surprising Hannah with her response.

"Are you sure? I don't want to force you . . ."

"No. I'm startin' to think you're right. Some stories need to be told," she said, arranging her thoughts for a moment before starting. "I never knew I was adopted till I was pregnant with your daddy. My momma, Florence Patton, lost eight babies after my brother was born—some kind of problem with her blood and the baby's blood mixin'."

The row of tiny headstones flashed through Hannah's memory, digging up another memory right after it. "Oh, what is that called? Rh factor? My friend Karen had that when she was pregnant with her second baby. She had to get shots. It seemed kinda routine. I had no idea it could be so deadly."

"Scientists eventually figured out what it was, but it was too late for my parents. I was always told that I was their miracle child. But when I was pregnant with my first baby, I told my doctor about my momma's struggles bringing a child to term, and he told me what he thought had likely been the issue. When I went to ask my momma about it, she wouldn't say a word, not one. She was in poor health by that time and had turned ill-tempered. I was desperate to know more, so I asked Daddy. At first he told me that he wouldn't know such things, but then he came to my house the next day and sat me down and told me the truth.

"He got deeply serious, the most serious I've ever seen him, and said, 'Mable, you are a grown woman. I don't care what your mother says, it's time you heard the truth.' Which scared me into silence because Daddy never went against Momma. Never. So I sat on the maroon armchair in the front room—you know the one—and listened.

"I already knew the first half of the story, but I sat there as he worked his way through it. He said that Momma was once a lovely and sweet-natured girl. They fell in love at sixteen and eloped together. The Patton family owned a cotton distribution company that worked with the new railroad that came through town and made money fast. My parents built the big house on Summit Ave., the one with the dark-blue siding and columns out in front. The Hermans bought it in '84, and I think it sold a few years back.

"Anyway, back then there was one thing my momma wanted more than anything, and that was children. Right away, within the first year they were married, she had my brother and was pregnant again within a year, but that baby was stillborn, and my momma was brokenhearted. She told my daddy that the only thing that would heal that fissure was a healthy child.

"So they tried again, and again the baby died. Five more babies were born, some would make it all the way to delivery but then die a few hours later; others came too early and couldn't survive. Finally, after endless years of loss, not just of the babies but of my momma's health and patience, she had her last baby, a little girl. I'd always been told I was that little girl, a miracle child. He confessed that morning that the Mable Patton who'd been born on that cold spring night died in my momma's arms like all her other babies, and she told my daddy she wanted to die too.

"The next morning, Daddy said that he left the house and didn't come back for two whole days, and when he did he had a baby—a little girl. Me. He never told me where I came from. Your papaw liked to joke that he'd bought me from the whorehouse in Memphis, but I always believed I was born to a teenage mother at the Home for Wayward Girls. In the end it didn't matter where I came from; Daddy said that Momma nursed me as if I were her own, and no one ever mentioned the fact that the real Mable was buried six feet under."

Mamaw told the story like a fairy tale read to sleepy-eyed children at bedtime, like she'd distanced herself from the emotion enough that it was just a story to her. Hannah let all the pieces finally click fully into place, making a detailed image in her mind. It all made sense—why Evelyn's voice sounded so familiar and why her plight felt so real.

Evelyn was Mamaw's birth mother and Hannah's great-grand-mother. Hannah wasn't a spiritual person in general, and if she were checking boxes on a survey asking for her religious preference, she'd probably check *agnostic*, but she believed in genetics and in the undefin-able "something" that connected family through generations. Hannah sat up, rod straight, her body filled with a light that burned with understanding.

"Mamaw, I think I know who your birth mother was." Fumbling with excitement, Hannah took out her phone and showed Mamaw the documents. Mamaw grabbed her glasses from the side table so she could make them out. It had to be true. Impossibly true. After a few minutes of Hannah vomiting information, proof, and backstory, Mamaw closed her eyes.

"You mean your Evelyn is my . . . ?"

Mamaw stopped before saying the phrase that meant stepping out of the tolerable fiction her family had built around themselves for the past nine decades.

"I really think so." Hannah said each word with purpose and wiped away her grandmother's tears, waiting to find out if they were from sorrow or joy. Hoping to bring her more toward the side of joy, she took out her phone again. "And here is the insane bit. You have a brother," Hannah said, looking up a picture of Jack Dawson. Mamaw's lower lip trembled as soon as she focused in on the image. She touched the picture and traced the line of his jaw.

"He looks a bit like Sammy, don't you think?" Mamaw shuddered and removed her glasses, but didn't move to wipe away her tears. Hannah used a tissue from the bedside table to dry her grandma's face, wanting to know what was going on inside her mind.

"He kinda does, you're right." Hannah stared at the photo. There was something in the crinkle of his eyes and the creases around his mouth, the cut of his jawline, that brought up a younger man laughing at Thanksgiving dinner in a way that would make an outsider wonder if he'd ever experienced sadness. Hannah knew better—still waters did not mean safe waters. She flipped to the next picture, this one of the whole Dawson family. "And you have an aunt and nieces and nephews. You have a whole family out there," Hannah declared, like a doctor calling out the gender of a newly born baby. Mamaw smiled but then recoiled.

"I don't think they'd like to meet me," she said in a very small voice. "I'm sure they'd rather leave the past in the past, and all that."

Hannah wanted to scream *OF COURSE THEY WANT TO MEET YOU*, but she wasn't sure. The Dawsons had invested so much in keeping Evelyn's rape and subsequent pregnancy a secret, it was unlikely they'd jump for joy at the connection being made in such a concrete and provable way as modern-day DNA evidence.

"Well, maybe, but I wonder if all of them would feel that way."

Peter's face came to mind. He was her—what was the connection—second cousin? The idea was both disgusting and hilarious. No wonder he'd felt so familiar. Pete would want to know. Pete had to know. Maybe this wasn't as much of a dead end as it had seemed at first glance.

"I can't do that to them. It's not fair."

"Not fair? Are you kidding? Mamaw—let me tell you about Evelyn's life and fairness. What's not fair is that no one even knows she exists. It's not fair that the Dawsons have thrown money around for decades to hide the fact that before he became governor Fred Dawson impregnated an unwilling teenager who tried to end her own life out of desperation. It's not fair that this is not the first or the last time a powerful man will force a young woman into sex and then discard her. The Dawson family doesn't need *you* to protect them, Mamaw."

Hannah desperately wanted her grandmother to see her value, that it was no less than her brother Jack Dawson's. In the original narrative, Evelyn had been seen as disposable. And her baby a secret to be swept into hiding. Their stories, Hannah thought, shouldn't be so easily deleted.

"And that's why you wanted to tell Evelyn's story?" Mamaw asked, unhurriedly.

Passionate emotion constricted Hannah's reply at first, knowing the opportunity to share this particular outrage had passed. She coughed and answered concisely.

"Exactly."

"Hmm, well." Mamaw stared at the Google images of the family she hadn't known existed for the entirety of her long life. "Maybe you should."

Hannah stared, amazed. Her grandmother, so afraid of truth that she couldn't bring herself to visit her own son's headstone, wanted to air her family's dirty laundry. The desire inside Hannah to write the truth was nearly overwhelming, but it was impossible to fulfill. Finding out the truth for Mamaw and the rest of the family would have to be enough.

"I can't, though. Remember? I signed the nondisclosure agreement. There is no way I can . . ." Hannah noticed something as she explained the impossible situation they were in. Every statement about the article used a personal pronoun that referred to Hannah. Hannah kept saying "I . . . I . . . I . . ."

"Wait, Mamaw!" Hannah gasped. "I have an idea." She pushed her knees up against the side of the bed, turning her phone off. "I can't write the story, but you could." She pointed at her elderly grandmother, unfolding her finger slowly.

"Me?" Her voice pitched, and her warm eyes widened, wrinkles rippling across her cheeks. "Heavens no. I can't do that."

"Listen. Yes, you can." Excitement bubbled inside Hannah. It could work. "It could fail . . . yes, but it could possibly work. I won't push you, but you are a writer. You taught this stuff at the women's college, and it's *your* story. If Evelyn could do it, you can."

"I'm an old woman. No one wants to hear from me." She stared at her hands, neatly folded in her lap, the IV taped down to her nearly translucent skin.

It killed Hannah to see how little her grandmother knew of her own value. Was this what women had become used to? Men became more powerful, wise, and experienced as they grew older. Women became . . . irrelevant.

"I think you're wrong," Hannah said, her last push before giving up on the idea, at least for now. "I think a lot of people would like to hear this story from you."

Mamaw listened and then closed her eyes for a moment. "I'll think on it," she mumbled. Almost immediately, her head bobbed like she was wrestling against pure exhaustion, and Hannah knew she'd stayed too long. Hannah collected her things and then pressed the button on the hospital bed to move it into a more comfortable resting position.

Mamaw needed her beauty sleep before Mr. Davenport's visit, and Hannah would be back for another visit before she and Pam returned to Chicago.

With a kiss on her grandma's forehead and a quick sniff of gardenia, Hannah wiggled into her jacket and then put her bag over her shoulder. When she'd come to this town, the bag had been empty besides a notebook with not one mark inside. At various times during her stay here, she'd thought she was leaving with a bag full of files that would result in a good story, that would get her back her old job, her old boyfriend, and her old life. But it turned out she was carrying far more than papers, or articles, or even boyfriends, or past lives. She'd collected a life story, one that ended with tragedy but lived on in flesh and blood and in rejected articles in the basement of a small-town newspaper.

She hoped Evelyn's plight would be told, and she hoped her grandmother would tell it, but what Hannah knew for certain was that Evelyn's story wasn't the only one out there. If her satchel, full of one story, was heavy enough to throw her off balance and change the way she stood and walked as the strap dug into her shoulder, then what could the weight of ten . . . or more stories do?

CHAPTER 37

Ten months later

Hannah drove down Main Street in Senatobia. American flags were everywhere—big ones on top of light posts and small ones shoved into the ground along the side of the road. The hotels were full in town, restaurants bustling with patrons. It was beautiful to see the city so alive. The larger-than-usual crowds were not the only unique sight. Large television vans lined Main Street and filled random parking lots. Hannah knew who they were here to see.

Today Mamaw was going to officially meet her birth family. She wrote the piece, and Guy worked as editor and consultant prior to submission. Hannah stayed away from the project, which was made easier by her return to Chicago, but the entire time she felt like a father from the fifties pacing in the waiting room while his wife birthed their baby. But what Guy and Mamaw created together turned out better than any story Hannah could've developed on her own.

The only way Hannah did help was by introducing Mamaw and Guy's piece to her former editor, Tom, at the *Tribune*. She'd gone to visit him when she moved back to Chicago in December and shared with him the real reason she'd been AWOL during her last days employed there. She'd hidden from that truth for so long, surrendering her position rather than allowing her father to tell her editor about her mental state, which would've allowed her to take a leave of absence rather than be let go. Her December confession to Tom was not made in an effort to get her old job back, but to fill in the backstory of how she came upon the Evelyn idea and to build the bridge between the major newspaper and the two individuals who were now in charge of the story.

Tom fell in love with the pitch, and working with Guy and Mamaw, they ended up collaborating on a six-part feature article detailing Evelyn's story and the secrets Hannah had learned about the past and the present as well. The article was published right as the presidential primary season was starting. Jack Dawson won by a landslide and accepted his party's nomination.

Which is exactly what Pete had predicted would happen. When Hannah shared the news of his long-lost aunt, Mable Williamson, and the circumstances surrounding her birth, he was fascinated but also concerned about the backlash. Shelby tried to pay off Mamaw and manipulate Hannah with offers of a campaign job, but they refused. It was time for Evelyn's truth to come out.

In those prepublication days, Hannah braced for a legal battle with the Dawsons, but it never came. Pete explained that after much convincing, Shelby had finally agreed not to push Monty to enforce the NDA, as had become standard practice for many companies in cases of sexual harassment or assault in the post-#MeToo era.

Besides, with a simple DNA test, it was impossible to deny that Mable Williamson was Evelyn Kensley and Fred Dawson's daughter. Faced with an impossible-to-stop leak of information, the Dawson family changed their tune. Instead of attempting a long-term cover-up like Fred and eventually Shelby had with the *Record*, Pete encouraged his aunt Shelby, Mamaw's aunt, to embrace Mable and her grandchildren as a part of their family.

Hannah liked to think Shelby and the rest of the Dawsons had been so welcoming out of the kindness of their hearts, but she'd been observing the Dawson family long enough to have picked up on the fact that they didn't do anything that wasn't helpful to Jack's or Pete's political careers as well. A touching special interest story was exactly what Jack Dawson needed to nail down the nomination, and what Pete needed to win his reelection campaign. Soon after the article came out, Monty closed up shop at the *Record*, and Tonya Sellers took over the entire building for her boutique. Hannah never found out the entire reasoning for the swift liquidation of that news outlet, but she could guess. The money had run out.

The Dawsons weren't the only ones to benefit from the popularity of Mamaw's article. Hannah started a podcast where she could tell not only Evelyn's story but the other hidden stories of normal, everyday women throughout history who had faced some of the same challenges as Hannah's great-grandmother. And just before heading down south to Mamaw's great reunion/photo op, she received an offer to write a monthly column at the *Chicago Tribune* about the stories she shared on her show twice a month.

But every time she returned to Senatobia, it felt more and more like coming home. Hannah had spent most holidays in this little town since moving north. Guy and Rosie felt the most like home, next to Mamaw, of course. Hannah knew that everyone in town was expecting them to end up together, but after the kiss in the woodshop she and Guy hadn't kissed again. Like protagonists in a TV sitcom, they clearly cared about each other, but neither one had been willing to take the risk and say anything about those feelings. So they remained close friends, really close friends, but everyone knew better.

Mamaw's house was rented out to a young family, so Hannah had taken a small studio apartment above one of the little shops in town, sharing time between Chicago and Senatobia. It had no air-conditioning, and sometimes she had to run the water for a few minutes to get rid of all the rust deposits, but Hannah could see the courthouse from her window and got to watch the magnolias bloom in the spring, so she kept renewing her short-term lease.

She also had made a special visit in January to speak on Guy's behalf during his grand jury trial, but the charges were dropped that day for lack of prosecution, his record expunged and job restored.

But the past few months had been busier than ever, and today was the first time since July that Hannah had found her way home again. The presidential election was six weeks away, and Uncle Jack wanted to squeeze a few more drops of good luck out of the Evelyn ordeal. It seemed that standing firm, telling the truth, and making amends were the key ingredients in clearing the negative effects of the scandal.

Hannah pulled her rental car into the parking lot of the Sunrise Nursing Home. After her stint riding a bike everywhere, she'd made it a point to never be in Senatobia without access to a vehicle.

The parking lot was already full, and Hannah was relieved to find one last space around the back of the large white structure that was built to look like a classic plantation home. The end of September in Illinois was a time of crisp winds that predicted frozen, subzero winters. However, here in Mississippi, it was still a time of sticky humidity and temperatures in the nineties. Hannah wore a nice pair of slacks and a loose-fitting tank top that allowed some air to circulate against her skin. She wore a low heel, which was not her usual footwear, but knowing that pictures were going to be taken and published all over the world she'd decided to take her effort up a notch.

Hannah had arranged for a beauty team to visit Mamaw earlier that morning to set her hair and do her makeup and dress her specifically for the event. Writing brought a vivacity back to her grandmother that seemed to jump-start her recovery. She'd adapted to her new way of life well, making friends easily in her new home, and with Mr. Davenport, her ever-doting beau, never too far away. He'd moved into the assisted-living wing of the facility, and they were engaged and planning a holiday wedding. Hannah still attempted to apologize for her part in her grandmother's injuries, but Mamaw still responded, "Oh, hush." Seeing her vibrant grandmother in a wheelchair made Hannah think of how Evelyn had come to be in the same situation at the age of fourteen.

The bullet that Evelyn had sent through her right breast and into her spine did end up killing her, in a way. The last document that Guy had texted Hannah on the day all the puzzle pieces finally fell together was Evelyn's death certificate. It had been tucked in the back of the envelope of records she'd given him and Rosie. Upon closer inspection Hannah discovered the reason the *Tate County Record* had never received Evelyn's last letter was because she had passed away before she could send it. She was only twenty years old. The cause of death listed on the medical report was an intestinal blockage, which turned out was a common cause of death for people with paraplegia in the first half of the twentieth century. Hannah often played a game with herself, listing the ways things might have been different if Evelyn had been born fifty or even eighty years later, and then listing the ways her situation would've been the same. Just another reason she started her podcast.

Hannah was beeped into the rear entrance of the nursing home as she showed the security guard her ID. Security was tight because of the senator's visit, but on most visits Hannah came and went freely, familiar with the staff and many of the residents there. Nancy, Mamaw's former day nurse, greeted Hannah at the front desk. She was a newly hired supervisor at the facility, and her personality fit perfectly in this place.

"Hey, Hannah, good to see you," she greeted Hannah, as cheerful as ever, hair in the helmet shape she'd perfected, and her pink scrubs stretched across her swollen belly, six months pregnant.

"Look at you!" Hannah declared as she approached, amazed at how much she'd grown, only barely hearing the good news before she'd left in July. Her engagement ring now had a matching band with it, and the sight of the sparkles and baby bump didn't make Hannah cringe and look for the closest Wi-Fi connection so she could stalk Alex. Instead, she just felt happy. "Boy or girl? Or do you not know yet?"

"It's a little girl," she said, hand resting on her stomach affectionately. "I love your podcast, by the way," Nancy said, handing Hannah her pass.

"Oh, you've been listening?" Hannah was always surprised when she found out that people listened to what she had to say. It made sense, logically, that she must have an audience of listeners and readers, because numbers and reports on her computer said it was so. But whenever she had the chance to see them face-to-face, it made the world feel like a more connected place than Hannah had let herself imagine.

"Yeah, I . . ." She lowered her voice and leaned toward Hannah. "Something like what happened to your great-grandma happened to me when I was in school. No one wanted to talk about it. I . . ." She paused.

Hannah waited patiently for Nancy to find her words. This phenomenon was the most surprising result of Hannah's success—it happened on airplanes, in elevators, and once even in a public bathroom, a grand outpouring of trust and this borderline desperate need to share their experiences. All they wanted was for someone to listen—listen and believe.

"I understand why she did it, you know," Nancy said when she found her voice again. Then she mouthed the words "Why she shot herself." She continued, whispering still. "God forgive me, but I considered it for a minute or two—you know, when things were really bad. I thought for sure nobody would ever want me after . . . after that."

Hannah blinked back unexpected tears. Usually, she was better at holding in her emotions in these moments, not wanting to make someone else's trauma about her. But Hannah envied Nancy when she moved here a year ago, loathed her 'cause she looked happy and pretty and perfect. But even Nancy had a story like Evelyn's.

"Oh my, I'm sorry. Don't ruin your makeup. You have to look pretty," Nancy said, grabbing a handful of tissues.

"Gosh, no. Don't be sorry." Hannah blotted her eyes, careful not to wipe off too much makeup. "You're amazing, that's all."

"Oh, hush. I'm no such thing." Nancy batted at Hannah, shifting away from the serious nature of her confession. Hannah was used to this too, a minimizing of the trauma after sharing in a victim's effort to keep themselves from being retraumatized. Nancy changed the subject. "Hey, I just saw your family get in the elevator, so you'd better get going."

"My family?" Hannah asked, scanning the lobby. Brody and his crew had turned down the invitation to join in on the family reunion, not agreeing with all of Jack Dawson's politics. It'd take some time for his guard to drop. Her mother thought it would be best to let Hannah and Mamaw experience the spotlight together. And Carla, who both Hannah and Mamaw considered family, was in Arkansas helping her daughter with her three kids. Mamaw had insisted that every bit of the rent on the house that wasn't used on Sunrise should go to Carla, which made it possible for her to finally retire. Even with all the people joining her life, Mamaw missed Carla, Hannah could tell. Hannah missed her too.

As far as Hannah was concerned, that was the entirety of her family, so she didn't know what family Nancy was talking about.

"The Dawsons. They walked by while we were talking."

In no way did Hannah consider the Dawson clan her family. The only one who came anywhere close was Pete, and she was glad he'd be here today. They'd become close friends over time, and she knew that if she'd taken the time to look, he had probably already texted asking where she was.

"Let's have dinner this week, okay? I'm here for a bit now," Hannah said, heading toward the elevators.

"Sounds great! Good luck!"

Hannah pushed the button to the second floor and hoped that she was the only one who could tell how sweaty she had become. Usually she'd take the stairs to get to Mamaw's room, but there was no way she'd encourage her body to get any warmer than it already was. When the elevator doors opened, she took two rights and a left to arrive at Mamaw's bedroom.

Inside, half the room was dim, and the other half was bathed in lights. Introductions and photographs were already taking place on the bright side. There would be a public press conference in about an hour down in front of the nursing home, where the Dawson family would welcome Mamaw into their family officially. It had been a long journey of tests and changing opinions and articles and busy election schedules. But eventually every test had come back with the same results: Jack Dawson was Mamaw's half brother, though he was twenty years her junior, and when they spoke or had their younger pictures placed side by side, like was happening on most news shows, it was quite obvious. That made Pete Hannah's second cousin. She always grimaced good-humoredly at that thought after the amount of flirting that had taken place between them in the early days of their friendship. He found it hilarious.

"Hey! There you are," Pete whispered, greeting Hannah with an extra-squishy hug. On the production side of the room were lights and cameras, as well as Jack Dawson himself, talking with his sister quietly, his wife, Pete's mother, by his side, and Mr. Davenport, Mamaw's new fiancé and perpetual companion, holding her hand on the other side of the bed. Out of the shot was Shelby Dawson, who watched from her wheelchair, still very much in charge of the Dawson family despite her age.

"You look amazing," Pete said like he always did when they saw each other after it had been a while.

"Let me remind you that I'm your cousin," Hannah said, who'd made the joke an obscene amount of times since the DNA results came back.

"Second cousin. Which is not illegal. You can even marry your second cousin."

"But still gross," Hannah said, elbowing him in the ribs lightly.

"Some people think that vegetables are gross. I like to think they're good for you."

"What does that have to do with anything? You are such a politician."

"Is that supposed to be an insult?" he muttered.

"Hell yeah, it is," she whispered back.

Shelby, who likely heard their hushed banter, scanned the back of the room.

"You come from a long line of politicians, so . . . you might want to rethink your prejudice."

"You do realize how messed up it is that you called me part of your family and talked about the legality of marrying me in the same conversation?"

He bounced his head back and forth, eyes rolled up in his head like he was thinking.

"Yes, yes, I do," he said, and they both convulsed with laughter, well above a volume that Shelby would likely find acceptable, and then hid from her glare like schoolchildren.

"Your grandmother is a delight, by the way. I wish I'd had her as my aunt growin' up instead of Aunt Shelby. My God, that woman is mean."

"Pete. Hush." Hannah put a finger to her lips, serious. "She definitely has you bugged."

"Hannah, is that you?" Mamaw called out, her voice hugging her from a distance.

"Yes! Hey! You looked busy." Hannah stepped into the lit part of the room, where Mamaw sat propped up in bed. She hugged her and kissed her cheek ever so lightly, so she didn't leave a mark.

"I'm never too busy for you, darlin'," Mamaw said, grasping Hannah's hand in hers like she was holding on for dear life. "This is my amazing granddaughter, Hannah. She's the one who made all this happen."

Jack Dawson, a large man with white hair and a broad smile, held out his hand. He already knew Hannah, even though they'd never met; she was sure of it. "I've heard a lot about you, Hannah."

"As have I," she said, shaking his hand.

"I would take any story you've heard from Peter with a grain of salt," Aunt Shelby chimed in.

"As long as you'll do the same for me," Hannah bantered back, finding it interesting that she was related to these strangers.

"Thank you, from the bottom of my heart, for finding my sister for me. It is lonely in this world without family," he said, and she'd wondered if he'd practiced that line. She decided to play along and hope that he was at least partially sincere for Mamaw's sake.

After a bit more small talk, Hannah checked the time. "I have to run out to an appointment. I'll be back in an hour for the big shindig, okay?" she told her grandmother.

"Oh yes, dear, do what you need to do. I'm in good hands."

"Yes, you are," Jack's wife chimed in, and Hannah was glad to see that she could talk.

She kissed her grandmother goodbye, and as Mamaw held Hannah a fraction closer than usual, she whispered, "You've made me so damn proud, Hannah girl. And I know your daddy would agree with me."

"I think he'd be proud of both of us," she said in return, knowing it would be true. Then she added, surprised and impressed, "And—you swore!"

Mamaw swatted her away playfully. "I'm not planning to make a habit of it, but I think I've earned the right."

"Hell yeah, you have," Hannah shot back, standing at full height but trying to stay discreet, not wanting to embarrass her grandmother. She hugged Mr. Davenport and made a few rounds of handshakes. Then she snuck out while Pete was distracted talking to a pretty nurse. Making it out to the street without getting stopped again, Hannah looked around for her ride.

"Hey there, beautiful, need a lift?" Guy rolled up in his silver Honda Civic, elbow hanging out the window.

"That is a super-creepy pickup line," she said, wondering if he could tell that seeing him made fireworks go off inside her body. She tried to hold in her smile and act coy, walking around to the passenger side of the car and angling the air-conditioner vent right at her face once inside. It always felt like home with Guy. Always.

"But it got you in my car, so I think that means it worked."

"Just drive."

"Where are we off to?" he asked, grinning uncontrollably and taking more than one extra-long look at her fancier-than-normal outfit.

"It's a secret." She gave him a mischievous look. "Go straight. I'll tell you when to turn."

It was a quick drive, just under two miles. Hannah made sure to wait till the very last minute to tell Guy to turn every single time, which was likely dangerous but reminded her for the five hundredth time why she was about to do what she was about to do.

"Stop!" Hannah shouted, and Guy slammed on the brakes dramatically, making a skidding sound that she'd thought only existed in movies. "We're here."

They'd stopped in front of a dilapidated two-story Victorian-style home. The windows were boarded up, and parts of the roof looked to be missing.

"Get out," she ordered playfully, shoving him toward the direction of his door. "I'll meet you on the other side."

When she rounded the front of the car and climbed up onto the grassy knoll next to the road, her heels sank into the grass, and she grabbed for Guy's arm so she didn't fall down. He caught her, his arms wrapping around her waist. She took in a short, sharp breath and didn't pull away, loving the way his support felt. She put her arm around his midsection as well, so they were connected.

"Do you know what this is?" Hannah asked, pointing at the barely standing structure.

"I should pretend I don't, but I looked this up a long time ago when I was helping Mamaw with the article. This is Evelyn's house, right?"

Reason 501, she thought, finding it beyond attractive that he'd taken the initiative to find this place.

"Yeah, it is. All right, here is a question you don't know the answer to." She turned away from the house and put her other arm around Guy till they were face-to-face. She'd been so cautious over the past months to not cross this line, to be friendly but not too flirty. She'd pulled away when she wanted to lean in, but if he was willing, she was ready for more. Even with the heat and the sweat, she didn't mind the bonfire that permeated through his T-shirt and soaked into her skin.

"I'm having a hard time thinking about much of anything with you standing this close, looking this good," he said, somehow pulling her closer when it seemed like there was no remaining space between them.

"I have to say, I find it distracting too. Oh no, I just forgot what I was going to say!" She let her arms drop and faked trying to walk away, but Guy held her against him.

"You're not getting away that easily. I'll try to remind you. This is Evelyn's house. You brought me here. You are temptin' me something fierce. Now—your turn."

She knew he wanted to kiss her; she could read it in his eyes by now. It had been nearly a year since they had first kissed, but she thought about it every time they were together. His eager lips. His hungry grip on her hips and waist. He must have thought of it too, or he wouldn't be looking at her like he could devour her.

"Do you know who owns this house?" she asked. This wasn't how she'd expected things to go, but standing so close to Guy only made her more sure. She'd been alone for some time now, and it wasn't terrible. She took care of herself and didn't have to worry about losing everything in a breakup or a fight or a slip in her mental well-being, or even because of some indiscriminate disease. But the more she got to know Guy, the more he filled her empty spaces and she enjoyed filling his, the more she knew that being alone was only safer if you hadn't found the right person to trust.

"Umm . . . let me see if I can remember who lived here last . . . I can call Nick down at the land office and see what I can find out."

"Shhh." He stopped talking, raised his eyebrows, waiting to hear what she had to say. "I know who owns it already. Just ask me."

"Oh, okay. So, who owns it?" he asked, dutifully.

"I do."

"What?" He stared at the house and then back at Hannah. "You know you can't live in that house, right? It's pretty broken."

She smacked his bicep. "I'm not going to live there. I want to renovate it, restore it. Eventually, I'd like to turn it into a museum dedicated to women like Evelyn, like women from my podcast. And I was hoping you might want to help me."

"Oh," he said, his grip on her going slack, very little emotion in his response. "You want to hire me? I see. My father usually handles quotes and big jobs like this."

"I mean, I do need a handyman." She pulled him in again, not wanting to let go now that she had him in her reach. "But I want to do it together. Like, *together* together. Like—we kiss and hold hands and go on dates kind of together."

"Did you say kiss?" His eyebrows shot up, and his hands immediately returned to her waist, where they belonged.

"Mm-hmm."

"I like the sound of all that," he said, dipping his head down till their lips touched. Hannah ran her hands up the back of his neck and pulled him down toward her, parting her lips slightly, inviting him to deepen the connection. Her lips moved along with his in a lovely, easy dance that felt like the first time and the millionth in the same instant.

"Does this mean you are going to stick around for a bit?" he asked when they separated momentarily.

"Yeah, I think it's about time I gave staying a try."

"I think you're gonna like it."

She looked at the crumbling house behind her and the road she'd ridden on her bicycle on her way to work every day for the months she lived with Mamaw. She almost felt closer to her father here than at Columbia College, or even in the house where he died. There was Dr. Williamson, PhD, whom Hannah mourned and missed every day. But the ongoing heritage of Patrick Williamson, outside his children, came through this town. He'd left as a teen, thinking the only way to avoid the mistakes of his ancestors was to escape. He'd run away from Senatobia to find his purpose. Hannah ran *to* Senatobia to find hers—which only seemed right.

She returned her gaze to Guy and nodded.

"Yeah. I think so too."

ACKNOWLEDGMENTS

First, I need to say thank you to all the essential workers who bravely went to work and made life possible the past year. It was a hard year for everyone, but I was able to stay home and work from my computer while you all went out and did the hard tasks. I have a deep respect and awe for all of you.

The complications of writing during a pandemic were more than I'd expected, so I need to also say a deep and heartfelt thank-you to the internet. I know it sounds like a joke, but I'm serious! Without Google Maps, Ancestry.com, Newspapers.com, county websites, helpful librarians, and the existence of email and social media, I would not have been able to write this book with any amount of accuracy, since in-person research was impossible at the time. I'm grateful for such technology, and I also hope that with the use of those tools I've been able to convey this story with as much veracity as possible during this strange time in our world.

In that same vein—thank you to Kelly Haramis for your insights into the world of journalism and the *Chicago Tribune*. Your experience there and willingness to give feedback and information was priceless. Thank you for all your assistance and for chatting with me over Facebook Messenger at the drop of a hat.

And thank you to Torrice Albarakat for your consulting prowess. Your ability to speak boldly and share your undiluted thoughts on important topics relating to racism, injustice, and equality was so deeply appreciated. The way this story and the characters transformed under the influence of your input and insight was beautiful and exciting to me. I hope the future brings more opportunities for collaboration . . . especially once we don't have to teach algebra AND attempt to be creative at the same time.

To my writers' group, coaches, and castmates at Improv Playhouse—you have become such an important part of my life. To our little band of performers who have worked together, following guidelines and restrictions—thank you for being my emotional support system, whether you knew it or not. Your dedication to art and creativity keeps me going.

Shahab Astabraghpour—I know it was kismet that we became friends when we did. I'm so grateful for your slight obsession with Memphis (but in a good way) and familiarity with that area. The details you were able to provide were not just informative but inspirational at a time when everything having to do with research felt impossible. Thank you as well for checking in with me as I was working; for encouraging me when I felt stuck; for providing me with references, phone numbers, and deep thoughts; and most of all for always being there to make me laugh when I needed it. I know you think you didn't do much to help— I'm pretty sure you're wrong.

To the women I look up to and cheer for: Karen Schaffroth, Nora Benjamin, Lorena Vazquez, and Sarah McFeggan—I have learned resilience and determination from each of you. And I have also learned what it means to be a true friend. Thank you for always being there for me, showing up on my doorstep, putting up with my random texts, and always knowing the right thing to say. I wish every woman could be as lucky as I have been to have such a powerful group of women standing beside me through life. You mean the world to me.

Thank you as well to my fellow authors at Lake Union Publishing. You are such a lovely and supportive group, and you give the BEST advice. Thanks for making me feel normal in my writing neurosis and helping me push through the stumbling blocks of this creative life.

Thanks to my developmental editor, Tiffany Yates Martin. You challenge me in such a productive way. I love the way we work together and the way you encourage me to make my stories the best they can be. You are an insanely hard worker, and I feel lucky to have enjoyed honing and beautifying so many books together. Here's to many more transformations in our future.

I would not be where I am today without my amazing agent, Marlene Stringer. You have always been such a great support to me, but during this worldwide crisis you were there to care about me not only as your client but also as a person. Your words of care and advice meant the world to me and pulled me through some hard times and self-doubt. Thank you for seeing the best in me and being a voice I can trust unwaveringly.

Thanks to my editor, Chris Werner. Your perceptiveness and insight were priceless with this story. Thank you for being so hands-on and for keeping me on my toes. I am always grateful to have the opportunity to work with you and your awesome team at Lake Union.

I know I'd be far less sane without the support and care of my friend and castmate, Lorena Vazquez. Thank you for being a constant in my life. If they had PhDs in friendship, you'd for sure have one. You support me, encourage me, challenge me, and push me to be more every single day. Literally—every day. Thanks for every meme, quote, taco, adventure, laugh, and tear you've brought to my world. I love being each other's cheerleaders. Let's keep doing all the scary things, okay?

Thanks to my sister, Elizabeth Sadler, for taking my phone calls and listening like a pro. Thank you for wanting to know about the real Evelyn just as much as I did and trying your hand at research in some really amazing ways. I don't know how I'd ever write a book without you, if I'm honest. Even though you are my baby sister, I look up to you. You are a crazy-impressive working mom who shows me that it is possible to have professional and parental success. Thank you for always picking up the phone and teaching me what it is like to have a secure base. I love you.

Thanks to my parents, George and Cindy Sadler, for your love and support and for being truly amazing with my kids. Dad, thank you for helping with virtual learning during this pandemic. Also, thank you for having hours and hours of conversations with me about Mississippi, your childhood, and growing up in the South. Also, thank you for supporting the whole idea of this story, even though parts of it were based off your family history. I know we have been fascinated by Evelyn's true story for decades, and it's been such a joy to let it inspire this book.

And most of all, I'm grateful to my children: Johnny, Brandon, Thomas, and Maddie. We have been the most "together" we've ever been other than when you were babies. It's been . . . interesting. Ha! But even with the struggles of shelter-in-place, virtual learning, and limits on what used to be normal life—thank you for showing me that you are growing into humans I'm crazy-proud to call my own. You all are so creative and bright, and I love you endlessly. I am on the edge of my seat waiting to see what greatness you will bring to the world. You *could* start with a cure to COVID-19 . . . I mean . . . if that's not asking TOO much.

And to my great-aunt, the real Evelyn: Thank you for writing your story down eighty years ago and trusting that one day it would find a way to be shared. You had a hard life. I'm so sorry you felt like you had so few options that a loaded gun seemed to be your only choice. The world is still not perfect, I'm sorry to say. But some things have changed and continue to change every day. We are working hard to make sure that no woman has to experience the hardships you did. It might not happen in my lifetime or my daughter's, but I have to believe that as long as we listen to voices like yours, each generation will find new and growing strength, support, and compassion.

ABOUT THE AUTHOR

Photo © 2019 Organic Headshots

Emily Bleeker is the *Wall Street Journal* bestselling author of *What It Seems, The Waiting Room, Working Fire, When I'm Gone,* and *Wreckage.* Emily is a former educator who learned to love writing while teaching a writers' workshop. After surviving a battle with a rare form of cancer, she finally found the courage to share her stories. Emily currently lives with her family in suburban Chicago. Connect with her or request a Skype visit with your book club at www.emilybleeker.com.